What Others Are Saying

Carina and her story are so monumental that readers will live with her memory for a lifetime.

—Lindy Hudis, producer, IMPACT Motion Picture

A great, romantic, sweeping, historical saga in the tradition of *Zhivago* and *The Godfather!*

—Dan Gordon, writer/producer, *Wyatt Earp*, *The Hurricane*, and *Murder in the First*

Memorable characters and exciting action fill this epic tale.

—Gary Chafetz, co-author, *The Morphine Dream*

Beauty and viciousness—two words that explain both the character and story of Don Corina, which is a mesmerizing journey of a woman who will do anything to survive in a world of war and crime. There are not enough of these powerful female characters in stories today.

—James Cotten, director, *La Linea (The Line)*

You know Don Corleone, now meet Don Carina, the first woman to assume ruthless control of a Mafia crime family. Set in Naples during the desperate times of World War II, Don Carina will stop at nothing to protect the ones she loves. A great story.

—Hudson Hickman, producer, *MacGyver*

A most amazing saga!

—Sharri Williams, author, *The Maybelline Story and the Spirited Family Dynasty Behind It*

Infectious reading.

A thrilling read! An important book.

Unforgettable!

A fascinating, and elegantly told story.

DON CARINA

WWII Mafia Herione
Ron Russell

BETTIE YOUNGS BOOKS

Disclaimer:
This is a true story, and the characters and events are real. However, in some cases, the names, descriptions, and locations have been changed, and some events have been altered, combined, or condensed for storytelling purposes, but the overall chronology is an accurate depiction of the author's experience.

Cover design by Tatomir Pitariu
Photo of Ron Russell by Cathryn Farnsworth

Bettie Youngs Books are distributed worldwide. If you are unable to order this book from your local bookseller or online, you may order directly from the publisher.

BETTIE YOUNGS BOOK PUBLISHERS
www.BettieYoungsBooks.com

Library of Congress Control Number: 2010915367

ISBN: 978-0-9843081-9-4

10 9 8 7 6 5 4 3 2 1

Printed on acid-free paper

AUTHOR'S NOTE: *Don Carina* is based on actual people and events in Southern Italy before and during World War II.

Naples endured more air attacks, starvation, and hardship than any Italian city during WWII. The citizens of Naples suffered more than a hundred air attacks, a brutal German occupation, and deplorable living conditions. After three years of uninterrupted Nazi rule over Europe, Naples was the first major city to be liberated by the Allied troops, but Neapolitans continued to experience many more hardships throughout the remainder of the war and for years thereafter.

A MESSAGE FROM DON CARINA: Many whisperings I've heard over the years of how the Prince of Napoli met his end, none of them accurate. Various versions of the astonishing events in my life have been softly spoken to me as well, by people who were unaware that I was the one they were rumoring about. But here and now I've laid down the truth about those years. I don't know who will read this account, but it's enough that deep within me I needed to clear the waters, to separate the fact from the fiction, as Napoli is a city rife with myth.

CONTENTS

ACKNOWLEDGEMENTS

To begin, I had a mother, a shocking revelation to some people. Peggie Russell gifted many years of encouragement to me and her deep love of reading helped inspire me to become a writer. I wish she was still alive to see the publication of this book.

Three dear friends added so much to flushing out the story and voice of this novel: Bill Stenton, Pam Goldstein, and Rebecca Smith.

Bill Stenton is one of the most talented people I've ever met. Bill is a highly accomplished composer, artist and human being. He is also one of the finest writers alive. His novels are so exceptional I expect to find all of them on bookstore shelves soon. His notes after reading Don Carina were pure platinum and the book owes much to him.

Pam Goldstein is another phenomenal writer that helped the book in so many ways, especially her insight into the love story between Carina and Domenico. Her continued input during the writing of the book provided me carts full of useful ideas that found their way into every chapter.

Rebecca Smith is my business partner at SunCafe organic cuisine, the restaurant we own together, and my long time dear friend, the person I most trust in the world. Her feedback was absolutely invaluable, and helped clean up many rough edges and bring focus.

I'd like to express my gratitude to the editors that provided their invaluable input on Don Carina: Andrea McKeown and David Alan Kirk. The time and care they committed to my novel is most appreciated. I'd like to give a special thanks to another editor Peggy Lang who added some very deep insights that helped me create new layers of power to the book.

A somewhat awkward thank you goes to Selina McLemore, a senior editor at Grand Central Publishing, for rejecting the novel but providing me the nicest and most encouraging rejection letter that I've ever received. After I made changes, Ms. McLemore even consented to reread the novel a second time. While the novel ultimately didn't fit at GCP, her encouragement, suggestions and enthusiasm for my work gave me great confidence in it.

Finally, Bettie Youngs, of Bettie Youngs Books, deserves an immeasurable thanks for her guidance, publishing wisdom and patience for bringing *Don Carina* to print! When all is said and done, Bettie loved this book and believed in me . . . and was the one who brought my book to life.

SOUTHERN ITALY, 1946

Meticulously, I placed the blush on my cheek. I wanted to look my best on this solemn night. My husband loved to see me all dressed up and I wanted him to be pleased with me. The final coat of crimson lipstick glided onto my lips and I pursed them to make sure they were smooth and wet.

With a wiggle, I shimmied into my black rayon cocktail dress. The soft fabric felt sensual gliding over my fair skin. I opened the box on the floor by my vanity, pulled out my red stiletto heels and slipped them on. It had been years since I'd worn them or anything else so elegant.

The mirror revealed my dark mane needed straightening after putting on the dress. I brushed it up and carefully wedged the silver comb Papa had given me into my thick black hair to hold it in place. With all I had lived through, I felt older than my thirty years; but, I still could turn heads. As I wrapped my ruby scarf around my neck, I took a final look at my reflection and saw no obvious imperfections; but, I still felt nervous and wondered how God would see my actions on Judgment Day.

Leaving the bedroom, I went down the long hall, stopped by the bar, snatched the brandy carafe and a couple of glasses, and went down the stairs to the basement door. The click of my heels counted out the twenty-one steps. At the landing, I stopped to gain my composure and took a nervous little breath. I'd certainly done this to quite a few men, but this was my husband.

After unlocking the door with my free hand, I entered the large basement and made sure to re-bolt it. My husband sat on the couch with his back to me. He didn't turn towards me when I entered, which was a blessing.

Looking around the rather stark cellar, I regretted that I hadn't made this living area cozy. The cold stone floor needed the warmth of a rug and the cool walls had no festive paintings to allow one to escape into another place and time.

I set the glasses and carafe on the table in front of the couch. For the first time, I turned toward my husband. He was expressionless.

"Brandy?" I offered. I took his lack of response as a "Yes," and poured us each a drink. Ever so slowly, I moved towards him. He didn't take the drink, so I placed it next to him on the table.

Now, my gaze never retreated from my husband's handsome face. With a swing of my hips, I straddled him, face to face.

"I'll always protect you, my Prince." I pulled him against me, bringing his head to my bosom. His chest expanded with each tranquil breath. It had been years since I had felt him against me and it seemed both sweet and disturbing.

Reflecting on our past together, I drew my long silken scarf across his body and wrapped the strong cloth around his arms. He didn't respond. The silky fabric felt so soft and harmless. I caressed his freshly shaven neck, swept my hand up to his temple and ran my fingers through his black hair, now speckled with gray.

"Through the war, the Allied air attacks, the Nazis, I've watched after this family well," I whispered. "I've done everything necessary to protect it. I've told you all under the seal of Confession."

I smiled, but my throat tightened as I pulled my stiletto from its hidden sheath in my belt. Placing my arm across my husband's chest, I said, "I always have and always will do what's best for you and the family. I love you, *principe*."

I chose to believe that the look of contentment on my husband's face acknowledged his agreement. During the last four years, ever since the bombing, he hadn't uttered a word. Trapped within his secret world, he stared vacantly into a reality I could not see.

I kissed his cheek. Even in the dim light of the basement, the stiletto blade glimmered like a diamond as I brought it around and slid it into the great artery in his thigh.

Chapter 1

BOTTOM OF THE BOOT

Fall was approaching Reggio Calabria, at the bottom of Italy's boot. Papa liked to say we were so close to the tip of the boot that we could watch the country's toes splash in the warm Mediterranean Sea.

Restless this night in 1932, I ventured into the hall and headed for the banister that led to the parlor downstairs. My sewing basket would provide me the needed distraction that would relax me enough to fall asleep. But before I made it to the stairs, I noticed the light under Papa's study door. I smiled. He would be able to put me at ease.

I knocked, but he didn't answer.

"Papa?"

Not an utterance. I turned the handle and nudged open the door. He sat behind his desk, lost in a book.

"I can't sleep." I moved over to the desk. My talks with Papa had always calmed me, even on my most restless nights, but his eyes were frozen still in the dim light.

"Papa?" I shook his shoulder. The book fell to the floor, and his body shifted loosely in his chair.

"Papa!" I started to scream for help but held myself back, remembering that his heart had stopped once before. Putting my ear to his chest, I hoped to hear it still pounding, even if only quietly. There was nothing. "No! Please, don't go!" My tears began to flow and I clutched his cool hand, trying to will his soul back into his body. "Come back, Papa."

His eyes stared with unnerving intensity, and I followed his lifeless gaze to the statue of the Virgin Mary on the edge of his desk. "You left me to be with her, Papa?" It was his time to join the angels. I started to call for my mother but thought better of it. This would be my last chance to be alone with him. I wanted him to myself, to make sure his soul was safely in Heaven, so Mama couldn't disrupt his journey. She had upset him enough in life; I would not let her disturb his death.

It comforted me to know that he had escaped this world and Mama's strong grip. I had often considered taking such a door to free myself from Mama's world. Quickly, I crossed myself.

"But why must you leave me, Papa?" Tears trembled along my cheek. My teeth clenched and my hand formed a fist, as a burst of anger rippled through me. I punched into the leather chair near his head. "You are selfish to die and leave me here alone with Mama." I instantly regretted snapping at him. I didn't want to face life without him; he was the only one who could protect me and my twelve younger brothers and sisters from Mother's anger. With him gone, that responsibility would now fall on me. Life rarely seems fair, and it certainly didn't that day.

My anger died as rapidly as it had flared. *Papa wouldn't be so selfish. God decided that he was too gentle for this harsh life.* I swept the tips of my fingers over his noble face. "Rest well."

As I leaned over him, my tears sprinkled across his hand. Wanting to lose myself in the darkness, I extinguished the flame from the oil reading lamp on his desk. The smoke from the wick slowly danced with the incense from a thurible, escorting my prayers to heaven. I sat on the floor beside Papa and clasped his tightening fingers, holding onto them as the night grew ever more still. His body was cooling. Wanting only his touch, I cuddled his smooth hand against my cheek and sat as motionless as my dear father.

After many hours, the morning sun disturbed our communion and the holy sanctuary of the night. When I heard the sounds of my younger brothers and sisters stirring, I kissed his cheek one last time. "Goodbye, Papa. Our time is over."

Now, for the first time in my life, I had to face a day without Papa's protection.

Chapter 2

DOMENICO'S RETURN

I took a bolstering breath as I finished binding my charcoal hair and picked up the exquisite silver comb that Papa had given me on my last birthday, my sixteenth. He had had it engraved, "To my little grown-up." Tears blurred my vision as I kissed the comb, made the sign of the cross, and pushed it into my thick hair.

Mama came into my room, short, stocky, her black eyes hard. "Carina Cunzolo, you better be useful today."

"I'm always a good girl, Mama."

"Hmmm," she grunted. "Watch after your brothers and sisters. I need—" Uncharacteristically, her words caught in her throat with a hint of emotion.

"Don't worry, Mama. I'll watch after everyone."

"Pray to the Virgin Mother to get us through this day." She touched my shoulder, and I flinched. She started to say something, but then turned and headed downstairs.

Looking out my second-story bedroom window, I noticed the chestnut and olive trees starting to bend under the hot Sirocco Winds, which had arrived from the deserts of Northern Africa across the Mediterranean and warned of the arrival of fall. I could see all the way down the hill to Reggio Calabria and past it to where Italy's toes met the sea. The vista was beautiful, but for me it had always felt like the view of a prisoner peering from a jail cell.

Our rambling house shuddered with uneasy whispered tones. The usual playful sounds of my brothers and sisters were conspicuously absent. Everyone hid in the protection of their rooms, reluctant to venture downstairs and face the reality of this day.

Uncle Salvatore called out, "Children! Come down, please."

I gathered the five youngest of my twelve brothers and sisters and funneled them down the stairs. Already I felt sticky from the heat. My other siblings gradually drifted downstairs as well.

Several of the little ones cried when they saw Papa's body in the coffin. I tried to comfort them, biting my lip to keep from weeping myself.

The coffin was surrounded by four women in black praying with their rosaries. During each of the three days since his death, starting before sunrise and continuing to midnight, these women had been kneeling by Papa and praying for his soul. I didn't like them being so intimate with him, as they didn't even know him.

In addition to these women, Mama had hired a large funeral band and numerous paid mourners for the day. Few people in the South could afford such funeral preparations, but Mama had the power of the lands. The extravagant arrangements would keep her status in the South secure and ensure that everyone would think highly of her. I doubt she had given nearly as much thought to the man she was burying.

Almost a hundred guests had already arrived. They stood about in clusters, murmuring amongst themselves. Although I kept my eyes on my youngest siblings, my ears were dedicated to listening to what those voices were saying. In a house so often full of silence, I had long ago learned the value of stalking conversation as stealthily as a hunter.

I sidled close to a group of women, who were too busy whispering amongst themselves to notice me.

"Guglielmo did much for Calabria, but his drinking and smoking . . . Saldino's whore houses—scandalous."

"Gino told my husband he even gambled away much of Lucilla's lands."

"One thing's for sure, she can't handle things on her own."

"Do you think she will make Carina a black widow?"

"Perhaps. Carina might end up cursed, the youngest woman in the South who knows how to read."

"Ssh, ssh," shushed a woman in the group with the harsh eyes of a crow when she noticed me standing nearby. She turned toward me. "Hello, dear. My heart goes out to you this tragic day."

After each woman had given me the obligatory sympathetic smile, they flocked together again and migrated deeper into the gathering.

I walked over to Uncle Salvatore, who had just welcomed the priest. Salvatore was the only adult in our dour family who could still summon a smile. He had a kind face that put people at ease, yet when necessary his powerful voice demanded respect from even a noble, and his quiet elegance warmed a room like the light of a cathedral's stained glass. I adored my uncle, even though I'd seen him less than a dozen times in my life. When I was four, I had visited his Hotel Augustus, an elegant palace outside Rome surrounded by rolling green hills and regal mountains with the Eternal City shimmering like a mirage in the distance. This was an image of Heaven that I would hold to firmly for many years.

He embraced me and offered a consoling smile. "My brother often wrote to me and said how much you meant to him," he said. "How much you've helped to care for this family." He paused. "I know how difficult it's been for you, Carina."

"Uncle, what's a black widow?"

"Where did you hear such a thing?"

"I heard some women—"

"Don't pay attention to such gossip," he said, cutting me off abruptly.

"Is our family in trouble, Uncle Salvatore?"

"Don't worry, Carina. Let God's hand lead us." He gave me a pat on my shoulder, but I could feel the uncertainty in his touch.

In that moment I felt my first deep concern for the future. I started to feel the weight of our family's circumstances on my thin shoulders. Little did I know that I would take the central role in its destiny.

More and more people Papa had known began to arrive. A parade of black marched into our house: farmers from Mama's lands, magistrates, police, government officials, judges in high hats, several "Men of the Round Cape"—other notaries who dressed like Papa. Men of importance were in uniform; others wore black. They all had a black armband or black button prominently displayed on their lapels out of respect for Father. Dust from the Siroccos, swirling outside like a thick fog, had left its mark on everyone.

People arrived with elaborate displays of flowers in surprising shapes: a lyre, a half-moon with a star, a cross, a rosary, a Roman pillar, and a clock face with its hands stopped at the estimated time of Papa's death. When someone of stature died, people fought to outdo one another with flower arrangements that had religious or celestial meaning.

I knew Signore Saldino had arrived when I heard an automobile approach, as he was one of only three people in Reggio who owned a car.

When he entered the house, people backed away like vinegar separating from olive oil and lowered their heads. Nearly two meters tall, he was an imposing man with a box-square body and a brutal wide face centered around a huge mass of a nose.

Saldino's twenty-year-old son Domenico carried a huge arrangement of flowers shaped like the gates of Heaven. He was tall like his father, but the similarities ended there. I hadn't seen him in several years, since he'd gone away to university. During that time he had left boyhood and grown into a handsome man, with a face sculpted from character, the eyes of a sensitive poet, waves of dark hair, and an athletic physique.

Signore Saldino tipped his wide-brimmed hat to Paolo, my other uncle, who owned a small newspaper up north, in Cosenza.

Paolo helped Domenico place the arch of blooms by the other flowers that were multiplying in the corner of the room. "Signore Saldino. Very benevolent of you to come," he said, a little nervously.

"Of course I would come," Signore Saldino boomed. "Such a terrible loss. Signore Cunzolo did so much for Calabria and the region, constructing churches and helping the poor. My deepest sympathy to you and your family." He gestured to his son. "Paolo, do you know my son, Domenico?"

"I'm so sorry for your great loss," Domenico said to Paolo, as they shook hands. I wished he was touching my hand—and then, I admonished myself for thinking such selfish thoughts on the day my father would be transferred to his final resting place.

Mama entered from the kitchen, a little flour still speckling her hands. It seemed silly to be baking bread on a day like today, but Mama never broke routine. On her stocky form she wore her blackest dress with four additional garments underneath to fill it out, according to custom; in the South, women of wealth wore multiple dresses in place of petticoats to show their stature. She also wore a long dark-colored veil that hid her face. Her heavy work shoes poked out from under the dresses as she walked.

Signore Saldino took off his hat. "I'm terribly sorry for your great loss, Signora Cunzolo. Your husband was a fine man."

"Thank you for your words of respect, Signore Saldino."

He smiled and then moved on as more people stepped forward to offer Mother their condolences.

Domenico approached, and his presence enveloped me. "I'm deeply sorry about your father, Carina." He placed one of his elegant hands on my arm, and the skin warmed all over my body.

"It means a great deal to me that you would come today, Domenico."

"I know how much he meant to you."

Domenico's father motioned for him. All of a sudden, a line of people had appeared in front of Papa's coffin. Signore Saldino stood near the front of it.

"We'll talk later," Domenico said, before going to stand by his father's side. Many years had passed since we had last consoled each other, as children, but Domenico's presence still felt comforting.

I positioned myself halfway up the stairs, so I could watch people pay their respects to Papa. The lid of his casket, which displayed his gold Examiner insignia, leaned against the wall nearby.

Mama walked up to the casket and stared down at the man with whom she had brought thirteen children into the world. Into his rigid right hand she placed his gnarled pipe and worn, veined leather tobacco pouch, two of his most valuable possessions. Papa had always ordered special blends from faraway places; smoking was expensive, but his pipe had burned constantly, filling the house with wonderful sweet-fruit or woody aromas. I yearned now for the comfort they brought.

Next, Salvatore looked at his motionless younger brother and mouthed a silent prayer. He placed Papa's favorite book, *The Three Musketeers,* next to his body. He noticed me peering down from the stairs and winked. Paolo followed him and tucked a small flask under

Papa's suit coat. I managed to return a despondent smile before he was replaced by Mr. Saldino, who snuck a pair of dice into the lining of the casket.

Doctor DiScullo, our family doctor, also mouthed a short silent prayer. When he looked up from Papa, he seemed startled to see me watching him. He smiled awkwardly and returned to his wife, who was standing in the far corner of the room.

As other people passed and gazed at Papa's form, some cried, many delivered a goodbye peck on his cheek. Some even kissed his lifeless lips. I didn't need to look into a box to see Papa, I felt him everywhere.

The priest quieted everyone, then dipped his right hand into a small bowl of holy water and made the sign of the cross. When he started speaking in Latin, I knew Mass had begun.

After the priest finished, Salvatore and Paolo, along with six of Papa's business associates, picked up the casket and carried it out the front door.

As the rest of the guests filtered outside, I gathered up the youngest children, held hands with little Bruno, and headed for the door. "Sergio, take your little sister's hand," I told my middle brother.

"I don't want to touch a girl," he protested. "They're poison." After his refusal, I couldn't get any of the four brothers younger than Sergio to take anyone's hand, as they always followed his lead.

My sister Gianina came to me with her tears, barely able to catch her breath. I comforted her under my wing. "We'll get through this, Gianina," I told her.

"With Papa gone . . . I'm afraid, Carina . . . I'm afraid of life alone with Mama," she whispered to me.

I nodded.

The wind still spun about fiercely, whipping Mama's long black veil like a serpent preparing to strike. An elaborate hearse-cart lined with flowers awaited its passenger. Hitched in front, eight magnificent black horses stood adorned with long white feathers in their manes. They danced restlessly in the relentless wind. A knot gripped my stomach as I watched the men place Papa's coffin into the cart and secure it with rope.

My oldest brother, Antonio, moved to the cart behind Papa's. I joined him to hoist the little ones up and secured them for the ride down the hill to the cemetery in town.

Mama, Paolo, and Salvatore took their places directly behind the hearse. Mama stood stiffly in the buffeting wind, her face betraying no emotion whatsoever.

The procession started with a dramatic roll of drums. The man standing in front of the hearse held a large black flag that snapped in the wind. At the end of the drum roll, the sixteen-piece band, comprised mostly of brass instruments, began to play and the man with the flag started to march to the beat.

A dust cloud blurred the road ahead. The cart that held my siblings lurched forward and I jumped in. The dust storm blurred my vision but not as much as Papa's death had. I didn't cover my face with a scarf to protect myself, like most of the women. I wanted to feel the dirt of the earth pummel my skin, to distract me from my new world without Papa.

Behind us, Signore Saldino, Domenico, and some of Papa's business associates marched a body's length from our cart. I stared into Domenico's deep dark eyes for a few seconds—far too long; he would think me a harlot. Tossed by the wind, his jet-black hair rounded into curly waves across his forehead. His intense gaze turned to me and seemed to take control of me.

I had first met Domenico when I was ten; he was twelve. My brother, Giacomo, had been struck with scarlet fever, so Mama sent Papa and me into town to bring back Dr. DiScullo. We found the doctor talking with Signore Saldino and Domenico. To save time, Signore Saldino offered to drive us to the house in his car. I sat with Domenico in the back. Up until then, I had never spoken to him but I'd seen him in church. I was scared for my brother, but Domenico reassured me and showed real concern for my brother. Giacomo survived the fever but it left him with a jerky spasm of his hands.

Later that year, despite all my duties watching after my brothers and sisters, Mama enlisted me into the children's choir at church, determined that I needed to earn every point possible to win God's favor. After choir practice, Domenico and I started spending time together. We'd walk along the beach and explore the rocky shoreline as we commiserated over the harsh treatment we both received at home. It felt comforting to share my troubles with him, and spending time with him made my heart dance. Meeting a boy unescorted would have earned me a severe beating if Mama ever found out, but fortunately it was one of the few times her omniscient powers failed her.

A year later, Domenico's father sent him to a highly respected school in Cosenza. I didn't see him much after that, but I thought about him often. He was the only person in the world, outside of my brother Antonio and my two uncles, whom I trusted. Now he was bringing me comfort once again by sharing Papa's death with me.

The black river of humans flowed like molasses into flour down the dusty hill. We passed Mama's crops: wheat and grapes, as well as olive, Bergamot, and orange trees. No one spoke as we navigated the twisting curves leading into town.

Spartacus Summit now stood in front of us. Locals always enjoyed telling the tale of how Spartacus, the famous gladiator slave who defeated three different Roman armies, once stood on top of the large boulder. With his hodgepodge army of a few gladiators, tens of thousands of escaped house slaves, and various criminals, Spartacus defeated the mighty Romans in battle after battle for many years, eventually arriving at this spot in Reggio Calabria. From his vantage point atop this rock, Spartacus surveyed the Mediterranean Sea and discovered that he had been betrayed. The pirate captains he had commissioned to take the 90,000 men and women in his care across the sea to freedom had double-crossed him in favor of the Romans and never delivered his transport ships.

As we entered the outskirts of town we passed small farms with tiny old houses, many of which were owned by Mama and worked by itinerate farmers. Other structures, damaged in the massive earthquakes of 1905 and 1908, remained abandoned.

The unmistakable marker of the blue-domed ceramic-tile roof of the church came into view as we rounded the final hill into town. Papa had helped pay for the construction of the consecrated structure more than ten years earlier.

The thick flow of people in the procession was now covered with mushroom-colored dust; its musty smell tickled my nose. The wind finally subsided as we entered town. I noticed the frayed clothing of the farmers who worked Mama's lands; they wore shoes with holes in them, tattered pants, and threadbare fabrics. The people of Southern Italy had been poor since the time of the Romans. Only in stories about the North did people live in marble houses, wear fancy gowns of satin, and enjoy some sense of freedom.

The cart stopped at the graveyard behind the church, and everyone gathered around the grave that waited to swallow Papa. Mama had already taken her position near the huge granite headstone, which displayed a porcelain picture of Papa in his best suit and Sunday hat. I wondered what the engraving said.

I saw some people look my way and whisper amongst themselves, but this time I was not able to listen in. Only later would I learn that these relative strangers knew more about my father's indiscretions and my family's history than I did.

Mama motioned to me, obviously irritated by the lack of structure in the way the children were positioned at the grave. I quickly organized everyone into a line of military precision. The priest signaled for quiet, and the murmur of voices hushed. The finality of the moment made me tremble; I found it difficult to breathe, and my vision blurred with tears.

On cue, at least two dozen women began to wail—mourners Mama had paid to properly reflect her position. Her lands stretched from the tip of Italy's boot all the way to its heel on the Aegean Sea by Greece. What would people think if she skimped on the number of weeping women?

The pallbearers lifted Papa's coffin from the cart and placed it on three pieces of rope laid out on the ground by the grave. They each took an end of rope and lifted up the bier, moved it over the grave, and carefully lowered Papa into his new confined home. I couldn't bear to picture my dear Papa so restricted.

The priest said a few more words in Latin and sprinkled holy water into the grave. I lowered my head and watched the earth absorb my tears—the earth they shared with his body.

After laying Papa to rest, everyone returned to our house and people lined up to give Mama their condolences. Many tears dampened her cheeks as they kissed her, but none were her own.

As Signore Saldino came up to her, I heard him whisper, "If I may be of service to you, feel free to call on me, Signora Cunzolo. Without a man in the house, who will oversee your lands and handle your business arrangements?"

"A kind offer, Signore Saldino," Mama replied.

"The least I can do." He moved on.

I made my way through the crowd of people giving me sad and pitying looks. As I passed my uncle Paolo, who was talking to several men dressed in various uniforms, I patted him on the back. He smiled but continued his conversation as if I were not there. In a way, I wasn't. Girls could hardly be expected to comprehend the discussions of important men.

"Mussolini is making Italy strong again," one magistrate said to Paolo. "He led us out of the Depression caused by the Great War. Italy will once again become the center of power in the Mediterranean, like in the days of the Roman Empire."

Paolo frowned. "I wish I felt as sure."

"Don't you remember before Mussolini?" said a soldier full of admiration for his leader. "Now the trains run on time, new roads make travel easy, and the nation's work is getting done."

"I hope you're right, gentlemen," Paolo said, turning to gaze out the window.

I spotted my brothers Luigi and Bruno going into the parlor, so I followed them inside before they could stir up any mischief. From the moment I stepped into the room I could feel Domenico's eyes on me.

"*Ciao*, Carina."

"*Ciao,*" I managed to squeak.

"Much time has passed since we last saw each other. I'm sorry our reunion is marked by sadness."

"Yes, a long time." Mama had told me never to show a boy my interest in him—he would think me wanton.

"I've thought a lot about you since our walks on the beach. Thinking of those times with you always brings a smile to my face." He didn't look *at* me, he looked *into* me.

"Really?" I couldn't believe anyone thought about me. "Someone told me you attend the university in Napoli now."

He nodded. "Yes. I'd enjoy meeting with you sometime."

I couldn't find my way back out of his dark eyes. I stood paralyzed and powerless, as if a *strega* witch had surrounded me with her magic.

After what seemed a lifetime, I finally managed, "Mama would never let me go out. Perhaps you could come here . . . for dinner."

Sergio popped over. "I'm going to tell Mama. You're not supposed to talk to boys."

"You're going to be quiet, little brother." I grabbed him by his shirt collar.

"You don't scare me."

"I'm hungry," Luigi piped in.

"That's because you're a little pig," Bruno said then mimicked a pig eating at a trough.

We all laughed. "You've got your hands full now," Domenico said. "I'll look forward to hearing from you soon, under happier circumstances." He put a hand on my shoulder. "I'm truly sorry about your father."

"Thank you."

He bowed his head, and then melded back into the other guests. I couldn't stop myself from noting the way his body moved with such confidence and grace.

"Carina's in love, Carina's in love," Luigi teased.

"Stop it, Luigi, or I'll make sure you won't be able to sit down for a week."

On the way to kitchen Doctor DiScullo and his wife crossed our path. "I can't believe how grown up you're getting, Carina," he said.

I smiled. He was always so kind to everyone.

"Your skin is radiant. You're the picture of health. Such a lovely young lady. I worry about how all of you will get by without your father watching after you." He laid a comforting hand on my shoulder.

"On a day like today especially, its difficult facing life without Papa," I admitted.

"You're almost a lady. You'll be getting married soon and starting a family of your own."

I nodded. Most women in the South married before reaching age twenty. What else could a woman do?

He turned to his wife. "Isn't she a fine young lady, dear? I hope our little ones turn out as well."

"Yes," his wife absently agreed.

My brothers began a pushing match. I gestured toward them. "I better fix them something to eat before someone gets hurt."

"I'll watch Luigi and Bruno for you," he offered

"Thank you, Doctor DiScullo." I turned toward my brothers. "You two wait here and stay out of trouble." They nodded, but I feared for the doctor's sanity.

When I went into the kitchen, I found several people rummaging around in the cupboards and sneaking bites of food. Since I was mostly hidden by the floor-to-ceiling cabinet on the other side of the room, no one noticed me, and I took care to remain out of sight. Eating at a funeral was considered rude, but it had been a long day, so stealing a few bites was proper decorum. I grabbed a loaf of Mama's bread and assembled sandwiches for my brothers, as well as for the doctor and his wife.

The kitchen raiders gobbled down bread and cheese, whispering to one another with every step.

"It's always been a bit of a mystery how Lucilla got the lands in the first place."

"Where's her family?"

"They were gypsies, after all," one of the women said. The others chuckled as the group scurried out of the kitchen through the far doorway.

At the same time Gino, one of Papa's lawyer friends, and another man came into the kitchen through the same opening. They did not appear to be interested in food. I made sure I was out of sight

"Does Lucilla know yet?" Gino asked the other man.

"I'm uncertain what she's been told. I don't believe so."

"The news should come from me. I hate to say anything today, but it must be done."

Their voices dropped and I left the room with the sandwiches, worried over what new secrets were about to be revealed. My brothers each grabbed a sandwich.

Luigi started to devour his and Bruno made pig snorting noises, holding the two halves of his sandwich up by the sides of his head as if they were big, floppy ears. I had to laugh. Even the Doctor giggled at how goofy he looked.

"Here's one for you, too, Doctor and Signora DiScullo," I said, holding out the plate.

"That's very sweet of you, Carina," the doctor said.

I didn't reply, as I was distracted by seeing Gino hand Mama a document. She didn't study it, of course; she couldn't read. She simply marked an X on it. But as their conversation continued, she grew more and more upset. Noticing her distress, Paolo came over and tried to calm her.

Her shout rose over the rumble of conversation in the room. "I don't care who he is! He's no longer welcome in my house. His gambling games and brothels have brought shame to my family and his!"

Everyone froze as Mama hurried toward Signore Saldino, shouting, "You've disgraced my family, Saldino! You'll find no absolution for your sins!"

"Lucilla, this is Signore Saldino," Paolo said, noticeably afraid of how Saldino might react. "I am so sorry, Signore Saldino."

Signore Saldino held up a hand to indicate his understanding, and then calmly said, "We will leave now. The widow is distressed, understandably. Women are ignorant; they have these emotional outbursts. We can look past such things on such a traumatic day; after all, we must feel sorry for her. Who will look after her now?" He then stared into Paolo's eyes and said softly, "But see that she does not say anything she might regret about me or my family in the future. I ask this as a personal favor."

"Yes," Uncle Paolo said, wringing his hands. "Yes, I'll make certain she doesn't."

Signore Saldino turned toward the door. Someone helped him with his overcoat. He turned to Domenico and motioned for them to leave. Domenico's eyes caught mine as he crossed the room to his father, and I could feel his disappointment that he had to leave. How could we ever be together now?

"Get out of my house!" Mama cried, eyes burning, one hand clasping the locket that hung around her neck; the locket with Papa's picture inside. "You've always been a curse on this family! Get out!"

Everyone remained hushed, waiting for her next words.

"Never again do I want to hear the name Saldino! Never!"

Chapter 3

THE BLACK WIDOW

A week had passed since Papa's funeral. Normal routines had returned, even though our spirits still faced a long journey to recover from our loss. The view out my window was clear all the way down to town and across the Straits of Messina to Sicily, where Domenico lived. In the other direction, the sun's reflection created brilliant golden tones along the peaks of the Apennine Mountains, and there was no trace of the Sirocco Winds as the cool breezes of fall had begun to flow down from the mountains.

After breakfast Antonio and Giacomo went to pick olives with Umberto, while my younger brothers played with their wooden toy horses. My sisters Gianina and Santina huddled around the fireplace in the parlor and played tea time with their dolls.

I kissed my fingers and pressed them against the picture of the Madonna on the mantel, which sat beside the one of Mussolini. Mama had told me that Mussolini deserved prominence because he made Vatican City a country for the pope in 1929 and restored the Church's right to teach religion in schools.

Mama poked her head out of the kitchen. "Carina, come here." I started toward the kitchen. "No one interrupt us," she added, glaring at the other children. I thought through my recent actions, considering if any of them might have displeased her.

Once in the kitchen, Mama directed me to sit. With nervous

anticipation I complied; the cedar chair felt as cold as her tone. Her hand gripped the kitchen table as she seemed uncertain how to begin. "You know how important family is, Carina?"

"Of course, Mama."

"We must do what's best for family."

"Yes, Mama. Are we in trouble? I heard things at Papa's funeral."

"What things?"

"Well . . ."

"Go ahead. I should know what people say about us."

"That Papa drank, smoked, gambled, and . . . that he sold off much of your land."

Mama was quiet for a moment, and then said in a hushed tone, "Gino, the attorney, says it's true. Saldino supplied the vices and Papa gave in to them."

"So, Signore Saldino—"

"I told you never to mention his name! What's wrong with you, spiteful girl?" A scowl eclipsed her face and for a moment I thought she was going to strike me.

"I'm sorry, Mama. It won't happen again."

"It's difficult . . . Paolo and I talked again last night . . . Decisions were made . . ." Mama wavered between thoughts. "Do you know what a black widow is?"

"It sounds scary."

"Don't be silly. We all do what's best for the family. What else is life good for?"

"Yes, Mama."

"We have no one to look after things. A black widow helps look after things."

"I don't understand."

Mama stood up. "With Guglielmo gone, you will become a black widow, Carina."

Tears started flowing down my cheeks. It sounded as if I was being sent to prison.

"Don't cry," Mama ordered, as she gave me a quick cuff to the back of the head. "A black widow must be strong."

"But what *is* a black widow?"

"You'll learn to read, write, and work with numbers."

"Girls don't read."

"Of course not, but you'll learn so you can take care of this family. That's what a black widow does; she becomes the man of the house after a family loses its father. It's the way of the South."

"I already help take care of the family."

"Yes, but you'll be educated and learn to manage the lands. Papa didn't do best for our family—he brought shame on us. We've lost much property, and the vultures continue to take more. You must learn to protect us, with the wolves sniffing at the door. Paolo and Salvatore say they'll help as much as they can, but you must take Papa's place at the head of the family. You'll become the *paterfamilias*—the patriarch." She picked up a dishtowel and began to twist it. "There's one more part of being a black widow: As women can't be allowed to read and educated, except for nuns, a black widow must give up . . . a normal life."

"A normal life? I don't understand."

"Dense girl. You can never marry."

"But to get married is one of the sacraments of the Church!"

She slapped the towel on the edge of the metal kitchen sink and my heart pumped faster. "It's been decided. You will do as I say! No more questions. A tutor will teach you. I just hope he finds a brain in that ugly head of yours." She went over to the window and looked out. "You're better off without a man, anyway. Men are evil. They wound you. They're selfish and can't be trusted."

I buried my face in my hands and filled them with tears. My body trembled with dread at the thought of my future. The life of a nun, without the company of God. I had been condemned to purgatory.

I sat in my father's big, crinkled leather chair in his study, waiting for the tutor's arrival. I thought about my future as a black widow; beatings from Mama seemed more appealing—at least they ended. Never would someone love me. Never would I care for my own child. Never would I know life. My future held only loneliness and servitude. More than anything else that Mama had subjected me to over the years, I resented her for this the most. I vowed to have my day.

As much as I missed Papa, I hated him for dying and putting me in this position. He would want me to care for the family. So much responsibility made me wish to face my final judgment and join my father in the afterlife.

My eyes drifted around Papa's study. From behind his imposing desk, the room seemed menacing with its tall mahogany bookshelves lining every wall. The books looked down on me from their shelves, taunting and laughing at my ignorance. I looked away, out the window, to avoid their glare.

One of Papa's books on the desk drew my attention. Big, thick, and lifeless. I touched its leather cover with my fingers and drew away. What could this dead object teach me about living life? Women cooked, sewed, and took care of the family. Of what use were books? Why men found benefit in them baffled me.

Mustering my courage, I opened it. The letters looked strange—so many filling each page. How would I ever learn to tell them apart? How could anyone make sense of an entire book?

The splendid smells of Papa's pipe still lingered in the air, along with the scent of wood bookshelves and leather-bound volumes. His study had always seemed intimidating, but I'd always savored the aromas.

I heard steps from the hall as they approached the door, then Mama's and a strange man's voice exchange a few unintelligible words. The surprisingly heavy thump of Mama's petite, ninety-pound footsteps faded away, and there was an endless pause before the door opened.

A short, chubby, bald man with squinty eyes came into the room. He was dressed in a shabby, wrinkled brown suit, and carried a worn leather briefcase and a blackboard that was tucked under his arm. He placed them both on the floor against the side of the desk.

"My name is Signore Moretti," he said, looking around the room but avoiding my eyes altogether. "Until recently I taught at a school in Cosenza." Finally, he turned his gaze to me and studied me thoroughly, as though assessing whether or not I was worthy of consideration. "I have never had the displeasure of teaching a girl before. Do you want to learn, little girl?"

Uncertain how to respond, I said nothing.

"Well, tell me the truth."

I shook my head.

"I wouldn't think so. Yes . . . hmmm. I don't know if it's possible for a girl to learn. Do you know the letters?"

"No."

"Numbers?"

I hesitated, then again shook my head.

"Hmmm," he droned, disapprovingly. "Let's see if that pretty little head of yours has a brain." He pulled a book out of his briefcase and set up the blackboard on the small end table by the leather chair. He leaned the blackboard against one of the bookcases and began writing letters on it with chalk. I recognized the third symbol.

"That's the letter 'C,'" I called out triumphantly. "Our name, Cunzolo, starts with 'C.' Papa showed me that."

"Yes," Signore Moretti grunted, unimpressed by my knowledge. "Well, let's see if we can learn the other twenty-five."

For the next several hours he scribbled symbols on the chalkboard and quizzed me on the names of the letters and the order in which they appeared in the alphabet. It was all very confusing. If I couldn't even learn the alphabet, how would I ever learn to read?

Signore Moretti asked me once again to recite the ABCs, and by letter "P" I wanted to scream.

Suddenly Mama burst into the room. I hoped she had come with lunch; instead, she brought hysteria. "Paolo . . ." She couldn't continue.

"What is it, Mama?"

She took a deep breath. "Paolo is dead."

I screamed, but no sound exited from my mouth. Uncle Paolo *also* dead?

"He killed himself," Mama went on in a rush. "Holy Mary, Mother of God. Pray for us sinners now and at the hour of our death. Mary, Mother of Jesus!"

"Why, Mama? Why?"

She didn't answer, just kept whispering desperately, "Holy Mary, Mother of God. Pray for us sinners now and at the hour of our death."

Mama had calmed down enough by bedtime to expect us all to follow the normal ritual before going to bed. She waited for us in the parlor. The little ones entered first, then the oldest, ending with me. We each kissed Mama's hand and asked, "Forgive me, Mama, if I've offended you in any way today." Mama would wave us on if we hadn't, or caution us on the proper behavior to please her if we had.

"You *will* learn everything your tutors want you to learn," she said to me. "You cannot fail."

"I know, Mama. I'll do my best."

"Don't want your best. You will do everything this family needs," Mama insisted.

"I will." I had enough welts on my back to know what it meant if I failed her.

"Salvatore lives far to the north and cannot help us. We have no one else. This family stands alone. You must watch over our welfare."

"Yes, Mama." I kissed her hand, but the kiss tasted of the rage that filled me. I wanted to care for my siblings, but she deserved no respect or credit. Yes, she worked hard in the kitchen, but her meals were seasoned with malice. She never talked of the past, but she was so filled with hate that there was no doubt of its horror. It seemed odd that we knew nothing of our family lineage from her side. Whenever one of us asked a question about her family, she either refused to respond or said, "Who needs to look at the sadness of the past?" The only mention of ancestry was of Roma gypsies who had come to Calabria a thousand years ago, or my great, great grandfather, who she claimed was King of the Gypsies.

Antonio waited for me at the bottom of the stairs on our way up to bed. "Scared of being a black widow?" he asked.

"I'm terrified I'll let everyone down."

Antonio hugged me. "Don't worry, you keep this family together." It felt good to be held by someone who cared about me. He was a good brother. He might be a miser when it came to words, but he gave generously of himself for the benefit of others, a trait he had inherited from Papa. Being tall but without the proper strength or weight to carry it, he sagged to one side or the other. His eyelids always appeared heavy, as if he fought to keep them open. Someone who didn't know him well might mistake him for a passive young man without fire, but Antonio held an inner strength few others could claim. And no one could doubt the power of his loyalty. He was the person I trusted most in the world.

I said, "I wish Papa had . . . done things differently. Uncle Paolo told me Papa died more from unhappiness than his heart. He said Papa felt guilty about giving into his weaknesses with Saldino."

"Maybe he wanted to escape Mama." Antonio's breathing seemed uneven. He coughed and rubbed his throat.

"I heard Uncle Paulo owed money to Saldino. I think that's why he killed himself."

Sergio sprang out into the hall from his bedroom. "Mama said never mention Saldino's name. What weaknesses did Papa have?"

I wagged a finger at him. "Hey, you little sneak. Stop listening to other people's conversations."

"No one tells me anything. I'm old enough to know what's going on."

"No, you're not, you little *saputo*," I said, giving him a shove toward his room. "Go back to bed, Sergio."

He stuck his tongue out at me and then ran downstairs. Antonio's breathing became more uneven, and now he was struggling to take a breath.

"Oh, no. Your asthma." I rushed him into his room and grabbed the brown bottle from the top drawer of his dresser. I quickly dribbled a few drops of the chestnut-leaf elixir into his mouth as he labored to inhale, and then I opened up the window to let in some fresh air. His body started to relax, and his breathing gradually improved. Excitement and anxiety seemed to bring on the attacks.

"Better?" I asked.

He nodded. I saw Mama stomp up the stairs and head down the hall with her whipping belt in hand. Sergio peeked down the hall from the staircase. Mama waved the thick leather belt in the air as she yelled at Antonio, "I told everyone in this house never to speak of that scum from Sicily! The belt will remember you to never to say his name again."

I hurried over to her as she started in on Antonio. "Mama, it was me! I was the one talking about Saldino. Antonio told me not to say his name. It was me."

"No—" Antonio tried to speak but lacked the necessary air.

Mama cracked me across the back with the belt. "*Never* speak his name! How can I make it clear to you? Never! Never! Never!" She smacked me several more times around my arms and back with the thick belt. Antonio tried to stop her, but she stormed off as quickly as she had descended.

Sergio now peered at us from his doorway. When I turned toward him, guilt surfaced in his face and he hurriedly shut and locked his door. The *spettegolare* rat.

Ignoring the throbbing burns on my back, I attended to Antonio until his normal breathing came back.

Despite Mama's beating, the Saldino name flowed from my lips many more times after that. Especially when I had to face one of the biggest decisions of my life—which involved the family name Mama most hated.

Chapter 4

FURTHER EDUCATION

The morning sunlight filtered through the lace curtains over my bedroom window and illuminated the pages of the novel. I was lying on my bed with my body draped over the pillows and the book propped against the headboard. Almost two years had passed since Signore Moretti first introduced me to the alphabet; now I held a book in front of my face night and day. Like one of those new deep-sea divers that go underwater for hours, I used books as my lifeline to the world. They had replaced real life ever since I'd become a black widow.

When I asked about my progress, Signore Moretti grudgingly admitted that I was his best student. I immediately absorbed anything he exposed me to. He concentrated my studies on math and business fundamentals, as I needed that knowledge to run Mama's affairs. Noticing my quick progress, Doctor DiScullo volunteered to help tutor me as well. He visited once a week to cover biology and a little medicine that would help me care for Mama's animals. He even taught me some English, Latin, and German. We discussed philosophy too, though I never told Mama, as she would have beaten me for wasting my time on such a useless thing.

Reading Papa's books transported me into the exciting lives led by those who lived in the North. In Rome, Venice, and Milan people lived in palaces and villas, and enjoyed the freedom to socialize with whoever they wanted and go wherever they desired. I envied their liberty. People in the South lived strictly by tradition and propriety.

My new knowledge began paying off as soon as I started to organize Mama's affairs. I created charts and tracked the payments of farmers working her lands, which came in the form of crops, wool, milk products, cloth, and other items, as no one ever paid with money. It surprised me how much joy I found in getting her business affairs into proper order.

I usually accompanied Mama into town when she went shopping, since she relied on me to negotiate for her. One particular day, Antonio, Giacomo, and Mama's long-time servants Umberto and Zola helped us load the wagon with wheat, wool, and chestnuts. We planned to exchange them for heating oil, a textbook I had ordered, and several bags of cement for a watering trough to expand the goat herd.

After we finished loading, Mama stood by the cart giving last-minute instructions to Umberto's wife, Zola, who would be remaining behind. "Now I don't want Santina to eat any of the cannoli I made. Remember, Dr. DiScullo said it was bad for her stomach condition. Make sure Giacomo cleans out the stalls and get Sergio and Luigi to help him. I want them to have more responsibilities, they're old enough. Also be sure Gianina helps you fix dinner. You know how she tries to ignore her duties. We'll return before sundown, so hold dinner for us."

Although almost two years had passed since Papa's death, Mama—the eternal widow—still dressed in black every day. "What would people think if I didn't mourn for Guglielmo?" she would say. Yet in all that time I had never seen her cry. I think she hoped the grim reaper might forget to come for her if she remained in constant mourning.

Antonio and Giacomo finished loading the crops onto the wagon while Umberto bridled the horse. Umberto had to help Mama and me onto the wagon because our skirts, with three dresses layered underneath, always presented difficulties. Once we were seated, he climbed up to the driver's seat and we started our journey.

I began to read my book on royalty from Roman times to the present. What a life the royals led! "Mama, you own a lot of land stretching over two hundred miles. You tell us stories about great, great grandfather, King of the Gypsies. Why aren't you a countess?"

"What silliness do you speak?"

"You own the land. Why do you still bake, clean, sew, and milk cows?"

"Because it's the duty of a woman. What kind of nonsense question is that?"

"In the North, women with means don't work. They go to balls and fancy dinners."

"They sound like whores, drifting about unescorted."

"These women come from noble families with long histories," I said. "Why don't we ever see or hear from any of your family, Mama?"

"The past is painful. Most of them are gone. What reason is there to talk about it?" She turned away, signaling me to drop any further discussion.

As we passed through the main street of town, I noticed many of the men on the street turning to look at me. Men are silly, I thought. I didn't know why they stared.

We pulled up to Calabria General Store. The windowed door gave a raspy groan as we entered. The scent of freshly ground cinnamon filled the air. Signore Verduci and his wife were working behind the counter, and several people, including Doctor DiScullo, were milling around the store.

On seeing Mama, the proprietor put a finger up in the air to punctuate his enthusiasm. "Oh, Signora Cunzolo! It's good to see you looking so well."

Mama gave him a half-smile and nodded. Most people showed her respect, but I never saw her give much in return.

"Hello, good Doctor," I said, happy to see him. Although not a handsome man, the doctor shone with kindness.

"How's your anatomy coming?" he asked.

I pointed to my shoulder, my arm, and then my hand. *"Susipere, brachium, manus."*

"Very good, Carina. Your Latin is coming along." He pointed to the top of his head. *"Cranium."*

I pointed to my head. *"Cranium."*

"You soak up everything. You're such a bright student, my little chestnut."

"Thank you, Doctor." He always spoke to me with such encouragement, while Mama gave me the rod for progressing too slowly and questioned the time I was wasting on learning useless information.

Signore Verduci helped Mama with her order, but the usually sullen shopkeeper was smiling at me as he did so. Was there something in my teeth? I ran my tongue over them. In the past year, he often looked at me that way. Signora Verduci poked her husband in the side with a broom handle and got him back to work.

I looked down at my book. "I've read about it, but what's Rome really like, Doctor?"

"It pulses with the fast beat of a circus, so many things happening all at once. Beauty and history assault you on every street in the Ancient City, and people race about like ants."

"*Bel niente*—sweet nothing. Two thousand years ago it was the first city in the world to house more than a million people."

"There wasn't another for a thousand years," he confirmed. "I'll tell you more when I see you tonight for your lesson." The doctor gave my arm a squeeze. "Ciao bella, Carina."

"Ciao, Dr. DiScullo."

"*Arrivederci*, Signora Cunzolo," he said to Mama as he moved to the door, but Mama only returned a cold nod.

Behind me, two girls giggled and whispered, "That girl is reading!"

"How silly, she'll never find a husband," the other replied.

Mama handed a bolt of black fabric to Signora Verduci. "Three yards." Signora Verduci measured the fabric, cut it, folded it and wrapped it in paper with a string around it. Mama never paid with money, and no one expected her to. In fact, I never saw her with currency in her hand; she didn't trust it. What was a piece of paper compared to wheat, vegetables, cloth, lumber, and other real goods? It was an arrangement that suited most people in the South.

The shopkeeper's wife spoke up. "My nephew is visiting from the North. I think he'd enjoy meeting Carina. Would the two of you like to come to dinner at our house to meet him?"

"No, no, I'm sorry," Mama said firmly. "Carina's a black widow. No point in her meeting any young men."

Signora Verduci nodded solemnly. "I understand, Signora Cunzolo."

After I had negotiated an exchange for Mama's crops with Signore Verduci, Mama ordered, "Go to the butcher and get some of those sausages I like while I finish here."

"Yes, Mama. Ciao, Signore and Signora Verduci." They waved to me.

I left the store and started toward the butcher's shop, when I felt a shiver ripple up my spine. Instantly, I knew who was behind me.

I turned to see Domenico standing an arm's-length away.

"Hello, Carina."

"Domenico!"

"I saw you and your mother come into town, and I've been waiting for a chance to speak with you. Carina, meet with me."

"You know I can't do that. I'm forbidden to even mention your family's name." I pulled him to the side of the building so we weren't so visible.

"But you want to see me, don't you?"

"What I want doesn't matter." I cherished the time we had spent together as children. Other than my brother Antonio, Domenico was the only person I had ever shared my deepest thoughts with, the only person willing to share the burden of my responsibilities. He made me feel as though I existed in the world for some other reason than to simply follow Mama's orders. I hadn't seen him since he had gone back to college after Papa's funeral. He had grown into a man.

"Your mother's hatred of my father has nothing to do with you and me." He leaned toward me and placed his hand on my arm. I felt guilty that I loved the touch of his hand on me. "Meet me at the Spartacus Summit at dusk tomorrow."

"I can't meet a man alone."

"Your mother will never give you permission to see me. Please come."

"I can't."

"I'll be there. I pray that you will, too." His tone was assured, as though he knew I would come. He grabbed my hand and kissed it before rushing off.

Mama came out of the general store but didn't see Domenico walking away. She looked at me quizzically. "Where are my sausages?"

That evening, Dr. DiScullo arrived at our house with a book in hand. Antonio and Giacomo had placed the dining room table on the moveable hearth after dinner, and most of the family now sat around it roasting chestnuts. I grabbed a few to share with the doctor during my lesson, and then ran up to him and kissed him on the cheek. My mood was still high in the clouds from my encounter with Domenico.

"How is Calabria's man of healing?"

"Well, thank you. How's my little sponge of knowledge? Where have you traveled in your books this week?"

"England and the Caribbean. I just finished *Treasure Island*. And now I'm reading one of Papa's books on Europe's royalty."

We walked up the stairs to Papa's study. Tuesday night was the doctor's regular evening to tutor me, after attending his patients in the area. I looked forward to Tuesdays because he always made studying fun; he was interesting, well read, and traveled—a refreshing change from Mama.

"Can you name the first royalty of Rome?" he asked as we walked into the study.

"The first Roman emperor was Octavian."

"Correct, my little chestnut. He proved himself a great leader, bringing peace to the Roman Empire after a hundred years of civil war. He reduced class inequities, stimulated trade, and brought the armies under control of the State, rather than the old method of each general forming and controlling his own army. This led to two hundred years of internal peace within the empire, an achievement no other Roman leader ever accomplished. Many governments around the world still govern under his methods."

"*Bel niente,*" I said, marveling at what life must have been like in Rome. "Doctor DiScullo, all these books show me that there's more to life than this house on top of a hill at the bottom tip of Europe, the far end of nowhere. I want to go out and live!"

"Where do you see yourself, Carina?"

"Someday I want to run a beautiful hotel in Rome, like my Uncle Salvatore, a magnificent place where the rich and famous come to holiday. I'd have a lobby appointed with beautiful marbles, elegant drapes and furniture done in luxurious velvets and silks. A place where people throw fancy balls and lavish parties. I'd employ all my brothers and sisters, so they'd have the freedom of their own money." I also imagined Domenico helping me, but didn't mention that.

Doctor DiScullo gave me a broad smile and ran his hand over my hair. "A grand dream. You're far too smart and beautiful not to get what you want."

Chapter 5

ECSTASY AND AGONY

For the next twenty-four hours, I dreamt of Domenico. As I picked at my dinner I sensed his presence on Spartacus Summit, drawing me like a magnet. The very thought of him made me burn inside, and I had to remind myself that I was a black widow and that my family was counting on me. Besides, what kind of woman meets a man alone at night? I knew: the kind of woman Mama hated.

"I'm going into town for evening Mass with Umberto and Zola," she announced after dinner. Antonio and Giacomo told her they had to finish repairing the sheep stable before the shearing. Since she hated any embarrassing disturbances during Mass, Mama didn't make the younger children go with her. I wasn't so fortunate. "Carina, come to Mass."

"I want to, Mama, but I need to work on the payment schedule for the farmers who work your land in the east."

"Well, that's important," she conceded, as she took her coat and headed out the door.

I watched from the window until the carriage passed from sight, then ran out of the house and down the hill. The scent from the orange trees smelled heavenly. Each step toward Spartacus Summit was both exhilarating and terrifying.

The setting sun radiated behind the summit. A tail of smoke curled up from the top boulder.

Suddenly, faced with the reality of actually meeting with Domenico alone, I froze. Unable to take another step forward, I couldn't return home, either. This was my one opportunity. I wanted to feel his strong arms around me, protecting me from the world, if only for an instant. Perhaps his embrace would become a memory I could carry with me for a lifetime. Surely God would see this one transgression as a venial sin that wouldn't affect my soul. I didn't care what Mama did to me, I had to look into Domenico's eyes.

I hurried to the summit and climbed up the boulders. Other than a few cypress trees that grappled to grow within the cracks, the summit was barren. I reached the top breathless. The final light of the sun outlined Domenico as he paced around the campfire he had made. The smoke from it smelled comforting. Deep in thought, he used a stick to stir the embers.

"I don't know why I came," I blurted.

He turned. The warm glow of the fire accented his chiseled features and accentuated his electric eyes. "Because you want to be here with me," he said, moving toward me.

"What can I want as a black widow?"

"Things change. We can make them." Domenico continued closer, but I backed away.

"How can you be so forward?"

"In our situation, if we wait for propriety, our lives will be over."

"My family's counting on me."

"I love my family, too. My father wants me to go into his business. But I won't live my life that way. I want nothing to do with my family's past." He motioned with his arm, as if pushing the past behind him.

"What *do* you want?"

He was silent as he thought it through. "I want to make a difference in people's lives. I want to help." He paused, looking up at the sky and then back to me. "And meeting with you has clarified that I want to be with you."

"How can you say such a thing?" His brazen words thrilled and shocked me at the same time. Just being within a few feet of him made my heart race to the point I thought I would pass out.

"Because," he said, as if realizing it himself for the first time, "I know, together, we can accomplish great things. I want to share my life with you, Carina."

"Domenico . . ." I could not find anything to say. Desire, temptation, guilt, need, panic, longing, and love created a whirlpool of confusion in me.

"Let's run away," he went on, "before it's too late. I want to taste your lips on mine, feel what it's like to run my fingers through your hair. I want to see you the first thing in the morning and for you to be the last thing I see at night. I want to look into your beautiful blue eyes and see your love for me."

"I know you could make me happy." I felt so naked before him, I had to turn away, but he pulled be gently back towards him.

"You see, Carina? You want us to be together, too. We could go to the North where no one knows us."

"You could leave your family?"

"If I stay, I'll lose my soul."

"My family needs me." I sighed with despair. "I'm the *paterfamilias* now."

He grabbed my hand, shook my ring finger. "What about your sacrament to the Church? To be married?"

I melted at his simple touch. "Yes, but a black widow must—"

He waved his hands in protest. "Forget that. Forget the traditions of the South. Meet me tomorrow and we'll go to the North."

I wondered why he wanted me, of all people, but trembled with fear at the thought of asking.

"We can start new lives in Rome," he said.

My eyes grew wide. "Rome. Really? Maybe my Uncle Salvatore would let us stay at his hotel, maybe even work for him."

Domenico ran the charred point of his stick down the boulder's surface to make a vertical line. "Come to this point." I moved to it cautiously. He marked another line, closer to him, and then motioned me to move toward it. I took two steps. "We'll just keep moving little by little until we come together."

He captured me in his arms and held me with the force of a man in love. I let go of my will, wanting to feel possessed by him. My body filled with desire for him. He pointed to the sky.

"I arranged this for you," he said with a grin. The moon glowed brightly now, sharing the sky with the dimming orange sun.

"It's beautiful."

"Not compared to you."

Our lips met and his kiss took me to a weightless, timeless realm. The taste of his mouth made me hunger for him. I'd never known such longing. We held each other for eons of time before I finally whispered, "I must go." His arms released me and I took a couple of steps toward the path.

"Meet me here at dusk tomorrow," he insisted. "Commit to our love."

I rushed back and kissed him again, praying that it conveyed my love for him and hoping it didn't violate any Church law. Our souls seemed connected through our lips. "I'll give you my answer tomorrow."

He smiled. I pulled from his embrace and headed onto the path. After a few steps I stopped and turned to fill my eyes with his image one last time.

"I won't be able to sleep," he shouted.

"Nor will I."

I drifted home in a euphoric daze. The familiar landscape around me now glowed with new textures and vivid colors. The orange blossoms overwhelmed my nose. Was a life with Domenico possible?

I saw Umberto putting away the cart and knew Mama had returned.

When I entered the house, Mama was pacing like a crazy woman and screaming, "My face is lost! The shame!" Her skin burned brick red. She ran to the fireplace, grabbed a large scoop of ashes, and smeared her face with them. "God, take me! I cannot live with the disgrace!"

Could she have seen Domenico?

She spotted me, and her expression instantly transformed into rage. A rush of fear filled me as she charged at me. Grabbing me by the hair, she shouted, "The disgrace!"

"Mama! I've done nothing wrong!"

Still yanking me by my hair, she led me past the kitchen and pushed me into the storage room, where I fell against the table inside. She snatched her beating belt and an intense loathing came to her face.

Dear Lord, how could she possibly know of my encounter with Domenico? I grabbed her arm to stop her from unleashing the strap on me, but my feet slipped out from under me and I fell to the floor.

Holding the belt by the opposite end from the buckle, Mama swung it at me. I cried out in pain as the metal buckle hit me in the genitals.

"You've ruined this family! You can no longer be accepted as a black widow. No one will respect you or this family ever again." As I struggled to get to my feet, she swung the belt at me again. It ripped into my dress and pain lit across my side. "You must hide in shame the rest of your life!"

"I did nothing wrong!"

She lashed at me even harder. I blocked the blow with my arm, but the buckle ripped into my wrist and opened a large gash. I began to bleed.

"You whore! You filthy whore! You were with him. You let him touch you." Mama took another swing, which I partially blocked with my hand. Blood from my wrist splattered across the table and several droplets hit my face. "The best we can hope is to sell you as a maid to some family far away."

"What are you talking about, Mama? I've done nothing."

"You let Doctor DiScullo touch you! Now he is dead! He took a shotgun and . . ." Her words swirled about me like a haze. "In his suicide note, he said he was consumed by you, that he couldn't go on any longer without you."

She took a firmer grip on the belt, which gave me time to get to my feet. As she swung again, I grabbed her arm and pushed her against the wall.

"What will people think?" she shouted as we struggled. The ash on her face gave her the complexion of a corpse. "They can only think that you and the doctor . . . You've ruined this family, you filthy whore! You can't represent this family any longer. There's only one thing to do . . . send you away—far away, so everyone forgets you ever existed."

I finally wrestled the belt away from her. She turned and dashed out of the room, but I followed her into the parlor. I reeled back with the strap, tempted to give her some of her own medicine, but threw her tool of abuse into the fire instead.

"You'll never beat any of us again, Mama!"

"You filthy whore!" she yelled. She mumbled something—a gypsy hex—spat at me and hastily left the room.

Blood was still dripping from my wrist, and the pain of Mama's lashings throbbed across my body. I ripped off a torn section of my dress and wrapped it around my wrist. I sank to my knees and remained motionless for a long time, unsure if my paralysis stemmed from the damage Mama had inflicted or the news of the sweet doctor's death. If I had contributed to it in some way I could never grant myself absolution, nor could God, I was sure. Certainly this was a nightmare that I would soon wake from.

Prison bars can be made of many materials; simple cotton curtains can sometimes lock you away from the world as firmly as iron bars. After the suicide of the doctor, I was captive within the four walls of my room. I couldn't find the courage to face anyone, and Mama didn't release me from my penitentiary for fear my presence would corrupt anyone exposed to it.

Over the days that followed, through my bedroom door, Antonio related the gossip from town about Doctor DiScullo. Many stories centered on my seducing him and losing my virginity; this and other lies even reached the newspaper. Antonio told me, "I overheard you were pregnant by the doctor, and that's why he killed himself."

"Is that what you think?"

"Rumors in Calabria are just that."

I wanted to believe in my goodness, but wasn't convinced of it. The doctor was dead, people blamed me, and perhaps they were right to do so. Perhaps God was punishing me for my plan to betray my family by running away with Domenico. I could not be certain why the doctor took his own life. The answer to that question was known only to the doctor and his Maker, but I knew he had never touched me, I didn't entice him in any way, and I wasn't pregnant with his child. But none of that mattered. In Calabria, once a thing is thought to be true, it never fades from the memory of its people. Mama was right about one thing: my life would be hell if I remained in the South. But what choice did I have? A woman's future there was determined by her family, which left my destiny in Mama's hands.

As I began to get dressed, I caught site of my nakedness in the mirror. I inspected my body. My alabaster skin had never seen the rays of the sun, and, I had grown many new curves in the past year. My eyes were unnaturally large and dark; perhaps they cast some gypsy spell on all those who looked into them. I studied the way my long black hair brushed along my shoulder. With my fingers, I grazed my cheekbone and then my neck, my shoulder, my breasts. For the doctor to perform such an unforgivable sin in the eyes of God, I must be evil. I turned the mirror toward the wall. "The way men look at me . . . I must be unholy. I drove the doctor to this terrible act."

Grabbing the ugliest dress in my closet, I threw it on and pulled a sweater over it, added my heavy, gray wool coat and planted my floppy rain hat on my head. For a long time I sat in quiet reflection, praying to the doctor and God for forgiveness. The sun beamed outside, but a dark storm rained in my room.

As night descended I looked toward Spartacus Summit. As it had for each of the past nine days, a campfire burned atop the boulder. Why did he still wait for me? I loved Domenico; I couldn't bring my shame on him. I couldn't corrupt him with the evil I carried inside myself.

Chapter 6

RUSSO'S INVASION

A heavy knock fell on the front door, the first contact with the outside world since Doctor DiScullo death. I crept out of my room and peered down from behind the banister. Mama opened the door to a man in his late thirties, who was dressed in a fancy silk suit. He had a handsome face, but his build was slight and he was no taller than me.

"*Buona mattina,* good morning, Signora Cunzolo," he said with a charming smile. "I am Vincenzo Russo. I wrote to you about Carina." His dense Napoli accent made him difficult to understand.

"Ah, yes, Signore Russo," Mama said.

"I must apologize, Signora, but I couldn't wait for your reply. The matter's too pressing, so I came to see you in person."

"Well, come in, Signore Russo." Mama took his hat and hung it on the coat rack by the door. Signore Russo nodded to Antonio and glanced at Santina and Isabella playing on the floor nearby.

"I was surprised to receive your letter. My priest read it to me," Mama said. "Of course, he comes to see me often."

"Well, as I stated in the letter, I've come to make you a proposal."

"Come into the kitchen and I'll make you coffee." Mama led him to the kitchen door. "We can talk privately."

"Thank you. So kind of you, Signora Cunzolo."

As they exited, Mama smiled. A distinguished appearance and good manners had always impressed her.

I snuck down the stairs and asked Antonio, "Do you know who he is?"

"No."

Mama poked her head out of the kitchen, and I quickly ducked around the corner. "Get Carina and bring her to the kitchen," she called to Antonio before closing the kitchen door behind her. Mama hadn't spoken to me since the doctor's death more than a week ago.

Cautiously, I stepped into the kitchen and stood by Mama while she filled the visitor's coffee cup. The warm, nutty smell filled the room. Mama glared at me with narrowed eyes as she placed a bowl of chestnuts in front of the stranger. "Please help yourself to some chestnuts, Signore Russo."

Seemingly from nowhere, he produced a stiletto and flipped it open. The slim tapered blade looked razor-sharp. Within seconds he had skillfully peeled a half-dozen nuts.

Mama returned the coffee pot to the stove and led me by my shoulder with her hand. "As you can see, she is not an unattractive girl."

"No, she is quite beautiful," he said, looking at me from top to bottom. Then he spoke to me directly. "The photo of you in the newspaper didn't do you justice."

Mama pointed to various parts of my body. "A good sturdy girl with strong hips, womanly curves, and a tiny waist. Good bone structure. She works well in the kitchen and makes her own clothing." I felt my face burning. She was valuing me like an auctioneer at a horse auction.

Signore Russo looked me over while popping chestnuts into his mouth. Without shifting his gaze, he continued to peel more with his blade.

"She's a hard worker," Mama continued. "Good with children— being the oldest of thirteen."

"Mama, I don't even know this man. Why are you saying these things?"

"Hush, Carina," Mama said, in a stern but polite tone, not wanting her guest to see her angry. "Signore Russo, after the death of my husband, our family is in need. I planned to make my daughter a black widow, but . . . Well, what I'm trying to say is that I must be compensated."

"I came here to marry your daughter. I'm not accustomed to being told what terms to adopt. He jammed his knife into the table and let it stand there like a claw. "May I suggest you take what I offer?"

This man wanted to marry me? Surely even Mama wouldn't stoop so low as to trade me for some small amount of security. She didn't even know this man. But when I looked at her face I knew she would do exactly that.

Russo's voice became soothing. "As I wrote to you, because I have considerable standing in Napoli, I could help you look after your holdings here in the South. If our two families work together, we can return your family's pride and respect to the status it deserves."

"I'm sure you could help us a great deal."

"Yes. After all, Napoli is only two hundred miles from Calabria. I would take an active role in helping you manage your affairs."

"Thank you, Signore Russo. You offer much." Mama looked over to me as if wondering why I was still standing there. "Go to your room now, Carina."

I wanted to say something, anything, to protect my future, but I followed the path women have taken for thousands of years in the South. I kept quiet and did as I was told.

Once back in my room, I threw myself on the bed. Tears distorted my vision for an hour. I asked God why had I been born. For this?

Mama opened my door. "Pack your clothes. You're moving to Napoli."

"Mama!"

"You will marry Signore Russo this Saturday."

She might as well have told me I was moving to the moon. "He's horrible. They don't even speak the same language in Napoli. I won't go."

Mama lunged forward and slapped me across the face. "You have no choice. You're lucky to become a wife, mother, and housekeeper after what you did with the doctor. I don't know why anyone would want a whore like you. Russo holds power in Napoli. Only the influence of the Cunzolo family name gives you this hope of redeeming yourself." She dragged my storage trunk from the foot of the bed and opened it.

"What choice does a spoiled whore like you have?" she went on.

"Pack your things, but no books. You can't let him see that you hold the shame of knowing how to read. Be grateful this marriage might bring some comfort and respect back to your family. You'll do as he says. It's your duty." Then she turned and left the room.

I sat there and looked at my books on the shelves along the wall. They no longer mocked me. They called to me, "Rise up and follow us into the world."

Crossing over to them, I longingly touching the covers of *Treasure Island* and *Anna Karenina*. "Farewell, my friends."

I turned to the window and gazed toward Spartacus Summit. The nightly fires signaling Domenico's love had stopped burning two days ago. Thoughts of his piercing gaze, his wavy black hair, and his silhouette swept through my mind.

"One day I'll have the chance to control my own fate," I told myself.

Chapter 7

WEDDING A STRANGER

"In nòmine Patris, et Filii et Spìritus Sancti." In the name of the Father, the Son, and the Holy Spirit, the priest spoke in a loud clear voice. He wore robes of white with fine gold embroidery. He left me and entered the church to take his place at the altar.

The cathedral was full but I had never felt more alone. Jesus, the Virgin Mary, and God himself had all abandoned me. I stood at the doors leading into the unfamiliar church with its unfamiliar priest, in an unfamiliar city, about to marry a stranger.

The Duomo, the cathedral of Napoli, and its Chapel of San Gennaro, named after the patron saint of Napoli, had seen 1,500 years of weddings and funerals. The organ music began and I entered the church. The scent of lilac candles drifted over me as I proceeded down the aisle. The ceiling spanned so high above me that I started to lose my balance as I looked up at its elaborate carvings. Granite pillars formed eight high arches that flanked Uncle Salvatore and me as we walked toward the altar, where I would declare my eternal allegiance to a man completely foreign to me.

The priest continued. *"Confiteor Deo omnipotenti et vobis, fratres, quia peccàvi nimis cogitatiòne, verbo, òpere et o Signoreinaiòne, mea cupla, mea culpa."* I confess to Almighty God, and to you, my brothers and sisters, that I have sinned through my own fault.

"For everything there is a season, and a time for every matter under heaven:
   a time to be born, and a time to die;
   a time to plant, and a time to pluck up what is planted;
   a time to kill, and a time to heal;
   a time to break down, and a time to build up;
   a time to weep, and a time to laugh;
   a time to love, and a time to hate;
   a time for war, and a time for peace."

Pain pounded in my chest. How much must one sacrifice for family?

"I lift up my eyes to the hills—from where will my help come?" the priest asked.

My immediate family and more than a hundred of Russo's guests sat quietly in the cathedral to witness our sacramental event. Looking around, I saw many unfamiliar faces, not one of them with the courage to step forward and stop this farce. I put my hand on the necklace Papa had given me—a small gold key that he'd told me was the key to my dreams.

"Let love be genuine. Hold fast to what is good. Love one another with mutual affection. Outdo one another in showing honor . . ."

Russo's guests included an odd assortment of people: a man with only one finger on his right hand, another who could not speak, tough-looking men, women in dresses that showed their legs. Whenever such people had approached my mother in Reggio Calabria, she would cross to the other side of the street.

"Do not repay anyone evil for evil, but take thought for what is noble in the sight of all."

Russo's brother Alonzo was a husky, dimwitted man who couldn't remember my name; he kept calling me Sophia. His other brother, Benito, in his early thirties, was much taller than Russo or Alonzo. He stank of alcohol and I presumed that his large gut, one typical of older men, came from drinking. A jagged scar cut along his right cheekbone. When I was introduced to him he became fixated on my bosom and stared continuously at it.

"Carina and Vincenzo, have you come here freely and without reservation to give yourselves to each other in marriage?"

I gained the courage to glance at my husband-to-be. His features were handsome and his skin almost as delicate as a woman's, and an aloofness enveloped him like a protective shell. I feared he would want to have sex often. My whole life, Mama and the priests had warned me of the evils of this sinful act.

"Will you love and honor each other for the rest of your lives?"

A voracious fear gnawed at my bones. I forced the slightest nod to the priest.

"Repeat after me," said the priest, "I, Carina Maria Cunzolo, take you, Vincenzo Julius Russo, to be my lawfully wedded husband."

Panic rose inside of me when I realized there was no breath in my lungs to speak, so I whispered, "I, Carina Maria Cunzolo, take you, Vineto Juliano Russo . . ."

Russo laughed quietly. "By the end of the week you'll know my name." People in the audience chuckled.

The priest gave Russo his instructions and asked him to repeat them in front of those present. Then he placed a ring on my finger and I moved a ring toward his. The priest indicated that both of us should take a small candle, and then he guided us to light a large one.

"What God has joined, man must not divide." The priest blessed us and sprinkled our joined hands with holy water. The holy sacraments of the church now bound me for life to this man, but I felt nothing but fear. I wanted to run out the door to freedom, but paralysis seeped into every nerve in my body like a scorpion's sting.

The priest pronounced us husband and wife. Russo awkwardly kissed me as I kept my eyes closed, imagining that it was Domenico kissing me, holding me, loving me.

People applauded and congratulated us as Russo dragged my stiff body down the aisle. Outside the cathedral, Russo paraded me in front of dozens of important-looking people, saying, "Isn't she lovely?"

My mother was nowhere to be seen.

That evening, after a brief reception, I found myself sitting in the back seat of a luxurious automobile with my new husband, who paid more attention to his flask of liquor than to me. With streetlights casting scowling shadows at every turn, we bumped along the mysterious bustling streets of Napoli without speaking. I listened to the hum of the wheels on the road and searched the street ahead of us trying to avoid thoughts of my future.

"Did you enjoy the wedding?" he finally said.

"It was nice. Very nice," I replied, and then another silence engulfed us.

The streets outside buzzed with life; people drank, ate, and laughed in sidewalk cafes. They walked, road bikes, and drove their cars. In Reggio Calabria, you rarely found a soul stirring after nine o'clock, and you could count the number of cars in town on your fingers. Russo's driver, Carlo, turned onto a quiet street that led uphill. The higher we traveled, the more city lights I could see twinkle below us.

We stopped in front of a large building that looked like a hotel. Carlo, a gorilla of a man with a kind face, opened the car door for us.

"This is your new home, Carina," Russo said.

"*Bel niente!*" I said, eyes wide.

The house consumed half a city block. Lights attached to an iron fence illuminated the structure, casting shadows that stood along the facade like Praetorian guards protecting their Roman emperor.

We entered the front of the house through carved double doors. Carlo followed behind. A bitter-faced older woman greeted us at the door. "Did everything go well, Signore Russo?" She didn't even glance at me.

"Yes, Amelia." Russo held out his coat but dropped it on the floor, too inebriated to pass it to her. She picked it up and folded it over her arm with care.

"May I get you anything, sir?"

"You may go to bed."

Once Amelia had left the room, Russo turned to Carlo. "Thanks for your help today, Carlo. I won't need you anymore tonight."

Carlo nodded to him and to me, and then left us alone.

Russo led me down the hall. We entered the bedroom, lit only by the faint glow from a single small window. With a gentle hand, he sat me on the bed. He smelled of alcohol, and I fought the impulse to move away.

"Welcome to our bedroom, my beautiful wife," he said.

I began to tremble. The act of making love remained a total mystery to me. Mama had explained nothing, other than to say that I should clench my teeth during sex to fight off the pain.

Russo took off his shirt, sat down beside me on the bed, and kissed my neck as his hands slid from my ankles all the way to my hips, pulling up my skirt.

He moved to kiss my lips and saw my tears. "Are you still a virgin?"

"Of course," I said, unsure if this would please or displease him.

He wiped my tears away with the sheet. "Don't worry, my pet. Lie back and relax." He stroked my hair gently. His tenderness surprised me. I started to calm down, imagining Domenico's touch comforting me, and then the words of many priests filled my mind to remind me of the mortal sin of lust and my body tensed again.

"It's all right. Enjoy yourself," he murmured.

He caressed my neck and shoulders, but the priest's words were stronger than his touch. My body remained unyieldingly rigid.

"If you like, we'll wait and take it slowly another time," he offered.

I nodded vaguely, surprised by his thoughtfulness. I felt ashamed for not pleasing my husband but more terrified of offending the priests and God. He reclined me back onto the bed and petted my head.

Just as we were dozing off, a knock on the door roused us. Irritated, Russo flung open the door and growled at Carlo, "You disturb me on my wedding night?"

"Forgive me, Prince," Carlo said, then cupped his hand by Russo's ear and whispered something.

"You're kidding. That asshole," Russo cursed. He turned to me. "Carina, I'm sorry. I must take care of something." He joined Carlo in the hallway but left the door open. I heard them move down the hall.

After a minute or two, I expected him to return. Stillness.

I started to call out, but didn't know what to call him. Again, I had forgotten his first name. "Russo, are you there?" I cried tentatively from the bed. I saw a glow from the hall and heard footsteps approach. "Russo?"

"Signore Russo asked me to see if there was anything I can get for you, madam. He had to go out." I jumped upon hearing Amelia's voice through the open door. The glow of her candle placed her just outside of my view.

"No . . . no, nothing. Thank you." It embarrassed me to imagine that she had been in the house while Russo touched me. I prayed she wouldn't be the next time.

"Yes, Signora," she said impatiently, then the sound of her footsteps faded down the hall and the bedroom fell black again.

The dark silence unnerved me. It took me a long time to fall into an uncomfortable sleep.

Chapter 8

THE SACRAMENT
OF MARRIAGE

A beam of morning sun pierced through the curtains of the small bed-room window and prodded me awake. I jumped and called out, "Dear God!" as I jolted out of my restless dreams into the nightmare of my reality.

I heard someone running down the hall, and then Carlo burst through the door with a pistol in his hand. His eyes quickly scanned the room. "What's wrong?"

"I'm sorry. It was nothing . . . a nightmare. I'm sorry." I couldn't take my eyes off the gun.

Carlo looked around the room one more time, then slid the pistol into a holster under his black coat. He looked as though he wanted to say something but finally just nodded and closed the door behind him.

I found myself trembling. Why did Carlo carry a gun? What danger did he think I in? Clearly, he lived in the house. And evidently Russo still hadn't returned. Where had he gone so late last night? I didn't even know what my husband did for a living.

The cavernous bedroom provided no clues; showed no sign that anyone actually lived in it—nothing on the night stand, nothing on the dresser, nothing hanging on the white-plaster walls.

After finishing an examination of the closets and drawers, I decided to take a bath. To my surprise, warm water came out of the faucet—no need to heat it on the stove, as we'd always had to at home. The soothing water relaxed me. I closed my eyes, and my mind drifted to the nagging questions about my new life, the most immediate being *What is a wife supposed to do all day?* I got out of the bath, dressed, and headed down the hall. No time like the present to meet Russo's domestics.

I was young and afraid, but my soul would be damned to hell before I'd let my new staff know it.

Russo did not return home until late that afternoon. I was back in the bedroom, sitting in the chair by the window. I looked up when he entered carrying a bouquet of beautiful pink roses. I quickly hid my book, *Tales of Gulliver's Travels,* by the side of the chair.

"What are you reading?" he asked, smiling.

"Oh, I wasn't reading. I was just looking at the illustrations."

Russo laughed. "Carina, it's all right. This isn't Reggio Calabria. It's good you can read. You can help our children with their schooling."

I smiled. "I read everything I can find."

He reached into his pocket and handed me a hundred-lira note from a large roll of money. "Have Carlo take you to buy some books."

"Thank you! And thank you for the glorious roses."

"Enjoy them." He smiled and handed me the flowers. "You can call me either Vincenzo or Russo, my pet." After kicking off his shoes, he emptied his pockets onto the dresser, little scraps of paper plus a large wad of bills. He went into the adjoining bathroom and scrubbed his hands for a long time.

I jumped up and perused the items from his pockets. The bits of paper were scribbled with names, numbers, amounts of lira.

I heard Russo finish washing up and hurried back to the chair. He came into the room drying his hands with a towel.

"Where did you go so late last night?" I asked.

"Business never sleeps, my pet."

"So late, though."

Russo glared at me, and I knew the discussion was over. He said, "What do you want Amelia to cook us for dinner?"

"Anything you like, Russo, but shouldn't I be doing the cooking?"

He poked through his scribbled notes. "Where the hell is Del Lagio's telephone number?" he said, then added distractedly, "Amelia does all the cooking." He turned to me and noticed the disappointed look on my face. "Well, maybe you can share that responsibility." He searched his pockets a second time and found the scrap of paper he was looking for in his shirt pocket.

"Excuse me. I've got to make a call," he said, and left the room.

He returned a few minutes later. "Amelia says dinner will be ready in a few hours." He walked over to me and stroked my hair. "We have plenty of time," he murmured, running his fingers down my back and kissing my neck.

He continued to caress me, and then his hand cupped the underside of my breast. My body pulsed. I couldn't help it. Mama had taught me to fear the horror of sex, but I liked Russo's gentle touch. I prayed that she had lied about sex, too, just as she had lied to me about so many other things.

"You're so beautiful, Carina," Russo whispered. Domenico had said the same thing, and hearing it brought a flow of confidence through my body. Russo slowly began removing my clothes, moaning with appreciation as he studied and kissed my body. My heart pounded with anticipation. I still yearned for Domenico, but it felt wonderful to have someone want me like this. My breathing quickened.

With care, Russo moved on top of me. "Ah, my pet, my little Carina. This first time will hurt a bit, but I promise you, not for long. Will you trust me?"

I nodded, although I wasn't sure what he meant.

His hand gently trailed down my abdomen, then lower still. Finally, his fingers moved between my legs. My body jerked with an intense rush of sensation. "No!"

"Yes, Carina," Russo said calmly, as he continued to caress me. "It's all right. This is the way of love between a man and a woman. Trust me to do this."

The warm sensation between my legs grew stronger and stronger, like a tightening knot. Dear merciful God in Heaven, I thought. This kind of feeling must be a sin.

"Ready?" he asked softly.

I nodded again.

He inserted one finger inside me, and I jumped. "Shh, little one," he whispered. "It will make it easier." He started gently massaging me.

The pressure inside me was excruciating, exciting and frightening. All at once my body began convulsing with an exquisite delight. "Oh, Russo!" I shuddered over and over again.

He kissed my eyes and lips. "Now you are ready for me, Carina."

He spread my thighs. "Wrap your legs around me," he instructed. I did as he asked. He held me firmly with his hands as he pushed himself into me, fast and hard. I cried out with pain and pleasure. "The worst is over, my little pet," he said, as he kissed my tears away. "You'll never feel pain again, unless I want you to. Is it subsiding?"

To my surprise, the pain was almost gone. I managed to whisper, "Yes."

Slowly, he pressed in and out of me. A new fire began to burn inside me, even more delicious than before. I moaned with the pleasure of it. "Russo," I murmured.

He groaned, his movements becoming fast and fierce, his breathing hard and quick. I cried out as his seed spurted inside of me, and I felt myself contract around him, drawing him farther in.

Eventually, I opened my eyes and looked at him in wonder. "Mama said sex was a horror."

Russo laughed. "And what do you think?"

"It's wonderful."

"Good." He smiled. "We'll do it again soon." After stroking my back for a few moments, he rolled over and fell asleep. I had barely caught my breath.

I found Russo at the dining room table the next morning, reading the newspaper and enjoying a breakfast of *Pagnotta di Santa Chiara,* a crusty bread that Amelia had stuffed with spinach, Feta cheese, and roasted bell peppers. He seemed ravenous, as we never had made it to dinner the night before.

"Good morning, my pet," he said, in a familiar tone that made me feel self-conscious and awkward. He smiled when I blushed.

"Morning." I needed a good confession to cleanse myself.

Russo laughed. "Eat up," he said. "I'm sure you're as hungry as I am."

The pagnotta smelled delicious, so I cut off a piece and bit into it to focus on something besides his grinning face. Mama used to make the same dish using dough made of potato and wheat flour, with a little yeast and pepper. She would stuff the pagnottas with tomatoes and anchovies before baking them. Amelia's tasted different, but equally delicious.

Russo was absentmindedly rolling a coin back and forth across the backs of his fingers. He walked it from one finger to the next.

"Russo, would you go to confessional with me today?"

He chuckled. "Confession? My presence might strike God down with a heart attack. You go yourself. It's not far."

"A woman alone on the street . . . people would think I was a whore."

"Carlo will escort you." Russo smiled, stood and patted me on the head. "All right, my little pet. I've got to get to work."

"I still don't know what you do for a living."

"I'm in imports and exports, this and that . . . I'm a captain of industry," he said, with a grin.

After he left I put on a floor-length black dress with an embroidered flower pattern just above the hem, my thick stockings and my sturdy, black lace-up shoes. I found Carlo waiting for me outside the front door. He gave instructions to a man who seemed to be guarding the front of the house, and we set off.

A light morning fog lingered over the hill. For the first time I got a good look at the house I now lived in. It was big—very big—two to three times larger than Mama's sizeable house, with a fancy iron gate protecting the front door and the small front yard. Like all the houses atop the hill, Russo's house was boxy and the color of the bubbly drink at our wedding reception. It looked like a sandcastle with just a few small windows cutting into its straight, unadorned walls.

Carlo stayed behind me as we started down the hill, until I insisted that he walk by my side, an order he reluctantly obeyed. Even in the fog it was warm outside, especially in my heavy dress. We could hear the city breathing below us: fog horns and bells from the harbor, the drone of traffic, the toot of horns and, as we advanced down the hill, the buzz of people starting their day.

By the time we neared the base of the hill, the haze had burned off and the city was revealed. At that moment, I realized that the impressive cities I had read about in books weren't fiction, and I stopped and stared in awe. Napoli stretched out along the Italian coast and spanned many kilometers, with buildings colored in austere grays, whites, yellows, and somber reds. Almost all of the structures near the water stood the same height: six stories tall. The dual peaks of Mount Vesuvius stood behind the ancient city, watching over the metropolis of more than two million people.

The Bay of Napoli sparkled with a blue that rivaled the sky's rich tone. A long jetty stuck out from the coast at the central point of the bay's shoreline. At the end of the point, an enormous fortress built of sandy gray stone clung to its own small island.

I pointed to it. "What's that building in the bay?"

"The Castel dell'Ovo on the Isle of Megaride," Carlo told me. "For twenty-five hundred years the Castle of the Egg has protected the city." Already, I had decided I liked Carlo. He wasn't handsome, but he had striking eyes that absorbed everything they touched. And despite his size and obvious strength, he seemed a gentle soul.

"How does it protect the city?"

"In 550 B.C., several generations before the Trojan War, the Etruscans founded Napoli and battled the Greeks here. A curse hung over the city for centuries, until the Romans took over. The Roman leaders called on Master Virgil, who wrote the *Aeneid* and was believed to be a wizard, to dispel the curse. According to legend, Virgil hid a magic egg inside an amphora placed into an iron cage that he hung from a truss in the crypt under the Castel dell'Ovo. It's said if that egg ever falls and breaks, the castle and the entire city of Napoli will sink into the sea."

"A 2,500-year-old egg? That must be one stinky castle."

"It would certainly make a lousy omelet," Carlo said, and we laughed. A misty uneasiness drifted between us and the muscles in my body tightened. I had shared an intimate moment with a stranger. I sighed as I imagined roaming the city with Domenico, then felt guilty for having such a thought the day after losing my virginity to the man who was my husband. I really did need to get to confession.

"It's an imposing castle, isn't it?" Carlo said, apparently noticing my discomfort.

"That was twenty-five hundred years ago. Who's lived there since?"

"Louis XII King of France, but it passed to the Spanish the same year and they ruled Napoli for the next two centuries. Napoleon took the city at the turn of the nineteenth century and placed his brother Joseph here to rule from the castle."

"How do you know all this?"

"History's my hobby, Carina. Greek pioneers founded the city, then the Romans conquered it and built a thriving port." He pointed to the busy harbor. "The city became the center of tourism for the Romans, and the wealthy built vacation villas here. The city has seen many conquerors since then, but Garibaldi came in 1860 and declared the city part of the Kingdom of Italy, and it has seen peace ever since. I'm sorry, I'm rambling away. I sound like a travel guide."

"No, it's fascinating. I read that the last emperor of the Roman Empire died here."

"Augustus, the first emperor of Rome, built a villa here. Five centuries later, Romulus Augustus, the last Roman emperor, was conquered by the German barbarians and imprisoned for thirty years in the Castle of the Egg, where he died."

At the far south end of the bay, a large island shone like a jewel in the water. "What's that island?"

"The Isle of Capri. It has a long history too, including the palace of the Roman emperor Trajan, but I'll save that story for another day."

I smiled. The history lesson had helped me relax, and I was glad we shared a thirst for knowledge.

As we approached the bottom of the hill we left the residential area and entered the bustling city. The noise overwhelmed me; countless bicycles whizzed by, cars and trucks beeped their horns, people shouted from windows, and merchants hawked their fruit and vegetables to passersby.

Still, I felt more comfortable now. "Can we walk awhile before we go to the church?" I asked. "I'd like to see some of the city."

"Certainly."

We stepped onto a very wide street. "This is Sacca Napoli Road," Carlo said. "It's the main road that cuts Napoli into east and west."

As we stepped onto the busy street, a collection of foul odors attacked my nose. Rotting food and refuse sat stagnant in the gutters along the street. A woman threw a bucket of slop from her second-story window. I gagged at the stench of human waste.

Women wore short vibrant-colored dresses with hems as high as the knee and matching dyed high heels. Some women dressed in skirts and puffy blouses made of bright colors or floral patterns. Their faces were layered in makeup and lipstick. Many walked alone. All of them would have been considered harlots in Reggio Calabria. I found it shocking, but knew that these women enjoyed a freedom the women of Calabria would never know.

It amazed me how many people filled the streets. Everywhere there were men in uniform: soldiers, militia, and National Gendarmerie, police who wore Napoleon-style hats, red-striped trousers, and long swords. They always traveled in pairs to lessen the chance of being bribed.

There were also beggars harassing people on every corner. Construction workers, street vendors, merchants, delivery men, women with children, and men in suits all rushed about like Mama's chickens at feeding time. Yet, some people just sat in chairs on the street in front of their homes sipping a cup of coffee and watching the parade.

As we walked along, several people recognized Carlo and moved out of the way to make us a path. It seemed odd, since no one else appeared to receive such treatment. Carlo kept an eye on two men in worn out fedoras who seemed to be following us. Every time Carlo looked their direction they stopped and acted like they were checking out a vendor wears.

"Who are they?" I said.

Carlo ignored my inquiry and kept walking.

A bicyclist nearly ran me over. "Hey, watch out!" Carlo yelled.

The bicyclist started to give a rude gesture, but then seemed to recognize Carlo. "Oh, I'm sorry. Please forgive me." He peddled off down the road, looking over his shoulder several times.

At every corner, even on the streets outside the marketplaces, vendors sold warm chestnuts, pizza, pastries filled with cheese, and fresh fruit and vegetables displayed in wooden crates stacked high with colorful produce. I noticed one vendor selling a huge bunch of bananas and ran over to him. I had seen the exotic fruit only once in my lifetime. This vendor also displayed a large, thick, odd-looking fruit with prickly thorns on the outside with what looked like a green straw hat on top.

"Try a bite," the vendor offered, handing me a slice of the yellow fruit.

I bit into it. The juice made my tongue tingle but the fruit tasted sweet at the same time. I liked it. "What is this?"

"Pineapple," the man replied. "A tropical fruit. You like some?"

"I don't have any money." I felt rather helpless.

"It's taken care of," Carlo interjected. He paid the vendor and handed me a stick stuck through many pieces of pineapple.

"Thank you. Would you like a bite?" I held up the offering to Carlo, but he shook his head. We started walking again. "There are so many vendors. How do they all make a living?"

"Everything's for sale in Napoli," Carlo said. "And everyone seems to make their way. A merchant's living is as good as bread."

Suddenly, a man clutching a camera bag started running as a well-dressed tourist shouted, "Stop thief!" In a flash, the man ran by us and gave Carlo a glance of recognition. People turned their heads to follow the action, but no one moved to grab the man before he turned down an alley and disappeared.

"Do you know him, Carlo?"

Carlo hesitated. "No. No."

We arrived at the Duomo. The two men behind us were no longer visible.

On entering the cathedral, I dipped the two fingers of my right hand into the *font* and crossed myself with the holy water, a ritual so second nature to me that it came more unconsciously than blinking. Once in the confessional box, I unburdened my soul.

But I would soon learn that it wasn't my soul that was in jeopardy; my husband was the one who needed the absolution of Confession and the power of Holy Communion, to accept Christ's body and blood to release him from his sins.

Chapter 9

THE PRINCE

Several months had passed since I'd first laid eyes on Napoli. I had gotten into the routine of going to church every few days, with Carlo as my escort, but little else filled a day. I'd cared for twelve younger brothers and sisters without ever seeing an idle hour, but now I faced large empty voids in every day.

My husband, though, led a hectic mysterious life. Russo came and went at odd hours of the day and night, never telling me where he was going or what he was doing. Business associates, including relatives that he employed, often came over to meet with him in his office at the house. Most of them were boisterous men, but they talked in hushed voices when discussing business.

Russo and I were having coffee one afternoon when Amelia announced the arrival of Gilberto, Russo's cousin and business associate. Russo told her to show him into the office. After finishing his drink, Russo met with Gilberto. I snuck over to the gaming room; a few weeks before, I had discovered an opening inside the closet that looked into Russo's study. I peeked through the small gap.

Gilberto was a crook-nosed man with coin slots for eyes. He stood half a head taller than my husband and weighed half again as much. As usual, Russo was playing with his coin, making it disappear and reappear in his hand, as he talked with his cousin.

"Say, boss, what do you say to a woman with two black eyes?" Gilberto asked.

"I don't know, Gilberto."

"You don't say anything, you've already told her twice!" Gilberto erupted with laughter.

Russo stood stone faced. "So what's the take this week?"

Gilberto handed him a large wad of bills. The Prince flipped through it. "This is it?"

"Things have been slow."

"Things have been slow a lot lately, Gilberto."

"I gave you your full cut, Prince."

"What? Are you talking back to me?"

"I'm just saying I gave you—"

Russo slapped him hard across the face. "You don't *give me* anything. I pay all the expenses for keeping everyone out of trouble—the police, the judges, the politicians. How do you think I built this organization? How do you think you even have the opportunity to profit? You don't *give* me my share; I earn every lira of it."

Gilberto hung his head. "Of course. No one questions—"

"I take care of my guys. Benito tells me things have been going good for you. You've been holding out on me, your own family." Russo struck him hard again with the back of his hand. Gilberto stumbled back.

"No, no, never. I wouldn't!"

Russo slapped him again. I couldn't understand why Gilberto didn't fight back. It seemed so odd to see such a slight man as my husband intimidate a much larger man, but Russo was boiling with anger. His attack was so fierce and full of animal rage that I began to worry for his cousin's life.

"You would cheat your own flesh and blood?" Russo yelled. Gilberto shook his head, but Russo struck yet again. This blow knocked Gilberto into a stack of boxes that fell and obstructed my vision.

But from the sounds behind the wall, I knew Russo was continuing his assault. "I keep your territory free of competitors! I make it possible for you to live the good life! If I tell you to kiss a dog's ass, I expect you to kiss it and thank me!"

My hands were trembling and my heart pounding. Then I heard

another thud of fist to flesh, a moan, and the heavy thud of a man falling to the floor. For a moment there was a terrible silence. Then, to
my relief, Russo said, "Now get out of my sight, and leave the back way.
And may I suggest you show me the proper respect? Until you treat me
with respect, you'll receive none."

The door slammed and the room fell silent just before Amelia rang
the dinner bell.

After taking a few deep breaths to compose myself, I hurried into
the dining room and sat down. My hands were still shaking; I was completely unnerved. What kind of man had I married? Mama's beatings
had been vicious, but Russo's attack could have been lethal. I prayed
my husband's anger would never be turned against me.

I heard him washing up in the bathroom down the hall. The water
ran a long time. He came into the room after a few minutes, but I
couldn't look at him.

Amelia began serving the food. "Oh, it looks wonderful," Russo
said with delight, as she scooped a generous helping of ravioli stuffed
with ricotta and pine nuts onto his plate. After taking a bite, he said,
"Ummm, *molto squisito*," then kissed his fingertips in appreciation. He
seemed totally unaffected by his brutal encounter.

"Yes, it is," I agreed, still afraid to look at him.

"What's the matter?"

"Nothing, nothing." I glanced at him, my gaze fixed on the side of
his forehead, where small drops of blood dotted his skin.

What?" he asked, noticing my stare. He wiped his forehead, saw the
blood on his fingertips, and cleaned his face with his napkin as though
it was nothing. "So it looks like we're in for a little rain."

Other than commenting about the weather, I sat silently through
dinner, and then went immediately to the bedroom to ready myself for
bed. I prayed he wouldn't touch me, that he'd go out, as he so often
did. When I came out of the bathroom, though, he was lying in bed.
But at least half of my prayer had been granted; he had already fallen
asleep.

Who was this man beside me in bed? After years of my mother's
whippings, I had vowed that no one would ever raise a hand to me
again, but here I was, married to a man capable of vicious cruelty. He
assaulted Gilberto with such icy calm that I was certain he hurt people

often and with far more brutality than what I had witnessed. My heart sank at the realization that Russo could easily kill a man, might already have done so. Loving him was out of the question. I considered running away before he could hurt me too, perhaps to Uncle Salvatore's hotel in Rome. Domenico might still want to run away with me. No, I reminded myself, not after the scandal.

And of course now I was married.

With my back to my husband, I lay motionless, afraid to stay awake and terrified to fall asleep.

Russo got up early the next morning. I pretended to be asleep while he quietly dressed and left. During the night I had spent many hours thinking about Domenico, and had decided to go to the university to see him. If nothing else, he could provide me with guidance.

A knock on the bedroom door shook me from my thoughts. I jumped with guilt.

"Yes?"

"There's someone here to see you," Amelia said with disdain. The tone in her voice told me she hated me for invading what she saw as her territory. "You should hurry."

"I'll be right there." Who could it be? I didn't know anyone in Napoli.

At the front door I found my brother Antonio leaning against the wall trying to catch his breath. Dried blood from a cut above his eye trickled down his temple, and his shirt was dirty. Carlo helped him inside.

"Antonio!" I cried. "What are you doing here? Are you all right?"

"I ran away," he gasped. "Had an asthma attack . . . Mama beat me."

Carlo and I helped him into a chair. "Do you have any of your medicine left?"

Antonio held out the nearly empty bottle. After helping him take a few drops, his breathing gradually improved.

"Why was she so angry?"

"I asked Saldino for a job. She heard."

"Good Lord!"

"How else can anyone find a job in Calabria?"

"Mama wants to run all our lives," I said bitterly. "Even if you hadn't approached Saldino, she'd probably never let you work for anyone within her domain. How would it look? A Cunzolo working! Well, you can stay here. We'll find you a job in Napoli, outside Mama's reach."

I worried all afternoon about what Russo would say, but when he returned home he surprised me by showing sympathy and compassion for Antonio's plight. He insisted that Antonio stay with us.

But when I asked him if he would give my brother a job, he refused. He didn't want one of my brothers working in his business.

That was fine with me. "But you know many people, Russo. Surely you could find him a job as a waiter or something."

"Well, the owner of Caffe De Sica owes me a favor, my pet. I'll speak to him."

So the next day Antonio started as a waiter at the Caffe.

A week after Antonio had settled in, I decided the time had come to go see Domenico. As close as I was to my brother, I hadn't told him about my feelings for Domenico, my plan to meet with him, or that I was considering leaving Russo. To keep Carlo from following me, I snuck out the bedroom window and down the alley.

The week before, I had called the university and learned Domenico's schedule. I arrived at the Science building at the university after lunch and lingered by Domenico's classroom, waiting for his class to let out. As the time approached two o'clock, I began pacing, my eyes on the big clock on the campus tower. The minute hand moved more and more slowly as it approached the hour.

Finally, the clock struck two. I walked down the hallway by the door, but the doors to the classroom didn't open. I put my ear to them and listened. Not a sound. I opened the door a crack and found the room empty, except for an older gentleman with a beard, who was working on some papers at the desk in the front of the room. The door creaked as I stepped inside. The man looked up.

"Oh, I'm sorry to disturb you." I turned to leave.

"No bother. Nothing much to do, now that the semester's over."

"The students are gone?"

"Last Friday was the last day of exams. Who are you looking for?"

"Domenico Saldino."

"One of my favorites. He graduated and went back to Sicily."

I stood there, dumbstruck, my heart pounding. His parents lived in Sicily, hidden to the outside world—no phone, no known address, no way to contact Domenico.

I finally managed a nod to the professor, and then turned and ran down the hall. I kept running all the way across campus. Down the streets of Napoli I ran until I found myself on a small, unfamiliar, empty street. Leaning against a wall, I sobbed for a very long time. I'm still not certain why, since I really never expected Domenico to run away with me, and I doubted that he could have provided any advice that would have changed my situation with Russo. Still, I cried bitterly.

When I finally arrived home, I went around to the back of the house and started to climb in my bedroom window so Carlo wouldn't know I had been out without his protection. I was halfway through when a hand grabbed me from behind. I gasped and tried to pull myself inside, but I couldn't move. Carefully but forcefully, the hand pulled me back outside.

Carlo stared at me with narrowed eyes. "Where have you been? I've been worried."

"I'm sorry, Carlo. I needed to go out alone for a walk, to think."

"You're my responsibility."

"I'm sorry I didn't tell you."

"It's dangerous for you to go out alone."

"Dangerous?"

Carlo hesitated before speaking. "There are people who would like to hurt Signore Russo; through you, they can hurt him."

Hurt him. Who wanted to hurt Russo? I had lost any chance to be with Domenico, now it seemed I faced a dangerous future.

Chapter 10

THE FAMILY BUSINESS

Over the next few weeks, I resigned myself to staying with Russo. After all, he had shown me nothing but kindness. In fact, he made me feel special. Perhaps I had overreacted to what I saw him do to his cousin. Perhaps Gilberto had deserved his punishment.

A few weeks after Antonio started working at the caffe, Russo announced, "Carina, it's time for Antonio to move out. He's a young man and needs to live on his own, make his own way."

I protested. "But we have so much room, and I love having someone to chat with when you're away."

"I'm a man, Carina. I need my privacy. Congini owns some apartments and owes me a favor. I'll get your brother a nice place for a good deal."

So, once again I found myself alone most of the time. Although I loved working in the garden and learning how to arrange flowers in the big urns situated all around the house, it wasn't enough. I was lonely and bored. The servants were polite but kept their distance, and Russo was off doing business at all hours. When he was home he could be quite entertaining, but he often left me alone for days, never explaining where or what he was doing or when he would return.

One morning while he sat at the table eating his breakfast, I gave him a big smile.

He grinned. "Is someone enjoying her afterglow?"

I pushed him playfully. "Don't let Amelia hear you. You'll make me blush." He grabbed me around the waist and pulled me to him, gently bit my breasts through my gown. I squirmed out of his grasp. "Stop it, you naughty boy. Are you going to be home for dinner tonight?"

"I doubt it, my pet. I'm meeting with some business associates from out of town."

"Will you be home by the time I go to bed?"

"Why? What did you have in store for me?"

I gave him a little playful slap. "Nothing. You're a bad boy."

"I may be late, though."

"How does the import business keep you out so late at night? What are you doing?"

"You have to work your ass off to stay ahead of the competition." He tried to hug me, but I moved a step away.

"What do you expect me to do? I'm bored just sitting around here day in and day out."

"My pet, I want you to put a woman's touch on our house. Redecorate and turn this into a home."

"That sounds like fun." Looking around at the sterile dining room, I frowned. "This house really isn't a home, is it?"

He smiled. "No, that's going to be your job. Certainly we'll have little *bambini* running around soon; they should have a warm home." He pulled me close and I kissed him.

I dove into my project with purpose. Despite Napoli's fame as part of the sunny Italian Riviera, only a few small windows allowed light into our house, giving it the feel of a fortress instead of a home. I never even knew the time of day.

To lighten up the gloomy castle, I had the kitchen and dining room painted a soft yellow. I found that I enjoyed shopping the city for curtains, furniture, and rugs. The wide variety of Napoli shops made every conceivable style of furniture. I looked forward to living in a warm home, rather than the cold cave we inhabited now.

But redecorating didn't fill all of my time. Still a curious young girl, I fed my inquisitiveness. When Russo emptied his pockets and swept his little notes into the top dresser drawer, I read the names, monetary amounts, or meeting times scribbled on them. When his brothers or cousins who worked in the business with him came over, I kept an open ear. Russo's private office at the house always remained locked. He told me not to renovate this room, but that didn't stop me from exploring it.

Since I'd found the peephole in the adjoining room's closet, I had spied on Russo in his office several times. While working on my remodeling one day, I uncovered a panel in the gaming room's closet that opened into his office.

I had been puzzling over the five large chests on the floor of his office, so, once in the room, I investigated them. The two midsized ones were unlocked and filled with postcards of women. I picked up one, a photo of a very pretty woman partly hidden by feathers pasted onto the card. When I blew on them, the rest of it came into view, revealing that the woman was naked. Hundreds of such postcards filled the boxes. They made me blush but I studied them and compared their bodies to my own. Mother Mary, I didn't want to confess this sin in the confession box.

The other chests were locked. While searching Russo's desk for the keys, I came across some cryptic notes of times and locations for deliveries. In the back of the drawer, a small compartment held a ring of keys.

One by one I tried the keys in the chests. The largest trunk, old and worn, opened. It was filled with furs: coats, stoles, hats. In the two smallest trunks, I uncovered dozens of fancy watches and pieces of jewelry. Russo had told me he imported goods.

The large metal cabinet mounted securely to the wall couldn't be opened with any of the keys. I searched for a way to break into it but failed.

Later that week, Russo's not-so-sharp brother, Alonzo, came over with two boys about ten years old. One boy was tall for his age, and the other had the thickest mop of hair I'd ever seen. Both wore shabby clothes with a piece of rope tied around the waist of their pants in place of a belt. Russo led the three visitors into his office. I waited until they entered the room before going to the peephole in the billiard room.

Russo used a key attached to his trousers to unlock the metal cabinet. I suppressed a gasp. Dozens of guns hung inside it, along with various knives and weapons I had never seen before. No one needed so many weapons, I thought, unless they were in the military . . . or doing something illegal. A nervous chill rippled through me.

Russo handed a pistol to Alonzo and nodded knowingly. Alonzo tucked it in his coat pocket, and then handed Russo an envelope of money. "This is it?" Russo asked irritably, leafing through it.

"Yeah," Alonzo replied uneasily. Russo stared at the boys until they began to squirm. He walked around them, getting closer and closer. Finally, he leaned over until his face was inches from theirs. "Now, my dear boys, you would never hold out on our friend Alonzo, would you?"

"No, signore," mumbled the taller boy.

"We . . . we wouldn't, Prince," said the other.

Russo turned back to Alonzo. "So what's the problem?"

"Nick and Forenzo are my two best *Scugnizzi*," Alonzo said. "I thought you could give 'em some guidance. They got more and more problems getting the goods."

Nick, the tall boy, spoke up, "Yeah, everybody's nervous and careful these—"

Alonzo thumped the kid on the back of the head. "Don't talk to the Prince unless you're spoken to."

"It's all right," Russo said, as he began rolling his coin over the back of his fingers. With his free hand, he patted Forenzo on the back. "I think people are spooked by the talk of a coming war. Boys, did you know I worked the streets when I was about your age?" They shook their heads. "I started by lifting wallets. It's an art. Develop your skills, be the best. Exactly what problems are you facing?"

"Well . . . you see . . . it's several . . ." Forenzo stammered nervously.

"Not many tourists around anymore," Nick interjected. "The *pescare* we see hold onto their wallets tighter than a flea bites a cat."

"Yeah, button down p . . . pockets, or ch . . . chains on their wallets," Forenzo added.

"Right. Well, let me see if we can come up with a few new moves for you," Russo said. He stood there thinking a minute, walking his coin back and forth across his fingers, and then flipped it in the air. It landed in Forenzo's shirt pocket. "Here you go, try this one. Find a woman in an outside café with a nice purse. Even if she doesn't have much cash, at least you can dump the purse for some good *scarol*. Most women put their bag on the chair away from the street to keep it from getting lifted by *Scugnizzi* like you."

The boys grinned. I almost laughed and gave myself away.

"One of you enters the restaurant," Russo continued, "the other comes along the street and asks her for the time or a kiss. The kid in the café walks by the table and pinches the purse. Simple. Clean, but it works."

Their grins widened.

"Here's another that works like butter on bread," Russo went on. "Alonzo, you'll need two of your men to work with them."

"Sure, they're in if it'll make a buck," Alonzo said.

"No one's used it for awhile," Russo said. "Work it at the Piazza dei Martiri. Highbrow foreigners still shop there, along with some of our snooty, blood-sucking Italiano brothers from the North. I wouldn't mind setting them back a few lira. One of you spots up a male tourist—the richer the better. Ask him if he needs help with directions. It's even good to be a little suspicious. When he gets aggravated or anxious, Alonzo's men come up dressed like detectives in suits. They flash badges and say, *'Polizia!'*" Russo grabbed Forenzo and shoved him against the wall. "One grabs you just as you start to run and pats you down."

"I don't get it," Nick said.

"While the one *La Madama* arrests you, the other fake one asks the tourist for ID," Russo explained.

"I see," Forenzo said. "He checks the tourist's ID, and p . . . palms his *scarol* and watch."

"This is a smart one," Russo said, turning to Alonzo. Then he continued, "The fake detective tells the tourist, 'You're in a bad area. This kid's a known thief.' When our cop sends the tourist on his way, nine times out of ten he thanks the officers."

"Beautiful," marveled the tall boy.

"The b . . . best," Forenzo agreed. "P . . . Prince, what's the most amazing thing you ever st . . . stole?"

Russo put his hand to his mouth, after a moment a big grin came to his face. "I once stole a forty-ton cargo ship."

"*Cazzo!*" Forenzo exclaimed. "Shit!"

"Honest. A British ship pulled into the harbor, and when the captain and his seamen came ashore, my boys tied up the two remaining guys left on board. We navigated the ship to a different part of the harbor and hid it behind some construction scaffolding. Remember, Alonzo?"

"Yeah, Vincenzo. That was a good one," Alonzo said with a dumb smile.

"We unloaded tons of sugar from the hull and refilled the bags with white sand, then stacked a few bags of real sugar on top. After I recovered the ship for the captain—for a price—they set out to sea. There must've been some lousy tea parties in Merry Ole England when they got back!"

"Son of a bitch," Nick said with amazement.

"Watch your mouth," Alonzo scolded.

"*Fantastico,*" Forenzo gushed. "I w . . . wish we could work a b . . . big drop."

I had to smile at the enthusiasm of the boys and Russo's intriguing scams. An importer, indeed.

"Someday, boys, someday. For now, may I suggest you make next week more productive for all of us?" They eagerly agreed. Russo grabbed his brother by the shoulder and gave him a warm embrace. "Now get out of here and get to work."

"Thanks, good brother," Alonzo said.

"You are the p . . . Prince," Forenzo stuttered with a gap-toothed grin.

They started to leave the office, so I quietly hurried out of the gaming room and down the hall. As they went through the hall to the front door, I waved to Alonzo. He smiled at me before leaving with the boys.

Russo massaged my neck. I turned to meet his eyes. "How's Alonzo doing?"

"He's fine."

"We should have Alonzo and Benito both over for dinner, and I'll cook a nice meal for them. Bachelors need a good home-cooked meal now and then."

"That would be very nice, my pet."

I looked for little ways like this to please Russo. When he was home, I followed his least little suggestion.

"I would like dinner now," he'd say.

"Let me get it for you right away." I'd rush to serve him.

"Where are my slippers?"

"I'll get them immediately."

"I think it's time you go to bed."

"Whatever you think, my husband." I would head off to bed. I never disagreed with him or disobeyed his directives, initially. I felt protected under his care. Once I'd complied, though, I'd often sneak back to eavesdrop on his conversations with his colleagues.

Before long this became almost pointless, because little by little Russo opened up to me about the true nature of his business. When he curled up in bed his usual commanding presence relaxed, and he'd start revealing the pressures he faced every day. He'd ramble as if he were just thinking out loud.

"My little pet, you can never trust Napoli women. They always try to trick you and steal what they can.

"You have to take what you want. No one in this life is going to give you anything.

"When you're on top, someone always nips at your heels, looking to take you down, ready to grab what you built. Always some new guy who wants what you have, like the Pollini Brothers. The Pollinis! Upstarts! They have no morals. They steal from our country's own soldiers. They don't help the poor and they extort money from simple shopkeepers."

When he talked about his street scams, though, his eyes lit up like a young boy's. "Those who can't hold onto what they own don't deserve to keep it," he said. He was proud of devising ways to extract money from the people he called "suckers." While describing his scams, Russo played with his gold coin. With a snap, he would launch the coin into the air and catch it on the back of his hand, where it twirled like a top. One time, after a little cajoling, he showed me the trick to running run a coin across my knuckles.

Tricks and scams. While my husband's crimes were shocking, I must admit I also found them intriguing. It all seemed very exciting.

I wasn't the only one who thought so. A few months after starting work at the restaurant, Antonio told me he could barely live on his wages as a waiter. He told me that through talk he'd overheard at the café, he knew about some of Russo's street businesses. He pled with me. "Could I work for Russo? I couldn't hurt anyone, but I could sell stuff." With a little questioning on my part, he finally admitted that he hoped to increase his income because he'd met a girl.

To my surprise, Russo no longer opposed the idea, so Antonio quit his waiter job and started selling fake watches and furs on the street. He made triple what he'd earned as a waiter.

"Do you like working on the street, Antonio?" I asked.

"Rich tourists, a few less lira in their pockets doesn't matter. Plus they get a good story to tell back home."

For a long time, I'd watched after Antonio and my other siblings. Most young men were joining the army, but with his asthma Antonio couldn't pass the physical. I wanted more for him than scamming tourists, but it made me happy to see him independent and out from under Mama's rule.

A few months after Antonio showed up at our doorstep, Giacomo, my next oldest brother, arrived looking for a job. Being very fit and knowing how to sail a boat, despite his jerky hand condition, he was quickly assigned by Russo to smuggle alcohol in from France and Greece.

Every week or so I'd learn of some other business Russo had his hand in. One night, hesitantly, I asked him about his brothels.

"It's a very honorable business that dates back thousands of years," he said defensively. "A wife shouldn't ask about such things."

But Russo's sins fascinated me. Prostitution, gambling, pick-pocketing, selling fake merchandise, and, I'm sure, other crimes he had yet to disclose . . . the more I learned, the more I wanted to learn. Never would I have imagined such things would hold such fascination for me. I had always fantasized about living a quiet life as a wife, mother and good Catholic, baking bread . . . maybe for Domenico. But Russo's world offered such an exciting alternative.

Then Russo revealed a secret that took me into yet another world. The underworld.

THE UNDERWORLD

Late one afternoon Russo led me to his study, pulled back the Italian flag draped across the wall and revealed a small door. When he opened it, a curious little room carved from stone stood before us. "Go ahead. Go in. I want to show you something amazing," he said, as he grabbed the lantern just inside the door and lit it.

I slowly entered. A stone staircase led down from the landing. I looked over the shaky railing. The stairs seemed to drift down into infinity, well beyond the reach of the lantern.

"This is the reason I bought this house," he told me. "I want to show you the womb of Napoli. Few people ever see Napoli's 'sottosuolo,' the city's belly."

I hesitated. "I don't think I want to go down there."

"You'll love it, the history. Something special for All Souls Day." The night before, November 1, we had gone to the cathedral for All Saints Day, one of the few times Russo had accompanied me to church.

He took my arm and we started down the tightly spiraled staircase. Step by step, it felt as if we were exiting the world of the living and descending into the realm of the dead. As we sank deeper into the shadows, a feeling of dread came over me, afraid of what he might show me.

"This place might even save your life someday. It's saved mine," Russo said. "It's the largest underground city in the world, but few have seen it."

Once again I looked over the railing—down, and then up. I could no longer see the top of the stairs, and the bottom still wasn't visible. My foot caught in a gap and Russo grabbed my shoulder to keep me from falling. By the time we reached the corridor at the bottom, I found myself out of breath, as much from apprehension as from exertion. I filled my lungs with acrid air.

"The crafty ancient Roman bastards built this section to get water around the city," Russo explained. After I caught my breath, he led us down the passage carved in stone. The footing was surprisingly flat and easy to walk on, but the silent, sinister halls spooked me. Each footstep echoed back to us, and whenever we stopped the absolute silence hurt my ears.

A chill vibrated up my spine as the ancient past engulfed us. Many small tributary passageways, sheathed in shadows, fed into the hallway, but we kept on a straight course. At points, the opening narrowed so tightly that we had to shuffle sideways to fit through it, with the surprisingly warm walls pressing against us. I wanted to run back to the surface, but I continued following Russo obediently. I wondered what would happen if his lantern went out.

"Don't worry," he said. "It's not much farther."

The passage opened into an immense room of yellow stone. My jaw dropped as I entered the cavern, which stood so tall and wide that the lantern light was unable to illuminate the top of the ceiling or the far wall. I wobbled, trying to get my equilibrium in the disorienting space. The walls sloped into arches and curved over the ceiling. I touched the wall: desert dry. The fresh, clean-smelling air here surprised me.

"Tufo sandstone formed from the ash of Mount Vesuvius," Russo said. His murmurs echoed all about, making it sound as if ghosts haunted this underworld. "The Greeks, Romans, and Spanish excavated it to build their temples, palaces, and villas above us."

I looked around in awe. "I'd heard of Napoli's underworld, but I never imagined this."

"Some of these tunnels date back five thousand years," said Russo. "The Napoli on the surface was built from this stone by the fuckin' Greeks and Romans. Cutting the huge stones out left this underground city."

He led me to the far wall. "Look at this." He held the lantern up to the wall to illuminate a beautiful, vividly colored painting of a chariot race. Another painting displayed men and women in robes in front of a grand building with pillars.

We moved on into a colossal tunnel. "This was built to fit oxcarts and chariots. Crazy Romans lived down here."

"*Bel niente.*"

We continued walking until the passage opened into a street made of *piperno,* a black volcanic stone Carlo had told me could be found only in Naples. Soon, ancient structures surrounded us. "The Romans built this street hundreds of years before Christ," he said. He pointed to long, thin indentations in the stone street. "Wagon carts made these grooves in the stone." He swept his arm toward various buildings. "Look, the baker's shop with its dome oven, the laundry with channels to drain the water, and tubs for dying clothes. There's the *aerarium,* where the city's treasury was kept."

He took me by the hand into the back and pointed to a series of crevices in the stone. "These holes held iron bars in the windows to protect the city's coffers."

"You can feel the people still walking the streets."

We approached a large two-story structure. "This is the best," Russo said. "The Roman marketplace, a *cryptoporticus.*"

"A what?"

"*Cryptoporticus,* a covered shopping bazaar invented by the Romans—all your market needs under one roof."

We entered the building, which remained surprisingly intact. A series of sales counters built in stone flanked the wide hallway. Behind each counter, a series of nooks in the stone offered storage to the proprietor. One couldn't help but imagine Romans in togas buying and bartering for cloth, exotic spices, fresh bread baked in the stone ovens, and statues of Roman gods used to protect homes from evil. And I couldn't help but think that Domenico would wear a huge grin at seeing such wonders.

"I'll show you something even more incredible," Russo said. We swept through several tunnels, each ending in high archways, and finally entered a room where rows of boxes stood along the wall. As various other objects began to come into focus, a shiver penetrated my spine. Hundreds of small open compartments stacked five high filled the room, and each held a human skull.

"Monks built these burial chambers hundreds and hundreds of years ago for victims of the plague," Russo murmured. "During the plagues, fifteen hundred deaths a day overwhelmed the holy grave-yards of the churches. People dug graves in the middle of the streets to bury the dead."

"It's spooky."

Russo chuckled. "When the epidemic ended, the city overflowed with unburied bodies. Priests dumped them into the underground and sealed these caverns with lime. Last century, priests reopened this burial ground so people could visit their relatives. People began to pil-grimage here to select and adopt a skull of one of the unknown dead. They prayed to these *pezzentelle*—little begging souls of Purgatory—for miracles and for grace. It's said that the prayers of the living lift the nameless dead from Purgatory into Paradise."

I shuddered, feeling the presence of souls all around me, invading their solitude. *The nameless dead.*

"Are you scared?" Russo grinned, but then noticed that I was shak-ing. "Very well, we'll go." He put his arm around me and led me through yet another group of tunnels, shadows lunging all around us. "Most people have forgotten about the underground world of Napoli, but it still serves a purpose. When a Byzantine general laid siege to Napoli, he used the tunnels to sneak his men, horses, and weapons into the very heart of the city. That's how I use it. My men know entrances throughout the city. By using them to escape and travel around, we can appear and disappear instantly."

We walked up a steep pathway, and the corridor split into two. Russo pointed at one of the paths with "Materdei Hill" carved in the stone over the archway. "That way is the Church of Holy Mary of the Carmelites. You can access the underground from the south side of the church, and pass from the present day above into this ancient past in a few steps."

He led me down the other path to steps that ended at a door. He extinguished the lantern and pushed the door hard. Outside, night had fallen, but thousands of tiny flames created a heavenly glow. The doorway placed us inside a graveyard, where hundreds of people stood holding candles. Everyone in Napoli seemed to be visiting a departed relative on this All Souls Day.

A flickering sea of flames illuminated our path. As we walked, splashed by candlelight, emotion-filled faces floated by us. The tears of mourning were washed in the light of the flames and glistened like stars. People placed flowers and baked goods on the graves of their relatives. My heart panged as I thought of Papa.

At one well-manicured grave accented with a large bouquet of flowers, Russo stopped and knelt. Two impressive gravestones marked the site. One read, "Isabella Russo, Faithful Wife and Mother, Born 1888 Died 1916 While Giving Another Life to the World." The other, "Giorgio Russo, Born 1884 Died a Hero 1916."

"*Madre, Padre,* I introduce you to my wife, Carina. You will like her. She is good for me." His voice was soft and reverent. Russo kissed two of his fingers and touched them to the top of both headstones. He looked to me. "Let's head back."

He remained reflective and quiet on the walk back to the house. It moved me to see his guard down, to see him vulnerable.

That's why I was surprised to find myself uneasy. I kept thinking about Russo's words to me as we entered the underworld: "This place might even save your life someday." Why would I need saving?

Chapter 12

ABDUCTION OF INNOCENCE

Autumn moved into Napoli on the backs of rain clouds. On the first clear day that dawned, I asked Carlo to escort me to church. As we walked, women sang from the balconies of their apartments as they hung their wash over the long cords drawn from terrace to terrace. It didn't matter if a person sang well or not, it seemed a requirement for citizens of Napoli to sing operatic arias, popular songs of the day, or old folk melodies. The voices drifted through the streets and turned all of Napoli into one huge theater.

The food vendors that lined the streets provided refreshments for the entertainment; unfortunately, the pervasive foul odors of the gutters made it difficult to enjoy the tasty temptations. Centuries of waste excreted into the ancient boulevards created a constant stench that permeated the city. It made one question the wisdom of eating spaghetti after seeing fresh pasta hanging outside on wooden racks to dry in the rancid air.

As we walked toward the cathedral I spotted the fruit vendor from whom I had purchased the pineapple several months before. I asked him for another helping. "No pineapples, no bananas, signora. I don't sell such things," he replied nervously.

After we moved on, Carlo explained, "Mussolini banned the import of bananas and other exotic produce. He wants only domestic fruit sold—another of the Duce's rules to keep Italy free from dependence on any other part of the world."

Even with Carlo beside me, I noticed men staring at me. Some were brash enough to whistle. Perhaps it was my fault; I had started dressing like a Napoli native, in shorter, tighter skirts and peasant blouses. Although I felt naked in such outfits, not conforming to the popular local dress caused me even greater embarrassment.

We walked along the upscale Via Tribunale near the Piazza Dante. In Italy, one knew Christmas was approaching when one heard the sound of the *zampogne,* a musical instrument similar to Scottish bagpipes. Strolling musicians filled the street, with Christmas music emanating from their pipes.

Presepe, Christmas nativity cribs, were already on view, even though today was only the first day of December. People displayed the cribs in their front windows, and many shop owners exhibited especially elaborate ones.

I peered into one of the shops. "These are so much fancier than any I saw in Reggio Calabria."

"It's sad they commercialize Christmas in such a way."

"St. Francis of Assisi made the first crib," I pointed out.

"A great saint to respect. But the way people compete to create the most beautiful cribs, using gold and gems, it ruins the sacred spirit." He threw his hands into the air. "The tradition has lost its old charm."

I stopped at a bakery to look at the treats, and decided on a tall round cake filled with raisin and pieces of candied fruit.

We were walking along the street nibbling on pieces of the cake when an automobile screeched up to the curb next to us. Carlo was turning toward it, one hand dipping under the lapels of his jacket, when two men jumped out of the car and knocked him to the ground. One of the men turned a pistol on him and fired. I felt the heat from the blast.

"Oh, my God!" I screamed, dropping the cake and lunging toward Carlo.

I didn't get far. The men grabbed me and hauled me to the car, my heels dragging furrows through the cake on the street.

"Hurry up! Get her in!" shouted the driver.

They tried to force me into the back seat. I screamed and thrashed about, and then braced my legs against the door jamb, making it impossible for them to push me into the vehicle.

Over their shoulders I saw Carlo stagger to his feet. Swinging just one of his huge arms, he grabbed both men from behind. They released me to fight him. With his free hand Carlo held his pistol, and as the driver turned toward with gun drawn, Carlo shot him in the head. The driver fell against the steering wheel, causing the horn to wail.

Carlo holstered his pistol and then, with incredible strength, grabbed the other two men by their necks and smashed their heads into the side of the car. They toppled unconscious to the street.

That was when I realized Carlo's pants glistened with blood.

"Carlo, you're hurt!"

"I'm fine. Come. We need to get you out of here."

"Shouldn't we wait for the police?"

"It's not safe." Carlo grabbed my arm and rushed me away, propelling us both into a full sprint even though his face clenched in pain.

"Carlo, you're bleeding badly! We need to stop."

He didn't reply, just guided me to an old battered door at the end of an alley. With a heave, he opened the decaying door to reveal stairs leading down. *This place might save your life someday.*

We plunged into Napoli's underworld, but Carlo didn't reduce his speed until we were safely home.

Russo called immediately for the doctor. Carlo seemed calm, but his face was chalk-white and glistening with sweat. While waiting for the doctor, Russo helped him tie a cloth around his leg to slow the bleeding.

Seeing Carlo hurt made my stomach churn and my head pound. I rubbed my cheek with my hand. "Carlo, how can I thank you enough?"

He shrugged. "I'm just glad I was there."

"You risked your life for me. You saved my life."

"Please, Carina," he said, pink staining the paleness of his cheeks. "I couldn't live with myself if something happened to you while you were in my charge."

"I owe you a great debt, Carlo," Russo said.

The doctor arrived and examined Carlo. "It doesn't look bad. The bullet passed through."

I let out a sigh of relief. "Thank goodness."

The doctor placed his instruments on the table. Russo turned to me. "Why don't you go lay down, my pet? You've been through a lot. Carlo will be fine. I'll bring you up a cup of tea in a moment."

I nodded and started down the hall, but stopped a few steps away and turned back to listen. I wanted to understand exactly what had happened.

"Who was it, Carlo?" Russo asked.

I couldn't hear Carlo's reply.

"I'm calling Benito and Renzo," Russo said, with a calm intensity. "I want this handled immediately."

Russo stepped into the hallway and stopped, startled to see me there. I pulled him away by the arm.

"What's going on?" I whispered. "Why did those men try to kill Carlo and kidnap me?"

"I'm sorry you had to go through this," Russo said in a low, calm voice, "but trust me, nothing like it will ever happen again."

"Both my life and Carlo's are in danger. Why?" I emphasized the question by shaking my hands at him.

"Carina, I told you, dogs always nip at your heels when you're at the head of the pack. I'm the Prince of Napoli. I run this city. This crime against me will not go unpunished."

"The crime was aimed at *me*. And what about Carlo? They tried to kill him!"

He took me in his arms. "Carina, I promise you nothing will happen to you or Carlo."

His confident tone made me believe him. In Russo's arms I felt protected.

He whispered in my ear, "Carina, I ask you to swear that you'll never divulge any of the secrets you may learn about me."

Secrets worse than those I already knew? The thought made me uneasy, but I knew what my answer must be. "I swear to you, my husband, nothing will ever leave my lips."

He smiled at me, patted me on the head, and kissed me. "Now, go to bed and relax, my pet. I'll have Amelia bring you some hot tea. As soon as the doctor finishes with Carlo, I'll check on you."

Russo gave Carlo time off to recover from his wound.

To speed up his healing, I made Carlo minestrone soup and fresh baked bread. It was all I could think of to do. "Here's a little something to start you on the road to wellness."

He smiled. "That's very sweet of you."

"Carlo, how can I ever thank you enough?"

"Please, Carina, it's my job to protect you. Let's not speak of it again."

I respected his wishes, but the memories of that day haunted me.

A couple of weeks later, Russo asked me, "Honey, wouldn't you like to go to church?"

"I really don't feel like going into town."

"My pet, there's no reason to be afraid."

"I know."

He hesitated, his face thoughtful. "I can give you a pistol to carry, if it'll make you feel safer."

"Maybe I would feel better." I was unsure if I really meant it, but Russo immediately led me to his office and unlocked his gun cabinet. I pointed to a gun with a round lump on the top of its barrel "That's an odd-looking pistol."

He picked it up. "This is a Luger; they're used by German Gestapo officers." But he put it back and selected a small, gray-metal handgun with a wooden handle. "This Colt's the right size for you." He handed me the petite pistol. It was heavier than it looked; or perhaps the gun's purpose weighed on me.

Over the next week, Russo spent his spare time teaching me how to use the gun. After living under the constant threat of Mama's whip all I wanted was to find peace, yet here I was learning to shoot a weapon in order to protect myself from the dangers that pervaded Napoli—especially for the wife of the Prince.

Chapter 13

INVITATION TO THE COURT

While Russo dressed for work, I washed the sleep out of my eyes and dried my face.

"How would you like to go to the Royal Christmas Ball next week?" he asked as I returned to the bedroom.

My eyes flew wide. "Really?"

"Yes, my pet. I thought you could use a distraction to help you forget that nasty incident with Carlo."

"Is it a fancy ball, like the ones I've read about? Will we meet dukes and Princes?"

Russo grinned. "It's at the Royal Palace, hosted by Vittorio Emanuele the IV—the other Prince of Napoli. I'd say that's pretty fancy."

"Oh, no!"

"What's wrong?"

"My father taught me to waltz when I was little, but I don't remember how."

"Then I'll show you." Russo held out his hand. I took it, and he pulled me into his arms and started to lead me across the floor

"But we have no music."

Without skipping a beat, he turned on the radio and danced me around the bedroom to the music of a big band. "The woman must trust the man to lead her," he said. "She must be completely under his control."

I enjoyed feeling his strong, sure movements, which compelled me to follow his will. "Yes. I see."

"Give your body to me, my pet. Trust yourself to my protection." Even though we were the same size and his eyes met mine at the same level, his forcefulness exhilarated me as his torso pushed against mine, leading me about. "Everyone will be there. Mussolini himself is coming. It's time I showed off my beautiful bride." He broke free of me. "More lessons later. Do you have an evening dress?"

From the closet I produced my fanciest, most formal outfit—a black, high-collar long dress with endless loops of lace.

"Oh, no!" he said. "We're not going to a funeral. That will never do! We'll buy you something festive, a beautiful gown."

"I wish I had more time . . . I could make one."

"Don't be silly. We'll go to Fortunato's; he owes me a favor. We'll buy you the most expensive gown in his shop. Everyone at the ball will be envious of me having you on my arm." Russo smiled. "And you deserve a special evening."

The kidnapping still haunted my thoughts, but maybe a fancy ball would help chase it away with beautiful memories.

I danced around an imaginary ballroom, giggling, and Russo laughed as he watched.

The morning of the ball I awoke from dreams of palaces and dancing in a fancy gown to inexplicable uneasiness. The truth was that even after more than a year in Napoli, I still felt out of place. I wanted to fit in at the ball, but how could I? The fanciest event I had ever attended was Papa's funeral. I would always just be a farm girl from the South.

Even though the ball didn't begin for another half-rotation of the earth, I tried on my dress again and practiced walking in my new shoes. I was determined to not have any mishaps.

Almost a week earlier, Russo had taken me to Fortunato's salon, which offered the latest fashions from Paris, Milan and Rome. True to his word, he bought me the most expensive dress after Fortunato told him that the Italian designer who'd made it was the most famous dressmaker in the world. That was all Russo needed to hear, but the dress seemed too wild for me. In the South, I had never worn clothes with much color, and this bright pink satin gown seemed to blaze with its own light. Its color reminded me of cotton candy—much too dazzling for good taste. The top portion was form fitting and then flared into a graceful full skirt that fell nearly to my ankles. It was so silky against my skin it felt as if I was wearing a cloud.

"Look how your skin glows," Russo said when I first tried it on. He looked mesmerized. "You're stunning. No one will be able to take their eyes off of you."

Signore Fortunato insisted that I have matching shoes, and presented a fantastical pair in glorious pink with a tiny bow and a mountainous high heel. I'd never seen such open shoes with straps going every which way. I wasn't even sure how to insert my foot, but Signore Fortunato's lady assistant slipped them onto my feet and strapped them up. They pinched my toes, but I didn't say a word. Signore Fortunato called them *stilettos*. I had seen women all around Napoli wearing them, but I was certain I would topple over at any moment. I paraded around awkwardly. "Wrap them up," Russo told Fortunato.

Now, practicing one more time for the ball, I danced in front of Russo in my new dress and shoes. He watched me as he sat on the dressing bench at the foot of the bed, putting on his socks and shoes.

"I made the right choice with that dress. We'll get noticed," he said.

I looked down. "It's amazing. I'll feel like a Roman empress . . . Could we move to Rome some day?"

"What brought that on? Why would you want to move to Rome?"

"Rome is the city of life. It's sophisticated, full of culture, art, freedom—"

"When were you in Rome?"

"Well, never. I got as close as my uncle's hotel just outside the city. I've read a lot about it, though."

"I'm doing quite well in Napoli, thank you. In fact, I'm looking to expand to the South using some of your mother's properties."

"Why do you need to expand?"

He chuckled. "You need to take everything within your grasp so people cannot give you orders; you tell *them* what to do. *You* have all the power. No one can touch you then." He looked at his watch, and then stood and put on his coat. "The Marseilles shipment never arrived."

"Oh, that's too bad. I know you were waiting for the penicillin and morphine."

"I think I need to find a new supplier." Russo sounded discouraged. "It's getting tougher and tougher to get shipments through. With all this talk of war, many things are in short supply."

"Italy lost half a million people in the Great War. Why does anyone want another one?"

"I'm worried about business. Soldiers and police are everywhere grabbing shipments for themselves. Expansion to the South will help, although there's one competitor down there who remains a thorn in my side."

"Couldn't we leave the South some day? Run a fancy hotel in Rome?"

"A hotel?"

"Where people throw fancy balls, and the rich and famous stay. I'd love to live in the Eternal City. A woman can be something there."

"Women can be something?" He laughed. "I need to keep you busier so such foolish thoughts don't enter your pretty little head." He headed toward the door. "I've got business in Salerno now."

"Don't be late for the ball."

"I'll be back soon enough," Russo assured me, and then he snapped his fingers and made the coin he was playing with disappear. He kissed me on the forehead and left.

I twirled around on my shoes for much of the morning, until I felt sure-footed in them; but after I finished that exercise, time dragged as I waited for the big event. When the gala was less than an hour away, I began to panic. Russo still hadn't returned. I would be furious with him if he didn't show up. At that moment, the thought hit me: *If someone wanted to kidnap me because I'm Russo's wife, how safe is* he?

I grew exhausted from anxiety before I had ever set foot in the ballroom.

Chapter 14

ONE GRAND BALL, ONE MUSSOLINI, AND ONE SHOCK

Traffic backed up as we approached the Piazza Plebiscito, the site of the Royal Palace. A flow of fancy cars and fancy people clogged the Piazza entrance.

Because Russo had returned late from his trip to Salerno, he had decided to change his clothes in the car to save time. I noticed a couple of splotches of dried blood on his shirt. I pointed them out. "What happened? Are you hurt?"

"I'm fine, my pet, just fine," he assured me, as he pulled his coat sleeve over his shirt cuff. "There was an accident on the road coming back and I stopped to help."

I didn't believe him, but on a day like today I really didn't want to know the truth. I changed the subject. "How did you get invited to the Royal Christmas Ball?"

"Let's just say someone owed me a favor."

It seemed everyone in Napoli owed Russo a favor.

Carlo drove our Alpha Romero into the circular Piazza. "The church to our left emulates the Pantheon in Rome," Carlo explained, pointing to the monumental structure. "And over here is the palace of Salerno."

"Glorious!" I gushed on seeing the royal residence sparkle in the orange glow of the setting sun. Surely God lives in such a place in heaven. Red brick combined with black stone covered its façade. I counted twenty-one windows on each of the top two floors that looked out from the palace onto the piazza. Nine archways with statues topped with crowns stood under them, shouldering the mighty structure above them like Atlas holding the world. The Royal Palace had been the seat of power for both the Kingdom of Napoli and the Kingdom of Sicily until being absorbed into the Kingdom of Italy in 1860.

"Each statue represents one of Napoli's kings," Carlo said.

A National Gendarmerie with his red-striped trousers, long sword, and Napoleonic hat directed Carlo to let us off. Hundreds of impressive cars filled the piazza.

Women dressed in the latest designer gowns made their way toward the palace. Their diamonds, rubies, and sapphires sparkled in the setting sunlight. The men escorting them wore elegant clothing, many draped in black capes. A good number of them were in olive-green dress military uniforms splashed with colored ribbons and medals.

Carlo opened the car door. Russo stepped out and eyed the fancy cars. I stumbled as I stood up on my stilettos, but Carlo steadied me. He winked at me and whispered, "Don't worry, you'll be fine."

Russo turned toward me and smiled. "Are you ready to go in and make every man jealous of me?" He took me by the arm and we started toward the magnificent structure.

We entered the palace through large arched doors. A tidy row of soldiers in pristine uniforms greeted us and checked our invitations. They threw their right hand forward in the Roman salute, which Hitler's troops would later adopt. My eyes widened when I stepped into the entrance hall. The pink marble staircase started as one structure, but then broke off into left and right sections, each wide enough for three couples to stand comfortably on a single stair. Beautiful carved panels, arched stained-glass windows, and carved marble accents decorated the staircase. Spectacular flower arrangements of roses, orchids and exotic flowers I didn't recognize blossomed along the corridors and their delicious scent permeated the halls. This palace held no resemblance to Mama's large but simple house. This must mirror God's throne.

We followed other guests up the stairs toward the ballroom, a group of people creating a magical moving kaleidoscope of colors, textures, and patterns of light. The buzz of conversation reverberated in the stairwell and the hall, and filled it with palpable life.

The royal-red grand ballroom exhibited a thirty-foot-high sculpted ceiling, huge crystal chandeliers and, across the far wall, a glorious fresco of an ancient Roman battle. Hundreds of colorfully dressed guests accented the room. A small orchestra played a waltz, but no one was dancing. A huge regal throne made of red velvet with a gilded frame, surrounded by red carpet, pulled your attention to the front of the room.

Decorative figures of animals sculpted from ice graced the long tables flanking either side of the throne. One table held dishes I didn't recognize. I asked the server about them and he pointed out several. "This is imported Russian caviar, these hors d'oeuvres are French *foie gras,* aspic, filo stuffed with brie." The other table was laden with rich desserts which were described to me as: strawberries coated in Belgian chocolate, éclairs, Swiss tortes, and of course Italy's famous cannoli, which had been assembled with such artfulness that I wanted to frame them rather than eat them.

"What would you like to drink?" Russo asked.

"Champagne, please." I felt like a Princess out of a fairy tale. "Pink champagne! I read about it once."

Russo laughed. "All right, my pet. Pink champagne it is." He gave a gentlemanly bow before venturing off.

A refined-looking middle-aged woman approached me. Though tiny and not in the least beautiful, she carried herself with dignity. Her flowered scent wafted over and introduced me to her. Her baby-blue gown was made of some brushed fabric I couldn't name. An arresting, maroon velvet coat with gold lapels like a man's that draped to the floor gave brashness to her outfit. Her hair was pinned up tightly and topped with a funny black hat that reminded me of Napoleon's. She wore gloves with fingernails painted on at the tips—most odd. As unbelievable as her outfit seemed, I had to admit that it made an impression. She looked at me and then at my dress. "Lovely gown, my dear," she said, with a mischievous grin. "It was made for you. You look radiant."

"Thank you." I smiled nervously. My dress still seemed outrageous to me, but not nearly as shocking as hers. "You certainly stand out, as well."

"Thank you, dear." She chuckled.

"My name's Carina Maria Russo."

"Ah, one of my names is Maria, as well. I usually go by Elsa, but you may call me Maria." She smiled.

"It's nice to meet you, Maria."

"You're the loveliest lady here, Carina Maria," she told me.

"Thank you." I felt myself blush.

"Well, enjoy yourself, dear. Please don't spill anything on that beautiful dress. Remember, in difficult times like these, fashion must always be outrageous." With that, she winked and merged into the crowd.

An older woman with a sagging face came up to me excitedly. "Do you know who that woman was?"

"She told me her name was Maria." Suddenly I was afraid that I had made a mistake in etiquette with a royal.

"Yes, Maria Elsa Schiaparelli. You're wearing one of her gowns. She's the most famous clothing designer in the world."

"Dear Lord!"

Just then Russo returned with the drinks. The woman looked startled to see him. "Enjoy your evening," she said, and retreated back into the crowd.

About ten paces away, to Russo's left, I noticed three women in their thirties who didn't seem to fit in. They were looking at us and whispering among themselves. They turned away when they saw me watching them.

"Carina, I want to introduce you to someone," Russo said, as he placed my arm through his and led me through the crowd. As we passed the three women, I could hear their gossip.

"That must be Russo's wife."

"She's awfully young."

"Do you think she worked for him?"

We approached a well-dressed man with medals draped across his coat, although his attire was governmental rather than military. He stood a head taller than Russo.

When Russo slapped him on the shoulder the man turned and said, "Russo. How are you, you old scoundrel? And who's this luminous lady with you?"

"Aldo Fortuno, this is my wife, Carina," Russo said proudly.

A broad smile came to Aldo's face. "So she does exist. A great pleasure to finally meet you, Carina," he said, taking my hand and kissing it. His soft, manicured hands told me he hadn't worked a hard day's labor in his life.

"Very nice to meet you, Signore Fortuno." I gave him a slight nod.

"Aldo, you're looking tired and old," Russo joked. "You must be working too hard."

"These days, if you're employed by the government, you always work hard. I need more projects with you, Russo, to build my nest egg."

"Well, there might be something soon, but I'm having a hard time getting shipments right now. Are we going to have another war?"

"Don't worry. If war comes, it'll be over quickly. Mussolini continues to bring a new Renaissance to Europe. He'll bring back the prosperity of the Roman Empire throughout the Mediterranean."

"I'd settle for one undisrupted shipment of medical supplies from Marseilles."

"The communists and socialists tried to ruin this country, but Mussolini's returned our prosperity and strength. Our future is as good as bread with Il Duce."

"You sound like a walking advertisement for Mussolini," Russo laughed.

"Not a hundred miles from where I was born," I added, "Mussolini is building a great new city: Mussolinia. My papa took us to the opening ceremony when they started construction. He said it would help many men who couldn't find work get back on their feet."

"Yes," Aldo said, "a very progressive idea. Mussolini's restored respect for Italy throughout Europe. Britain and France called on Italy during the Great War to help bring peace to Europe, and Italy lost many soldiers." A flash of sadness drifted across Russo's face, but Aldo didn't seem to notice. "Our war allies proved untrustworthy, though. They refused us the Austrian land they had promised us. They slighted us after we helped them push back the Germans. It cost Italy dearly, and we won't forget their betrayal. Mussolini will set things right."

"All this talk of war and politics, Aldo," said Russo. "Carina's here to celebrate."

"What else does anyone talk about these days?" Aldo replied, and then smiled at me. "But for the beautiful lady we'll make an effort. What do you think of this affair, Carina?"

"I've never been to anything like it. It's overwhelming."

"Aldo, at last," said a voice from the crowd. Its familiarity made me tremble.

Aldo turned. "Ah, you've made it. Signore and Signora Russo, may I introduce Domenico—"

"Hello, Carina," Domenico interrupted. He shook my hand. "I noticed you in that lovely pink dress the moment I came in."

I managed to smile but felt dazed. His dark bottomless eyes penetrated into me, as they always had. More than a year had passed since I last saw him, yet he still made my heart race.

"Ah, you two know each other," Aldo said.

"Yes, we met in Reggio Calabria . . . as children," I explained.

"Our families . . . knew each other," Domenico added.

Aldo asked, "Russo, do you know Domenico, as well?"

Russo wore an odd expression on his face. "Ah, no. I haven't had the pleasure." He smiled tightly and shook Domenico's hand. With the difference in height, Russo looked like a child next to Domenico, despite being twelve years older. "Good to meet you."

"And you, Signore Russo."

"We were just discussing Mussolini's accomplishments for the country," Aldo offered.

"Well, I'm not always so sure Mussolini has the country's best interests at heart. He's rather ruthless."

"Surely you don't believe the rumors about how he gained power," Aldo said. "Just the gossip of socialists and jealous rivals. He gained power from his strength to lead Italy out of a troubled time, not through brutality. Right, Russo?"

Russo smiled. "Right. Nothing but rumors."

"Well, Mussolini did make the Lateran Treaties with Il Papa," Domenico conceded, as he removed his coat.

I nearly passed out. Under his coat, Domenico was wearing a priest's frock. He continued, but I didn't hear clearly.

"For nearly sixty years the government and the pope feuded over the Church's role in the welfare of the Italian people. When Mussolini took power he agreed that Church doctrine would be taught in schools. He even pays my salary, and he set Vatican City up as an autonomous country."

"Leave it to a priest to see the how the Church benefits from our leader," Aldo chuckled.

Domenico touched Aldo's shoulder for emphasis. "I do thank Mussolini for that, but I worry that more people worship him than our Savior."

"People see immediate visible benefits from Il Duce," Russo said. "Jesus only offers the promise of a hereafter, and who knows if He'll keep His word?"

A highly decorated officer in uniform approached us. "Good evening, everyone."

"Captain Scolari keeps the streets safe for us all," Aldo teased him in greeting.

"Sorry to intrude, but may I borrow your husband for a moment, Signora Russo? I believe he has some information for me."

"Certainly, Captain Scolari," I said, and the two men stepped a few paces away and huddled in conversation.

"I better sit in," said Aldo. "We don't want them plotting against the government." The three of us laughed. "Excuse me." Aldo joined them.

"I can't believe you're a priest, Domenico."

"I've always wanted to make a difference in people's lives. I teach in the school next to the Duomo."

A long, awkward pause followed. "Is your family well?" I wanted to say so much more but dared not. Certainly, my heart's thumping could be seen by everyone it was beating so strongly.

"Yes, fine. My father surprised me by being very supportive of my decision to go into the priesthood."

"Good."

"I hope you're happy, Carina."

I looked away. To answer truthfully would force me to acknowledge to myself that I wasn't happy being married to a man I didn't love—not the way I loved Domenico. It was a fact I couldn't face.

"Carina, we were both so naive when I asked you to run away with me."

"I wish I'd said yes," I whispered in a rush of emotion.

Domenico chuckled. "Kind of silly to be up on that rock burning a fire every night."

"Not to me." I looked into his eyes.

He shook his head, brushing it off. "Youthful infatuation. Now you're married. Do you have children?"

"Not yet," Russo answered. I jumped at hearing his voice, afraid that he'd overheard our conversation. "But soon, we hope." He handed me a plate of hors d'oeuvres.

"I'm sure you'll be blessed," Domenico replied.

Russo studied him intently, then looked at me.

"Well," Domenico said, "if you'll excuse me, I should get to my duties. I'm helping Father Denosi collect for the orphans' fund."

"Here, let me get you started." Russo pulled a large wad of cash out of his pocket and handed Domenico 100,000 lira.

"Goodness, that's very generous, Signore Russo!"

"I'm happy to help the orphans. It's a tough life. I know firsthand."

"Well, thank you. Now I must get to work. Good to see you, Carina."

"You, as well." I smiled politely but wanted to throw myself into his arms. In the secret world of thoughts and desires, I imagined I was not alone in living a parallel life to my real one. I hoped Domenico and I at least shared a life within that realm.

"So good to meet you, Signore Russo, and thank you again on behalf of the orphans." Domenico bowed his head to us, then turned and disappeared into the crowd. Russo glanced harshly at me.

Before he could speak, a buzz swept through the room, and people began moving toward the entrance. We drifted with the crowd.

"What's all the excitement about?" I asked.

"Only one man can create a rumble like this," said Aldo, who had also returned.

Mussolini walked into the room as if he owned the world. He wasn't a handsome man, but his presence was electric. His powerful build filled his military dress uniform, which was crossed by a gold sash. Numerous medals draped across his chest.

Several officials escorted him to the platform next to the throne. He waved to the crowd, and a thunderous cheer erupted.

One of the officials stepped up to the microphone. "It is my great privilege to introduce the man who led us out of an impoverished era, the man who leads us to a bright future. Winston Churchill said of this man after his visit to Rome, 'Anyone can see he thinks of nothing but the lasting good of the Italian people.' The man the British newspaper *The Manchester Guardian* calls, 'The greatest statesman of our time.' I give you Il Duce!"

Mussolini approached the microphone to the roar of the crowd.

"Ah, it is good to be with my fellow countrymen," he began. "We stand in the middle of the 1930s and must choose a direction. It's a perilous time. The scourge of socialist doctrine continues to infect much of Europe. It is the doctrine of the weak: weak minds, weak bodies, weak spirits. I say to you, it is better to live one day as a lion, than a hundred years as a sheep!"

The crowd shouted its approval. My body pulsed with excitement at the force of his delivery.

"Socialism is a fraud, a comedy, a phantom, blackmail. Much of Europe languishes in its lurid, placid seduction. It will breed decay and misery. It must be rooted out and destroyed.

"If every age has its characteristic doctrine, a thousand signs point to fascism as the doctrine of our time. It is the doctrine of strength, power, leadership. Blood alone moves the wheels of history. Look back on history and find a great civilization that wasn't built on the blood of others.

"Through expansionism we will bring back the prosperity of Italy's past. We won success in Ethiopia this year. If war comes to Europe, it will not last long. We possess the will to fight. Those weakened by socialism do not. Life is hard! Sometimes we must forego our own happiness and comfort to give every effort within us for the good of our country, our great State of Italy!" He lifted his arm, his fist clenched in triumph, and shouted, "To the new Roman Empire!"

The crowd roared. Mussolini thrust his arm once again in a gesture of victory. I, like everyone else, applauded wildly as tears ran down my cheeks.

Some dignitaries motioned Mussolini to sit on the throne. He waved them off, but they insisted. He laughed but finally sat down.

"*Viva o Re! Viva o Re!* Long live the king!" the crowd shouted joyfully. Mussolini, clearly amused, waved to everyone.

A group of Italian Army offices began to sing *Giovinezza,* and more and more of the gathering joined in to sing the rousing march. Mussolini nodded in time to the music.

"Greetings heroes, greetings immortal country, your sons are reborn with faith in the ideal. The value of your warriors, the virtue of the pioneers, the Dante Alighieri's vision today will shine in every heart. Youth, youth, spring to the beauty of Fascism, savior of our freedom.

Within our borders we the citizens are remade and the maker is Mussolini.

For the glory of peace and the time to shame the one's who denied this country.

Youth, youth see the beauty spring from the harsh life your song sings. The poets, artisans, Princes, and paupers sing the proud unswerving faith to Mussolini.

There is no poor neighborhood that does not send their forces, that does not fly flags to the redeeming vision of Fascism.

Youth, youth see the beauty spring from the harsh life your song sings."

Thunderous applause rose up at the end of the song. Mussolini made his way down from the platform to mingle with the crowd as the orchestra began to play.

"Let me introduce you to Mussolini," Russo said, leading me through the crowd.

"You've met Mussolini?" I was certain he was kidding me.

"We're well acquainted. I've helped him out a few times."

"He comes to you for help and guidance?"

All of a sudden I was standing before the great man.

"Il Duce. You're looking very fit," Russo said over the drone of the crowd.

"Ah, Signore Russo." Mussolini grinned in recognition. "It's good to see you again."

"Yes, the years pass by."

"Good productive years for both of us," Mussolini bellowed.

"For you, certainly more than myself." Russo motioned to me. "Il Duce, I'd like to introduce my wife, Carina."

"Signore Russo, you've outdone yourself," Mussolini said, then kissed my hand.

I smiled nervously. His energy and command shook through me like the quakes of the south. Standing so close to him, I realized how he had built such an army of devoted souls. "What did you think of my speech?" he asked.

"It was inspirational, Il Duce. I'm thankful the country is in your hands."

Mussolini laughed heartily. "Russo, I think you have a diplomat here."

Russo smiled. "I'm learning more about her all the time. Perhaps you would honor us with a visit sometime."

"I'd love to. Would you like that, dear?"

"She'd love it, Il Duce," Russo said before I could answer.

An excited high-strung man grabbed Mussolini's hand and shook it vigorously. "Il Duce! Il Duce!" he shouted over the crowd, tears flowing down his cheeks.

Mussolini patted him on the head like a father would a child. He turned back to us and said, "Farewell, Signore and Lady Russo. I must give all my children attention." He motioned to the entire gathering, winked at me, then let the crowd absorb him.

When the orchestra began playing a waltz, people moved to the dance floor.

"Would you care to dance?" Russo asked me. I smiled and gave him my hand.

He led me around the floor with grace. "Why are people watching us?" I asked.

"They're admiring the beautiful woman in pink, my little pet," he said, with a gentle smile.

As the dance ended I noticed Domenico standing by the refreshment table. He seemed distressed, and two other priests looked to be consoling him. "I wonder why Domenico looks so upset." I headed toward him.

"He looks as though he's in pain," Russo said, following close behind me.

"What's wrong, Domenico?" I asked.

"Domenico's father, Mr. Saldino, was found shot in Salerno today," one of the priests informed me. "The police think it was a robbery."

"Dear God, Domenico." I gently placed a hand on his arm. "I'm so sorry."

"It's such a shock," Domenico managed.

Russo came close and whispered in my ear, "Domenico Saldino? His last name is Saldino?"

"Yes, why?"

Russo snickered. Fortunately, Domenico was too overcome to notice.

"Why are you amused?" I whispered in Russo's ear. "That's cruel."

"It's just that life has so many ironies."

"My mother's here in town," Domenico said. "I must go to her. Please excuse me." He headed for the exit. The other priests followed him.

I turned to my husband. "Imagine. His father shot."

"I'll go get us a drink."

Without warning, a large man, his face flushed red with anger and alcohol, grabbed Russo by the arm. "How did a puny low-life snake like you get into the Royal Ball?"

"May I suggest that you show me no disrespect, especially in front of my wife?"

"What you did to my brother . . . You're nothing but a blackmailer."

Russo raised an eyebrow. "You mean I spread malicious truth and vicious facts."

"I'll never forget what you did to him. You're nothing but a street thug, you *bidonista*."

"May I suggest you apologize for such a vulgar comment?"

"May I suggest you go back to the sewer where you belong, you filthy rat?" the man said, and tried to push Russo.

Russo fired his fist into the man's throat. Shocked and gasping for air, the man fell to his knees, clutching his throat.

Leaning down, Russo lowered his voice to a deadly whisper. "I didn't like your apology. I warned you not to disrespect me in front of my wife." He stepped on the man's finger and I heard a snap, like Mama breaking the neck of one of the chickens outside her kitchen window. The man's hand recoiled and he still struggled to breathe, his face a sickly blue as he wheezed and clawed at his throat.

Several people, including two guards and Aldo, rushed to help him. Russo slipped over to me and said, "Let's go."

The man finally found his breath, pointed at Russo, and gasped, "Him! He attacked me!"

One of the Gendarmerie grabbed Russo.

"Ridiculous," Aldo said. "I saw the entire incident. He assaulted Signore Russo, and the gentleman was merely defending himself. Release him."

The guards bowed to Aldo's authority and freed Russo. Then they bowed to Russo as well before withdrawing.

"I think it's best if you make a low-profile exit, let things blow over," Aldo said quietly to Russo. "Follow me." He led us to a small side door.

I sat in silence on the drive home, my gaze fixed on the streets of Napoli. I wanted to be as far away from Russo as possible, but he sat just a few centimeters away.

"Who is this Domenico to you?" he asked.

"We knew each other as children."

"Don't lie. I have eyes that see very clearly."

I didn't say anything. Russo pulled a string of rosary beads out of his pocket.

"What are those?" I asked.

"They're your priest's one precious asset."

"Why would you take Domenico's rosary beads?"

There was fire in Russo's eyes. "I take a man's wallet, I take his possessions, I take his life. Anything I want is mine! People call me the Prince of Napoli because I own this city. I own you. You are *mine!* I know when someone looks with lust. I know lust. It's my business to know lust."

I was both frightened and furious. "Like when you sleep with your prostitutes? Because I know you do."

"Priest or not, he'll be looking for comfort after the death of his father. You will not be his comforter."

I ignored him and looked away. He pulled my head around and forced me to look at him.

"I can make a call and have him dead in a minute! You are married to me. In the sacred Cathedral of Saint Januarius, you pledged your devotion to me. You will never speak to Domenico Saldino again."

"But he—"

He cuffed me across the face. "You will never speak to him again, or I'll kill him."

I nodded, and no further words were spoken. But the air remained thick with rage.

Chapter 15

THE GREAT ESCAPE

Russo was right. In the eyes of the Church, I had given him my soul. Marriage was one of the most sacred sacraments. For better or worse, Russo was my husband. But my husband's warnings only made me want to defy him.

A few days after the ball, I asked Carlo to take me to church for Confession. I also wanted to offer Domenico my condolences. Carlo took his customary position outside to wait for me.

Inside, I asked a priest if I could speak to Domenico. It was late afternoon, so I knew he had finished teaching. He appeared a few minutes later.

"I wanted to say how sorry I am about your father, Domenico." I reached out to him and rubbed his shoulder. His muscles relaxed.

"Thank you, Carina."

"How's your mother taking it?"

"She's having a tough time, but she's strong."

"How about you?" He nodded that he was all right. "Have the authorities learned what happened?"

"The police say it was robbery, but the only thing missing was my father's Saint Christopher medallion."

I shook my head. "Well, my sympathy to you and your family." An awkward pause set in. "I've come for Confession and counsel, Domenico."

"Let me get a priest for you, Carina. You shouldn't be confessing to me." He started to walk away.

"No. I must confess to you." I pulled him into a confessional box. "I'm frightened. I'm married to an evil man."

"Then you must help him to be a good man," Domenico said.

"I love another man, a man I've always loved."

"Carina, don't."

"I know you're grieving over your father, but I've been grieving over you. I confess . . . I have lust in my heart. I confess . . . I love you." I caressed his cheek and swept my hand along his temple.

He did not pull away. "Just because I'm a priest now doesn't mean I'm not filled with desires, Carina. These clothes don't shield me from yearning for you, but we freely made our choices, and now we must live with them." He moved away from me.

"Freely! I've never been free. I've worn chains my entire life—first in mother's prison, now in Russo's. Mama forced me to marry Russo. If only we'd lived in the North. Choice doesn't exist in the South."

"You didn't have to follow the traditions of the South, Carina. You could've made different choices."

"Let's run away, Domenico. We can find a way." I enveloped him and kissed him as if my life depended on it, as if tomorrow wouldn't come without him. Through his lips energy surged into me. My body pulsed. Maybe with the right man I would feel whole.

Domenico returned the kiss. He held me tightly, breathing deeply, as if trying to consume my essence. But again, he pushed me away.

"No, Carina! You gave a solemn commitment before God to this man. I'm a priest. It is my duty to protect your bond with him. For us . . . it's too late."

He rushed from the confessional and moved toward the door of the rectory. Then he turned and gazed at me. I thought he was going to run back, but he hurried to the door and disappeared.

Weak, I stood there unable to move, unable to breathe, unsure how I would find the strength to take a single step.

The following morning I had no desire to get out of bed. I felt indifferent, numb. No part of life seemed worth living. Mama was right, God hated me. I stared at the ceiling, hoping it might cave in on me and end my existence.

There was a knock on the front door. I heard Russo's voice, and then Domenico's. Leaping from the bed, I crossed to listen at the bedroom door.

"Signore Russo, I just wanted to thank you and Signora Russo for your generosity to the orphans' fund," Domenico said. "You're very kind." They exchanged pleasantries, and then Russo thanked him for coming and sent him on his way.

In my heart, I knew Domenico had come to deliver more than a thank you. I dressed in a rush, intending to hurry after him, but waited until Russo had left for work. Of course Carlo escorted me, but on this walk to the church, uncharacteristically, I didn't say a word.

In front of the altar, Domenico knelt in prayer. Except for a couple of old women praying in the back pews, we were alone.

I waited for him to finish his prayer and cross himself. "I heard you came by the house," I said.

He turned, startled, then took a few steps toward me. "Yes. I was hoping Russo wouldn't be there." He looked deep inside me as only he could.

"You came to see me?"

"I can't stop thinking about you, Carina."

My heart pounded with anticipation. "Domenico, Domenico, Domenico," I whispered. I wanted to say more, but I could think only of his name. He loved me! He wanted me! God had answered my prayers.

He pulled me into the hallway that ran along the inner wall of the chapel, and then into a small room off the corridor. "Let's do it," he said. "Let's run away. Let's go to Rome or America or—"

"Anywhere!"

He embraced me and for the first time since Papa died, I felt completely loved and completely safe. In that moment I was truly awake and alive.

We held each other for a long time without speaking. Slowly, reality returned, and I began to doubt whether or not we could run away.

"Every time I'm with you a smile grows inside me and feeds my soul," Domenico murmured. "Who can explain such things?" He looked off, as though he were peering into the future. "I see us together one day, on a hilltop in the countryside."

"Domenico, it's such a far-off dream. How can we ever get there? How can I even divorce Russo?"

"As your mother forced you into the marriage at a very young age, I believe you'll be able to obtain an annulment. It's good that you don't have children."

An annulment. How would Russo react to that? I closed my eyes, unwilling to think about it. "What about the priesthood?"

"Carina, God did not give me this love for you only for me to squander it away. Happiness is worth sacrifice, and you make me happy." He pulled me close and pressed his cheek against mine. "We can go to Rome, as you've always wanted. We'll make a new life there."

"Yes. We'll start a life that's free of the past." His kiss gave me strength and his arms gave me sanctuary. "I will come to church every day until we can run away."

"We'll plan to leave by . . . let's say . . . Friday. That gives us five days." His euphonious voice always reassured me. It would be a contented life, listening to that voice.

I nodded, but then my heart sank. "What about my brothers? They work for Russo. Who knows what he'll do to them!"

"They may have to leave with us. Let me pray over it. Perhaps we should all go to America."

"America. My brothers will never agree. Oh, Domenico, how can we do this?"

"If God has willed this, He'll grant us the answers, Carina," Domenico said, with fierce conviction. He melted me with a loving smile. "Now go home and pray, my love!"

I continued my daily trips to church, where Domenico and I planned our escape. He had looked further into the possibility of an annulment and felt the Church would grant me one, but I was more worried about Russo's reaction. As always, Carlo continued to watch over me, which didn't concern me; a daily trip to the cathedral wasn't cause for suspicion.

As the day of our planned flight approached, the butterflies I'd felt in my stomach for more than a week multiplied. Feeling sick, I curled up on the bed and drifted off to sleep.

I found myself standing with Russo on the bank of a river teeming with huge fish. Domenico stood on the other side. Russo took off his clothes and dove into the water, sinking out of sight. For some reason I put on his clothes. Across the river, Domenico was now sitting in a canoe, waving for me to come across. But the water was too fast and deep. Wolves and bears came out of the forest, nipping at my heels. I ran for my life.

I woke as Amelia came into the room carrying fresh linens. The nightmare had left me nauseous. I ran into the bathroom and vomited.

"What's the matter with you?" Amelia asked, as she began making the bed.

"I've been queasy lately. It's not like me . . . I've always been healthy as an ox."

"Silly girl, you must be pregnant," Amelia said, her tone filled with loathing. "Are you completely ignorant? When did you last have your monthly bleeding?"

I stared at her blankly.

"Are you still bleeding every month?" She pointed toward my privates. "When did you last bleed?"

"Not for some time." Please, I prayed, don't let me be with Russo's child.

"And you have a jumpy stomach and trouble eating?"

I nodded numbly. "I must go to the doctor and be sure before I tell Russo." I turned to Amelia. "Promise you won't tell him, Amelia. I want to be the one."

She gave a halfhearted shrug. "If that's what you wish."

A little while later, I snuck out of the house without Carlo and went downtown to see a doctor, who confirmed the bad news. I held back my tears until I reached the street and then collapsed against an alley wall and cried.

"God, why are you punishing me this way? You know I love Domenico. Am I so evil that I deserve this misery?" My anguish turned to rage. "Fine! So be it. But I don't respect You anymore, God. Do You hear me? You betrayed me! We are now enemies!"

Bound by my burden, I walked toward the cathedral. Each step sent a cold bolt of pain through my body. I forced my legs to take me inside, where I started to weep all over again. And then I saw my beautiful Domenico.

Smoke from the many burning candles drifted about him as if he were floating inside a cloud, and their vanilla scent made me dizzy. He was talking to an old woman just outside the confessional. After a moment, he noticed me and smiled. The woman nodded at something he said and then walked away. He came over and pulled me into one of the side rooms.

Looking into my eyes, he said, "Don't worry, my angel. I know how difficult this is for you, but we'll get through it. We'll be fine."

"Domenico, I . . . I am . . . The doctor said . . . well . . ."

"Are you all right?"

"No. I'm not all right. I'm with child."

Domenico flinched. "Dear God." He took me in his arms, and my tears soaked into his priestly robes. "Perhaps we could . . ." he started, but couldn't find a way to complete the thought. I was pregnant with my husband's child; the Church would never allow an annulment now.

"I can't see God's providence in this," I moaned as I pulled away from him. "There can be no talk of a future for us."

Domenico searched my eyes. "But, darling, if only we . . ." His throat tightened.

I watched him struggle to think of a way to keep us together, but he reached the same conclusion I had. He pulled me back into his arms. A tear fell onto my cheek and streamed down my face. This would be the only thing we could share.

We held each other a long time, knowing that soon our lives would go forever in separate directions. It would have been less painful to cut off my arm than leave his embrace.

The steeple bell rang, announcing evening Mass.

Domenico took a chain with a small gold cross out from under his robes and clasped it around my neck. "I've worn this next to my heart every day since my mother gave it to me when I was twelve. Wear it and feel close to my heart, Carina. Through it, I'll always feel your heart beat."

I took off my necklace with the small gold key and placed it around Domenico's neck. "Papa gave me this key to unlock my dreams. Through it, we'll always share our dreams."

Again we fell into other's arms. But this time his embrace didn't send me soaring; it yanked me back to the solemn reality of the earth's wretched gravity.

Chapter 16

BIRTH AND DEATH

Although my physical body continued to live, my soul had died in Domenico's arms. But as always, other souls depended on me. I vowed to dedicate myself to my child.

Russo was ecstatic to learn he was going to be a father. Every day a new bouquet of flowers arrived in my bedroom. Candies and exotic foods that I mentioned would appear within the hour. Even Amelia was ordered to treat me like royalty.

Domenico and I still saw each other when I went to church. We exchanged glances, but all they did was acknowledged the future we had lost. Maybe I should have started attending another church, but never seeing Domenico again would have killed me.

My cravings during pregnancy were endless. I had an insatiable appetite for pizza, cannoli, biscotti, mozzarella cheese, and other foods native to Napoli. I wanted eels in capers and butter, fried squid, octopus soup, and anchovies. I ate anchovies every day, followed by cream-filled cannelloni. Russo couldn't sit at the same table with me without turning sickly green. Food had become my drug to numb me.

Still, as my belly grew, so did my excitement about the little person kicking around inside me. As the expected day drew closer, Russo also became more excited. Coinciding with the event, he grew a mustache, which gave him a look of distinction. He told me that he added his furry lip because having a child made him feel like a true grown-up for the first time in his life.

Two years to the day after our wedding, the Virgin Mother blessed me with a lovely girl—Adriana. Just as I had been reluctant to join Russo's world on our wedding day, Adriana also fought to stay out of it. I labored for forty-two hours before she finally emerged breech. Mama had hidden away when giving birth to my younger siblings and never spoken about giving birth. The intense pain of it was a surprise to me. The midwife worried when I bled so profusely and grew weak. She called Russo's doctor, who seemed amazed that I'd lived through the ordeal. Despite the agony I'd suffered, I couldn't stop smiling at Adriana, my little *angelo*.

After such a difficult birth, Adriana turned out to be a perfect baby—gentle and sweet. From the beginning she was the most attentive infant I'd ever seen, and immediately won Russo's heart. To me, she had only one flaw: she had the wrong father.

A week after she was born, Russo announced that he planned to hire an English nanny.

I protested. "After caring for thirteen brothers and sisters, why would I need help from strangers for a single child?"

"Only the best for our daughter," he declared. "My position in the community demands it. She'll have the finest of everything. Only the elite can afford an English nanny."

I came to the conclusion that he wanted the best of everything for our child to compensate for his own deprived upbringing. Despite my objections, a nanny showed up the next day. Russo hadn't even asked my opinion on the applicants.

A few months later, when I leaned down to pick Adriana, she reached for the nanny instead. Within a week, without Russo catching on, I made sure the nanny felt so uncomfortable that she decided to leave. I then convinced Russo not to replace her. I alone wanted to be the influence in Adriana's life.

Russo's attitude toward me also began to change. He lost some of his playfulness in the bedroom. He was still sweet and continued to exercise his marital prerogative, but not as often. Giving birth had changed my body, and his reduced amorous appetite made me feel less attractive.

It seemed I had just given birth to Adriana when I found myself in labor again. Our son, Giorgio Caesar Russo, named after both Russo's father and the great Roman general, was born on All Saints Day ten months after his sister. With only fourteen hours of labor, Giorgio's birth felt like a gentle spring rain compared to Adriana's agonizing delivery. He roared out full of energy, and he was all boy. He flailed about constantly and rarely slept.

Two years later, our second daughter, Lucia, arrived. She was a quiet baby like Adriana, but didn't have her older sister's awareness.

Domenico baptized each of our children, so in this small way he shared some of the most important moments of my life.

As time passed, I lamented losing my figure but worried more over bringing children into a world filled with talk of war, as the Nazis had struck fear in all of Europe. I also feared that we lacked the intimacy a mother and her children should share. I was strict because I wanted my children to excel, but sometimes I wondered if Mama's poor example had affected my ability to be a good mother. Once the children were old enough, Russo hired tutors for them.

I was undergoing an education as well. Now that we were a proper family, Russo began to confide in me more and more, usually at the end of a long tough day when we were nestled in bed. He'd say, "My little pet, you're the only one I can let my guard down with." And then he'd divulge some of the problems he was facing with his lieutenants or tell me how the madams of his whorehouses were trying to cheat him.

While I found most of his business dealings repugnant, I was also fascinated. Gradually, as I began to understand more, I felt free to offer suggestions on how he might handle someone in a situation, or how to better organize himself—always careful to make him think it was his idea. I enjoyed seeing him implement many of my recommendations, and a sense of pride swelled within me over these small accomplishments.

Eventually I felt comfortable enough to joke with Russo by imitating him. "May I suggest you do it this way? You owe me a favor." At first he'd act upset, but then he'd roll with laughter. One time I even put on his hat, coat, and a potato peal across my upper lip as a mustache. "I want to speak to my lieutenants," I said in his voice.

"Take that hat off," he insisted. "I'll never be able to sleep with you again. You look like my reflection."

I began to help him organize his notes. During my brief time as a black widow under the tutoring of the doctor, I had learned to organize and track what people owed Mama. Putting things in order came naturally to me, and I excelled in math, so I set up better bookkeeping records for his various businesses.

Taking Russo's wrinkled notes scribbled on envelopes, scraps of newspaper or wrappers from chocolate candy, I created time schedules for pick up and delivery of shipments, as well as loan payment due-date tables for collections and payments. He supplied me with the financial numbers for each business area: his importing and distribution company, gambling and entertainment clubs, street scam operators, and various other business operations. I kept track of where the money flowed and provided him with information on each individual lieutenant so he could see if their profits had increased or fallen since the previous accounting period.

As his trust in me increased, Russo fed me more information. Eventually, although I never dealt with anyone except my husband, I learned the names and positions of all his employees.

I discovered how Russo used Napoli's *Scugnizzi,* the many homeless boys roaming the streets. He employed them as pickpockets, information collectors, or smugglers. *Scugnizzi* means "spinning top," which signified how these boys twirled around the city looking to beg or steal enough for their next meal. Almost no one gave the Scugnizzi the time of day, but Russo helped many of them get off the street by providing them housing in several old warehouses he had fixed up with beds, showers, and kitchens. He also used them and their vulnerability to make money for himself, but he clearly cared about them, having been one himself after his mother and father died during the Great War.

With my help, Russo's various operations ran more smoothly and his profits shot up. He had never been good with details, and loved being rid of tracking the financial side of things. Although I learned a great deal about the finances, Russo told me little about the actual operations, which suited me fine. I wasn't sure I wanted to know more than I did.

We had attained a fine balance. Now, when Russo talked about the business, I felt I shared a stake in it. And Russo was amazed by how effortlessly I made things run. My feelings for him became like those you feel for a business partner: We worked for our mutual benefit but mostly lived separate lives. He seemed to feel similarly about me.

It wasn't my dream of a life with Domenico and owning a hotel, but at least I held a certain amount of independence and freedom.

Chapter 17

MAMA'S DISGRACE

One day, looking for some papers in Russo's desk, I opened an envelope and found a Saint Christopher medallion tucked inside. The inscription on the back read, "L. Saldino."

When Russo came home that night, I held it up to him. "How did you get this?"

"I think you can guess how," he replied irritably.

The medallion cut into my palm. "Did you kill Luciano Saldino?"

"That bastard was a constant pain in my ass. His operation always bumped into mine. So, yes, I took care of him. As fate would have it, I met Domenico at the Christmas Ball the same day I met his father in Salerno." Russo smiled. "Being there when Domenico found out his father was dead . . . an irony."

"The entire south of Italy, and there wasn't enough room for both of you?"

Russo's face reddened. "Luciano Saldino killed my sister!"

My fingers loosened. "What? You had a sister?"

"When our father died, Saldino recruited Bettina as a prostitute in Salerno. He roughed her up one night during a session. She died at that scum's hands. She hadn't even reached her seventeenth birthday. So don't tell me the bastard didn't deserve to die!"

I looked down at the medallion. There was no mistaking the genuine pain in Russo's voice. Mama had hated Luciano Saldino as well, and even his Domenico had left home to get away from him. Maybe he *had* deserved to die.

Russo and I never spoke of the matter again, and I saw no reason to tell Domenico.

Far bigger problems were overtaking us, and the entire world.

On September 1, 1939, all of Europe fell into a state of shock when the German war machine invaded Poland. But the turmoil barely touched Russo's businesses. Despite Mussolini's connection to Adolph Hitler, Italy was not a participant in what would be known as the *blitzkrieg* sweeping across Europe. We were a refuge, a warm, basking nation to the side of the action and danger.

Russo took advantage, and so did my brothers. Giacomo enjoyed the smuggling business, especially when it involved travel to foreign countries. Antonio excelled at selling fake watches and furs to the declining number of visitors on the streets. My other five brothers now also worked for Russo in one capacity or another, and even Gianina and the rest of my sisters had moved to Napoli. Everyone had left Mama behind.

"I thank you, Carina," Antonio said to me one day.

"For what?"

"Because of you, my life's better than I ever hoped."

"You feel that?"

"Mama raised us to serve her. Thanks to you and the Prince, I make good money . . . enough to get married."

"Married? You're thinking of getting married?"

He blushed. "I haven't asked her yet. I saw her a dozen times in a café before I got the nerve to talk to her."

I laughed. "Does she have a name?"

"Leola," Antonio said, a dreamy look on his face. "She's beautiful, a tiny thing, and so sweet . . . she looks after me."

"I'm happy you're happy."

My brother grinned. I mussed his hair and gave him a big hug. He deserved some happiness.

Every now and then Mama came to Napoli, allegedly to visit her grandchildren, although she never paid them much attention. That was fine with me. I suspected she came mostly because people expected it of her.

She never failed to remind me about "a woman's proper duties." She reeled in horror when she discovered that I continued to read books. "Why would a wife and mother need to read? It's an insult to the husband who provides for her." *An insult to the husband?* I thought. Her ways had only made Papa miserable.

Although Mama never seemed to enjoy herself when she visited, she did take pleasure in Russo treating the entire family to dinner at a nice restaurant. Everywhere he went, people gave Russo the royal treatment, and he made sure Mama received the same. She loved being kowtowed to because of our status.

At the same time, Russo helped Mama manage her lands—something I was sure helped him as much as Mama.

Over the years since Papa's death, Mama had learned that her lands had dwindled to about a third of what they had once been. Papa had gambled much of it away, and Mama's ignorance of business had cost her a great deal of property. Not long after Papa's death, Mussolini passed a law giving itinerant farmers the right to petition for ownership of property after working it for five years, unless the original landowner produced proper proof of possession. Russo helped Mama secure her land rights and even overturn some of the itinerant farmers' claims, with the assistance of some of his government connections. Since then, she'd trusted him completely. She liked having him take charge so that she didn't need to think about any of it.

Of course, Russo had used her influence and lands to expand his operations into the South. He opened brothels and gambling houses on her properties. It was almost funny. If Mama ever learned that she, like Saldino, ruled over whorehouses and wagering establishments, she would die of shame. I never dreamed Russo's whorehouses and gambling games would bring me such pleasure.

When life is good, proceed with caution. Smooth roads turn quickly to rough gravel. This I had learned the hard way, and over the next few years God would teach me the same lesson over and over again. Like nearby Mt. Vesuvius, a violent eruption was bubbling, and it was about to spew chaos through all our lives.

Chapter 18

THE WAR COMES HOME

A dozen of Russo's top lieutenants—now including my brothers Antonio and Giacomo—sat around our dining room table. Russo had brought them all to discuss the changes in business caused by the war raging in Europe, and Amelia and I had prepared a nice meal for the occasion. The men gulped down dinner as though they were starving, and then lit cigars or cigarettes as they drank more wine and started their meeting. I lurked inconspicuously at the edge of the room, not a difficult trick as the smoke thickened. I longed for the sweet aroma of Papa's pipe; the rancid odor of the cigars left me queasy. Still, I remained, and listened.

Gerrani spoke first. "It's finally happened; the war is affecting business. No one's on the streets these days, other than *testa di cazzo* soldiers, police, and militia. My Scugnizzi can't find a *merda pieno* wallet to pick." He pretended to pick Benito's pocket, which brought laughter from the others.

Russo's cousin Gilberto was visibly drunk. "Exaaactly!" he slurred. "I've never seen sooo few people on the streets, with or without shit filled wallets. Not a tourist in sight. Other than soldiers, Napoli is a ghost town."

"Well, don't have your *testa di cazzo* boys come into my section of town!" Gerrani said.

"We wouldn't touch your stink hole territory, but we could do a better damn job with it."

"*Vaffaculo!*" Gerrani gave Gilberto his middle finger. "We've had to run your freeloaders out of there."

Gilberto started to rise to his feet, but knocked over his wine glass.

"May I suggest you two stop squabbling?" Russo said in a quiet but stern voice. He had confided to me that he'd had to bail Gilberto out of several sticky jams over recent years. When his cousin drank, his tongue wagged, and Russo was tired of cleaning up his messes. "May I suggest we're here to improve this situation, not fight amongst ourselves?"

"There are a lot of fucking scared people in Napoli," Benito said. "Food is growing scarce. No one feels safe. Many are leaving for the countryside."

"Some of my street guys enlisted or were swallowed up by the army," said Renzo, another cousin of Russo's. "There's no question Italy will enter the war soon." At close to fifty, Renzo was the oldest member of Russo's family in the organization, but he might also have been the most physically fit, next to Russo.

Russo tapped ash off the tip of his cigar. "Renzo, Benito, you're both right. Everyone who isn't tied to Napoli is leaving. Most of our servants have left. It's time to adapt. We need to shift our business mostly to smuggling—medicine, alcohol, guns, gasoline, and food luxuries like chocolate, sugar, butter, and other rationed or scarce items. Money always flows through the black market during a war." Russo rolled his gold coin over the back of his fingers. "Of course there's always profit in whorehouses, especially with all the soldiers in town. Use your Scugnizzi to drive soldiers to our establishments." He looked up. "Let's not fight against the trend; let's go with it."

"Take advantage when we can," Benito added. "The way the German's *blitzkrieg* overran Poland and France, this war will end in less than a year. It's as good as bread."

"Probably a few months, Drain," Gerrani countered, using the nickname Benito had earned from his drinking prowess.

"After that," Russo said, "business will be bigger and better than ever! Lots of profits after a war."

"As good as bread," Alonzo piped in, smiling dimly.

Russo patted him on the shoulder. "Yes, brother."

Carlo rushed in and turned on the radio in the dining room. "Listen! Italy's at war."

"... and all military personnel have been ordered to report to their command. As everyone knows, Germany continues to occupy France. It's been more than a month since the German war machine overran ... Wait, I have word that Il Duce is about to address the nation from Rome."

There was a moment of anxious silence as we waited to hear what would happen next. Finally, Mussolini spoke. "On land, sea, and in the air, black shirts of the revolution and of the legion, men and women of Italy, of the empire, listen! An hour signed by destiny is ticking on the skies of our country—an hour of irrevocable decisions. A declaration of war has been given to the ambassadors of France and England. Our conscience is absolutely tranquil. The entire world is witness to the fact that fascist Italy has done everything possible to avoid the sting that is now beleaguering the world. All within the State, nothing outside the State, nothing against the State. Believe! Obey! Fight!" The sound of cheering crowds rose wildly in the background.

The announcer returned. "Again, Il Duce has declared Italy at war with France and England this historic day, the tenth of June, 1940."

"There's still resentment from the Great War," Renzo said.

"*Leccacazzi!*" Russo spat. "France and Britain promised Italy lands from German territory for our help and then ignored their agreement after the war. We lost half a million men—including my father—helping to save France's ass, and they gave it to us!" Russo thrust his torso in a vulgar way.

"*Meretrici* won't ignore us this time," Gerrani said. Many of the men laughed and nodded in agreement.

"Damn right. We'll show 'em," Alonzo said.

"With Italy allied with Germany, the war will be over before San Gennaro's verdict in August!" Benito shouted. Everyone laughed.

I prayed to the Virgin Mother the war would end even sooner than that.

The military soon drafted into service more of the younger men from Russo's organization, including my brothers Sergio and Bruno. Even Giacomo, who had served several years earlier in Ethiopia and was now registered in the reserves, was called to return to duty. Only Antonio was spared, thanks to his asthma.

Still, the announcement of war prompted Antonio and his girl-friend, Leola, to elope. "When a little happiness comes your way, accept it and be grateful," he told me after the wedding.

Not long after declaring war, Italian forces attacked British positions in Northern Africa in the hope of taking over Egypt. Amazingly, in October 1940, only a few months after entering the war, Mussolini demobilized 600,000 of the nations 1.2 million soldiers stationed in Italy so they could tend to the crops of a starving Italy. Two weeks later, Mussolini attacked Greece through Albania—not the best plan to undertake when you've just cut your reserve soldiers by one half. Within a month the Italian army experienced defeat in the Balkans at the hands of the third-rate power of Greece. Worse still, strained by its invasion of Greece, Italian forces lost most of their control of Northern Africa to the British. It seemed unthinkable, but it looked to me as though God had abandoned Italy, the country that housed His own emissary, the Pope. I started to lose faith that His hand didn't reach as far as the mortal plane. Perhaps only after death did He protect and receive His children.

One thing was clear: the war would not be wrapped up in a few quick months.

Il Duce quickly recalled the discharged troops back to service, but the Army's recent defeats had permanently wounded the hearts of Italian soldiers. Many of those called back into service had experienced enough of the war in Africa, or the horrors and humiliation received in Greece. Most failed to report to duty, and many active-duty soldiers deserted.

My brother Giacomo returned from Africa a decorated, injured, broken ex-soldier. Russo placed him back into the smuggling business. According to Giacomo, after being in battle, outrunning navy patrol ships on foggy nights felt safe.

Sergio, my sister Gianina's twin, deserved less than a hero's welcome when he returned home. After watching his commanding officer force his battalion into a Greek ambush and then desert his dying men, Sergio decided he'd had enough of the army and returned home without mentioning his departure to his commanding officer. At my suggestion, we told everyone he had been discharged because of injuries to his shoulder. A jagged scar made the statement credible, even though he'd worn that wound since falling from a tree while playing pirate with Giacomo when he was nine.

Sergio joined Russo's troops rounding up customers for the brothel near the train station. I didn't like how he constantly mouthed off, calling every woman a slut or bitch. "You're just another whore who sucks the life out of her husband and takes his money," Sergio slurred to me at a party Russo hosted for his men. I made sure that no one who heard his comment repeated it to my husband; Russo would have punished my brother severely.

Not surprisingly, German soldiers were soon stationed throughout Italy. The German Luftwaffe arrived first, flying bombing missions out of Southern Italy and Sicily on British troops in Northern Africa, assaulting enemy ships in the Mediterranean, and protecting military supply ships bound for the African coast. Just a few months earlier, in February, the first convoy of the newly formed German Afrikakorps, under the command of Generaloberst Rommel, left Napoli for Tripoli on Libya's coast. German units began showing up all around Italy, but being a strategic harbor, Napoli saw the most activity. The Nazi Gestapo started working with the local police.

From the moment the Germans arrived, Russo saw them as an enemy, not an ally, of Italy. Still, business went on, and as my husband had predicted, the smuggling operation quickly became the focal point. Medicine, gasoline, alcohol, and food items like cheese and beef brought tremendous prices. Much of the medicine and food came into Italy from France and Turkey on a fishing boat Russo had stolen. Driving trucks from neutral Switzerland through the dangerous mountain passages of the Italian Alps provided another source of banned goods.

But the most desired smuggled commodities were human beings. A long list of people wanted out of Italy: Serbs and Gypsies escaping persecution in Yugoslavia; communists hunted by the fascists; people on Mussolini's or Hitler's enemy list; people just looking to escape the devastation of the war; and of course, Jews. Sadly, most refugees didn't have the means to pay for the service.

By this time most Italians would have gladly left their homeland as well. Food, money, and jobs were more scarce than a kind word from Mama. Fear became the only commodity available in abundance. Russo seemed immune to it, but I devoured enough for both of us. At church I would genuflect lower than usual during the Holy Communion to receive as much grace from God as possible.

One night Carlo and I took the children for a walk. The city was under a blackout, so the moonlight provided the only light. We wandered through an area of cramped six story apartments. With practically every step, a new cooking aroma or sewer stench assaulted my nostrils.

"A single block of these dwellings probably holds more people than the entire population of Reggio Calabria," I said as we exited into a major street.

"That was the Vicaria district," Carlo explained. "Three thousand people per acre. It's said to be the most densely populated spot on earth."

I jumped at the screech of air-raid sirens. Even though I'd heard these warning wails dozens of times before, they always made me flinch. Their horrid moan accomplished its purpose: to fill you with panic.

But I quickly shrugged it off. For months, the government radio station had warned us of an oncoming aerial attack by the British. Each time we would rush to the nearest shelter or, if we were home, to the caves under our house. And each time the alert proved to be just a drill.

This particular night, Carlo and I dutifully herded the children toward the bomb shelter under the Cathedral of Napoli. Russo was away on business in Salerno. He planned to come back the next day, All Souls Day, to visit his parents' graves, which I had already dressed in preparation for the holiday.

People were walking toward the air raid shelter at a modest pace, as usual. But I noticed there seemed to be a lot of activity down at the harbor. And then an announcement blared over the civil defense loudspeakers. "*Attenzione! Attenzione!* This is NOT a drill! This is NOT a drill! This is NOT a drill!"

Even though the air was warm, an icy chill ripped up my spine. People began running for the shelter.

"It's fine, my dears." I moved a comforting hand over the back of each of my children. "We're just going to our little hide-out, like we practiced." I lifted Lucia out of the stroller and left it by the side of the road. Carlo scooped up Adriana and Giorgio . . . and we began to run.

"What's wrong, Mommy?" Adriana asked over Carlo's thick shoulder.

"Don't worry, my little *angeli*. Everything's going to be all right." But my gaze rose to the black sky.

Chapter 19

NIGHT TERRORS

Carlo and I dashed down the street with the children in our arms. For the first time, the drone of planes approached in the darkness, filling the night with their menacing vibration. Were they ours or *theirs*? I winced as the sky lit up with anti-aircraft cannons from battleships in the harbor. Spurts of shells shot up into the sky and hundreds of blasts exploded like fireworks above us, revealing the shadows of planes moving through the clouds.

Earsplitting whistles rained from the sky. Bursts of light exploded in the harbor, followed by delayed thundering booms, as bombs ripped into the skins of the ships and tore into the buildings along the docks. The cacophony of sirens, planes, and explosions rose to a deafening level. A nauseating fear filled me. How could I protect my little ones from this? While my two little girls screamed at the terrifying sounds, Giorgio's eyes opened wide in awe.

Although we had already been running as fast as I thought possible, our pace now doubled. A hundred yards ahead of us, a woman with two children at her side rushed toward the steps of the shelter under the cathedral. The howling whistle of a bomb grew, and the street erupted, catapulting the woman and her children into the air to the height of the rooftops. Limbs flew in every direction as their bodies broke apart. A gruesome rain fell down on us.

Carlo and I reeled back from the blast, and then raced toward the cathedral. In all the confusion and smoke, finding the entrance would have been almost impossible if it weren't for the many drills we had undergone.

Finally we were hurrying down the long stairway beneath the church, following a string of small light bulbs hanging from the ceiling. We descended forty meters into the underground world that Russo had introduced me to years before. The miles and miles of caverns, catacombs, and Roman aqueducts hidden below the city now provided safe shelter from more modern horrors.

The war had finally arrived in our front yard. People poured by the hundreds into the shelter. Priests directed them to seating or to the first-aid station. People huddled together in groups; many wept, some knelt in prayer. Every one of them wore terror on his or her face.

Carlo and I moved deep into the shelter before finding an empty bench. My heart leaped as I spotted Domenico, his priestly robes stained with dust and blood, attending to a little boy with a cut on his forehead. Domenico brushed back the boy's hair and spoke encouraging words. The boy gave him a hint of a smile.

Although we were deep below the street, the shelter still thundered from the bombing; clouds of dust drifted down from the ceiling like fog rolling in from the harbor. The face of each successive straggler who filtered down into the shelter revealed greater horror than the previous one. The smell of fear permeated the cavern, punctuated by sobbing and an occasional outburst of reverberating grief.

Adriana and Lucia kept quiet, except for an occasional choking sob. I stroked their hair and did my best to comfort them. Giorgio seemed more curious about the underground cavern than afraid of the bombing. Carlo appeared to be completely unaffected by the turmoil. After about ten minutes, my heartbeat returned to a semi-normal pace, which made me realize how fast it had been pumping before.

Just then, two men broke the somber tone of the shelter. "No Jews allowed in here!" shouted the large hairy one, gesturing at a couple snuggled with their young boy. The father, mother, and son were all dressed in tattered clothing, their faces gaunt from hunger. They posed no threat to anyone.

"Yeah, this shelter is for Italians only!" his smaller friend spoke up.

"Please. We just want to be left alone," the Jewish man said.

The big man grabbed him by the arm. "Well, get your filthy ass outside and we'll happily leave you alone."

I didn't take time to think. I rushed over and put myself in between the men and the Jewish family. "Let them be."

The man hesitated, apparently shocked that anyone—especially a woman—would intervene. "What business is it of yours, Jew lover?"

"They have as much right as any of us to be here."

"No, they don't. They're Jews," the smaller man spat.

"They're not causing you any problems, so take a seat somewhere else."

"They have no rights, and they're leaving now," the hairy man said, as he yanked at the Jewish man's coat collar.

By now, Domenico had walked up to the group. "All people are God's children, my son," he said evenly.

"Not everyone." The smaller man took the Jewish woman by the arm and forced her off the bench.

"Brother, don't do that." Domenico pulled him by the shoulder to move him away from the couple. I looked around, expecting some of the other priests to come over and help, but they were pointedly looking away.

The big man drew a fist back to take a swing at Domenico. From out of nowhere, Carlo clutched the fist and yanked it down behind his back, dropping him howling to the floor. The man looked surprised to find himself on the ground and in pain, as Carlo effortlessly twisted his arm in an awkward position.

The other man came at Carlo and instantly found himself on the ground beside his friend.

"Go find a place to sit and shut up," Carlo ordered.

The big man tried to take a swing at Carlo with his free arm, but Carlo diverted the punch and pushed the man's face into the floor.

"I said, take a seat."

The men pulled themselves from the floor. The hairy man gave us an obscene gesture with his fingers under his chin, mumbled something under his breath, and then they both disappeared into the crowd.

The Jewish man smiled gratefully at the three of us. "Thank you." He paused, as if searching for something more meaningful to say, then repeated, "Thank you." His wife's arms were still clamped tightly around their son. She seemed terrified of everyone around her.

"We're sorry that happened," Domenico said. "Of course you're welcome here. I'll bring you some water and bread. Is there anything else I can get for you?"

"No. We're fine. Thank you."

"Let me know if I can help," Domenico said, and then turned to me as we moved away. "How can people be so cruel? I hate what's happening to the Jews, especially the stories I hear from Germany."

I shook my head. "I don't know what's wrong with people."

"Hello, Carlo." Domenico offered his hand, and the two men shook.

"Good to see you again, Father," Carlo replied. "Well, I'll go watch after the kids."

"Thank you, Carlo," I said. "I'll be right there."

"Is everyone in your family safe?" Domenico asked as Carlo took his place next to the children.

"The kids are all right, at least no physical injuries, thank God. I haven't talked to my brothers and sisters." I caught myself not mentioning Russo, who was in Salerno, but I did wonder if he was all right.

"Well, you'll all be in my prayers."

I pulled him into a dark alcove where no one could see us. Right now I needed his comforting touch more than I could bear. I kissed him. To my surprise, he returned it. My mind went blank and my body grew warm.

"I think about you all the time, Domenico."

"Carina . . ." His voice filled with desire. But then he stopped himself, and his body visibly slumped. "What's done is done."

"I just wish I'd made different choices."

"Looking back, choices are easy. The trick to life is making the most of our choices." He paused. "You have three lovely children."

"Yes. I'd do anything for them."

"I worry about all the children of Napoli. I'm doing what little I can to help."

"I'm frantic about my children's safety. I don't know what I'm going to do. Do you think more bombings will come?"

"Most certainly," he said, looking soberly above us. "Well, you better get back to your family."

"Yes." I searched his intense eyes to see if he still loved me. Noticing my intense gaze, he gave me a soft, knowing smile which gave me my answer. I gathered myself, still intoxicated from being in his arms.

"I need to tend to Napoli's troubled spirits," he said as he surveyed those in his care. "If you need anything, I'll be here." After giving me one last faint smile, he returned to comforting the city's frightened souls.

After a sigh, I returned to my own flock and asked, "Is everyone all right?" The kids nodded half-heartedly. I sat down and embraced them. "Everything's going to be fine, my little *angeli*. God will watch after us," I told them as I gazed at Domenico's retreating back.

The thunder of bombs grew less loud, and an uneasy hush fell over the shelter. I leaned back and tried to relax. Bombs continued bursting above us, but I made an effort to feel safe within the womb of the city. I called upon Mary and asked the Virgin Mother to provide protection for my brothers and sisters, and for Russo.

The assault seemed to go on for hours, but in actual time it lasted less than half an hour. After the bombs stopped, a long uneasy silence lingered before the all-clear finally sounded.

Carlo and I carried the children out of the shelter. Heavy smoke assaulted our eyes from the fires burning all around us, and the smell of charred human flesh made me want to vomit.

The smoke played hide and seek with the destruction. Beautiful buildings that had stood proudly for hundreds of years now sagged sadly with gaping wounds ripped into their carapace. Military ships burned wildly in the harbor.

A solider lay dead in the street before us, his limbs twisted in impossible directions. Wounded people wandered aimlessly, searching for help or a comforting hand or a quiet place to die. A woman sat in the middle of the street holding her dead daughter, rocking her lifeless body in a reflexive attempt to comfort her.

I held my children close, but felt powerless to protect them in this new world of chaos.

Chapter 20

THE GESTAPO

Russo returned unharmed from Salerno the next day, despite the lack of available transportation after the bombings. He couldn't stop hugging the children and making sure everything in our home was still in place. He kept repeating, "My precious ones. I'll keep you safe." The more he said it the less convincing he sounded.

Amelia, our last remaining servant, had packed her bags. The second Russo returned and she was certain he was all right, she left for her sister's home in the country.

Russo began shoring up our house against future air attacks. He, Carlo, Mario and my brothers Giacomo and Antonio filled sandbags and stacked them against the walls.

One of my youngest brothers, Bruno, had recently returned from the war and become Russo's newest bodyguard. I now had more family members working in the organization than Russo did.

Bruno and Mario, Russo's mute guard, concentrated on filling the sandbags as Carlo, Giacomo and Russo packed them around the house to gird it against damage. Bruno worked as hard as anyone, but he loved to kid around. Every so often he would hand Mario a nearly empty bag, pretending it was heavy, or crack a joke. He kept everyone laughing.

In just a few hours the five men had managed to stack bags six layers high around the outside walls of the house. From down the street, it looked as if they had built pontoons around the structure and planned to cast off into the harbor.

Forenzo, the Scugnizzo who worked for Russo's brother Alonzo, came running toward us, out of breath. "Prince! Prince! I heard German soldiers talking . . . They're on their way here, to your house . . . with an Italian police captain. Looking for stolen medical supplies."

"Thanks for the warning, Forenzo." Russo handed him some cash. "You better take off." The boy nodded and ran down the street.

"What do you want us to do?" Bruno asked. "A little dance?" He performed a goofy tap step that made me giggle.

"Don't worry, just keep working," Russo said, and continued to place sandbags against the house. "We have nothing to hide . . . at least today. Jean Pierre thinks he can get his hands on a large shipment of morphine and penicillin in Marseilles sometime next month, though."

Since Italy had entered the war, Russo had taken extra care not to keep any incriminating items at the house. He knew that his activities would be under more scrutiny in a military State than in a civilian one.

Little Forenzo was right. A few minutes later, five Nazi soldiers marched up the hill to our house, along with a German SS officer and Russo's associate, Italian police captain Fortuna.

"Hello, Signora and Signore Russo," said Captain Fortuna.

I nodded to him. "Hello, Captain Fortuna."

"I'd shake your hand, Captain, but my hands are dirty," Russo said, showing him his soiled hands, and then went back to stacking sandbags.

"Sorry to trouble you," Fortuna said, "but Sturmbannfuehrer Major Kappel of the Gestapo would like a word with you."

"Oh? What about?" Russo asked.

Kappel stepped forward. He was a gaunt man with sunken cheeks and muddy blue eyes that cast a shadow of suspicion in whatever direction he cast them. "Usually a German officer would request a citizen to come to his office, Signore Russo; but I prefer to see where my constituents reside, especially the ones with such . . . colorful backgrounds as yours." He concentrated on a file in his hand. "I'm sure you wouldn't mind if we searched your house for a stolen shipment of German medical supplies meant for the Luftwaffe?"

"Not at all," Russo said.

"Hijacking morphine, sulfur, penicillin, and other supplies from the war effort is punishable by death to those involved. The injured soldiers of the Third Reich don't enjoy having their morphine taken away." The German officer held up a document. "I have the proper papers."

"Oh, I'm sure of that, Major Kappel," Russo said glibly. "I'm afraid the house isn't as neat as usual. All of our servants left us to go to their family homes in the country because of the war."

"Yes, this war can be an inconvenience," the major agreed. "It would be so much easier if countries simply acquiesced to German authority."

Russo stopped piling bags and walked toward the front door. "I haven't the slightest notion why you would want to search for the medical supplies in my home, but you're most welcome to do so," he said, as he opened the door. "May I offer you and your men some refreshments?"

"Thank you, no." Major Kappel motioned for his men to begin their search. They brushed past Russo and disappeared into the house like roaches scattering in Mama's barn.

"I have some excellent Napoleon brandy," Russo said.

"Well, perhaps one drink."

Russo turned to me. "Would you bring us a tray of glasses with the Cognac?"

"Certainly." I ducked into the house. His soldiers were already scouring the rooms I had worked so hard to decorate. I worried what they might find, but more than that felt violated by their intrusion. I grabbed the tray with the decanter of brandy and glasses, then hurried back outside and placed the tray on the garden table.

"Yes," Major Kappel was saying, "it's regrettable that Italy's military hasn't faired too well in Northern Africa and Greece. Now Germany must defend its ally, even on Italy's own soil."

"Yes, very regrettable. So, could you tell me again why have you come to my house?"

"We're just doing a cursory search."

"I'm sorry to disappoint you," Russo said, as he poured brandy for Major Kappel and Captain Fortuna. "I don't think I'd even know what morphine looks like. Dear, would you like a drink?"

"Thank you," I said, and he poured me one as well.

Russo handed everyone a glass then held his high. "Let us toast to the victory in Europe of two great allies, Italy and Germany."

"*Chin-chin,*" said Captain Fortuna.

"Yes, to good health." I clinked my glass with his.

"*Zum Sieg*—to victory!" Major Kappel said. Everyone drank. Kappel raised his eyebrows. "Ah, a very fine vintage."

"You know good Cognac, Major Kappel," Russo said. "Perhaps there are other things you would enjoy that I could offer you."

"Let me be clear, Signore Russo. Certain activities will be tolerated under German 'assistance' in Italy, but others will not. I have zero tolerance for anything that impedes the war effort, which includes obstructing or diverting any military shipments. Of course, certain recreational activities with the opposite sex that you control in Napoli will be allowed."

"I'm just a retiree. The war makes it impossible to earn a living." Russo's affable demeanor visibly cooled. "But if you're threatening me, I suggest you back off, Major, as I have powerful friends who—"

Major Kappel's thin lips flexed. "Signore Russo, no one has friends more powerful than the Gestapo."

At that moment, to my relief, the soldiers returned. "We found nothing, Major."

The major acknowledged him with a nod, his opaque blue gaze never leaving my husband's. "Please take my words to heart, Signore Russo. I would hate for anything to happen to you or your family. *Auf Wiedersehen,* or should I say '*Ciao*? Your language offers such a wonderful way of saying a less permanent farewell . . . and I am sure we will meet again."

A visit from the Gestapo was worrisome, but it was the air attack that gave Russo and me sleepless nights worrying about the safety of the children. For the first time in eight years of marriage, I saw fear on Russo's face.

Worse, I hated seeing how the war affected my *angeli*. Adriana hid herself in books, her face always buried in one, and she often erupted in tears without apparent reason. Giorgio turned aggressive, constantly hitting his sisters. He also started stealing. Lucia, now three, became so withdrawn that she almost never spoke. Most of all, it ripped my heart to see the fear on my children's faces. I hadn't always been the most affectionate mother, but now I smothered my *angeli* with hugs and kisses.

It seemed essential to get them out of the city, far from the threatening storm clouds of British planes. Germany, Italy and the Allies had agreed to declare Rome, the Eternal City, an open city free from wartime aggression. Russo and I considered having me take the children to my Uncle Salvatore's hotel in the countryside just outside Rome. I attempted to call my uncle, but the telephone lines were down and I couldn't even reach him by cable. Then Russo concluded that the longer the war dragged on, the more likely Rome—especially with the Nazis building up troops there—would become a target of the Allies regardless of any agreements, so I stopped trying to reach my uncle.

After much discussion, Russo and I decided to hide the children in a convent tucked high away in the Apennines Mountains, about thirty kilometers inland from Mount Vesuvius.

The Convent of the Sacred Wheel enjoyed a reputation second to none. I paid a large donation to the convent, more than Mother Superior Rosetta requested. I wanted to make sure she provided the best care possible for my children.

It took Carlo nearly an hour to drive up the curvy mountain road before we stopped in front of the remote sanctuary. A high wall surrounded the fortress, but the view off the mountain spanned the stunning valley below.

"Look, children, you can see the whole world," I reassured my little ones, now six, five, and three. The air smelled so invigorating up here, like the scented breezes in Mama's orange groves. It made me realize how polluted Napoli had become from the bombing, fires, and decay.

"Do I have to stay here?" Adriana begged. "Why can't I stay with you and Father?"

"You'll have fun playing with other children for a few months, until we can find something even better. It'll be a nice vacation."

"Will they have lots of toys?" Giorgio asked.

"Oh, there will be many toys." I bent down and straightened their clothing.

"Will we ever see you again?" Adriana's question shattered my heart and Russo's.

"Of course you'll see us," Russo said, and hugged her. A tear escaped his eye, which he tried to hide. "We'll bring you back home when it's safe. What makes you say such a thing?"

"People don't come back from the war, Daddy. My friend Antonia's father never came back, and neither did Aunt Gianina's husband."

It was true. Gianina's husband died in Northern Africa and many other people we had known hadn't returned from the war. My attempt to keep the children sheltered from its awful truths clearly hadn't succeeded.

"Papa and I will come to see you, and we'll be back together very soon. We're not going to get hurt because we're not going to fight in the war, and we have many friends in Napoli to protect us." I tried to sound convincing.

"My little *angeli*." I hugged each one of them. I squeezed Lucia so tightly that she let out a yelp.

We walked the children to the gate, where a nun took them inside. Russo put his arm around me as we turned away from the convent. Looking out over the panorama, he asked in a soft voice, "Did I tell you my father died in the Great War?"

"No, you never said."

"After enduring forty hours of artillery fire, he vaulted onto the battlefield." Russo's eyes welled but he didn't allow the tears to escape. "The Germans gunned him down. A few months later my mother died giving birth to my brother Alonzo. At fourteen, I was left alone to support and care for myself, Benito, and Alonzo." His hands contorted into fists. "This war will not take my family from me."

I put my arm around him. He was a strong man. From an early age, he had been forced to summon a man's strength. But how much power did one man's determination hold against a war between the most powerful nations on earth? What had been the fate of God's only Son, even with the powers divinely bestowed upon him?

BLACK MARKET AND BLACKEST NIGHT

The skies remained clear of British Halifax bombers for several weeks, until we began to think the bombing had been an isolated occurrence. But then the planes of death returned . . . again and again. The city sustained deep wounds and its people cried, "Why us?" Rubble replaced factories, government buildings, hotels, and houses along Napoli's streets.

With war now entrenched in the city, prices skyrocketed. A single egg cost most workers an entire hour's worth of labor. The price of a pair of shoes equaled a month's wages.

Russo's prediction came entirely true. Smuggling and the distribution of medicine, guns, ammunition, gasoline, and food replaced pickpocketing, selling fake furs and watches, and other street scams. The prostitution business remained a major profit center; Napoli suffered no shortage of soldiers, both Italian and German, who wanted a diversion from the stress of war.

Each day the war continued, more homes were boarded up and abandoned. People fled Napoli carrying whatever possessions they could fit into wooden carts, wheelbarrows, or on their backs. They hoped to find more livable conditions back in some remote village that they had felt lucky to have escaped from years before.

One day Russo, Carlo, and I went for a walk. Russo had decided to visit Gerrani, one of his top producers, whose auto repair garage was nearby. He wanted to check on a shipment of alcohol that Gerrani was scheduled to pick up. When we arrived, mounds of furniture, kitchen supplies and other household items filled the garage. Gerrani was distributing the items to his men for resale on the streets.

"Nice haul, huh?" he said proudly when he noticed us.

"Where the fuck did you get it all?" Russo asked.

"I have my Scugnizzi watch for people abandoning their houses. Then I go in and clean out what they couldn't carry out of town." He grinned. "Pretty slick."

The grin vanished as Russo swung an open hand hard into the back of Gerrani's head. "What the fuck's wrong with you? That's someone's home. That's sacred. *Merda!* What are you thinking?" Clearly, in my husband's mind, it was fair to steal a man's wallet, help him gamble away his savings in a crooked card game, or scam him out of his money, but entering the sanctity of his home was immoral.

"I'm giving you your cut!" Gerrani cried, rubbing his head.

"Well, your home remodeling operation is over. I don't want to ever hear about one of our guys ransacking a home. What are we—heartless animals?"

"Prince, the pickings are lean these days. This is an easy score for some quick cash. This could make us all some dough."

Russo lowered his voice. "It's over."

Gerrani was sharp enough to recognize when Russo had ended a discussion. "Understood."

Not long after that incident, Benito learned through one of his Scugnizzo that city officials were secretly collecting the city's public treasures, along with valuables from various churches, in order to hide them away from the threat of air attacks and Nazi plundering. He also learned that the famous sculptures, Renaissance paintings, and priceless Roman artifacts had found protection in the ancient underground, near the Villa Comunale fountain.

"Let's grab it all, brother," Benito said excitedly to Russo. "City Hall thinks it's a big secret where they're hiding this stuff, but we know. They're offering it to us. Only a few guards are stationed underground, and they don't know the passages like we do."

"No," Russo said.

"No? Just *no?*" Benito shouted. "This is the setup of a lifetime!"

Russo backhanded him. "I don't want to hear that kind of talk again. This is our city. Respect it." Amazingly, it seemed the war had brought out Russo's patriotism.

"*Cacare!* I can't believe you're going to pass this up."

Russo moved closer to him, until their noses were almost touching. "You're going to pass it up, too, Benito. You put this thought out of your mind, you understand?"

Benito looked away in defeat. "All right. Throw this away. What the *cazzo* do I care?"

"I guess you haven't heard . . . the Pollini brothers just had four of their men shot down trying to grab the same treasure. Is that the way you want to end up?"

Benito looked stunned.

The matter was never brought up again.

In March of '41, the government slashed civilian rations in half in order to send food to Nazi Germany as payment for bailing the Italian military out of its various debacles in Northern Africa and Greece. Ironically, Mussolini's government cut these rations the week before the traditional Feast of St. Joseph, the patron saint of all *frittaruoli*—pastry cooks. This year, no one decorated their houses with paintings of food, or hung large frying pans or loaves of bread on their doors. The customary shouting of bakers in front of their shops was absent. For hundreds of years, bakers had distributed their day's profits to the poor on the Feast of St. Joseph, but this year they had nothing to give.

Not just rationed food items, but all food supplies continued to dry up. Food replaced money as the currency of choice. A loaf of bread bought a nice statue of the Virgin Mary or a night with a beautiful woman. In fact, an increasing number of amateur prostitutes sprang up in Napoli, women from poor and wealthy families alike who now valued a full stomach more than their reputations. They competed with Russo's whorehouses, but there never seemed to be a shortage of customers.

Life in Napoli was difficult for everyone, but the Jews suffered most. Since the late 1930s, the government had systematically been removing them from society. Just before the war started, new laws came into effect nearly every month that controlled their lives. The government banned them from teaching, banned them from marrying gentiles, banned them from attending public schools, banned them from being listed in the phonebook, banned them from receiving an obituary in the newspaper, banned them from employing servants, and banned them from serving in the armed forces.

Forty thousand Italian Jews were legislated into the status of ghosts, and vanished. When Hitler began to have a greater influence on Mussolini, Il Duce ordered the Italian Jews to be removed to internment camps.

Russo contended that the anti-Semitic beliefs of both countries really boiled down to money. Governments simply confiscated wealth and property of an entire segment of society and silenced the dissenters.

Despite these dangers, thousands of Jews sought refuge from even greater German persecution in Italy. Because Italy was a German ally, crossing over the Italian border from Germany proved easier than anywhere else for a Jew. And most Italians didn't accept the government's anti-Jewish policies. In fact, I knew of many Italian families that were helping the Jews.

Allied bombs didn't discriminate based on your religious beliefs. As a strategic port and the only Italian city that could be reached by British bombers stationed in Africa, Napoli withstood more attacks than any other Italian city. Clouds of British planes hovered overhead like locusts and devoured it 200 times. British bombers distorted every aspect of life for the people who remained, Gentile and Jew alike . . . but no one experienced a conversion greater than mine.

Russo and I took a walk, with Carlo alongside us, and found ourselves on Veomero Hill. The vista offered a panoramic view across the gardens of the Villa Floridiana down onto the great sprawling city with Vesuvius looming over her. I looked out and realized how much I loved Napoli's bright colors, fast pace, and rich heritage. It saddened me to see the many scars inflicted on her beautiful physique by the war.

Russo and I talked about the children and considered how to bring us all together again without risking their safety. As we walked back down the hill into the city, the enticing aromas of the fabulous Neapolitan chefs preparing their evening meals met us. Even with food in short supply, people still found a way to prepare what little they had exquisitely.

When we returned from our walk I finished preparing my *pepperoni imbottiti,* peppers stuffed with breadcrumbs, olives, capers, and pepperoni. With Russo's connections, we enjoyed many food delicacies few others experienced.

After the meal, Carlo retired to his room and Russo enjoyed a cup of coffee over his newspaper. I sat down with a cup of tea and a book. It was nearly dusk when we decided to go to bed.

Without the usual warning sirens, the crackle of anti-aircraft fire filled the night. I looked out the kitchen window to see trails of anti-aircraft gunfire blazing in the dark sky. "Where are the sirens?"

"They must've been destroyed in the last attack," Russo said.

The whistle of falling bombs began—a hauntingly familiar sound. From the harbor, explosions of light and sound approached like a colossal wave crashing up the hill.

Russo grabbed me. "To the underground!"

Even as we turned, the house rose up from its foundation. The roof tore open and the sound of splintering wood ripped through the room. The blast deafened me and knocked me back twenty feet. As I hit the floor, debris covered me. A thick cloud of dust filled the house.

Gagging, I collected my wits and, without moving, took inventory of my limbs. I was bleeding a little and my head ached, but nothing seemed to be missing. The smoke and dust gradually cleared enough that I could see a gaping hole in the wall and roof. Through it, anti-aircraft fire and bomb explosions lit the night sky. The silhouettes of falling bombs looked like enormous raindrops.

I struggled to push the wreckage off of me. "Russo!" I cried.

No response.

As quickly as it had started, the hellish rain cleared from the sky. The underlying sounds of the aftermath came through the holes in our home: people screaming, fires snapping, dogs barking, a baby crying. The explosions of gas lines sounded like firecrackers compared to the roar of the bombs. A momentary gush of silence swelled and a nearby phonograph could be heard playing Puccini's *Turandot.* The orchestra tiptoed into a beautiful passage, and the tenor began to sing *Nessun dorma*. I heard Russo laugh.

"Russo! Russo!" I called. He kept laughing. Waves of dizziness washed through my head. I tried to sit up, but fell back onto the rubble and drifted into unconsciousness.

Chapter 22

"DEATH" OF A PRINCE

The first hazy stream of sunlight absorbed the night's blackness beyond the hole in the roof. A bird chirped happily. In a daze, I worked to orient myself, and then struggled to my feet. Dust and debris cascaded off me. The full impact of my pain struck me like several cars hitting me from all directions; but, other than a few scrapes, I didn't seem to have any real injuries.

"Russo!" I called. No reply.

Entire sections of the ceiling and dining room wall were missing, but somehow the remainder of the house appeared to have avoided serious damage. A glint of light on the floor caught my eye: the gold coin Russo always ran over the back of his hand. The blast had scuffed it up.

"Russo!" I cried again, and began searching for him amongst the debris in the dining room. Through the hole leading into the kitchen, I noticed a slight movement in the shadows. Working my way over, I peered inside the room and saw my husband sprawled out with his body propped against the wall, his eyes wide open.

"Are you all right?" I said. He didn't answer. I clambered awkwardly over the debris. "Russo? Are you all right?"

He giggled.

"Are you injured?" I touched his arm. He didn't respond. His eyes pointed at me, but did not appear to see me. "Russo, talk to me." He said nothing. I examined him, looking for injuries, but found none. "Vincenzo, please! Please, don't do this."

Nothing. Frantic, I waded through the debris looking for Carlo, and found him lying in the hallway just outside the dining room. I shook him. "Carlo!"

In a single lunge he jumped to his feet, then grabbed his head and moaned, slumping against the wall.

"Careful, Carlo. Slowly. Are you all right?"

"I'm fine. Is the Prince injured?"

"I'm . . . not sure."

We both made our way to Russo, but he didn't respond to Carlo's voice or touch any more than he had to mine.

I wet a towel with the cold beige water trickling out of the kitchen faucet and tried to clean both men up. "Do you think my children are all right, Carlo?"

"I'm sure they're fine."

"I wish they were safe with me."

He grunted. "They're safer at the convent."

When Mario arrived for his morning duties and saw the damage, he burst through the front door without knocking, and then let out a sigh of relief when he saw us. He pointed to the hole in the wall and shook his head in disbelief.

I gave him a reassuring pat on the shoulder. "I think we're all right, Mario."

"I'll go get the doctor now that Mario's here," Carlo said.

"Are you sure you're well enough to go?"

Carlo nodded and hurried off.

Russo, still staring blankly ahead, began to mumble. "Give police million . . . Need cover . . . Fuck Gerrani . . ."

Mario stood over his boss, visibly distressed that there was nothing he could do. I was fond of Mario, especially after Carlo had explained how he'd become mute. A bookie to whom Mario owed money had sent his debt collector to cut out Mario's tongue. Carlo knew Mario and had mentioned his plight to Russo, who not only gave Mario a job, but took over the bookie's territory. Mario worshipped the ground Russo walked on.

I gave him a reassuring smile. "Mario, it's all right. There's nothing either of us can do for him until the doctor gets here. Don't worry. I'm sure he'll be fine." I tried to sound calm but I was shaking with fear on the inside, like I had with my siblings after one of Mama's explosions.

Mario let out a loud, pitiful sound and put his arm around me.

I surveyed the damage while I waited for Carlo and the doctor. Only the dining room and kitchen appeared affected. The rest of the house seemed to be intact.

More than an hour passed before Carlo returned with the doctor, who had only been able to stay in business through the war because Russo had supplied him medicine from the black market. "My apologies, Signore Russo," he said as he made his way through the debris. "I'm sorry it took me so long to get here. I've been working on the wounded all over the . . ." His voice faded as he noticed that Russo was unresponsive. He turned to me. "How long has he been like this?"

"Since the bomb hit our house, I guess."

He shone a light into Russo's eyes, inspected his head and the inside of his mouth. He carefully moved each of Russo's limbs. When he tapped his knee, Russo's leg jumped. The doctor asked him questions, but Russo ignored him.

The doctor shook his head. "He seems to be fine, physically. He appears to be suffering from extreme shock. It's quite common with these attacks."

"What can be done?"

"Nothing, I'm afraid."

"How long will it last?"

"I can't say, Signora Russo."

"I need to know, Doctor."

"It's just impossible to say. It could be a hours, days, the rest of his life . . . I can't tell you."

A wave of dread filled me. I thought about Russo's colleagues, the way they'd react. "You mustn't tell anyone of his condition, Doctor! No one!" I was surprised by my own tone of voice, which mimicked the one Russo used to intimidate people.

The doctor looked both startled and nervous. "No, Signora Russo, I would never tell a soul." He finished putting away his medical instruments. "I'll come by tomorrow and check up on Signore Russo." He left quickly.

Carlo, Mario, and I puzzled over how to reach my husband, but there seemed to be no way in. His eyes weren't the eyes of the Russo we knew. To our surprise, he stood up—but then he walked to the corner of the room, unfastened his pants, and urinated against the wall. The three of us stared at one another.

That night, Carlo helped me get Russo ready for bed. Even though Russo's stature was undersized, he had always filled up a room when he entered. Now he simply looked frail.

When I lay down beside him, I found myself staring at the ceiling, expecting a bomb to fall through it.

"Please don't leave me, Russo," I whispered. "Not now. Not like this." He gave no response.

After catching a few minutes of sleep just before dawn, I awoke to find Russo washing his hands over and over again in the toilet bowl. I pulled him away and helped him wash them in the sink and dry them.

"Come along. I'll make you something to eat." I led him out of the room and down the hall to the kitchen. I sat him at the table, boiled some water and stirred oatmeal into it. I liked mine with butter and brown sugar, but such ingredients were a fantasy these days, and had been for more than a year. I had managed to acquire some roasted chestnuts, though, so I cut a few up and added them to the oatmeal.

Russo didn't say a word but surprised me by eating without assistance. I finished mine, and then left the room long enough to go to the bathroom. When I returned, Russo had vanished. I noticed that the side door was ajar.

As I ran outside I heard several women sniggering in the street, and one of them shouting, "Oh, my God!" When I reached the pavement, I saw Russo walking down the street, away from the house—naked, except for his socks. Carlo came out the front door and hurried after him. He threw his coat around Russo and brought him back.

Once inside, Carlo shook his head. "This is a very bad situation, Carina. It pains me to see him this way."

"I don't know what to do. But one thing's certain. We can't let anyone know what's happened to him. His enemies, and even his allies, would attack him like lions on an injured gazelle. I will not allow that."

I grabbed Carlo's arm. "Carlo, promise me you'll help me keep him safe."

Carlo nodded. "Of course, Signora Russo."

I awoke the next morning to find Russo's side of the bed empty. And he wasn't in the bathroom. "Dear God, help me," I prayed.

After a frantic search I found him by the sink near the maids' quarters. He was washing his hands again, as though intent on scrubbing away the sins of a lifetime.

I got him in his robe and led him into the dining room, relieved that at least he hadn't gone out wandering again. Just as I turned to start breakfast, he slipped out of his robe, snatched up his briefcase, and walked out the door. He headed for town—naked.

"Russo!" I ran after him.

He approached a shocked nun. "Captain Fortuna—I must pay him," he spouted to the world in general. "He doesn't respond well without his bribes."

I caught up and led him back to the house. Just as I got him inside there was a knock at the front door. I hurried to open it, whispering, "Lord, I hope You have a sense of humor about Your naked children."

Domenico stood there in his black robes. "Hello, Carina. I just wanted to make sure your family was all right; I heard your house was damaged in the last bombing."

"We're all fine," I said. "We sent the children to the Convent of the Sacred Wheel several weeks ago."

"That was wise."

There was an awkward pause. I wanted to confess the real situation to Domenico and let him take charge, but I'd learned that life seldom allows you to do what you want. "I'd ask you in, but now isn't really a good time. I hope you understand."

"Of course. I was just concerned. I'm glad everyone escaped unharmed." He turned to leave.

"Thanks so much for coming by, Domenico. It means a lot to me. Really."

When I returned to the dining room, I found Russo lying on the floor, gazing up at the hole in the ceiling.

I stared down at him, trying to think not like a wife but like my husband's advisor. I had heard whispers of what happened to associates in an organization like Russo's when they became a threat to the business's security. If word of Russo's diminished capacity leaked out, or it became known that he was babbling secrets, he wouldn't survive the day. Neither would I, the children, nor any other member of my family involved in the organization . . . which was almost all of us. Like an entrenched government during a coup, we would simply disappear.

For a moment I considered running away with Russo and the children to Uncle Salvatore's Hotel, but quickly dismissed the notion. The only people more ruthless than Russo's enemies were his friends. For as long as we lived, we would never be safe.

So I made the first of many difficult decisions to come.

The next day Carlo and I led Russo down the stairs into the darkness of the basement, where we had fixed up a bed, an eating area, and a makeshift toilet made from a chair with a large waste bin underneath. It wasn't much, but Russo didn't seem to notice. He sat down and stared into space as Carlo screwed a latch into the outside of the door at the bottom of the stairs.

I approached Russo, who was quietly singing a song to himself.

"Counting candy, on the sea shore.
Walking happy with dear Mother.
Miss my dearly like no other. Dear Mother."

It was gibberish, but clearly even a powerful man like Russo needed his mother. I whispered into his ear, "Husband, you've been good to me in many ways. In your own way, you watched over me and protected me. Now it's my turn to watch over you. I learned much from you, and I will not allow anyone to hurt you or our family. So until you wake up, you're going to stay down here in hiding. *Te amoro.* I love you." I looked for some response but saw none. "This is for your safety as much as ours. Do you understand?"

He just kept singing. I walked over to Carlo, who was waiting by the door.

"It's the right thing to do, Carina," he said. "I'll feed and care for him; you shouldn't have to worry about that."

"You're very good to me, Carlo. . . . And to him."

Softly, we closed the door on Russo. Carlo clicked the padlock onto the new latch we'd secured, then pulled a stiletto out of his pocket and handed it to me. "I think you should carry this now."

After only a moment's hesitation, I took the knife.

Chapter 23

TRANSFORMATION

Russo's delusional existence in the basement was gruesome, yet it seemed ideal next to the horrors of the world I faced above ground. How long could I keep Russo's organization afloat before the wolves started sniffing blood? The war had inflicted damage on everyone's earning power, which created a climate of dissatisfaction among the men, leading them to resent coughing up a cut to Russo. How long before people started questioning Russo's absence? I had to find some way to arrange a proper succession of power. But to whom? The options were not good. Alonzo didn't have the brains to take over the Prince's affairs, and Benito didn't have the sobriety. Russo's cousin Renzo was smart enough, but didn't have Russo's diplomacy; his impatience and temper always got him into trouble. Only Russo had held the mastery to keep everyone contented, or at least contented enough.

Nightmares visited what little sleep I could steal, with dreams of my brothers being hunted down one by one and their necks sliced open. Every night brought a different group of killers: men in Russo's organization; thugs from other organizations; the police he had bribed regularly; Major Kappel of the Gestapo. Every night a different set of faces produced the same result—my family lying slaughtered in the gutter.

Dark images filled my daytime thoughts as well. I imagined masked men invading our home, finding Russo running around naked shouting out the secrets of the Neapolitan criminal underworld. The masked men string us up in the basement and cut us open.

While pacing the house searching for answers, I passed by the mirror in the hall. I took two more steps, then stopped and walked back. Stood facing myself in the glass. Russo's hat and coat hung on the stand behind me—but in the mirror, the hat seemed to rest on my head.

I stood there a long time, staring.

For the week following the bombing of our house, I had been worried about this night. Everyone in the organization had been counting on the shipment of morphine and penicillin coming from Switzerland. I knew that Jean Pierre would deal only with Russo; he had met with my husband and Carlo a handful of times. The war had made everyone even more tense and suspicious, and anyone other than Russo himself would be unacceptable.

But of course allowing Russo to meet with Jean Pierre could be catastrophic. My husband might walk into the room naked and try to waltz with the man. But we needed this shipment, and Russo only needed to say a few words to get it.

On the night of the meeting, I could imagine exactly what Jean Pierre was thinking. The Napoli Harbor Hotel lobby looked seedy, with its wan lighting made even dimmer by windows painted over to comply with the blackout conditions. It was the perfect location to make a shadowy deal.

But when Jean Pierre walked in, the first thing he saw was a dozen or so guests mingling about in the lobby, amongst them a German Lieutenant and his assistant. This was bad news, but Jean Pierre was too experienced to show alarm. He strolled in and mingled with the other guests, and seemed not to notice the large man sitting on a couch across the room beside a much slimmer man slumped in a wheelchair.

A painfully thin man of about sixty years with rather nondescript features, Jean Pierre used his stature, looks, and advancing age to his advantage as a smuggler. He appeared completely non-threatening, almost fragile. Consequently, other than a casual glance at his beautifully forged papers, authorities rarely questioned or searched him.

The two Germans were no different. Without a second look in his direction, they went upstairs.

After a minute Jean Pierre strolled to the couch and sat, casually placing the blue case he carried under the nearby table near an identical case. Without looking around, he tried to get a look at the man in the wheelchair, but the shadows made it difficult. "I was sorry to hear you were injured, Russo," he said.

"I'll be fine." The familiar voice came from beneath the hat, accompanied by an equally familiar—and very Italian—flip of the hand. "Any problems?"

"None."

"I want to place an order. We need automatic rifles."

"Doesn't everyone? Very difficult."

"May I suggest you find a way? A lot of profit in it for both of us."

"I'll see what I can do. Now I think I'd better go."

"A safe journey to you."

Jean Pierre reached over and grasped the handle of the second blue case. He knew what it contained: several pointed bars of pure gold painted to look like ordinary railroad spikes. Collecting scrap metal was not a punishable offense to the Germans; gold was a different matter.

Russo was a clever bastard; Jean Pierre was glad the Italian wasn't badly hurt. "Be well," he said as he rose with the bag in his hand.

Once Jean Pierre had left the hotel, Carlo leaned over and picked up Jean Pierre's case. At a sedate pace he pushed the wheelchair outside, down the street, and around the corner. There he opened the bag, pulled out some books, and removed the false bottom. He turned it to display a bag full of medicine vials.

He smiled. "You did it."

"We did it, Carlo," I said in my husband's voice—the same voice I had used with Jean Pierre. The same voice, the same gestures, the same clothing. Who knew Vincenzo Russo's mannerisms better than I? I had imitated his voice and behaviors for years as a joke. But during the preceding week, with Carlo's assistance, I had practiced them intently and seriously. So what had the smuggler Jean Pierre seen in that gloomy hotel lobby today? Exactly the man he had expected to see—Vincenzo Russo.

A smile of satisfaction crept onto my face. For a moment I had become one of the most powerful people in Naples.

But what next?

Chapter 24

THE NEW BOSS

Seven men waited impatiently around the dining room table. On one side: Alonzo, Renzo, and Gilberto; on the other, my brothers: Antonio, Giacomo, Sergio, and Luigi, who now held positions of power in the organization. My brother Bruno, who had just started with the organization, joined Carlo at the door as a guard.

I feared we might need guards.

"Where's Benito?" bellowed Gilberto, Russo's cousin on his father's side.

Carlo shrugged. "I told the Drain personally about the meeting. He should be here soon."

I knew why Benito was late, since I was the one who had arranged a distraction for him to make sure he wouldn't be in top form by the time he arrived.

"Well," Gilberto said, standing in front of his chair, "what's this all about?"

"Please, sit down, Gilberto," I suggested with a smile. "We need to wait for Benito." Gilberto gave me a glare, uncomfortable having a woman telling him what to do, but then seated himself.

Finally Russo's brother entered the room, his gait unsteady. "Hey," he moaned in acknowledgment to the group. He kissed my cheek. "Little sister-in-law, I didn't know you'd be here. Get me some coffee, would you?"

I pulled back from the stench of stale alcohol that saturated his skin. Lipstick covered his cheek and shirt collar. The prostitute I'd arranged to sleep with him had obviously done her job. From past experience, I knew Benito wasn't as prone to eruptions of temper when he was exhausted, hung over, and up early in the morning.

Carlo moved toward Benito. "Why the hell are you late? It's disrespectful. Sit down."

Benito plopped into the open chair and let out a moan as he held his head.

"Rough night, Benito?" asked Renzo the Menace, another of Russo's cousins.

Benito raised an eyebrow, nodded slightly, and closed his eyes.

Carlo quieted the men in the room and started the meeting. "You're here to make some decisions about the future. First, Carina will give us an update on the Prince's condition."

"I thought the boss called this meeting. Where is he?" Renzo said. The world of the Camorra allowed only men. Women were banned, but I had to do what had to be done.

"Yeah. If the Prince didn't call this meeting, who did?" Gilberto stood up to emphasize his annoyance.

"That's why we're here," Carlo told him. "Please . . . sit down, Gilberto."

"Hey, I don't take no *merda*. I give *merda!* Russo should be at this meeting."

"He's not well enough," I said, striving to keep my voice calm. Gilberto was a rude *cafone,* and several times over the years Russo had apologized to me for his cousin's actions. If he hadn't been a relative, I think Russo would have gotten rid of him years ago.

Gilberto pounded the table with his fist. "I'm not doing anything behind my cousin's back. If he's not here, I'm leaving!"

When I nodded to Carlo to open the door for him, he looked flustered and sat back down. "Well, maybe I'll stay. Keep an eye on what goes on here for the boss."

Deliberately, I looked each man in the eye before saying, "First of all, no one is to say a word about what's discussed here today. If anyone repeats anything, he won't breathe another breath." The men looked at one another, eyebrows raised in surprise. "Do I have your oath?" I asked. "What's going on?" Benito said.

"Do I have your oath?"

They all nodded. Some looked bewildered, others almost amused, as if I were a talking dog.

"You're probably wondering why I didn't allow any of you, even Alonzo and Benito, to spend time with my husband since his injury," I said. "You all know that the bomb that hit our house last week injured my husband. What you don't know is that his mind sustained more damage than his body. I hoped he would come out of it, but he continues to grow worse. The doctor remains uncertain what to expect."

Murmuring swept through the room.

"Silenzio!" Carlo snapped.

I motioned around the table. "You may notice that several captains and other key individuals are missing today. That's because only family can know what I'm about to tell you. If people from the outside learn these things, we will face great danger."

"What's wrong with the Prince?" Benito asked.

"He doesn't recognize anyone, not even me. He talks gibberish. He's not the Russo you know."

The men appeared visibly shaken.

"No, not my brother," Benito groaned.

"Unfortunately, this circumstance allows us no time to mourn for him. We must make difficult decisions today about how to continue."

"Che cavolo?" Renzo said. "The Pollini brothers will come after us for sure without the Prince in control. They're already pushing into our turf by the docks."

"What about Gerrani?" Benito asked. "He's our own guy, and you know that *testa di cazzo* will try to grab the power with my brother out of action."

Giacomo nodded. "Russo was the only one able to keep him in line."

"And there are others," Renzo said. He was Russo's top earner, which probably gave him a bigger voice than anyone at the table, other than Benito. "Holy Mother of God, the organization will splinter into a dozen groups fighting amongst themselves. They'll all want control of their own territory. *Cazzo!* It will be chaos."

"No money when the streets are filled with blood!" Antonio added.

"I think we all agree that my husband has been the only one able to keep the peace. That's why people accepted him as the boss."

"*Merda!* What about the shipment of morphine and penicillin?" Renzo asked. "We've been counting on that for weeks."

"I've got Partisan freedom fighters waiting desperately for that medicine," Giacomo said.

"Don't worry," I said. "The shipment is in. I knew our contact would meet only with Russo and that we needed that shipment, so I met with him. I dressed as Russo in a wheelchair with Carlo pushing—"

"You what?!" Gilberto shot to his feet again. "Were you shot in the head and no one noticed? You endangered us all by—"

My brother Sergio also jumped to his feet, looming over me. "What the hell were you thinking, stupid bitch? You could've gotten us all killed!" He took a swing at me, but I had been expecting it. I kicked the back of his knee as hard as I could and shoved him on the shoulder, toppling my six-foot brother to the floor. Before he could get up Carlo was standing between us, gaze level.

Everyone in the room gasped. I looked down at Sergio. "I may be your sister, but I'm Russo's wife first."

Everyone else burst into laughter. Sergio's face turned purple.

"Where'd you learn that move, Sis?" Giacomo asked.

"I'm married to the Prince of Napoli. I've picked up a few things."

"Now let her finish," Carlo said as he guided Sergio back into his seat.

After revealing the bag full of medicine vials, which jingled like chimes, I spoke in my Russo voice. "Jean Pierre saw only Vincenzo Russo. Russo's hat, Russo's overcoat, and Russo's bag of gold. He heard only Russo's voice. As far as he's concerned, he dealt with Vincenzo Russo."

They all looked startled. "That sounded just like the Prince," Renzo murmured.

"The first order of business is that there will be no shorting on Russo's cut by anyone." I pointed to my accounting books. "I know everyone's share, and everyone's going to stay in line or there's going to be hell to pay. Now, we must decide how to continue. Where do we go from here?"

"One of us must be in charge," Benito said, gesturing around the table. "I'm Vincenzo's oldest brother. I guess I should run things."

"You run things, Drain?" Renzo laughed. "Run them into the ground, you mean. At a vital moment, you'll take off on one of your drunken binges with some slut, and we won't hear from you for a week."

"Thanks for your vote of confidence, Renzo. I feel so much love."

"What about you, cousin Renzo?" Alonzo said. "You could be boss."

Gilberto bristled. "What does he know about anything except selling dirty postcards to tourists? Can you see him dealing with the police, politicians, and government agents that keep us in the know and out of jail?"

Renzo muscled his shoulder into Gilberto's chest. "Normally I'd bust you in the jaw for talking to me that way, but you're right." He backed away. "I wouldn't know the first thing about how to deal with those fuckin' government types."

"I need a drink," Gilberto said as he grabbed a bottle and glass from the nearby serving cart.

As I had predicted, no one in Russo's clan was capable of diplomacy. They didn't trust each others' abilities enough to agree on a successor from their side of the table.

Under the table, I nudged Antonio's foot. He looked at me and nodded. "Maybe," he said in a clear voice, "we should just keep Vincenzo Russo running things."

"What the fuck are you talking about?" Benito cried.

"Keep Carina as the Prince," Antonio said, as I had earlier instructed him to do. He and Carlo were the only ones I had trusted enough to reveal my intent prior to the summit. And they had agreed with me that there was only one choice to run the organization, and with my plan of how to gain full cooperation.

"Are you crazy?" Benito shouted. "A woman running things?" Then he cradled his hangover-aching head.

"Benito's right," Sergio snarled. "A woman is not capable of running things. What the fuck does any woman know about business?"

Gilberto slapped the table. "It's out of the question. What's all this input from Carina's family, anyway? This should be strictly a Russo family decision."

"Get off it, Gilberto," Renzo said. "We can't pull this off alone."

"*Cavallo merda!*" Gilberto slammed his hand on the table again. "Russo built this business. There's no way we're giving power to the Cunzolos. How can we trust them?"

I strode around the table and stopped right in front of Gilberto. "Trust? You speak of trust? You've held out on the Prince in the past, and he's called you on it. I keep the books, and I know you're *still* holding out—but I didn't say a word. I didn't want to see you dead. So, *trust?* I don't think you're the one to talk."

Gilberto slid back into his chair and took another drink. His eyes would not meet any of the many eyes on him.

"Gilberto, you little *merda,*" Benito said.

Antonio stood up, and for once was not brief in his speech. "Listen to me. Carina knows the politicians and the police who help us, how to reach them, what the Prince pays them. No one else does. She knows who in the organization brings in how much; the entire money side of the operation. She knows all our black market suppliers and how to negotiate with them. Do any of you know these things?" Various men shrugged or shook their heads. "Carina even knows Mussolini. She knows every aspect of the organization, how everything fits together. Who else can say they do?"

No one spoke.

"I'd like to hear what Renzo thinks," Antonio said, as I had instructed. Renzo held a lot of influence in Russo's inner circle. His long tenure and track record as a top earner warranted him respect. If I was going to take power, my biggest obstacle was Benito. To bypass him I needed backing from at least one person within Russo's family. I had the feeling that although Renzo didn't want to become the boss himself, he wouldn't want Benito in power, either. Now was the test.

Renzo shrugged. "Well, she's already convinced Jean Pierre that she's Vincenzo Russo. And I for one was impressed with her imitation of his voice. And like Antonio said, she knows more about Russo and the organization than anyone else." He looked around the table. "And don't forget, we'll all be here to guide her."

"You're crazy," Benito said.

"What's your suggestion, then, Benito?" Renzo said. "Should we just let the shooting begin when everyone learns the Prince of Napoli is just as weak and stupid as a newborn baby?"

"*I* could pretend to be my brother," Benito replied indignantly.

"You're half a head taller than your brother, with half the brains. I'd rather take my chances with Carina."

"I'm going to flatten you, Renzo!" Benito wobbled to his feet but had to steady himself against his chair.

Carlo smoothly stepped between them.

"Stop!" I snapped. "We're here to find a way to survive and prosper, not to fight." I pulled out a piece of paper and put it on the table. "Here's a chart I made of Russo's organization. We need to decide how to handle the lieutenants who aren't here today."

Benito turned his back to me. "This is a Russo family matter, so butt out."

I grabbed him by the arm and spun him around to face me, nose to nose. "Don't you dare disrespect me! I'll put you down if I have to!"

"You? A woman?" He yanked his arm out of my grasp and reached for the chart. "Stay out of our business, bitch."

He froze as the point of my stiletto slammed into the table next to his hand.

"We're in this together!" I shouted. "We're going to do what's best for the entire family, Russo and Cunzolo. Got that?"

He hesitated.

"She's right, Benito," Renzo said. "We've got to work together."

Several seconds passed, then Benito shrugged and fell back into his chair. Everyone else stared at me as if I had just parachuted out of the sky.

"Carina can pull this off," Antonio said.

Renzo turned to Carlo. "Carlo, you're around Carina all the time, and you saw her at the exchange with Jean Pierre. *Can* she pull this off?"

"I think she's the only one capable of it."

"I say we back Carina," Renzo said with authority. Everyone nodded their agreement.

Almost everyone.

"Benito," I said. "You're such an important part of Russo's organization; we can't pull this off without you. It's only temporary. Can we count on you?"

He hesitated, and then laughed. "Parade you around in a wheelchair as the Prince? It's fucking crazy. Maybe that gives it a chance to work, at least until my brother comes to his senses."

I grabbed Giacomo's hat, put it on with the brim down, and then said in my Russo voice, "I can do it."

Most everyone laughed. Gilberto and my brother Sergio still held dour expressions, but the rest of the men seemed at least tolerant of the decision.

Antonio leaned close to me and whispered, "Are you certain this is what you want, Carina? Is this you?"

"It's who I need to be now."

He nodded his understanding.

When no one was looking, I let out an exhausted sigh. My hands were shaking, so I quickly hid them behind my back. It was like the time I had stood up to Mama and taken her whipping stick. I felt both terrified and exhilarated.

No matter what, I wasn't about to leave my fate, and my family's, to someone who wasn't up to the task. Everyone needed saving from the turbulent world we lived in, and I was the only one capable of becoming their savior. Until Russo recovered, I needed to take full power, piece by piece . . . but I knew these men. They believed women belonged in either the kitchen or the bedroom.

But what choice did I have? Between now and the day Russo recovered, I suspected I would be calling quite often for advice on one other woman: Mother Mary.

Chapter 25

ROLLING OUT
THE NEW REGIME

In a matter of weeks, Renzo informed me that Russo's captains and lieutenants were beginning to wonder about the seriousness of Russo's condition. Some were even speculating that he was dead. According to a man Renzo sent out to take the pulse of people in the organization, meetings were taking place and alliances forming all over town in anticipation of the fall of Russo.

Everyone in the inner circle of the family agreed: Russo had to make an appearance to dispel the rumors that he wasn't still in charge. That very evening I used make-up to darken my skin, draped Russo's hat brim over my face, and pulled on his overcoat, scarf, and gloves. This time I added a fake mustache as well.

Alonzo and Carlo stood on either side and pushed the wheelchair down the blacked-out street to Caruso's, a restaurant where a lot of our men hung out. The restaurant was dimly lit, as always, but in the gloom I recognized half a dozen of the men employed by Russo, and saw them recognize the figure in the hat and coat in the wheelchair.

The appetizing scents of fresh garlic, basil, and fresh bread distracted me for a moment until the waiter rushed over to me. "Oh, Signore Russo! It's so good to have you back." I nodded to him, and then ordered a glass of Chianti and one of Russo's favorite dishes, *tubettoni al pesce spada,* small pasta tubes mixed with pieces of swordfish.

After several weeks of being out of commission, Russo's appearance set tongues wagging around the room. Some of the lesser men in the organization nodded to me, while others felt comfortable enough to say, "Hello, Prince." I nodded and rolled a gold coin over my gloved fingers, just as Russo always had.

Gerrani, Russo's biggest producer, entered the restaurant with a couple of his men. He looked startled to see Russo. As he approached the table, Carlo stopped him. I nodded to Carlo to let Gerrani approach. He reached the far side of the table before Carlo putting a hand on his shoulder to indicate that he was close enough.

"It's so good to see you out and around, Prince," Gerrani said. "You look . . ." He paused as he studied me. "You look good. I hope you're feeling better."

I nodded and stared at him from under the brim of Russo's hat. "Stronger every day. I'm ready to get back into the action."

"That's good to hear, Prince." I could feel Gerrani sizing up Russo's condition before moving on to his own table.

Russo's cousin Renzo showed up for a brief meeting with "the boss." As a close family member and one of Russo's most important leaders, he had been my choice to give credence to my portrayal of Russo. We looked over papers and whispered so no one could hear us.

My brother Antonio arrived, as planned. Carlo made him wait while I finished my meeting with Renzo. Antonio paid "the boss" the proper respect by standing dutifully near the door, waiting for me to acknowledge his presence.

Finally I grabbed Renzo by the neck and patted him affectionately on the head, the way I'd seen Russo do it in the past. Then we kissed each other on the cheek.

Once Renzo had gone, I made Antonio wait while I enjoyed a few uninterrupted bites of my meal. Eventually I motioned him to the table. We talked softly, but I made it clear with a few raps on the table that I wasn't happy with Antonio. I slapped him briskly across the face and scolded in Russo's voice, "What the hell were you thinking? Just because you're my wife's brother earns you no special treatment. Now go."

Antonio skulked away. The murmuring around the restaurant convinced me that our act to make Russo appear strong was working. People saw what they expected to see: Russo in control. By day's end, everyone in the organization would hear that Russo was still firmly in charge of his organization.

My brothers were waiting for me at home. I stood up from the wheelchair and hurled Russo's hat off my head. "Antonio," I said, "can I pull this charade off?"

He rubbed his cheek where I had slapped him. "Well, you convinced me!"

"It worked beautifully!" Renzo added.

"But how long until someone figures it out?" Sergio asked.

Antonio murmured in my ear as he patted my shoulder, "Carina, you've got the inner strength and smarts to hold this organization together. No one else does."

Even crabby Benito appeared impressed. "Well, it's a fucking miracle . . . but I got nothing against miracles."

I did: you can't depend on miracles. I knew that a single display of Russo in public wasn't going to keep the forces anxious to tear down Russo's organization at bay for long. I needed to find a way to stay ahead of the pack.

My history lessons with the doctor came back to me. On his death bed, Julius Caesar had appointed Augustus, his adopted son, as his successor. But the Roman Senate ignored him; they planned to return Rome to the Republican government that preceded Julius Caesar. Furthermore, the Roman people, who saw Augustus as young and inexperienced, didn't recognize his right to the throne. Mark Antony, who held much of the power of Rome through control of his own large army, allied with Cleopatra and used his and the Egyptian forces to battle Augustus' army.

After Augustus' army finally defeated Mark Antony's rogue forces, Augustus took his place as the first emperor of Rome. He needed more than a decade to claim his station as Rome's leader, but his cunning and diplomacy finally paid off. Once in power, he restored peace to the empire after a hundred years of civil war and brought Rome the greatest economic prosperity it had ever experienced.

Like Augustus, I had to keep the allegiance of our troops until the end of the war. If we could survive until then, even if Russo never recovered and took his seat at the head of the organization's table, I was sure that prosperity would return and the infighting would subside. The future could be bright, if I could hold things together until the war had run its destructive course.

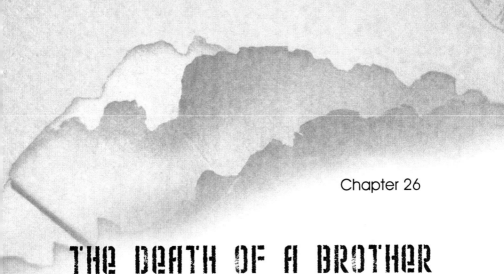

Chapter 26

THE DEATH OF A BROTHER

For a while, at least, our staged Russo appearance brought positive results. The family in our inner circle all reported hearing gossip about Russo retaking control. Several people who had been behind on paying Russo's cut immediately coughed it up.

But two lieutenants remained late in their payments. Russo had placed my brother Bruno in the position of runner—picking up payments, transporting packages—a typical entry-level position. I sent him to deliver a friendly reminder to the lieutenants that they had overdue accounts.

I was eating lunch at home that afternoon with members of the inner family when my brother Giacomo burst into the dining room.

"Carina!"

"What is it?"

"Bruno," he whispered, then turned slowly toward the door.

I rushed to the entrance hall to find Bruno hanging lifelessly in Antonio's arms, his shirt saturated with blood, a pool forming around his feet. Several members of both my family and Russo's surrounded him.

"Bruno's dead, Carina," Sergio said. "They butchered him!"

"No!" I embraced my baby brother as though I could pull life back into his motionless body. "Please, Bruno, breathe. Just breathe! Help him, Virgin Mother."

"It's no use," Benito said, as he entered the house. "He's gone." He pulled me away from my brother. I wanted to sob, but forced myself not to give in to the tears.

"Who did this?" I said.

"One of my guys found him behind Bianchi's Bakery," Benito said. "I think Gerrani did it. Didn't Bruno go to collect from him?"

I nodded as I stared at my brother's lifeless form.

"Gerrani is letting us know he's on his own," Benito said. "We can't hesitate. We must take Gerrani down now!"

"I'll take care of Gerrani," Sergio spoke in a deadly tone.

I shook my head. "No. I must handle this. *I* sent Bruno to collect from Gerrani."

"You, Carina?" Sergio sneered. "This is not knitting. It's no job for a weak woman."

"Gerrani has pushed his weight around too long," Gilberto said. "He's always stepping over the line. I'll enjoy taking him out."

"He killed my brother!" Sergio shouted. "I want to spit in his face as he takes his last breath."

Even sweet Antonio's face was red with rage. "Let me do it!"

"All of you, stop! We're not going to gun people down in the street and call attention to ourselves." I waved my arms. "I don't want war with Gerrani. It would be too costly. He's got a lot of good men under him, and I don't want to lose them. No. I'll take care of this my own way."

"What the hell do you know?" Sergio bellowed. "Women only know how to bitch, not take action!"

Gilberto pulled out his pistol. "We must show our strength!"

I raised myself to my full height. "If we operate like revenge-crazed idiots, the Nazi Gestapo or the Italian militia will put us all into the ground." I stepped toward Gilberto and stood toe to toe with him, the way Russo did. "Do you think Russo operated without thinking? Stop and use your head! We've got to be smart or it's over for every one of us."

His face darkened. "*Merda,* Carina! You want us to act like pussies!"

I very softly. "Go ahead, hit me. I can see you want to. Be a man."

Everyone, including me, held their breath. Gilberto pulled back, but when he saw that I was not going to withdraw, he slumped. "Aw, fuck it. All right, then, Don Carina—what do *you* think we should do?"

I stepped back. "I'm bathed in my brother's blood!" I could feel it drying against my skin through my blouse. "No one wants Gerrani's head more than I, but no one . . . *no one* . . . is going to move against Gerrani! It's my responsibility. It will be taken care of. Does everyone understand this?" I glared at each man until they had all conceded.

As Sergio exited, he bent close and whispered in my ear: "You are stepping beyond your place, Carina." He glared at me as he walked out, and an unnerving feeling filled me. I buried my face in my blood-stained hands. By my actions, I was responsible for killing my own dear brother.

Chapter 27

RETRIBUTION AND SOLIDARITY

With the war still raging and military forces working to keep order throughout the country, I knew that every move we made would be critical. Under all this pressure, power and alliances shifted in a heartbeat. Allegiances changed daily based on who seemed to be the most immediate threat or who offered the greatest gain. One false move and the powers controlling Napoli would grind us into the ground.

By killing Russo's collector, Gerrani had sent a clear message: he no longer considered his organization a part of Russo's. I wondered if he had recognized me in my Russo disguise at Caruso's. . . . Whatever the reason, he had decided this was the time to secede.

I had to do something about it, but I knew an all-out battle in the streets must be avoided. For one thing, Gerrani would be anticipating such an attack. But I mustn't wait too long, either. If Gerrani had killed one of Russo's family, Benito, Alonzo, Gilberto, and Renzo wouldn't have waited ten seconds to gun him down—but they had given me some authority on this matter, as it was my brother being buried. I needed to outmaneuver everyone to resolve this.

I discussed the problem with Antonio.

"Let me pull the trigger on Gerrani," he pleaded.

"No. If something happened, I couldn't live with losing another brother. I'm the one who sent Bruno to his death; it's my responsibility to deal with his murderer. Also, we must be certain that Gerrani is that man."

Antonio put his arm around me. His eyes filled with tears. "Bruno told the worst jokes."

"Like the one about the horse," I sighed. "How long should a horse's legs be? Long enough to reach the ground." We exchanged a melancholy chuckle. "He took great pleasure in placing a smile on everyone's face."

Antonio's lips attempted a smile, but it didn't quite form.

"I'll take care of this, Antonio," I said. "To everyone's satisfaction, except Gerrani's. Trust me. But you must also understand that with so many people depending on me, I have to plan things out and move carefully."

Antonio nodded. He seemed uncertain I could pull it off, but I knew I had to.

It took several days to map out my plan. Meanwhile, a host of other problems threatened to destroy Russo's empire: the Pollini Brothers continued to make inroads into his smuggling action; the Gestapo's fist of power and ever–present, watchful eye severely hampered our operations; and the threat of the German army gunning us down on a whim always seemed a possibility.

In addition to the outside threats, Russo's own pack of wolves, no longer fat and happy, wanted full bellies again. These men weren't used to living lean. The sparse pickings caused by the war made every-one in the organization want a bigger piece of the action. They craved the taste of a fresh, lucrative kill.

This made it all the more essential that I keep Gerrani's organiza-tion within Russo's group. Gerrani and his men had been top produc-ers, mostly working gambling and the black market. A visible battle with him would encourage other factions to fight for independence, creating an all-out civil war.

Every night in my dreams, gunfire rattled and the gutters of Napoli flowed with the blood of my brothers, my children, and me. Tributaries of red converged into a surging river. The scene changed to the horror of the fall slaughter, when Mama's itinerant hired hands cut the necks of my goat and chicken friends. The squeals terrified me and coursed through my bones. The dear animals that had comforted me from Mama's cruelty and shown me love were rewarded by dying in terror.

My dreams moved toward reality when Antonio informed me that Sergio was planning to avenge Bruno's death on his own. I rushed to his house. There was no answer when I rapped on the door. It was unlocked, so I entered.

"Sergio!"

I heard a gun cock. As I turned, Sergio stepped from behind the door and leveled his pistol at me.

"You can't stop me, Carina. I'm not waiting any longer. This must be done."

"Let me handle this, Sergio."

"Gerrani is a mad dog and he must die." Finally he lowered his P-38, picked up a handful of ammo from the coffee table, and continued to feed the weapon more deadly food.

I placed my hand gently on his arm. "You're going to get yourself killed, and your actions may take down the rest of us."

"You don't tell me what I can do." He jerked away from me and stalked towards the door.

"Yes, I do. I am in charge of this family!" I fought the urge to throw him to the ground and beat some sense into him. I was startled to find such violence inside myself.

He halted and spun toward me. "No bitch will ever control me like Mama!"

So that's where his hatred for women came from. "You must do this my way, Sergio."

He stepped forward and pressed his body into mine, driving me back a few steps. "I will avenge Bruno's death! He did not deserve to die!"

"No, he didn't," I said, and Sergio accepted my arm on his shoulder. "But I must do whatever is necessary for the good of Russo's organization, even if that means stopping you. Before we punish Gerrani we must be sure he is guilty. Of what use is it to kill an innocent man?" The image of Bruno hanging lifelessly from Antonio's arms shot into my mind. "But this, I assure both you and God: we will do right by Bruno."

Sergio hesitated, then nodded. "It must be done. It must." He rested his gun on the table.

The next day I telephoned Gerrani at his auto repair garage. It was Sunday, when I knew his men wouldn't be around.

"Yeah."

"Hello, Gino. This is Carina Russo."

There was a long silence. "Yeah, what can I do for you?"

"I wondered if we might get together today for a drink and to discuss a few things."

"Really? Now? Fine. Shall we meet at Caruso's?"

"I was thinking something a little more . . . intimate. Maybe your office?"

There was a pause. "That'll work. Come on by."

"I'll see you in an hour. I look forward to it. Oh, don't mention to anyone that I'm coming. A woman wants her discretion."

"Yeah, sure. Got it. I'll see you here in an hour, *ah bona*, beautiful woman," he added, in a knowing tone.

Several hours later, the loaf of fresh bread I had baked went into a bag along with a bottle of wine. After wiggling into my most form-fitting dress and tallest stilettos, I covered up with an overcoat, as a cool breeze was blowing up from the harbor this September night.

Bag in hand, I set out toward Gerrani's garage in the Piazza Dante. I went alone so he would feel safe and secure, sense no hint of a threat.

A few blocks from my destination, a pair of Gestapo agents stopped me and asked for my papers. My heart lunged against my ribs. The longer the war dragged on, the more security tightened. Every time you left the house it seemed that some military official, policeman, or Gestapo agent checked your papers and questioned you. By now, no one trusted anyone in law enforcement, least of all the Gestapo. Torture, rape, and murder were their tools, and they happily used them all.

"What's in the bag?" one of them asked.

I opened it. "Just some bread and a bottle of wine."

"How did you get those? The black market?"

"No, no. I baked the bread myself, and the wine was in our basement long before the war." The two officers looked unconvinced. I tried to sound pathetic. "Please. I'm taking them to a sick friend."

A moment passed. At the very least, these Nazis would impound my bread and wine, which would end up in their bellies. I didn't want to consider the worst case scenario. Then, surprisingly, the tall one waved me on with a wink. "Go on. Get out of here."

When I arrived at the garage, I was happy to see that none of Gerrani's boys were around. His office was all the way in the back, protected by a steel door. I knocked and Gerrani looked through the peephole. I held my coat draped over my arm, with both of my hands clearly visible. Gerrani might think highly of himself but he was not a fool; he would be suspicious of me and my motives.

He opened the door. "Come on in, baby," he said, as he checked me over to make sure I wasn't carrying a weapon. He searched my coat and looked in the bag, then put them on a chair. "Sorry, Carina. After some of the things that have happened, I'm being extra careful."

"I understand. It's a dangerous world."

"True. Is the bread and wine for us?"

"Yes, for a little later."

"I'm glad you called." He gave me his best seductive look. Six-feet-two and good looking, Gerrani was filled with self-confidence. His office smelled of stale cigars and cheap wine, but being in his presence was what made me ill.

"No one knows I'm here," I said.

"That's good, baby."

"Listen, no one sent me, but I want to play peacemaker for everyone. The Prince doesn't want war with your group. There's no benefit to anyone."

He shook his head. "You see, this is why I can't be a part of the Russo's group any longer. Allowing a woman to negotiate shows how weak he is."

"But I just said he doesn't know I'm here."

"Well, all the more reason a cripple like Russo can't keep an organization together. I'm better off on my own. When I saw him at Caruso's putting on a big show of strength, it revealed his weakness to me. He tried too hard. I'm sure it convinced everybody else, but not me. He's feeling vulnerable in that wheelchair. However, the organization could stay together if someone strong took charge."

"You?"

"Maybe. And what about you? You need a strong man, someone who can protect you. Don't get me wrong . . . Russo was a good leader. But . . ."

"What are you saying?" I knew full well what he was saying.

"Help me take control of the whole organization. I'll make sure you and your children benefit." He moved closer. "We both know why you're really here, Carina. You want another benefit that I can give you." He leered. "Don't you?"

He grabbed me and tried to kiss me. I pushed him away. "*Bastido!* Get your hands off me!"

He laughed and reached for me again. I moved away, putting the desk between us. "*Bella!*" he said. "Beautiful! Haven't you been lonely with your husband crippled?"

"What about the man you killed? What compensation are you offering for him?"

"Who did I kill? I didn't kill anyone."

"The runner who came to collect your dues."

"Russo's courier? Oh, yes, maybe I wanted to make a statement with that one. I don't want war, either, but I do want to run either the entire operation, or at least my own, without interference."

"You don't even know who he was?"

"Who—the runner? Just some new collector of Russo's."

"Here's a hint. His last name was Cunzolo."

He looked puzzled for a moment, and then his eyebrows rose. "One of your brothers?" I reached into the bag and pulled Russo's German Luger from the loaf of bread I had hollowed out.

Gerrani just laughed. "You're not going to use that, Carina. You're a woman. Come on. You're angry, but we can work it out so everyone's happy. You don't want to hurt anyone."

Without warning he grabbed for me across the desk, and I fired the gun into his chest. He looked down at his shirt by his shoulder, as it swiftly turned red. "Wait. You don't want to—"

I fired at his head, hitting him squarely in the temple. He collapsed face-down on the desk with a loud thump.

I watched, mesmerized, as the blotter absorbed his draining blood. Once it was fully saturated, a red stream dripped over the edge of the desk and began to pool on the floor.

Suddenly I felt sick. I wanted to vomit, to purge myself. "What have I done?" My hands trembled. Gerrani's face was distorted; it did not show the peace Papa's had when he died.

Suddenly a heavenly calm filled me. In this state of tranquility, I thought to myself, "I had no free will in this matter. This is not a mortal sin. I've merely followed the four cardinal virtues of prudence, justice, fortitude, and temperance."

Gerrani was an evil man and deserved to die. And I had held the power to kill him. I felt exhilarated. God would see the righteousness and prudence of my actions. I had averted a war and prevented the bloodshed of many. The ruthless justice of my action filled me with power. I had truly transformed myself into Russo.

From my coat pocket I pulled out the German SS pin that I had taken from Russo's gun cabinet. I pricked Gerrani's finger with the point to suggest that he struggled with a Gestapo officer, and dropped the pin on the floor near his desk. Then I pulled the cash out of his pockets and took his watch. After rummaging through the desk, I turned over the filing cabinet and took anything of value, trying to make it look as though a Gestapo agent had ransacked his office. After putting on my coat, I looked around to make sure I had remembered everything.

On the way home I stopped at the cathedral and dropped everything I had taken from Gerrani's office into Domenico's donation box for the war orphans. Then I knelt before the altar and prayed to the Virgin Mother. I felt a smile of joy radiating on my face.

I told my brothers, as well as Benito and Renzo, exactly how I had taken care of Gerrani. "The Nazis never investigate a crime an S.S. officer is suspected of committing. Doing it this way won't create bad blood between us and Gerrani's men. In fact, it will bring them closer to Russo, uniting us against our common enemy—the Nazis."

They seemed impressed. Even Benito tipped his hat and said, "Good thinking."

I was pleased with what I had done, but knew there was more to accomplish. The last thing the organization needed was more defectors like Gerrani. I asked Carlo to set up a meeting at the house with all captains and lieutenants, twenty-eight men altogether.

Dressed as Russo, sitting in the dim candlelight required by the blackout, I told the group, "I may be in this wheelchair, but that won't stop me from getting us through these difficult times. Every one of us has lost someone to the Nazis. Just last week one of our top leaders, Luigi Gerrani, was killed by a Gestapo pig. Those of you from Gerrani's group have lost a strong boss, but we'll do everything possible to help you, and we'll support you in every way." I lifted my glass of wine in a salute. "To Gerrani, a good man."

Gerrani's men raised their glasses. "To Gerrani."

I held out my hands, concealed in leather gloves. "Please, gentlemen, you are now a direct part of my family. Feel at home in my organization."

I had seen Papa hold meetings with important men in the south, and emulated how he had brought them together. I held up my glass of wine. "The war starves us of the days of easy living, but we don't starve for food like the rest of Napoli. I make you this promise. Everyone in our organization will be fed and have money in their pockets, even down to the last Scugnizzo and runner on the street. Better times remain ahead of us, but first we must stay unified to survive this war and the Nazis. It was true in Ancient Rome and it's still true today: united we stand, divided we fall."

"To Russo! He's never let us down!" shouted one of Russo's old-timers.

"To the Prince!" someone else cried.

"To the Prince!" came the chorus.

"To the bar!" I shouted, holding up my glass. Everyone laughed and began to drink. They forgot their troubles and were unified, at least for one night.

Carlo made sure no one got too close to me, and helped me examine the men for any sign of suspicion. Everyone appeared convinced by my ruse.

My first steps as the boss had been satisfying, although it surprised me that none of Russo's clan or my own had given me grief for taking such an important action without their approval. Their acquiescence gave me the confidence to take an even firmer grip over the operation, but I also realized that such quiet often anticipated the coming of a storm.

Chapter 28

ATTACKING A NUN

"Carlo, Mario, you must show me how to kill someone with a knife."

The two men looked at me as if I was crazy. "I must do everything possible to protect this family," I said.

"Don't worry, we can protect you, Carina," Carlo said.

"No, you can't! I must be ready for every situation. I'm not going to let anything happen to my family again. Somehow I'm going to get everyone through this war in one piece, and I'm going to keep this organization together."

So, reluctantly, Carlo and Mario began giving me a crash course on the use of weapons and the art of killing. They demonstrated various ways of using a stiletto, the basics of firing a pistol, and bare-handed fighting.

"Let me show you what to do if you find yourself without a weapon," Carlo said. "The most vulnerable parts of someone's body are the eyes, the throat, and the . . . the . . ." He couldn't bring himself to say it, so he pointed to his crotch. "Also, by grabbing the hair you can force someone's head back, which leaves other areas vulnerable." Carlo grabbed Mario's hair and pulled his head back to demonstrate how his neck, chest, and crotch became vulnerable. He pretended to jab Mario's exposed neck with his free hand.

"Another thing . . . if you're without a knife or a gun, one of your best weapons is your elbow." He demonstrated the movement toward Mario's neck.

Carlo pulled a stiletto out of his shirt sleeve. "These are the two basic knife holds—blade down, blade forward. Blade down is how people hold an ice pick, toward the elbow. This conceals the knife from your attacker." He demonstrated how using this hold hid the knife until you were ready to strike. "Unskilled knife users use this grip and hold their arm over their head to thrust down at their enemy, but this gives warning and is easily avoided or blocked. It's better to wait for your victim to get close, and then thrust the blade up across their arm, stomach area, neck or face.

"If you don't have time to conceal your knife, I think the classic underhand forward grip is best for you." He drew his stiletto from his holster and held it like a steak knife. "This grip is instinctual and works well if you're trying to fend someone off, because it keeps the blade between you and your attacker."

After two full days of studying the art of taking human life, I felt numb but prepared.

The Italian Army suffered further defeats on foreign soil, causing the Germans to deploy still more troops to Italy. Without question, the Gestapo now ran all aspects of law enforcement, and the Italian police officials on our payroll became impotent to help us. Despite this, I kept paying them in order to ensure their loyalty to us after the war.

The Germans installed an 8:00 P.M. to 8:00 A.M. curfew. Our business demanded many after-hour excursions, so I uncovered the one exception to the rule: a merchant permit, which allowed shopkeepers to conduct business at almost any time. After applying for the permit, I opened a food stall at the Piazza Antignano Market. It proved a good place to move some of our black market goods.

Even when I went out as Carina, I carried my Russo costume in a travel bag, just in case. When someone stopped and asked me about its contents, I simply stated that my husband had asked me to bring him his hat and coat.

All kinds of people used our organization to sell the goods they pilfered from the Germans. We moved loot as diverse as public statues, cemetery stones, telephone poles, scrap metal, even a stack of manhole covers.

Medicine remained the most dangerous item to steal. On my way to the marketplace one day, I saw three Gestapo agents search a young woman in the street. The officer of the group found a vial and held it up to the light.

"I had to buy sulfa on the black market for my daughter. She's dying!" the woman pleaded. "What else could I do?"

The officer raised his Luger and shot her in the head. She fell face down on the cobblestone street. The Gestapo agents chatted a bit, lit cigarettes and walked away, leaving the woman crumpled on the street like a discarded bread wrapper. Even so, I barely winced at the spectacle; the commonness of such deaths had made us all immune. We noticed but didn't react, and kept to our own business.

By now, various members of Major Kappel's Gestapo now paid regular visits to the house. Our loyal street Scugnizzo, Forenzo, usually preceded their arrival to warn us, but I made certain we were always clean of anything that could get us into trouble.

"Where do you live, Forenzo?" I asked one day.

"In Napoli, Signora Prince."

"I mean, where do you sleep?"

"I find places—I sleep well."

"Why are you so devoted to my husband?"

"The Prince of Napoli? Because the Prince showed me . . . he showed me how to make good money on the street. No one else gave me the time of day. The Prince . . . he was like me once, on the street. Now he's the Prince! A big man in Napoli. Maybe someday . . . someday I'll be like him."

I handed him a shiny new stiletto and some lira. "You're a good boy and loyal, Forenzo."

He grinned as though he'd just opened a toy on Christmas. "Thanks, Signora Prince. Thanks." After switching open the blade and waving it in the air, he wagged the bills at me with gratitude and hurried off. Seeing Forenzo always pained my heart, as he reminded me of my little ones still hidden away in the convent.

I hadn't seen my children since Russo left us. Taking his place in the business, dealing with one crisis after another, combined with continuous Allied bombings, had made it impossible for me to get out of the city to visit them. I so wanted to hold my little *angeli*.

Nights of lying awake had become standard, and I spent my time in bed worrying or dreaming of the day that Adriana, Giorgio, Lucia, and I would be together again without a care in the world. In my imagination, Salvatore's hotel was our safe oasis. I saw Adriana playing teatime with the children of famous hotel guests while Giorgio kicked a soccer ball in the field behind the hotel with neighborhood boys and little Lucia amused herself with her dolls by the fireplace.

When I could stand it no longer, I told Carlo we were going to visit the children. He merely nodded. Before we left, I checked on Russo and brought him his food.

"Hello, husband," I said. As usual, I received no response. He sat on the couch looking at the ceiling, oblivious to me and the world he'd placed me in.

"I'm going to visit our children, Russo. Do you want me to tell them anything?" He replied with a blank stare. I moved nose to nose with him. "Surely you want me to give them a kind word, or tell them that you love them." Nothing. Infuriated by his eternal vacant expression, I slapped him across the face. "*Bastardo!* How could you leave me to fight your battles? How could you leave your children?" Other than the slightest swivel of his head, he didn't even acknowledge the blow. Frustrated, I reached back to deliver another, but came to my senses and stopped myself, burying my face in my hands instead.

An hour later, Carlo and I left the house and walked to the outskirts of Napoli to an old barn well off the road behind a row of poplars. After the outbreak of the war, Russo had hidden our car here to avoid having it confiscated.

Carlo and I traveled on bombed-out roads with deep craters. Luckily, we didn't cross paths with either marauders or law enforcement—both of which were a threat to take your vehicle or your life.

When we finally reached the sanctuary, the calm silence seemed unsettling after the months of pandemonium we had experienced in Napoli. A gentle breeze rustled the leaves in the sprawling oak tree in front of the convent's tall fence. I walked to the famous sacred wheel. Many a mother had placed a bastard child on its turntable. With a simple half rotation, the child came under the protection of the nuns, who accepted every child offered without question.

I rang the iron bell in front, but no one responded. I rang it again. I rolled the gold coin across my fingers as I waited. A nun peered out of a slit in the gate. Frightened, she refused to let us into the convent grounds.

"Please, Sister, I'm here to see my children," I said. "I'm Signore Russo."

The nun disappeared, then returned with another nun, who recognized me from when I had dropped off the children. The huge gate creaked open, allowing me in.

"He must wait here," the elder nun said, looking at Carlo.

To my shock, the stench of filth saturated the institution. The place had been immaculate when I left the children here, but now the floors were dirty and the rank smell of used diapers assaulted my senses. Hungry babies cried in the nursery and the staff seemed much smaller. "Sister," I said, "do you not have enough food to feed these children?"

"We have what the Lord has provided us," she said serenely.

"Where has your staff gone? Where are all the nuns?"

She shrugged, pointed to Adriana and Lucia's room, then walked away.

The girls were playing on the bed with their tattered dolls. When they saw me they ran to me, yelling, "Mama, Mama!" I squatted and gathered them into my arms. Lucia started crying.

"We don't like it here, Mama," Adriana said. "We want to go home."

"I know, my dear, but it's not safe right now. I know it's difficult, but we must make the best of it. The war will be over soon." I tried to sound confident, but there was doubt in my voice. Adriana joined her sister in tears. "You must be brave, my little *angeli*." I looked closer and realized they were both dirty. "Why are you so filthy?" I asked, shocked.

"When did you last have a bath?"

"Uh, a month ago?" Adriana said.

"What!" I inspected them both and found both flea bites and live fleas all over them. A rustling came from the corner of the room, and I looked over just as a big, sickly-looking rat scampered under the bed. I jumped back in horror.

"He likes our room," Adriana said. "He keeps us company."

"Lead me to Giorgio's room," I instructed Adriana. Carrying Lucia,

I followed Adriana down the hall to an open door. Inside the room sat Giorgio, playing marbles on the floor.

"Giorgio," I said, "we're leaving. Right now."

"Hooray!" He jumped up and ran over to me.

I rushed the children downstairs and out the gate, where Carlo was waiting.

"Take them to the car, Carlo! I'll be right back."

I stormed back into the convent and into the Mother Superior's office.

"Why are my children dirty, skinny, flea-bitten, and fending off rats?" I shouted.

She looked up from her work, startled, and then stood. "We don't have the funds to—"

"I paid you plenty to feed my children and keep them clean—much more than you asked."

"The war makes it impossible. There's no food to buy, no soap to clean with. We try to grow what food we can, but it's difficult. We had to use some of your funds to keep others from starving."

"I'm not paying for everyone. I'm paying for *my* children, whom I brought here for protection."

She raised her chin. "It's my responsibility to see that everyone is fed, not just your brats."

I slapped her face. "How dare you! Do you know who I am?"

"Yes, I know who you are, and who you're married to. You're lucky I accepted the children of a *bidonista* in the first place."

This time I hit her with my closed fist. There was a crack, and blood trickled down from her nose. She doubled over, moaning. Three other nuns came hurrying in to see what was happening.

"Don't ever talk about my children like that again!" I shouted.

The three nuns grabbed me by the arms and yanked me away, but I pulled free and hit the Mother Superior again. This time two of the nuns gripped me by the arms and the third pulled me by the hair. As I started to break free a second time, a man who looked like a custodian threw a blanket over me and quickly tied it around my body.

Chapter 29

THE RETURN OF IL DUCE

It wasn't until I found myself in a Napoli prison later that day that I finally calmed down.

"Are the children all right?" I asked Carlo when he made an appearance late in the day.

"They're fine. Gianina's watching them at home." At that, my neck and shoulders relaxed a bit, but then he went on. "I tried to buy your release, Signora, but . . . Well, if it had been anyone but a Mother Superior . . . You gave her a broken nose and black eye. The Church's influence is stronger than ours, and they want to see you in prison."

"Call the telephone number taped inside the right top drawer on Russo's desk. Tell the man who answers that Carina Russo needs his help, and where I am."

"Should I ask for this man by name?"

"Only one person answers that phone. It's best if you don't know who it is."

Just as I had stood up to Mama all those years ago, I held no regret for what I had done to the Mother Superior. She deserved worse for treating my children so deplorably.

A day passed without word, although Carlo confirmed that he had called the phone number as I had directed. I wondered if my failsafe protection might be fallible after all.

But the next morning, a buzz circulated amongst the guards and I knew I'd be released from jail soon. Around noon a guard came for me. He put me in handcuffs and took me to the warden's office, sat me down in a chair in front of the desk, and left.

The warden looked up from his paperwork. "You have powerful friends, Signora Russo. Your release has been expedited." His tone was conciliatory. "I hope we didn't inconvenience you too much, and that the accommodations weren't too unpleasant."

"What else could you do? I have no complaints."

"I'm glad to hear that," he sighed. Then he noticed my handcuffs. "Oh, goodness. I'm sorry. Let me get those removed." He jumped up, opened the door, and called into the other room, "Get a guard in here immediately to remove these handcuffs!"

A guard instantly responded and unlocked the cuffs. "He's here," he told his boss.

The warden's eyes widened. "Already?"

From another room, I heard a familiar booming voice. "Here's the directive."

The warden ushered me out of his office into the anteroom.

Benito Mussolini stood there in his familiar pose: head cocked, back and chest thrust out. Several prison clerks were rushing to complete documents. One of them asked for his autograph, which Il Duce scribbled out hurriedly.

"Ah, Carina," he said upon seeing me. "You shouldn't go punching nuns."

"Yes, Il Duce. My boxing days are over."

"Good." Mussolini turned to the warden. "We will go now."

"Yes, Il Duce," the warden said. "A pleasure to meet you, Il Duce."

Mussolini nodded, then took me by the arm and escorted me out as two of his personal guards led the way.

"How is Signore Russo?" he asked.

"Fine, fine." Realizing he might want to deliver me home and see Russo, I added, "But he's . . . away at the moment."

"Yes, this war keeps everyone busy. I would've sent someone to help you, but fortune found me already in Napoli, so I decided to come over and help you out of your dilemma myself."

"I'm very grateful, Duce."

He opened the door of his limousine for me and we got in. After a long round of chitchat, which avoided the painful subject of war, we pulled into the impressive courtyard of the Palazzo Ravaschieri di Satrian, a beautiful Spanish mansion built in the 1600s. The four-story palace overlooked the bay with long banks of windows.

"It's almost time for tea," Mussolini said with a hint of a smile. "Come share a drink with your rescuer."

"Thank you."

We entered his large suite in the palace. A lovely fresco of sky and angels adorned the ceiling, which was illuminated by three large, matching crystal chandeliers. A huge tapestry lined the wall opposite the windows. Most of the beautiful Renaissance furniture had been pushed to one side to make room for the desk stacked with papers and maps.

"Please, sit," he said, motioning me to the sofa. "Normally I don't drink, but we must celebrate. Shall I add a little rum to our tea, my dear?"

"Yes, please. May I ask you a question, Il Duce?"

"Of course."

"I've always wondered . . . How do you know my husband?"

Mussolini walked to the bar, where a tea tray had been set out for him. "He did some . . . work for me early in my political career." He poured us each a cup of tea and added a dose of rum, and then handed me the fuller of the two cups. "Let us toast to Italy's victory, to our homeland, to beauty, and to love."

We tapped our cups and drank. "This is delicious." I gulped the remainder.

"Ah, let me get you more, my dear." He retrieved the tray, filled my cup with tea and more rum, and then sat down next to me on the couch. I clinked his cup again and smiled.

"I missed my little ones. It shocked me to find them in such squalid conditions at the convent."

"We'll get you home soon. How many boys, how many girls?"

"Two girls, one feisty boy."

"I'm happy you have children. Italy will always need good soldiers. How old is your son?"

"Giorgio is nine."

"He should join the *Balilla*. He'll learn the benefits of fascism and how to serve his country. It's good discipline."

"He is a bit of a wild one. A little discipline isn't a bad thing."

He leaned into me. "Wild is good, if you properly channel it."

"I'm sure you possess a wild streak of your own, to have accomplished so much for yourself and Italy." We laughed.

"I battle every day to pull Italy into the twentieth century. One needs the ferocity of a lion. I want this epitaph on my tomb: 'Here lies one of the most intelligent animals who ever appeared on the face of the earth.'"

I refilled both our cups with rum, leaving out the tea, and we chatted on. Il Duce began stroking my hair. I was nervous, unsure how to respond.

"You're *multa bella,* Carina," he said, now caressing my cheek. He kissed it, then the base of my neck. He rested his head on my shoulder, and I felt his warm breath against my skin. And then I felt it against my breast.

"Oh, Il Duce. You excite me." And it was true; my body had become eager for him. It had been along time since Russo and I had enjoyed each other, and I wanted to feel a man's strength within me. I ran my hand over Il Duce's balding head. He didn't respond. I looked down. He had passed out. I sighed. There would be no lovemaking with the powerful, virile Mussolini. Oh, how exciting it would have been.

With such thoughts in my head, I decided I needed to go to church and confess. I finished the bottle of rum and headed home.

Chapter 30

RETURN OF THE CHILDREN AND THE BOMBS

My stride became more and more brisk as I walked up the hill to the house. The children and Gianina were playing out front under Carlo's watchful eye. I ran to them, waving.

"Mama! Mama!" Giorgio shouted, as he ran toward me. The girls squealed with delight as we all hugged.

"How I've missed you, my little *angeli*," I cried. I walked to the house with the three of them attached to me, jabbering all at once.

"Oh, Mama, I was so worried about you," Adriana said.

"I was a big boy at the convent. I never got scared," Giorgio informed me.

"Did, too," Adriana contradicted.

Giorgio pushed her. "Did not."

"Mama," Adriana said plaintively. "It scared me seeing those people at the convent take you away."

"I know. I'm sorry I frightened you. I got out of jail today and I don't have to go back. That's in the past."

"You're not in trouble anymore?" Giorgio asked.

"We worked it out."

He looked indignant. "Daddy yells at me for talking at the dinner table, and you don't even get in trouble for beating up the head nun!"

"Mommy, Mommy, Mommy, Mommy," little Lucia kept saying the whole time, tugging on my dress. I patted her on the head and she smiled.

"Where's Daddy?" Adriana asked, voicing the question I'd been dreading.

"Yeah, where is he?" Giorgio said.

"We haven't seen him since we got home," Adriana said, and started to cry. "Aunt Gianina and Carlo won't tell us anything. You won't tell us because he's dead, killed in the war."

"Oh, no, no. He's just . . . away for a while on business," I reassured them. They looked dejected. "Of course he wants to see you, but he can't get away just yet. You'll see him soon. The war keeps everyone very busy. I wanted to visit you a hundred times at the convent, but every time I tried, the war stopped me."

"Are we going to be together now?" Adriana asked.

"Yes, my dear ones. We're staying together." I was uncertain how much truth was in my words. I turned to my sister and kissed her forehead. "Thanks for watching after them, Gianina."

"Sure. It's good to see some young life around here." Gianina still hadn't really returned to the living herself since losing her husband to the war.

"It's a beautiful day. Let's go down to the beach." I wanted to find some way to give them a little fun. It was October, but a spring-like day. Going to the beach seemed a little odd during a war, but safe enough in the daytime. The bombings had slowed and they almost always came during the night, anyway.

"Yes! Yes!" the children cheered, jumping about.

Gianina and I helped the little ones into their bathing suits, and then put coats over them in case it got cold. I grabbed a few towels and a couple of pails for sandcastle construction. We started down the hill toward the shore. Even war couldn't destroy the beauty of the bay, with Vesuvius protectively watching over the child it had created with its ancient lava flow.

The streets were missing the fruit and vegetable vendors that once lined every corner; they seemed barren without the colorful boxes of produce and equally vibrant merchants. Many of the clothing shops, bakeries and restaurants had been boarded up; those that still remained open offered limited selection and hours. Dairy products, beef, and pork had disappeared altogether. Nondescript meats, poultry, and fish had replaced them, and the few available fruits and vegetables always looked droopy.

A smile crept onto my face on seeing that Gallucci's was still open. The fine restaurant had been a fixture in Napoli since 1896. I bought everyone a bag of chestnuts cooked in a sweet Marsala wine that had been condensed into syrup, and we continued down to the shoreline as we ate our delicious treat.

The beach north of the harbor was quiet. We laid out our towels on the sand and stripped down to our bathing suits. Carlo looked out of place in his jacket and heavy shoes. At my insistence he reluctantly removed them and sat on a towel, but he still looked uncomfortable. He opened the book he had brought.

"What are you reading today, Carlo?" Gianina asked.

"*Book of the Kings of Egypt,* by Ernest Budge. A fascinating culture, ancient Egypt."

Gianina smiled but clearly found such intellectual interests boring. Marriage, children, and maintaining a house for the family defined her range of interests. Unfortunately, after the death of her husband my sister lacked all of these responsibilities, leaving her in a permanent state of melancholy.

Giorgio began building a sandcastle with the use of the pail I'd brought. Carlo helped by constructing an impressive pyramid next to it. Giorgio used the two structures to play army, culminating in the blowing up of the pyramid. After his victory he began the reconstruction period by adding two towers to his fortress.

"Someday soon, my little *angeli,* we'll own our own castle like Uncle Salvatore's hotel, Grand Palazzo Augustus."

"Tell us again about Salvatore's wondrous palace, Mama," Adriana begged.

"Well, it's just outside the Eternal City. Rome is so magical that God chose it to house His emissary, the Pope. It was the first city in the world to hold more than a million people. It's built in white marble. Emperors ruled most of the world from Rome for hundreds of years. In the distance, from Salvatore's castle, it sparkles like a jewel." I placed an additional section onto Giorgio's sandcastle, and then molded the sand into hills around it and topped them with seaweed. "Hills of emerald green surround his castle. The famous, the royal, and the wealthy from around the world holiday at the hotel. It's a grand place. Children, I can see you playing in a field of grass behind the hotel. A gentle breeze holds up Giorgio's kite. Lucia picks wild flowers. Adriana dances in the tall grass."

They gazed at me, transfixed. I wanted to give them such a sanctuary today and forever.

"Someday we'll live in such a special place, my little ones."

"I'm ready to go home," Gianina said.

I hugged my sister. "Of course, we'll have room for all our family and friends. You too, Carlo."

He smiled.

Pulling a pouch I always carried with me out of my pocket, I filled it with the fine sand from the beach.

"Why did you put that sand in the little bag, Mama?" Adriana asked.

"It's magic sand. It's like carrying a cloud in your pocket. It's a potion that makes you invisible." I emptied a handful into her pocket. "Now you own a magic cloud, too."

She smiled.

"Me too, me too," Giorgio pleaded.

I picked up a handful of sand and inspected it. "No, this sand isn't magical." I tossed it aside. Carefully, I looked around in the sand, then snatched a batch and scooped it into Giorgio's pocket. I gave a little to Lucia, too. "Now, that's authentic magical sand."

Giorgio peered into his pocket, eyes on fire. Lucia giggled, took a pinch of hers and threw it in the air so that it fell back over her head.

It had been a glorious day, lounging in the afternoon sun on the Italian Riviera as the wealthy of Europe had done since the time of the Roman emperors. But the sun was descending, bringing closer the hour of bombs.

"Gianina's right, it's time for us to get back," Carlo said. We shook the magic sand off our towels and started back.

Dusk had arrived by the time we reached the harbor. We found an open bakery and I bought another treat we could all share on the way home—a loaf of olive bread fresh from the oven.

The grating sound of air raid sirens destroyed our peaceful journey.

Once again, the British and Americans were on their way to pay us a visit.

We ran a few short blocks to the Duomo and hurried down the long staircase into shelter before the bomber planes dropped their deadly cargo. As we entered, I looked about for Domenico. I didn't see him, and hadn't for weeks.

We found an unoccupied spot and sat down. The raid seemed to frighten Gianina more than the children. She shook visibly, so I hugged her and stroked her hair. "It'll be all right. We're safe here."

I looked around the cavern. With the continuous bombings, people had gradually turned into expressionless shells. Joy, or even a simple smile, had become a rare sight.

Some sat on a suitcase or wooden crate, as if they planned to go on a trip, but these people weren't traveling. These people had lost their homes, and now their luggage served as their only furniture. For some families living underground, weeks passed without seeing sunlight. Some clever people, after losing their homes above ground, had built underground homes complete with DC battery power, showers and kitchen facilities.

Suddenly, Domenico was standing before me. Heavy circles hung under his eyes and an uncharacteristic glum, weary, dispirited expression had overtaken him. His left hand was lost under his priestly robes. Although it saddened me to see him so overtaken with dread, I warmed myself with the energy we shared.

"It's always good to see you, Domenico."

"Hello, Carina," he said, as he summoned a smile. "Hello, children. I've got a little secret for you. I know where some candy can be found."

Their eyes sparkled with anticipation. Domenico showed one empty hand, then the other, and then both. He turned his hands over and back again, and several wrapped pieces of colorful candy appeared, which he placed in their hands. More than the magic trick, it seemed a miracle to see something made of sugar.

A priest bandaging an injured woman called to Domenico, and he waved his acknowledgment before turning to me. "I must get back to my duties. Be well."

"God's speed," I said.

Over the months, each bombing attack seemed to last longer

than the one before. Tonight's attack rattled our shelter for so long I became convinced it would never end. But at long last the bombing gradually diminished like an opera fading to its conclusion, until an uneasy silence settled in. Gianina, the children, and many others in our cavernous crib fell into a fitful sleep.

I lay awake, my thoughts drifting to Russo, safely hidden in his basement cocoon. "Carlo," I whispered, "how did you come to work for my husband? You seem so different from him, such a gentle man."

"My parents and two sisters died in a shipwreck. I ended up a Scugnizzo on the street. Russo helped me survive. He lives by his own strict ethical code, even though it's not the same that society decrees. He would never hurt anyone unless they meant him harm. He's honest about what he does and he's always helped the poor and the weak, like the Scugnizzi. Russo has nothing to fear on Judgment Day."

"Yes, I guess you're right, Carlo."

"The world would be a better place if its leaders had Russo's ethics. These esurient leaders kill millions to satisfy their own lust for power. Hitler lies to his citizens to gain their support: He talks of regaining Germany's former glory; he waves the flag and cries for patriotism, and they rally around him in patriotic fervor." He sniffed disdainfully. "The rest of the leaders are nearly as bad. No one will win this war. Too many are dead, too much is destroyed. The masses die to provide more profit and power to a few arrogant men who pull the strings of the war machine."

I stared at him in amazement. "Carlo, as sharp as you are, why didn't you ever want to become a boss in the organization?"

"Why complicate my life? I offered my services as a protector only. I guard Russo, I guard you, I guard the children. I'm happy in that role. My job is clear and useful. Happiness is illusive and valuable. If you find a spot of contentment in this turbulent world it isn't wise to want more. Reducing desire is the key to happiness. I have enough to eat, a place to lay my head, and I take pleasure in my books. I'm content."

"Thanks for being my protector, Carlo." I put my on hand on his shoulder.

"It's always my pleasure, Signora Russo."

Carlo made a lot of sense. The war, Russo's condition, my involvement in the business, and the children all made life complex. Happiness and contentment seemed to be luxuries I couldn't afford.

"I'm going to stretch a bit, Carlo." I wandered off. As soon as I was out of his view, I drifted over to Domenico. He sat alone, his face resting in his hands, his body limp with exhaustion.

"Are you winning the battle?" I asked.

"I'm not even sure what I'm battling anymore," he replied as he looked up. "So much suffering, so much hunger, so much hatred. How does one make a difference?"

"It's an impossible world."

"I thought you had your children hidden away."

"I'm finding that during a war protecting my family isn't easy."

Domenico nodded. He looked as though he wanted to say something but was unsure if he should. I, too, wanted to confess—about Russo—but I couldn't.

I saw the trouble in his soul revealed in his eyes. "What is it, Domenico? Can I help?"

He tried to say something but held back.

"You can tell me anything, Domenico."

"I . . . I don't know if I can remain a priest."

"What?"

"Does this Church represent my God? The things going on in Germany, Croatia, here . . . and still the Pope says nothing!"

He looked both ways to make sure no one was watching, and then produced a small, tattered four-page newspaper from his pocket and handed it to me.

"Don't let anyone see you with this. Read it."

I did as he asked. It was an underground partisan newspaper from the North.

In 1941, Croat fascists declared an independent Roman Catholic Croatia. Hitler plans to grant "Aryan" status to the independent Croatia under the Catholic leader Ante Pavelic.

Since that time, a campaign of terror and extermination has been conducted by the Ustashe rebellion against the Serbs, Jews, Gypsies, and Communists. Pavelic's slaughter of Orthodox Serbs resounds as one of the most horrifying civilian massacres witnessed in history. Indiscriminate mass deportations and mass executions became one of the most characteristic features of the Ustashi. Whole villages were thrown into mass graves—alive!

The Pope met with Pavelic and bestowed his papal blessing on the Catholic Croatian leader. The Croatian Catholic clergy not only knew of the massacre of the Serbs and the virtual elimination of the Jews and Gypsies, but many of the priests took a leading role!

Monks and priests worked as executioners in concentration camps where they massacred Serbs. The Catholic fascists massacred hundreds of thousands of Orthodox Serbs and tens of thousands of Gypsies in the newly formed independent State of Croatia. In addition, at least sixty percent of the Jewish population has been slaughtered.

Not only priests but nuns were also sympathetic to the movement. Nuns marched in military parades behind soldiers with their arms raised in the fascist salute.

Dissenting priests, sickened by the carnage in Croatia, made sure that Pope Pius XII was aware of the atrocities with both written documentation and graphic photos of atrocity; but to date the pontiff has yet to speak out against those responsible.

Archbishop Stepinac was appointed spiritual leader of the Ustashe by the Vatican in 1942. Stepinac, with ten of his clergy, hold a place in the Ustashe parliament. Priests serve as police chiefs and officers in the personal bodyguards of Pavelic. The Orthodox are forcibly converted to Catholicism and we do not hear the archbishop's voice preaching revolt. Instead, it is reported that he takes part in Nazi and fascist parades. Even though news of their massacres has been sent to Pius XII, not once did Pacelli, the "infallible" Pope, ever show anything but benevolence toward the leaders of the Pavelic regime.

Reading it made me sick. I handed the paper back to Domenico, and he hid it under his robes.

He shook his head in disgust. "The Church blesses the men responsible for exterminating entire races of people, but if you miss Sunday Mass, the Church considers it a mortal sin! How can I represent such a church?"

"It's a difficult time to make sense of anything."

"Avarice, envy, wrath, lust, gluttony, sloth, lying, not keeping holy the Lord's Day, drinking to excess, hatred, disbelief in God—these

are some of the sins listed by the Church. These are the great sins?"
Domenico looked around the bomb shelter. "Not helping those who
suffer, not stopping those that cause the suffering, these are the sins I
see every day! Thou shalt not kill! This war, this suffering . . . these are
the sins." He pounded his fist against the wall in frustration, and then
collapsed against it.

"The weight of the war makes us question everything." I placed my
hands on his shoulders. It pained me to feel his anguish.

"Questions are not enough," he said. "I need answers."

Chapter 31

GOING BACK TO THE SOUTH

The all clear finally sounded and Gianina, Carlo, the children, and I returned to the outside world. A horrible world. A world I wanted to shield their eyes from. A world of death and terror.

I had to get my children out of Napoli and find a safe haven for them. In addition to the weekly bombings, rumors were spreading of an imminent invasion by the American and British forces that now controlled Northern Africa. The South still remained free from attack and troop build-up. It seemed the logical place to take the children. As much as I wanted to join them there, I knew I couldn't; too many people depended on me in Napoli. My sister Gianina agreed to stay with them, which put my mind at ease.

On November 2, we all took the train down to Reggio Calabria. Mama met us at the station. She was getting older but still worked in the fields and looked as strong as ever. I bought six chrysanthemums of different sizes and colors from a flower vendor.

"Let's go to Papa's resting place." I handed a flower to each of the children as well as to Gianina and Mama. We took Mama's horse-drawn cart to the graveyard.

The town seemed unaffected by the war. It made you wonder why everyone suffering in the city hadn't moved south, out of reach of the bombs.

Mama hadn't seen the children since the war had begun. She

couldn't stop looking at them. "They're so big," she kept saying. "All my children have abandoned me. The house is so quiet now." Of course we had all deserted her; cruelty does that. But despite her past behavior, I felt sorry for her. I knew all too well what it was like to feel alone.

It was All Souls Day, and there were many people at the cemetery tending to the graves of their ancestors and loved ones. Flowers— mostly chrysanthemums—small baked goods, and other offerings adorned many graves. Prior to our arrival, Mama had cleaned Papa's gravestone with meticulous precision, and placed a large white chrysanthemum on it.

As she laid her flower down and said a prayer, I looked around. Everyone seemed to be staring at me and whispering. I moved to readjust the silver hair comb that Papa had given me, but found it still in place. Something other than my appearance was drawing their attention.

I turned to Papa and prayed to the Virgin Mary to protect him. Carefully, I laid my flower on his grave, as if I had begun a sacred beatification of my father. In spite of all the responsibility he had left to me, I still saw him as a saint. When I touched the cold gray stone I felt his presence, and he smiled on me.

With a gentle nudge, I pushed the children toward the grave and instructed them to place their flowers on it. "It's All Souls Day, children. We pay tribute to our ancestors on this day. This is your grandfather's final resting place. He was a good man, and he would've loved the three of you very much. Say a prayer for him." Over the years, I had told them many stories about their grandfather. They placed their blossoms on the slab, and Mama and I completed one final cleaning of the tomb before crossing ourselves. I missed him so much.

Back home, Mama and her servants—Umberto and his wife, Zola— had prepared an All Souls Day feast big enough to feed half the town. As Zola did every day, she had baked fresh bread, along with the traditional pastries from *fave dolci*: sweet fava beans, also known as *ossa dei morti,* the bones of the dead.

"These pastries are used to commemorate the dead," I told the children. Their eyes grew wide. "The Greek philosopher Plato and the goddess Persephone received fava beans as offerings from their admirers. Ancient Egyptian priests refused to look at a fava bean because they considered them cursed. Ancient people believed they contained the souls of the dead and were shaped like the doors of hell. The ancient Greeks even used fava beans to cast ballots in elections, and the Romans used them to drive away evil spirits."

"I hope there aren't any souls in my pastries," Giorgio said, frowning. Gianina and I laughed.

"My sweet fava bean pastries are made with flour, sugar, almonds, eggs, and butter, children. No souls," Mama assured him, without as much as a smile.

Amazingly, Mama still used butter, something I hadn't tasted or seen in almost a year. Here in the South the farms still produced milk, although their output had been greatly reduced by the loss of farm animals to the war, as well as the lack of workers and children drafted into military service.

Everyone dove into the food with vigor. Conversation was kept to a minimum, other than the universal language of silverware clanking on porcelain.

Mama served Porcini mushrooms with white beans, tomatoes, garlic, rosemary, and sage along with *Pittanghius cu li viti,* turnovers filled with meat and spices. Her chestnut soup was as wonderful as ever. Most impressive of all, she had made *melanzana in agrodolce,* sliced eggplant scalded in boiling oil and then cooked in a mixture of sour wine, chocolate, sugar, cinnamon, pine nuts, raisins, walnuts, and cedar bark.

For the main course she'd made *Costoline di Agnello alla Calabrese,* lamb chops Calabria style. First, the lamb chop is pounded so flat on the bone it resembles a flag, and then it's baked with olive oil, lemon, artichokes, mushrooms, capers, and anchovies.

It felt strange sitting at the old family table, especially with less than half of it occupied. Part of me longed for the days when my brothers and sisters sat around that same table anxiously devouring Mama's cooking, after which Papa would light up his pipe. I said a silent prayer for him and a word of thanks to God for our meal.

After the clatter of utensils finally subsided, Adriana announced, "Grandma, that meal came from Heaven."

"Yes, Mama. That was a fantastic feast," Gianina said. "The best ever."

"Well, I should hope so, after all the time and effort I put into it," Mama muttered.

"Fantastico, Mama," I agreed. "Thank you, Umberto and Zola as well, for helping to prepare such a magnificent feast." Umberto and Zola beamed with delight. "I haven't seen so much food since . . . well, since I left home."

"With this never-ending war, I wasn't sure I'd ever see this much food again in one place in my lifetime," Gianina added.

Lucia came over to me and laid her head on my chest. "Mama, I have a stomachache."

"I'm not surprised," I said. "You ate enough for ten children."

"I can fix that." Mama went to the kitchen and added dry cherry stems to boiling water.

"These cures were passed down by Cosimo and Damiano, the great gypsy physicians who came to Calabria a thousand years ago. It was good enough for our ancestors, it's good enough for Lucia. It's part of being a Roma gypsy. Your great, great grandfather was—"

"King of the Gypsies. We know, we know," Gianina interrupted, having heard the stories of our ancestry countless times.

Mama rapped her on the back of the head. "Yes, and through his efforts we came to own all the lands."

Once the brew of cherry stems cooled, Mama served it to Lucia. Sure enough, her stomachache dissipated.

"Mama, this feast . . ." I said. "The farmers working your land still provide you lots of food, even with the war?"

"Not as much, but yes, they still make payment with their crops."

"If it's that much, let me have Antonio come down and pick some up once a month." Such premium food would bring a fortune on the streets of Napoli.

"Certainly he may come. I'm happy to help my family."

The morning after our feast, we prepared our little caravan for departure. Gianina and I packed up the canned food, olive oil, and other goods I had purchased from Mama. Before arriving in Reggio Calabria, I had instructed Umberto to buy an old horse and cart for us. I'd also had him buy a goat to supply milk to Gianina and the little ones. I'd paid a ridiculous sum for the animals, but everything was in scarce supply.

"I don't understand why Gianina and the little ones don't just stay with me at the house," Mama said. I didn't reply; how could I tell Mama I didn't want her to have any influence on my little *angeli*?

Instead, I had chosen a vacant parcel of Mama's land with a small house on it as refuge for the children and Gianina. I remembered visiting the place once with Papa. The itinerant farmer who worked the land then was migrating to the north with his family to work in a factory, and Papa wanted to wish them well. The farm seemed isolated and safe in the foothills of the mountains, about ten miles from Mama's house.

After five hours of slow travel over rough terrain, we finally arrived. The mud and straw house was Spartan—two small rooms, no running water, no windows, one door and a small fireplace for heat and cooking. A lumpy old bed, a few rickety chairs, and a table provided the only furniture. Austere, but an oasis in the midst of war.

A stream ran beside the rustic structure, supplying ample fresh water. Beautiful mountains added a fantastic view. The old grove of chestnut trees would provide plenty of food through the winter months.

Gianina and I unloaded the wagon as the children played around the brook. After we finished, I unpacked a shotgun from its case.

"What's that for?" Gianina asked.

"I'm going to show you how to shoot."

She shook her head. "I don't think so."

"Show me, show me! I want to learn," Giorgio piped up.

"I'll show you when you can lift it, Giorgio." He wasn't even as tall as the gun.

"I can lift it now," he said, trying to pick the stock up from the floor. I leaned on it to make sure it remained too heavy for him. His little seven-year-old muscles struggled mightily before he surrendered. "Well, maybe I'll be able to pick it up by Spring."

"Gianina, you're going to learn to use this shotgun." I jammed it into her arms. "You'll need it for hunting small game and for . . . protection."

We moved outside, where I showed her how to clean, load, aim, and fire the weapon. She resisted at first, but once she started shooting I couldn't get her to stop.

That night I slept with my little ones huddled around me in the lumpy old bed.

Early the next morning I stared out the door and watched the night fade into the glow of sunrise. The time had come for me to return to Napoli. Staying in the quiet countryside with the children and my sister was far more appealing, but wasn't an option. I dressed quickly and quietly, hoping to avoid a tearful goodbye, and started out the door with my pack slung over my shoulder.

"Mama!" Lucia cried, hurrying over and grabbing my leg. "Please, Mama! Don't leave me!"

I closed my eyes and summoned all my strength. "I must, my angel, but only for a little while. I promise."

Adriana appeared, her hair tousled, and joined Lucia. "Mama, you can't leave us again! I beg you, please."

Giorgio came running out too, and grabbed hold of me.

"You all need to be strong, little ones. I told you yesterday I must go back. You're safe here with Aunt Gianina."

They continued to cling to me, sobbing as if their hearts were breaking, as mine was. After a moment I broke away. "I must go."

"Don't worry about the children, Carina," Gianina said. "I'll take good care of them, just like you took care of all of us when we were growing up."

"Thank you." We hugged.

As I set out, from the corner of my eye I saw the children waving goodbye. "Ciao, Mama! We love you! Come back soon," they cried.

I didn't look back. I couldn't. I wouldn't be able to leave if I did. In a lope that advanced into a full run, I rushed down the road. "Just keep going," I told myself.

Before I knew it, I was at the train station. Several people looked familiar to me. Once they noticed me, they began whispering among themselves. It was clear that I could never move back to the far South. Here, I would never be anything but a whore.

"All aboard!" yelled the porter.

I stepped onto the train. As it jerked forward, I took a seat. Time to face Napoli again, but I had one final stop before going home.

Chapter 32

A DEAL GONE BAD

The train slowed and a burst of steam filled the small Salerno train station.

Through the windows I saw new posters hanging on the station walls. One featured a bloody Italian boy standing over his dead play-mate. In the background, an ominous American bomber flew over an Italian city in flames. The slogan read, "American bombers drop booby-trapped pens to kill our children." While I had never seen or heard of child-killing pens, after the wrath of a hundred bombing attacks on the city, dead children and parents were a familiar sight in the streets.

Another poster showed a German soldier with a frightening smile on his face, his arm stretched out to shake hands. "Germans are your friends," it told the viewer. I grimaced. Everyone knew to fear Nazis, no matter how many posters the government hung up to convince people otherwise. Despite the devastating American bombings, most Italians looked forward to the day they heard English rather than German being spoken in the streets. I got off the train as the steam dissipated in the late afternoon haze.

Before I left to take my children to the South, Cerelia, the madam at our Salerno Pleasure House, had called for Russo. I had replied in Russo's voice. "What's going on, Cerelia?"

"A German officer wants to buy all fifty soldiers in his unit unlimited access to our brothel, baby."

"That'll be costly." Such requests had become quite common.

"The lieutenant wants to make payment with penicillin, baby. He knows I just run the house, and he wants to meet the owner to make sure their payment is fully credited."

People used many forms of payment during the war. Cash was the least valuable currency, and medicine was the most prized. "All right, I'll meet with him, but tell him my name is Nick. No reason to provide a Nazi with accurate information. Also, I don't want to meet him at the house to exchange the penicillin. Too dangerous. Set it up at the Solerno Hotel."

"Right, baby. I'll call him as soon as we hang up. Why don't you come down to visit me anymore?"

"You know I'm married."

"Just because you're married doesn't mean you can't have a little fun. Don't 'ya love me anymore, baby?"

"Of course, honey, but the war keeps me busy." I hung up and sat motionless for a moment, not even breathing. How often had my husband cheated on me with his whores?

Now, nearly a week after that conversation, the time to meet the German lieutenant had arrived. I stopped at a public toilet to change into my Russo clothes, tuck my hair up, and put on his hat and coat. A fake mustache made the transformation complete: Russo stared back at me from the cracked mirror. I felt no need for the wheelchair. The German officer didn't know Russo, only that he was meeting a man named Nick.

The lobby of the hotel was nearly empty when I entered. The lieutenant approached me boldly.

"I'm staying in room 215," he said. "Let's conduct our business in private."

I nodded. We went up the stairs and opened the door. Inside, two of his men sat on chairs, and a small case rested by the corporal's feet. I didn't like it that we had company, but it was too late to back out. I looked around. The room was dimly lit, the only light a small lamp on the nightstand that cast shadows against the wall as we walked in. The paint was pealing from the wall. It fell a little short of a four-star rating.

"I understand you have some soldiers in serious need of R&R," I said in my Russo voice.

"I'd like to arrange for fifty men to receive unlimited access to your facility," the lieutenant replied. "You'll recognize them by our insignia." He pointed to the gold eagle pin with the number 22 on his uniform.

"Unlimited access for so many will be costly."

"That's why we brought a large amount of medicinal currency. Can you accept such payment?"

"If it's untainted and there's enough."

"Oh, I think you'll be happy with both the quantity and quality."

The lieutenant motioned to his corporal. The soldier brought over a bag, opened it, and pulled out a vial of penicillin for my inspection.

"Why don't you take your coat off and make yourself comfortable?" the lieutenant suggested.

"No, thanks, I'm fine," I replied, as I reached into the pockets and pulled out the chemicals and litmus paper I used to check the quality of penicillin. The German officer lifted his eyebrow in surprise. I mixed a drop of the chemicals with a drop of medicine and placed a strip of litmus paper onto the mixture. The paper turned bright blue—top quality penicillin.

"Your madam Cerelia was correct. I see you've dealt in penicillin before . . . Signore Russo."

I turned toward him. He knew the name *Russo*. What else had Cerelia told him?

The lieutenant was pointing his gun on me.

"Signore Russo?" I said. "Who's he?"

"Vincenzo Russo, you're under arrest by the Gestapo for trafficking in stolen drugs." The lieutenant nodded to his corporal, who began searching me for weapons. He frisked down my side first, and then he reached into my overcoat and ran his hands over my chest. Then he hesitated and did it again, grabbing my breasts this time as if to confirm his findings.

He drew back. "Oh, my God! It's a woman!"

"What?" the lieutenant said.

The corporal tore open my shirt and exposed my bosom. The three men stared open-mouthed, and then burst out laughing. The soldier holding the Luger returned it to his holster.

The lieutenant moved toward me, leering at my breasts. I pulled my shirt closed with one hand and hung my head. No doubt they thought me ashamed. No doubt they thought me helpless and weak, a silly female who had thought to trick the Master Race.

With my free hand I slipped the stiletto from its sheath on the inside of my belt and hid it against my wrist in an overhand grip.

"Pull off that fake mustache," the lieutenant said. "Let's see what we have here." The other men glanced toward him, and instantly I stepped to one side, rotated my wrist and drove the stiletto deep into the corporal's groin. His eyes bulged, his hands shot to his balls and he doubled over in pain.

To my surprise, the other two men exploded in laughter again. They hadn't seen the knife. They thought I had landed a lucky punch.

Then the corporal slumped to the floor, revealing the bloodstained knife in my hand.

The lieutenant rushed me. I swung the stiletto toward his throat and he jumped backward. For a moment I thought I had missed, but then came the gush of blood. Sagging, the lieutenant grabbed me by the coat, but I twisted out of his grasp, and he fell as I twirled toward the other officer.

The remaining soldier was fumbling frantically to pull his Luger out of its holster. With his right hand busy removing the gun, he was unable to block my swing. I stabbed at him from the right, aiming for his throat, but he turned and pulled away at the last second. The knife lodged deep in the muscle and bone between his shoulder and chest. The handle, slick with blood, pulled out of my grip. The soldier, who weighed twice what I did, gave up on the Luger and grabbed me by the throat. I couldn't breathe. I drove my fist down and found the stiletto still sticking out of his shoulder. As he scrambled to knock my hands away from the blade, I kicked him in the groin. Then I grabbed the handle near the quillons and yanked the blade across his chest with as much force as I could muster. "Die, Nazi scum!"

His grip loosened. His right arm went limp, the shoulder tendons severed. As I pulled away he sank to his knees, still pawing at my hands. He toppled forward, took a final gasp, and lay still.

I yanked the stiletto out of his chest. The blood on it was already growing sticky. I cleaned it and my hands on his shirt as best I could, then returned the stiletto to its sheath on my belt.

Only then did my eyes really see the blood on my hands, the blood all around me. Who was this person inside me? I'd just taken three lives! I slumped to my knees.

The pungent smell of death filled the room. My body shook, but beyond that I realized I felt no sorrow and no remorse. Why should I ask for forgiveness for what I had done? These were not men, they were Nazi demons. I spit on the lifeless body on the floor below me for all the Nazi injustices I had seen. Without doubt, the Church would grant me an indulgence and God would pardon me for this sin. Surely it was a good thing to remove evil from God's creation, and Nazis were evil.

I grabbed the case of penicillin and slipped it into my bag. At the door, I listened for movement in the hall. I heard nothing. I peered out. No one was in the corridor. It seemed surprising that no one had responded to the sounds of our struggle. With the ruthless Nazis in town, I guess an occasional scream appeared normal. Still, I dare not take the time to properly clean up and change clothes. I crept to the end of the hall, down the stairs and out the hotel's back exit.

The waning light of dusk lingered on the street. I walked casually toward the train station, berating myself for my stupidity. How could I not have seen the Nazi's trap? With Penicillin so precious, the exchange had been arranged too easily. Everyone from the baker to the ticket taker at the train station used stolen goods as currency, but still, I had allowed myself to become careless. Russo—the real Russo—would not have done so.

Police sirens disturbed the calm. From the end of the block I saw two police cars pull up in front of the hotel and both Italian and Gestapo officers run inside. I walked off the main road onto a side street and hugged the shadows as I hurried on to the train station. When the train whistle sounded, I jumped; the last train to Napoli was about to depart.

I stepped onto it, ticket in hand, just as it began to move.

Chapter 33

THE LONG RIDE HOME

My head bumped against the lavatory mirror as the train jerked forward. I looked at the withdrawing station from the tiny window. Several Gestapo agents had arrived and were frantically searching the depot, and asking questions of those who still remained. Perhaps they were looking for me, but perhaps not. I would never know.

I washed my blood-stained hands vigorously, changed out of Russo's clothes and pulled a dress out of my bag. I started to automatically stuff the pants, hat, and overcoat into the case, and then realized someone might find me with the bloody clothes. I needed to get rid of them.

Someone knocked on the door.

"Un momento!" I called.

Hiding the clothes in the lavatory would be too risky. It was getting dark outside, so it seemed safe to throw the coat out the window. As I thrust the garment through the opening the wind grabbed it, propelled it up, and then softly dropped it back to earth near the tracks. I prayed that no one had seen it flutter past. The pants and hat followed. After adjusting my dress, I picked up my bag and put my wedding ring back on my finger.

Another, more agitated, knock bashed the door. "Quickly! Quickly!" a female voice insisted.

I hurriedly checked myself in the book-sized mirror. The Russo mustache was still clinging to my upper lip. I ripped it off and tossed it out the window. One more look, then I grabbed my bag and opened the door. The impatient woman outside pushed her way in, giving me a dirty look.

I found a seat across from two older gentlemen, one gray-haired, the other bald. They were engaged in an animated verbal battle.

"No, no, no. I used to be two inches taller than you," said the gray-haired one.

"You're crazy, we've always been the same height," the other argued.

"I've shrunk a good two inches in the last few years."

"What are you talking about? I've shrunk more than you."

"You're crazy. Don't you remember all my back problems? I lost much more height than you."

"You're wrong. Stand up." They both stood.

"Now do you see?"

"See what? You're not standing up straight."

"You're the one slumping." With his hands, the gray-haired man adjusted the bald man's back to stand taller. He turned to me and asked, "Young lady. Which of us is taller?"

I hesitated to answer.

The man with no hair prompted me, "No, go ahead. Tell him."

"You look about the same height to me."

The man with the gray hair raised a finger. "See! See!"

"See what? I told you I shrank more than you." They sat back down. "And I have the aches and pains to prove it. . . ."

"Your aches and pains are nothing compared to mine," claimed the bald man. They continued to fight over who had the poorest health.

In the seat across from me sat a pregnant woman and her daughter, about seven. The girl reminded me of Adriana. The woman's belly bulged with full-term pregnancy. I hated to think that another baby was going to be born into this world.

Fifteen minutes outside of Napoli, I noticed two MVSN, Railroad Militia agents, making their way through the adjoining train car, checking papers. Mine were in order, but what if they wanted to look in my bag? Possession of medicine was a capital offense. They would likely kill me on the spot.

As I considered my options, I noticed the officers had become distracted by something outside the window. Passengers on that side of the train began to look up at the sky—and then were diving under their seats. I heard the rising drone of a fighter plane, leapt to the floor and curled under my seat.

The plane sprayed a round of bullets into the train. The sound of splintering wood and metal ripped through the compartment.

The MVSN agents fired their pistols out the window as the plane flew over, followed by shouts and obscene gestures. I heard the plane circle around for another attack. The Militia officers fired several rounds at the plane as it passed over a second time, but again bullets tore through the cabin. As the sound of the plane's engine faded, the two railroad MVSN agents maintained their verbal assault out the window.

After an excited self-congratulatory exchange over their bravery in fighting off the enemy plane, the agents continued their inspection. Gradually, people collected themselves and returned to their seats.

Then a scream ripped through the compartment. The pregnant woman was holding her bloodied daughter in her arms. The two agents rushed over.

As everyone huddled around the mother and child, I moved to the back of the car and onto the platform. Crouching, I peered around the corner of the train to see where we were. The central train station of Napoli was coming into view, and the train was slowing.

As I looked back into the compartment, I saw the MVSN men place a blanket over the little girl.

Outside, Gestapo agents on the railroad platform moved to their checkpoint stations as they readied for the train's arrival. Security was tight these days. It didn't look as though the agents were expecting anything out of the ordinary. Even if they were preparing to search the passengers for the person that killed three Gestapo agents in Salerno, they'd be looking for a man, not a woman. But I didn't want to take any chances. The penicillin was far too valuable to leave on the train and far too risky to take through the checkpoint.

After sizing up my options, I decided to risk jumping. The bulk of the train would hide me from the view of anyone on the platform; no one was likely to notice me.

As the train squealed to a stop, I leapt toward the tracks. My dress caught on the car's handrail, tightened, and slammed me back against the train. Dangling upside down, I hung from the side of the last car like an ornament on a Christmas tree.

Chapter 34

BETRAYAL

White steam poured over me from the train's air brakes and engine car, which helped conceal me as I struggled frantically to free myself from the railing that held my dress. Finally, I grabbed onto the bottom of the platform and pulled as hard as I could. The dress ripped and I shimmied down the side of the train with the valuable contents still safe in my bag.

I crossed the tracks to the quiet southbound side of the station. Two railway mechanics were working on the wheel of an idle train. A Nazi soldier I hadn't noticed before came over to the side of the platform and saw me climbing up from the tracks.

"Can I help you, little lady?" he asked in broken Italian, as he reached out to help me up. "What were you doing on the tracks?"

"Oh, I was trying to take a shortcut, but I guess it wasn't so quick."

"May I see your papers?"

I showed him my ID and merchant pass.

He looked at them, and then sized me up. *"Kommen Sie."* He took my hand and pulled me onto the platform, and then into a small utility room in the station. "Put your bag on the table and open it."

As I placed the bag on the table, the soldier, a plump man with a pockmarked face, stepped behind me and ran a hand slowly over my shoulder. I realized he wasn't interested in my papers or my bag. I tried to ease away from his touch, but he yanked me back against him and ran his hand over my breast, his breath hot in my ear. He had no intention of letting me out of the room until he had received his bribe.

Were all men so predictable, so simple? I let myself relax back against him. *"Un momento,"* I murmured, and began unhooking the belt on my dress. His breath grew even harsher. I heard him fumbling with his own belt.

With one hand I palmed my stiletto; with the other I reached into the little pouch I had carried to the beach. In one quick motion, I turned and threw a fistful of sand into the German's eyes. *"Sheisse!"* he cried, raising his pudgy hands to his face. I stepped toward him, released the stiletto blade, and jammed it into the center of his chest.

He fell without a whisper.

Fucking Nazis! Another surge of anger filled me, but I realized it wasn't the Nazis I hated most; it was God. Why had He burdened my soul with the responsibility of taking four lives this night?

At that moment I noticed a small gold chalice sitting on the table, partially wrapped in a thick protective cloth. This ornamented goblet, used for the Eucharist to hold the wine symbolizing Christ's blood, could only have been stolen from a church. I let out a breath. God had sent me a sign. He would forgive my blood-spilling if I returned this, the holy symbol of His Son's pain, to His protection in the church.

After wrapping the chalice in its cloth, I cracked open the door and peered out. No one was on the platform. The chill of the night air slapped me. My heavy breathing created little clouds. I walked down the ramp toward the street.

A door banged open and two German soldiers wandered out of the station house onto the platform. They headed toward the utility room. I picked up my pace. As they were about to open the door, one of them noticed me and shouted, *"Halt!"*

I ran out of the depot and onto the usually busy street—but the avenue was vacant because of the curfew; there was no crowd into which I could disappear. But I had another option. This was my brother Sergio's territory, and I knew he used the underground to evade the police, entertain gamblers, or even serve as a makeshift brothel when needed. At this time of night, there was a good chance he would even be down in the caverns. I ran down the street toward the entrance to the underground.

The clatter of two men running on the wooden platform punctured the night silence. I reached the end of the block and turned down the alley before they appeared at the street.

A dozen doors greeted me along the alley. Which led to the underground? The soldiers shouted to each other, their voices echoing down the street. I pulled on the oldest, most battered door. Thank Jesus!

I entered the reverent silence of the city's ghostly underworld.

In the darkness, I took a full breath and sighed. Inside my bag I found a box of matches that I always carried. I lit one and used it to ignite a makeshift torch some other underground traveler had left behind.

As I walked through the silent solitude, I reflected on my life. And not just mine—the war seemed to throw everyone from one desperate situation to another. We didn't live, we survived. The bloody evidence of the deaths of four men spotted my skin. Like Russo constantly washing his hands, I literally felt the dirt from my deeds staining my hands. I prayed for the safety of my children and hoped they would never learn of the sins forced upon their mother.

The sound of voices broke my thoughts. A fan of light seeped out from an adjoining cavern. I extinguished my torch and crept down the hall.

In the dim light of a lantern I saw a large, funny-looking woman prancing around in a poorly-fitting evening gown. A man sat on the ground before her, drinking wine from a bottle, watching and laughing. He shared the bottle with the woman. Her sequined dress sparkled even in the faint glow of the lantern. She started singing and strutting around, enthusiastic if devoid of ability. I knew the American song she sang; Papa had often played it on the phonograph. Because the composer's name seemed so odd for a man, I still remembered it: George Ira Gershwin.

> *Embrace me, my sweet embraceable you*
> *Embrace me, you irreplaceable you*
> *Just one look at you my heart grew tipsy in me*
> *You and you alone bring out the gypsy in me*

I love all the many charms about you

Above all I want my arms about you

Don't be a naughty baby . . .

Come to papa come to papa do

My sweet embraceable you . . .

As my eyes adjusted to the dim light, I realized the singer wasn't a woman but a man in a wig. I looked closer and nearly dropped my torch. The chanteuse was Sergio, my brother who as a child hated even to touch a girl. Now he stood before me dressed as one. The man watching him was Russo's cousin Gilberto. Next to them was an open piece of luggage with its contents strewn about. They had obviously pinched the suitcase, found the dress and wig inside, and started kidding around.

It took me a few moments to compose myself, but I managed to hold back my laughter. I couldn't resist continuing to watch their charade.

Sergio broke off singing. "Fucking women. Use all these props to lure us in so they can take our money." He tossed aside the wig and started pulling off the gown. He looked even more ridiculous with it half-on, half-off, his hairy chest exposed.

"Bitches," Gilberto said. "But we need to figure this out. I'm sure Benito will back us."

"Is he strong enough?" Sergio took off the dress. He had his pants on underneath.

Gilberto deliberated. "He's tough and he wants this change. I'm sure."

"Well, he'd better be ready. We can't do this half-ass. Everything is on the line. Carina doesn't use enough force, and makes us look weak." Sergio clinched his fist. "We can't make the same mistake."

"Right. You're right."

"The bitch must go!"

Fire filled my body. A day of ugliness had now turned to betrayal. I had taken care of Sergio his entire life, protected him from Mama, gotten him work with Russo—and this was how he repaid me?

"Carina has taken too much power," Gilberto said. "The agreement was just to have her appear as Russo, not make actual *decisions*."

"Exactly. What does she know, anyway?" my brother said with contempt. "I hate it. A woman has no place telling men what to do."

"When we talk to Benito, we'll offer to make him the boss in exchange for him giving us important positions. But . . . who will do the deed?"

Sergio pulled out a pistol. "It's my place to do this thing. But we can't breathe a word of this to my brothers. They're loyal to Carina."

"No, not a word can be spoken."

"We must be sly; we must not give ourselves away. After I get back from the next run to Switzerland, we will meet with Benito, tell him of our plan and finalize everything. We will hold the power."

"It's as good as bread." Gilberto grinned and shook hands with my brother. After they collected their cache and deposited it back in the suitcase, they picked up the lantern and walked off deeper into the underground city, away from me.

Exhausted, spent, despondent, I sat alone in the darkness. I had expected resistance to my taking power, of course—but I had not expected treachery, especially from my own flesh and blood.

I rubbed my hands over my face. How could I continue to play this role? Who was I kidding? Running such a huge organization, I couldn't . . .

I felt a crust of dried blood still coating my finger beneath my wedding ring. Russo . . . Russo would never allow such self-defeating thoughts to cross his mind. Whatever must be done, must be done; that was what he would say. There is no room for weakness when protecting the family. Only cold, calculating precision will keep the family safe.

These things, more than just a way of speaking and moving, were what I had learned from Russo.

Chapter 35

GESTAPO AT THE DOOR

I hurried to the Duomo, the weight of my day's activities and my brother's betrayal adding to the urgency of my quest. Along the way, I reached inside my bag and felt the cool gold surface of the chalice I had taken from the Nazi at the train station. By touch alone I could trace the sculpted face of the cup. When a priest poured wine into this vessel, it became Christ's blood. Merely holding it felt intrusive between the bond of priest and Christ.

I emerged from the underground on the south side of the cathedral. I would give Domenico the chalice and be done with it. But as I entered the chapel I realized I couldn't accept credit for returning this sacred artifact. That would taint my absolution. Only God must see my deed. The holy cup had to be reinstated anonymously.

Two priests were talking near the front of the great, empty hall. In the back pew, I knelt and said a prayer. After a few minutes, the priests left, and without hesitation I hurried to the altar and placed the covered chalice on the dais. Jesus looked down on me from his cross behind the pulpit, absolution in his eyes. Or was it scorn?

I heard the creak of a door opening behind me. Without looking back, I rushed out an exit and reentered the underworld.

After entering my house from the underground passage, I went to the kitchen sink and used the dirty dribble of water from the faucet to clean away the particles of dried blood that remained on my face and hands from the men I had killed that day. I noticed that my hands were trembling, but not because of the deaths. I was thinking of Sergio. My own brother wanted me dead!

I slammed the towel against the sink over and over again. I wished it was a club. Once I had exhausted my rage, I pushed my hair from my eyes with an unsteady hand. "It's all too much. Too much," I muttered. But God was not finished with me that night. Out of the darkness, Forenzo the Scugnizzi raced into to the window and stared in at me, wide-eyed and out of breath.

"Gestapo agents are on the way!"

"Hide," I said, and he sprinted out of sight.

I dropped to my knees and lifted up a section of tile in the floor, revealing the hidden compartment. I set the bag of penicillin inside it and had just finished replacing the flooring and rising to my feet when the kitchen door smashed open and two German soldiers leaped in, rifles raised. Major Kappel of the Gestapo and four more Nazi soldiers entered—shoving Forenzo in ahead of them. A moment later Carlo rushed into the room, only to instantly receive the butts of two rifles in the stomach. He grunted and collapsed to the floor.

"Don't hurt him!" I shouted.

Major Kappel stepped in front of me, a sneer on his lip. "Where is Signore Russo?"

"I don't know."

"No more lies!" He grabbed me by the hair and threw me against the wall. I managed to stay on my feet. Kappel stood staring at me, his hands on his hips and his feet on the tiles that hid the drugs.

As Carlo started to get up, one of the soldiers hit him in the chest with the stock of his gun and knocked him back down.

"Carlo!" I stepped toward him, and the major pushed me back against the wall.

"Three Gestapo agents were killed in Salerno today," he said. "Your husband was the murderer."

"Impossible."

The major motioned one of his soldiers to hold a gun to Forenzo's head.

"No, please!" Wildly, I thought about the stiletto in my belt. Oh, how I wanted to see more dead Nazis.

"Tell me where your husband is, Signora, or we'll add an extra orifice to the boy's face. Then to his." He indicated Carlo.

"I'll show you," I said hastily, then lowered my voice. "I'll show you something—but only a few people know about it, and I appeal to your honor as a gentleman to keep it a secret."

"What kind of trick is this?" He pulled out his pistol and held it to my head. "I should just kill you."

"All I ask is that you take a look. Station your guards outside the room—but I want only you to see."

"You had better lead me to Russo, Signora, or *they* die." He gestured at Forenzo and Carlo with the pistol. "Do you understand?"

"Yes. You will have your answer."

After squinting at me for a moment, he pointed to his soldiers. "You four follow me." To the ones guarding Carlo and Forenzo he said, "If anything happens, kill them—but fill it with pain." He looked at me to make sure I understood the consequences.

I nodded, and then led the men down to the basement door.

Chapter 36

DEALING WITH BETRAYAL

"They must stay outside." I pointed to his soldiers. Major Kappel looked into my eyes again, then signaled for the men to follow my instructions. I took the key off the nail in the wall and unlocked the basement door.

A single light bulb illuminated the dark room below. Russo stood by the sink washing his hands, his back to us. He didn't react to either Major Kappel or me as we entered the room.

"Signore Russo," the major said, pointing his Luger at Russo's back, "you are under arrest for crimes against the Third Reich, including theft and distribution of vital military drugs, as well as the murder of three Gestapo agents."

"He doesn't understand you," I said.

Russo dried his hands for a long time on a towel before turning around. The major flinched. Russo's hands hung at his sides like skinned birds, and his long, wild hair reminded me of the drawings of the composer Beethoven. His beard fell at least six inches below his chin—in a city of beardless men.

And he ignored the major. Picking up a sponge, he began cleaning the room with meticulous precision.

Kappel turned to me, eyes glinting with skepticism. "Is this some kind of trick?"

"The murders you mention—did anyone report a man with a long beard and wild hair leaving the scene?"

Kappel shook his head. Then he looked back at my husband, wring-ing the sponge out in a bucket.

I said, "He's been like this for a year."

"How did it happen?"

Apparently attracted by Kappel's pristine uniform and shiny but-tons, Russo approached the officer. With care, he took a button in his fingers and inspected it for a few moments. Then he released it, turned, and went back to his scrubbing.

"A bomb partially destroyed our house while we were in it," I said. "Since that night my husband has been trapped in his own inner world. So you see, it's impossible for him to have been involved in any murders tonight—or any other crimes. He hasn't left this basement in fourteen months. I swear to you."

"I see . . . but I can't believe it." Major Kappel shook his head. To my amazement he actually looked saddened by the sight of Russo; per-haps even he recognized how fragile every life was in this war.

"Pull a surprise inspection any day of the year, Major," I said. "You'll find him here busily cleaning."

"Wait . . . Doesn't Russo own the Salerno Pleasure House?"

A half-moment's thought convinced me that saying no would be risky. "Yes," I said, "he does."

"I'm glad you didn't deny it. We know he does." Once again he drew his gun on me. "Signora, it doesn't matter if Russo did or did not steal the drugs. Someone in your organization did, and killed our Gestapo agents as well."

I looked him straight in the eye. "During the war our only busi-ness has been the brothels. We never deal in medicine. Quite frankly, we've thought about it, but it's too risky." As my mouth spoke, my mind raced, casting about for an explanation of how the Germans had got-ten enough information to form their suspicions. It took me only a moment to figure it out. "Now I see," I said. "I can think of only one person who could have sent you on this wild goose chase." I paused to let Major Kappel come to the same conclusion.

"The madam," he said.

"She's setting Russo up to take the blame for her dirty dealings. . . . With Russo out of the way, she probably hoped to take over the whore-house for herself." I knew I'd given her a death sentence.

"Don't touch her," Major Kappel warned. "We'll take care of her." He paused. "As for your husband . . . I'm sorry, Signora Russo."

"Thank you, Major. But I beg you. Don't mention my husband's condition to a soul. I want people to remember Vincenzo Russo as he was."

The major nodded and gave my shell of a husband a final look. In the reflection of Russo's eyes, I believe Kappel witnessed his own frailty.

Now that the Nazis had taken over every aspect of running Napoli, it was difficult to get shipments into the city. The Germans were much more disciplined and watchful than the Italian Army, and not as susceptible to bribes. They just took anything they wanted.

During my absence, Giacomo had arranged to transport a large shipment of ammunition, motor oil, and other valuable street items from a contact in Switzerland. Before the Nazis, a few well-placed bribes would have allowed a Swiss driver to simply cross the border check and drive down the main road to Napoli. But that was no longer possible. Now we had to send men up via a circuitous route to pick up and return the goods. Giacomo was already driving south to get a load of food from some farmers, so the current trip to Switzerland had been assigned to my brothers Antonio and Sergio. When I added myself to the list of participants, I pretended not to notice the disapproval in Sergio's eyes.

"Why do you have to go?" he asked.

"Yes," said Antonio, but with a very different inflection in his voice. "It's dangerous, Carina. We have to take the most isolated roads, and you never know when they might be washed out or covered in ice and snow. Or if the Nazis will have set up a random checkpoint, or *briganti* are waiting to block the road, kill us and steal everything we have."

"All the more reason for another pair of eyes and another brain to be along. We need this shipment, brothers."

Neither of them could argue with that. They knew that before the war, a relatively straightforward operation like this would have been handled by one of Russo's lieutenants, but nowadays the commodities we were after were much too precious to entrust to anyone but family.

Except that for me, "trusted family" no longer included Sergio the cross-dressing traitor. I especially didn't want him alone in the Alps with Antonio, who doted on me; too many bad things could "accidentally" happen up there.

So we all went.

After two days of stealthy back-road driving toward Milan, we finally guided our truck up an abandoned pass through the Alps. It seemed crazy to risk maneuvering these dangerous roads, which as Antonio had warned were icy and posed the constant threat of encounters with Nazis or bandits. Even empty, the truck alone made us a highly valuable treasure, and therefore a target.

But we made it to the border unscathed, and crossed through an unguarded post off an old, closed road that had been revealed to Giacomo by his Partisan contacts in the Italian underground. The inaccessibility of this route had made it the choice of smugglers for centuries.

We reached Switzerland without incident. In the town of Brig we loaded the truck with oil, ammunition, and luxury items.

Soon we were heading back toward Milan with Antonio, the most skilled driver in the organization, behind the wheel.

Burdened with its heavy cargo, the truck strained up the snowy mountain road. At some points only a meter of snowy rock separated us from a near-vertical drop of a thousand meters; not even a guardrail provided protection.

As we approached the summit, snow began to fall so heavily we couldn't see to the front of the truck, and piled up so deep it covered the wheels. Antonio tracked the road by watching out his side window. We had no choice but to continue forward; trying to turn back to Switzerland would be just as perilous, and stopping to wait out the storm represented certain frozen death.

It seemed as though the rest of our lives might be spent reaching the top, but at last we crested the peak. No sooner had I begun to relax than the truck dropped down hard on one side, and stopped moving. Antonio fed the accelerator a little gas, but after repeated attempts he couldn't propel the vehicle forward.

The back of the truck was pitched to the right. I jumped out into the snow. The wind howled past me toward the top of the mountain. I asked Sergio for the shovel behind the seat. He handed it to me. Even wearing gloves and boots, my hands and feet felt like blocks of ice as I dug snow away from the back right tire.

A shadow loomed over me. I drew back. "Give me that," Sergio bellowed as he took the shovel from my hands and finished the job. I stood back and watched him—his face more than his hands. I saw no signs of deceit or ill intent.

Soon it was clear that the tire had fallen into a half-meter-deep hole in the road. Sergio scraped the last of the snow away.

"Try it again, Antonio," I yelled.

He gunned the engine, but the result was the same; the tire was buried too deep inside the icy hole to gain traction. As Antonio continued trying to rock the truck out of the ditch, I started pushing on the back bumper.

"Are you going to help?" I asked Sergio, who was just standing there watching me. Finally he stepped forward and added his weight to the effort. By then I could barely feel my extremities, and my lungs burned from the frigid wind.

But we kept at it, pushing and pushing while Antonio fed gas to the engine. Every time the truck moved a few inches up the side of the hole and I had hopes it would come free, it would suddenly drop back again.

"Hold on, hold on," I said, gesturing for Sergio to stop pushing. I took a careful look at how the wheel was lodged. "Antonio, when I say 'now,' put it in gear and step on the gas, but not before!"

"All right," he called back from the cab.

I turned to Sergio. "Okay, we're going to push, then pull—push, then pull."

He looked at me as if I was crazy.

"Just follow me." I started pushing the truck forward, and then grabbing the bumper and pulling it backward. Finally Sergio picked up on my plan. With coordinated effort, we got the truck rocking back and forth. When it hit the back end of the hole, I shouted, "Now!"

Antonio gunned the engine as the two of us pushed forward. With the full length of the hole available and Sergio and me adding momentum, the truck lurched out of the ditch.

Sergio and I scrambled back into the truck and Antonio guided it down the road. I worked to bend my fingers in front of the ane-mic heat from the vent, but my digits felt more like foreign objects stuck onto my hands than my own appendages. Sergio shivered and pounded his arms to warm up.

Our progress remained slow down the treacherous road, but, near the base of the mountain, we had cleared away from the blizzard and there was only a little snow on the ground but the wind still blew up the slope. As we made a turn around a pass, Antonio abruptly stopped the truck and turned off the lights and engine.

"What is it?" I said into the windy quiet.

"Don't tell me we're out of gas," Sergio groaned.

"Look; a campfire." Antonio pointed toward a faint glow in the for-est, not too far from the road. "Probably *briganti*."

"Do you think they spotted us?" I asked, involuntarily lowering my voice.

"I don't see any movement, and the wind seems to be blowing our sounds away from them. But they would only be camped here in this weather if they were hoping to attack a vehicle coming over the pass."

"Great," Sergio said. "Now what do we do?"

Antonio said, "Coast past them, light out . . . and pray."

"You're going to coast down a mountain road without headlights?" Sergio said. "You can hardly see the road with them on! Personally, I'd rather fight it out with the bandits."

"We don't even know how many there are," Antonio pointed out. "There could be a hundred."

"Then let's find out," I said. "I think Sergio's got a point. Antonio, you stay with the truck and be ready to leave fast; Sergio and I will scout out their encampment."

Sergio's face grew dour, but he followed me as I climbed out of the truck again. From the forest I heard the sounds of laughter and drunken singing; clearly the wine was flowing around the campfire.

Sergio and I crossed the road into the forest, heading toward the noise and the welcoming glow of a fire. "You take the lead," I said, although Sergio had already established his male prerogative and moved in front of me. He moved through the darkness silently, glanc-ing back at me every few steps. A week ago I would have assumed he was only showing concern for me; now I suspected sinister motives. It was terrible—I had nurtured him from his first day of life, and now his every move created suspicion.

From my belt I drew my stiletto, hiding it in the backhand grip. Sergio was no longer glancing back, though; he was moving toward the fire with caution. I saw four figures crouching close to the blaze, but couldn't be sure more were not hidden farther away, in the darkness.

I also noticed that Sergio now held a blade in his hand.

We took a long, slow step toward the *briganti* camp. Another.

No longer did I look toward the camp, I could only see Sergio's weapon.

When Sergio abruptly reversed direction and spun toward me, I stepped inside the arc of his arm and drew my blade across his throat. He stumbled, reaching out, his knife falling into the snow as he tried to clutch me. I grabbed him instead, cradling him in my arms as his blood flowed blue-black into the dirty snow. Leaning close to his ear I whispered, "I cared for you as a baby . . . my sweet embraceable you."

When I felt the life go out of him, I gently released his body into the snow.

When I climbed alone into the truck, Antonio peered out through the windows, then looked at me with blue-white eyes.

"Where's Sergio?"

I had no trouble producing shaking hands and unsteady breathing. "We ran into a sentry. He got Sergio. I cut the bastard before he could warn anyone, but we've got to get out of here. Now, Antonio! Now!"

But he just sat there. "Sergio? My god, we can't just leave him! He might still be alive."

"He's not alive. Now drive!" I pulled Antonio's foot away from the brake, and we lurched forward.

I couldn't stand the way he was looking at me. "Sergio's gone, Antonio. There's nothing to be done. Keep going. Coast on down the road, just like you said. And try not to drive us off the cliff."

He finally nodded as he recognized the seriousness of our own plight and turned his attention to the barely visible track in front of us. As we moved slowly down the snow-shrouded hill, I prayed for Sergio's soul, then for mine, and then for the truck not to go off a cliff. We picked up speed, Antonio using the parking brake when necessary instead of the main brakes as they produced less noise. He rolled down his window as we passed closer to the campfire and the sounds of merriment floated to us through the trees. Antonio's face burned with a fire of its own, and I placed a warning hand on his elbow. He turned his attention back to the road.

It took us several days to reach the outskirts of Naples, where we hid the truck in an abandoned barn we used for such purposes. The return journey had been spent mostly in silence.

Only as we entered the outskirts of Napoli in our regular car did Antonio break the silence. "I can't believe Sergio isn't with us."

I nodded.

"I still don't understand exactly what happened, Carina. Why would a *briganti* sentry attack Sergio and not call out to his comrades?"

"I couldn't see it all in the darkness. I don't want to talk about it."

"But he's our brother. I'm trying to understand."

"I don't want to talk about it!"

Antonio looked shocked. I had never before raised my voice to him, my dearest brother. "I just can't deal with it right now, Antonio," I said. "Okay?"

He nodded, but kept looking at me sidelong.

Our cargo had arrived intact, but I was clearly more of a wreck than I'd thought. An incident like my outburst with Antonio must not happen before the rest of the family. Another such sign of being out of control could mean my life.

My brothers and Russo's family were all shocked to learn of Sergio's demise, but here, as always, the general dangers and chaos of war conveniently brushed away suspicions.

I only prayed that I had not broken bonds of trust with Antonio. I was running out of family members.

Chapter 37

DOMENICO'S CONSCIENCE

With Sergio gone, I doubted that Gilberto would dare to make a move against me . . . but I couldn't be sure. The growing number of corpses at my hand made my body throb like Mama's beatings. I couldn't be sure of anything. I started to understand the burden Jesus felt caring for his flock.

The necessary routines of my life kept me from crawling away and hiding. I had to meet with the family to give counsel, keep the books, arrange shipments, and visit my merchant booth to keep the smuggled goods flowing out and the money in.

One day, after I'd been working a few hours at the stall, my sister Isabella arrived to relieve me, as she or my sister Santina usually did each day.

I was walking across the plaza when a hand touched me from behind. I knew immediately whose hand it was. "Hello, Domenico." I turned to find him looking gaunt and drained from carrying the weight of misery from so many souls. Still, even looking so drained, he filled me with energy just by being close to me.

"How nice to run into you," he said.

"Is this really a chance meeting?"

He smiled. "You know me too well, Carina."

"Let's take a walk," I suggested, and we strolled down to the beach. "It's a beautiful day. So quiet and peaceful. On a day like this you'd never know that war fills the hearts of most of the people in the world."

"I heard your brother Sergio was killed."

I hesitated. "This war takes so many," I said, furious with Sergio for putting me in such a position.

"How are your children?"

"Fine. I hid them in the South, near Reggio Calabria, along with my sister Gianina."

Domenico nodded. "Probably wise. Try being Jewish and hiding from this war. The stories from Germany and Croatia . . . I don't want to believe them." He placed his hands, once so elegant, now scraped with harsh work, on my shoulders. "Carina," he whispered, "you can't breathe a word to anyone of what I'm about to ask you." He looked into my eyes with that penetrating gaze that always made me feel faint. I had no choice but to nod. "I know your husband is a smuggler in addition to his other activities," Domenico said. "I've come to ask . . . *beg* for your help."

Secretly, I'd hoped his request involved the two of us running off together. "Yes," I said, hiding my disappointment. "Whatever I can do."

"It's your husband I really need. I want to . . ." He looked around and lowered his voice still further. "I want to get some Jewish families out of the country."

"How many people are you talking about?"

"Twenty I need to move right away, but there are others; I've been hiding them with Italian families in our parish. Russo would be paid for his assistance, of course. Some can pay well, but most don't have much to offer. I can add a few lira myself."

I felt a knot in my throat. "Let me see what we can do."

"Thank you." He surrounded me in his arms, a place I would have been happy to stay forever.

After my announcement, the room grew quiet, then erupted with angry shouts.

"What are you thinking?" Benito cried. He threw up his hands. "This is why a woman can't run things. There is no room for a soft heart in business."

Giacomo spoke in a more measured tones. "We've done many risky things, but never got into any trouble we couldn't buy our way out of. But not this. Not with the Nazis in control." My brother was a clear thinker, and I couldn't argue with his evaluation.

"We've got to take a pass," Renzo said. "It's too risky. If we're caught, no bribe's big enough to keep us from a firing squad."

I sighed. "Listen, I know smuggling Jews is dangerous—"

"Dangerous?" Now Giacomo's voice rose. "Suicide!" His hands jerked, and he slipped them behind his back.

"It's for a price," I said.

"Well, I for one am not going to risk my life for some stinking Jews," my younger brother Luigi said.

"You're right," I said. "All of you. It's too risky. Forget it."

Russo sat on the bed in his basement room, staring down at his reddened hands. When I entered, he didn't acknowledge my presence, and as always I felt a clenching strain in my muscles at the sight of his bewildered face.

"I hate to see you this way," I said. "You don't deserve it." I felt self-conscious talking to him, yet but compelled to include him in the decision. "Russo, I don't know what to do. Every day, Nazis cart Jews off to internment camps and certain death. Now we have a chance to help a few escape, but if we're caught . . . You've always stuck up for the defenseless, Russo. I've always admired you for that. Would you help them, despite the risks?"

His eyes remained fixed on his hands as he rubbed them together.

I bent down and gazed into his vacant face. "You'd love a good scam, too—to cheat the Nazis out of some Jews. You'd get a kick out of that, wouldn't you?"

He said nothing. A deep sadness took me, and I had to turn away.

"Help them." The whisper was almost inaudible.

I spun. "What?"

He stared at me blankly. I held his face with my hands to look directly into his eyes, and carefully I studied him. "Did you say, 'Help them'?"

He showed no sign of recognizing my words, or me.

So now I was hearing things. Hearing what I wanted to hear. Russo's voice had told me nothing.

But then I realized that his dead gaze told me all I needed to know.

Chapter 38

TRAFFICKING
FOR A JUST CAUSE

Above us, the city slept. Before us, the gloomy stone corridor seemed to stretch into infinity. The family clutched their meager belongings wrapped in cloth as they scurried down the hall behind Antonio and me, with Domenico following them. Antonio and I both carried pistols.

We arrived at our destination after twenty minutes of travel. The long, thin openings that had been dug out of the rocks allowed the first glow of morning to violate the cave's darkness. Peering out, I saw fishermen start their morning routine along the docks—untangling nets, loading bait, packing gear.

"Put these on," Antonio instructed the husband, wife, and two teen-aged boys as he handed them rubber slickers and hats. They put the old fishing gear on over their clothes. "Tuck your hair under the hat," Antonio told the wife. She obeyed silently.

"Thank you for all you've done for us, Father," the Jewish man said.

"No, thank Signore Russo, Carina, and Antonio. They're the ones getting you out of Italy."

"Father, we wouldn't have survived without your help and that of the Partisans," the husband said, but then looked to Antonio and me. "How can we ever thank you?"

"Just stay out of danger and find safety for your family. That'll be our thanks," I said. "Once you reach Marseilles, Antonio will get you to our contacts there. The route to Spain over the Pyrenees is difficult but quite safe."

"Carina," the man said, "perhaps as smugglers you would consider selling weapons to the Italian Partisans who helped us. They're desperate to acquire more guns to fight the Nazis. Father Saldino knows how to contact them here in Napoli."

"I'm sure my husband will be willing to talk to them," I said, and to Antonio. "You be careful out there."

He nodded and pulled on his yellow slicker. He led the family out of the cave toward the docks, Antonio carrying a box of fishing tackle. Domenico and I watched from the slit in the cave.

A light layer of fog lingered about the docks, waiting for the full sun to disperse it. Our group walked with several other fishermen toward the boats. The Jewish family held their heads low in the rubber hats as Antonio led them toward Russo's smuggling boat.

Domenico hissed softly and pointed out an MVSN Port Militia officer strolling along the dock about ten boats down from Antonio and the family. The officer passed by with barely a glance.

Antonio led the family onto the fishing boat and started the engine. As I prayed to Virgin Mary, they made their way through the harbor without incident. Domenico and I both sighed with relief.

"Isn't it nice living a life free of anxiety?" I said sarcastically.

Domenico chuckled. "Not a care in the world."

As we walked back toward home, I told him, "In addition to our fishing boat, we can take up to six of the less hardy travelers in our truck over the mountain pass to Switzerland. A final option is to smuggle people to the South. With my contacts there, we can hide them in remote areas, including the abandoned farmhouses Mama owns."

"Fantastic!" he said, embracing me. "God will reward you for what you're doing. I must thank Signore Russo as well."

"Domenico, I need to tell you something about Russo . . ."

"Do you think these Partisans will show up?" I asked.

"They're skittish but they need our weapons," Benito replied.

Dressed as Russo, I sat in the wheelchair and waited, along with Carlo, Gilberto, Benito, and my brothers Antonio and Giacomo, all of whom were holding various types of weapons. Everyone grew impatient. Our contacts were late to this meeting, which had been arranged through Domenico. Our lanterns added to the unease as our shadows jumped around the ancient cavern walls under the city.

"Just let me do the talking," Benito told me. Lately, he had asserted himself more and more in running the business. For the peace of the group I let him make non-crucial decisions, but I knew this solution would not last forever; he wanted ever more control.

"Yeah, let Benito do all the fucking talking," Gilberto slurred. Drunk again. Day by day he became more disrespectful of my authority. I wondered what he'd think if he knew I had killed his co-conspirator, my own brother Sergio.

Finally, three men arrived, carrying rifles. A handsome bearded man moved toward us while the other two stayed at the entrance with their weapons in hand.

"We were beginning to wonder if you were coming," Benito said.

He looked us over in the shuttered glow of his lantern. "Yes. I recognize all of you," he said, his gaze lingering on me. He checked out the rest of the cave, and then signaled to his two friends to come over. I imagined a Partisan's lifestyle didn't allow much relaxation, as they fought both the Nazis and the Italian Fascists. Groups had sprung up all over Italy to attack German units, now seen as occupiers by most Italians, rather than as allies.

"You can't be too careful," he continued, giving me a grin. "I go by Count Sureshot. This is Fast Talk, and he's Firecracker." Despite his beard and uncut hair, the Count seemed too elegant to be with this group of peasant Partisans. His regal posture, confident demeanor, and noble face framed with wavy black hair set him apart from the others. Surely he wasn't an actual count?

"We know your reputation, Signore Russo," Fast Talk said, "so we believed the rumors that you have rifles and ammunition." He spewed it all out as if it were a single word. I nodded, and everyone shook hands.

Despite their cautious behavior, the partisans seemed in good spirits. No doubt the main reason was that Allied forces had landed in Sicily just two days earlier, after establishing complete control over

Northern Africa. Soon, everyone agreed, they would drive the Nazis off Sicily; an Allied invasion on the mainland of Italy could not be long to follow.

"So what can you offer us?" Sureshot asked.

Benito said, "We have Carcano-91s and—"

Fast Talk groaned. "Please, not those ancient Italian bolt-action rifles! We don't need more of those pieces of shit. Our 'great' Italian Army has lost every battle they've fought using those relics."

Just listening to the speed at which words escaped his mouth tired me.

Benito shrugged. "Not the best, I know, but we can offer you a large number of them, if you need a quantity of weapons. We also have two dozen K98 Mausers—8mm, five-shot, bolt-action rifles."

"A little better, but don't you have any automatic weapons?" the Count asked. His eyes turned to me, hypnotic and powerful.

"We have six Soviet SVT-40 10-round, semi-automatic self-loading, rapid-fire rifles," Benito said. "Show them one, Antonio."

As Antonio handed over one of the Soviet weapons, I noticed a jagged scar on the Count's hand. He held the rifle up and looked down the barrel, checking for damage. Antonio started to show him how to load it, but he was already breaking down the weapon. He checked it inside and out before spinning it back together.

"What do you think, Count?" Firecracker asked. He and Fast Talk seemed jumpy, the way one would expect a Partisan risking his life every day to act.

"Hey, stop giving us shit," Gilberto said in a too-loud voice. "We've got top of the line artillery here." Even Benito looked a little pissed at his cousin for this interruption.

The Count ignored it. Unlike his compatriots, he seemed completely at his ease. As he handed the rifle back to Benito I noticed he was missing two fingers on his left hand. "It's a fine weapon and in good shape. I used one at the Russian front." For some reason he shifted his gaze to me. "Are they all in this condition?"

His steely eyes made me feel as if I should look in a mirror to make sure my mustache was on straight. "Yes," I said. "We also have three German MG34 machine guns." I motioned for Antonio to produce one from under the blanket, which he did.

"Excellent! A fine quality weapon, if you have enough ammunition."

"We have fifty clips for the MG34s." Benito motioned to a wooden crate filled with ammunition. "And we have some Walther P38 pistols, too."

"No, we're just looking for rifles and machine guns."

Benito shrugged. "That's all we got. A couple hundred rounds of ammunition for each type of rifle."

The Partisans huddled together and whispered amongst themselves. Then Fast Talk turned back and said, "We're interested in the machine guns, the Soviet SVT-40s, the German Mausers, and all of the ammunition you have for them."

Benito looked to me, as he wasn't good with figures. In my head, I calculated for a moment and announced, "130,000 lira."

Firecracker stiffened. "That's outrageous!"

"If you weren't Partisans, we'd charge you three times that amount," Benito snorted. "The Nazis confiscate more than half our shipments. No one else has any guns to sell you."

"Pay them," said the Count. "He's right, and we need them."

Firecracker shook his head but counted the cash out to Benito.

Benito smiled. "I hope you fuck up some Nazis real good with all this."

"We're also going to give you a *Panzerfaust*," I said in my Russo voice.

"A what?" Firecracker asked.

I gestured at Giacomo with my glove. He left, and a moment later returned with the tube-like weapon, stuffed inside with a very large warhead with metal fins. Firecracker saw Giacomo's hand spasm near the trigger and quickly took the object from him

"It's a German-made anti-tank weapon," I told them. "We have no use for it, but perhaps you gentlemen will."

"Good Lord, look at that." Firecracker inspected the weapon with the excitement of a little boy receiving his first soccer ball.

"Use it wisely, though," Antonio said. "It's made to fire once—no reloading. Please note the warning on the side." He pointed to the label printed in red: *"Achtung! Feuerstrahl!"*

Firecracker and Fast Talk looked at it, puzzled. The Count leaned forward. "'Beware! Fire Jet!'" He smiled. "I guess the back blast produces a little more kick than the rifles."

Everyone laughed, and Firecracker mocked the recoil of what it must be like to fire the weapon.

"Good luck, gentlemen," I said, lifting my arm in a partial salute. "Italy thanks you." The count gave me a curious little smile that made me feel uneasy.

Antonio, Carlo and Giacomo helped them load their purchases onto the cart they had brought. They gave us a final set of nods before disappearing down the dark passage. As they left, I wondered how soon Italy's future might turn, once again, toward the good.

"Only 130,000 lira," Gilberto muttered under his breath. "Fuckin' giving them away."

"It was a good price and they could not have afforded more," Carlo said.

I looked at Benito. "Were you okay with the price?"

He shrugged. "Carlo's probably right. They had no more than 130 in those dusty pockets of theirs." He turned to his cousin. "And I don't need any help negotiating from you, Gilberto."

"*Merda,*" Gilberto mumbled.

Gilberto seemed to be rubbing everyone the wrong way . . . and his loose tongue was worrying me.

Chapter 39

DRUNK, DISORDERLY, DEAD

One night around ten o'clock, during a week when the phones were working, my brother Giacomo called me. "Sis, Drain and I have a crap game running for some Germans down at the old warehouse below Cupa Caiafa Hotel. We're out of booze. Can you have some sent over?"

No one else was available and the warehouse was only about ten blocks from the house, so I gathered up some bottles, grabbed my coat, and set out to deliver the alcohol myself.

At the bottom of the hill, an Italian Militia man stopped me. "It's after curfew, young lady." He eyed me, checked my merchant's pass and peered into my bag. "What are you doing with all that liquor?"

I held the bag toward him. "May I offer you a bottle?"

He glanced both directions and took a bottle.

"Get to where you're going fast," he said as he disappeared into the darkness.

I dropped the booze off to Giacomo and Benito. Twenty German sailors were playing craps, with several prostitutes along for the ride. Benito took a bottle, filled everyone's glasses and took a few bills from the betting stack. One man shouted a toast in German, and they all raised and then tilted their glasses.

"Where's Gilberto?" I asked Giacomo. "I thought he was working with Benito."

"He got arrested when he went out for more booze," Giacomo informed me. "Just before we called you."

"What? How did that happen?"

He laughed. "Easy. He walked out the door, ran right into a Gestapo agent, and puked on him. They arrested him for public drunkenness. Benito was so pissed off, he said, 'Let him rot in jail for a few days.'"

I walked down Corso Vittonrio Emanuele Road to the police station. I wasn't sure what I wanted to do; I only knew I didn't like the idea of Gilberto's loose lips in a police station.

As I approached the building, I saw a Gestapo agent push Gilberto outside toward an Italian policeman at the top of the steps. "Here, watch this piece of shit. He needs some air."

Gilberto slurred, "Don't you know who I am? I'm Gilberto Russo! I work with the Prince of Napoli!"

The Gestapo agent hesitated. I moved a little closer, but kept my face turned away.

"And who is the Prince of Napoli?" the Gestapo agent asked.

"Only the man who runs this town. Well, he used to. Damn bitch does now." Gilberto swayed. "Wanna' know a little secret?"

"You're drunk." the policeman said.

Gilberto raised a corner of his lip. "How could you tell? I thought I was hiding it so well."

"Let's get him back inside," the Gestapo agent said.

My palms sweated and my heart pounded as I went up the steps behind them.

The Gestapo agent placed Gilberto in a chair by his desk so his back was to the room.

Without even looking up, the police officer behind the front desk said to me, "I'll help you in a moment, Signora." He continued to fill out paperwork as I inched closer to Gilberto.

"Hey," Gilberto said, "what'll it take to get me out of this dump? I can get you anything you want."

"Is that so," said the Gestapo agent as he filled out a form of some kind.

"Anything—booze, women, drugs . . . We can get it all." Then he put his head down on the desk.

The Nazi looked up. "Are you going to be sick again? Come on. Don't you dare fire a splatter shot here." He hurried Gilberto to the bathroom.

Once again I followed, looking around to make sure no one noticed me. At the men's room door I pulled my stiletto from its case in my belt. Then I eased the door open.

Urinals lined the back wall. On the left was a row of sinks; on the right, four toilet stalls. The officer was washing his face in the basin while the sound of retching came from one of the stalls. So did a putrid smell. I squatted and saw Gilberto kneeling on the floor facing the toilet in the second stall from the door.

The officer still had his face in the sink as I crept into Gilberto's stall and pulled my blade across his throat from ear to ear, making sure to cut both the main artery and the windpipe. In a gush of red, Gilberto slumped forward into the toilet. My actions—the smoothness of them—made me feel as nauseous as my victim had been. How could I kill a human being so easily now?

"Lord, man, how about a courtesy flush?" the Gestapo agent said. "It stinks out here."

I flushed the toilet and crawled under the divider into the next stall. From there I peered through the crack in the door until I saw the agent drying his face on a towel. I started to make my exit, but he tossed the towel aside, strode over and knocked on Gilberto's door.

"Hey! Are you about done in there?"

Once again I readied my stiletto. The agent pulled a comb out of his pocket, returned to the mirror, and carefully straightened the part in his hair. I started to hide the bloody stiletto inside my coat, then hesitated, bent down and placed my blade near Gilberto's dead hand. Flushing the toilet in my booth to cover up any noise I might make, I squirmed under the wall of the toilet, hid there until the Nazi went to opened a window, and slipped out of the room.

I got halfway through the lobby before the Gestapo agent ran out of the bathroom yelling, "*Wir erhielten Mühe!* Hurry! He's killed himself!"

I strolled out the front door and onto the street. I could not entirely prevent a smile from reaching my face. I had performed with precision under the fire of battle. I had done wonderfully well. Clearly, when it was necessary, I had both the strength and the will to play God; to do the difficult, necessary thing; even to decide who lived and who died. I . . . I . . .

Who was I?

I walked faster and faster, until I was almost running.

Chapter 40

PROTECTED BY
THE UNDERWORLD

No one in the organization seemed surprised to learn that Gilberto was dead, but none of them believed he had slit his own throat. "That would take too much energy for him," I overheard one of them mutter after a few glasses of wine. Instead, they assumed the Nazis had done him in and simply reported it as a suicide.

As to the condition of their other relative, the Prince, Russo's family had gradually stopped asking to see him. Out of sight, out of mind. His two brothers and his cousin Renzo had come to visit a few times in the first month, but the frequency of their visits lessened and finally stopped altogether. I understood; it was disheartening to visit a Russo that did not even recognize them. None of us could bear to see such a virile man in such a lifeless state.

Of course it didn't take a direct hit from a bomb, bullet, or shrapnel to get injured in this conflict. Many other people suffered wounds not inflicted by a weapon. The war had forced most people into an involuntary penance of fasting that some called "starvation." Disease and desperation killed many more. Near the front door of my house I kept a statue of Saint Christopher with a bowl in his hands, a common symbol in Napoli of a help offering. When deserting Italian soldiers,

Jews, or those who simply had an empty belly asked for assistance, I provided it.

But my motives weren't altogether altruistic. From these drifters I gathered important information for our smuggling business: bridge and road closures, troop movements, the contents of trains, and much more.

As I set up a deal for a load of sugar with one of my contacts at the open air market, the air raid sirens blasted their ominous call. I hurried to the familiar shelter under the Cathedral of San Gennaro, the church where I had married Russo. Bombings had become a part of life in Napoli. After three years of British attacks, the Americans had finally joined the mayhem eight months ago.

In the underworld, Domenico was working to bandage a young girl with a knee injury. Still, he looked up at me as I entered. No matter how busy he was, he always seemed to sense when I stepped into the shelter. Today was no exception.

Over the last few months, he and I had helped more than a hundred Jews flee the country. More than offering a simple prayer of intercession, we had saved lives. Although we had exchanged no words of love, this noble goal had brought us a mutual spiritual reward to share.

I found a place to sit but for some reason felt less secure than normal in the shelter. When the explosions began, I realized that this raid was different than the others had been, the bombs exploding at a more constant and extreme rate than ever before. Even in the shelter, the heat from outside grew intense and breathing arduous.

Perhaps the Allies were preparing the way for a coming invasion of Italy. It was possible, wasn't it? Allied forces in Sicily had already knocked the German troops to the edge of the island.

As the attack dragged on, I found myself staring at the ancient walls with their much more recent additions of graffiti. I remembered my Latin lessons from Dr. DiScullo; *gaffire* means "to scratch." Each time you reentered a bomb shelter you noticed more scratching in the wall; some of the most common were portraits of Hitler, Hirohito, and Mussolini. Other popular themes depicted battles or women.

On a visit to another shelter I had seen rooms named by theme. The "war" room depicted real sea and air battles complete with war news such as, "The Italian submarine Topazio sunk in the Mediterranean." The room also included portraits of famous bomber pilots such as the "accursed hunchback" or the *Savoia Marchetti*, rumored to use soccer game strategies to guide the release of his bombs. One elaborate etching showed air battles that had taken place over Napoli. In the "wedding" room you could read the inscription, "Anna and Romani married and honeymooned here July 11, 1943," with a picture of a uniformed soldier, his arm around a cute girl with a tall fancy hairdo. Another, more demanding, stone engraving read, "Permanently reserved for Signore Campagna."

San Gennaro, the patron saint of Napoli, remained the most popular subject scrawled into the tufa walls. For some reason, Napoli's citizens never gave up faith in their saint, even after all these years of depravation.

"Hello, Carina." I looked up to find Aldo, Russo's contact from City Hall, standing in front of me. He'd lost a lot of weight and spoke with an air of defeat, a condition most people carried these days. "How are you?"

I forced a weak smile. "Fine. Please, sit down, Aldo."

He sat cautiously, like a man twice his age. "How is Signore Russo? I've talked with him a few times, but I haven't seen him in a very long time. Where is he these days?"

For more than a year, I had impersonated Russo when dealing with Aldo over the phone to obtain information and favors from City Hall. "Oh, he's fine. He's just out of town a great deal lately, including today."

"It's a good day to be out of town," Aldo said, looking up.

I nodded. "How are things for you?"

"Let us say I look forward to a better tomorrow." He closed his eyes as a wave of explosions shook the room.

"Is there anything my husband and I can do for you, Aldo?" I asked after the wave passed. "You've always helped us."

"Can anyone help us these days? With the British and Americans in Sicily, Fascist power is crumbing rapidly. The Nazis control most of the government. I don't know what the future holds."

"Well, you watch after yourself, Aldo. Let us know how we can help."

"Thank you, Signora Russo." Aldo coughed from the dust in the air. Suddenly the lights went off. People screamed, even as the darkness intensified the terrifying reverberation from the bombing above us. Dust rained down, filling my mouth and lungs with grit. I wanted to run outside and scream at the planes, "Stop! You've won your battle. Let us die in peace!"

When the lights popped back on, they revealed many faces filled with an even greater terror than usual.

Aldo and I spit dust from our mouths. I said, "Maybe with the Allies coming, we'll be rid of the Nazis and this ridiculous war will end."

A weak smile came to his face, and he stared off into the distance. "Yes, there were once days without war, weren't there? It's hard to remember them." He stood and bowed his head to me. "Give my best to Signore Russo, and I hope the Lord looks after all of us."

"Good luck, Aldo. I'll be talking to you. I mean, my husband will talk with you soon, I'm sure." A shiver rushed through me, but Aldo didn't catch my *faux pas* as he slumped away.

The bombing reached a crescendo and people screamed for it to end. Then it did. I waited expectantly for more explosions, but only silence assaulted my senses. The all-clear didn't sound. Hours went by without us receiving the customary permission to reenter the city above, but no one seemed eager to face what was left of Napoli after this strike.

Finally, several priests informed us that the all clear sirens had been destroyed, and we could return to the outside world. I moved over to Domenico and we exchanged anxious looks. Two priests opened the shelter door, and the intense morning sun of summer beamed through the opening. It hurt my weary eyes, and I raised my hand to shade them from the light.

Then a heavy cloud of smoke rose into the sun, dimming the glare to twilight.

People slowly wandered outside.

Chapter 41

THE FIRES OF HELL

Domenico and I emerged from the temporary sanctuary and stood still, gripped by shock and disbelief. The sky, now tinted the color of tea by rising smoke, reflected the orange flames that burned away at Napoli's body. Fist-sized ashes fell down all around us. On all sides, entire blocks of buildings had been removed from Napoli's landscape.

"Domenico," I whispered, "Is it Judgment Day?" I felt like we were standing in the streets of Hell. I thanked God my children were safe in the south, and at the same time cursed Him for exiling me here.

Domenico said nothing, and we staggered forward. Charred bodies lined the streets like ghoulish statues. "This was no ordinary bombing," Domencio finally said. "This was a fire bombing."

He was right. Only an intense fire could have melted adult corpses down to the size of young children. "It's like a modern eruption of Vesuvius," I said.

Ash-covered citizens wandered about, not knowing what to do and with no place to go. No one spoke. Judging by their blackened clothing, some of these people hadn't made it to a shelter. Several lost souls had joined Russo by escaping reality altogether; they sat in the street staring at the sky. Crackling fires ate at the bones of buildings, and an occasional scream punctuated the reverent silence that hung over the city.

As Domenico and I turned a corner we came across a man sitting in the middle of the road in his comfy chair in front of a smoldering pile of debris that presumably, a few hours before, had been his home. He looked about as if he was waiting for a divine event on this day of apocalypse.

Several women wept as they called out and searched for lost children. One woman passed us cradling a charred baby in her arms as though it were still alive.

On the next street a diligent group of city workers and soldiers dug survivors out of a collapsed building. Beside the structure, a dozen bodies lay in the street next to the wounded, who looked bewildered and lost. Domenico and I walked over to see if we could help.

"Why don't you send for ambulances?" a man covered in ash was asking the city engineer who appeared to be in charge.

"There are only twelve ambulances in all of Napoli. Thousands have been injured. What good are twelve ambulances? We need a thousand, and that's just for the wounded. What do I do with the dead?"

"The dead will have to walk to the cemetery," the man of ashes responded.

"There's no other way," the engineer agreed.

"Yes, the dead are a real nuisance. Always more corpses. For three years I've seen nothing but corpses in the streets of Napoli, and they put on such airs, demanding our attention! Well, to hell with them. Let them walk to their own graves."

"To hell with them! Let them walk," the engineer said, resigned to the futility of his job.

Domenico went over to a dying woman and gave her Last Rites.

People drifted by like the living dead, dragging themselves toward destinations that they hoped still existed.

Across the street a group of men struggled to open the door to an underground shelter. Domenico and I hurried over, and he helped them pry it open. Finally, the door gave way. The odor of death knocked me back. Inside, dozens of people lay lifeless, suffocated. No survivors. Domenico crossed himself and said a silent prayer.

I overheard an Italian Army officer tell a government official, "I've heard about this in the bombings on Germany. The heat caused by this new kind of bombing by the Americans and British sucks the oxygen from the atmosphere and suffocates even people in shelters. Especially women and children. It makes air chimneys that make the flames rush around at typhoon speeds and rise to heights of four kilometers. Four kilometers!"

Domenico quoted, ". . . and they were given the keys to the well going down into the abyss. They opened the well, and from the well issued forth smoke and indeed the smoke blocked out the sun, and consumed all the air outside."

I kept shaking my head with disbelief. "The Allies may destroy us before they save us."

Once again our house had survived, with Russo still safely hidden in the basement. My brothers and Russo's family weren't so lucky; most of their homes had suffered damage from either the bombing itself or the after-fires. I arranged and paid for accommodations for everyone in the organization who'd lost their homes in the attack. Some had to move outside the city to find accommodations that were still livable.

From our Partisan friends, Count Sureshot and Fast Talk, we learned that the Americans had driven the Germans out of Sicily and were supposedly assembling a huge fleet in preparation for an invasion of Italy. Kesselring, the German commander in Italy, had placed all German units on alert.

On July 26, 1943, the unthinkable happened. The Italian government arrested Mussolini, ending his twenty-year dictatorship. Mussolini had given a great deal to the people of Italy—unfortunately, his thirst for war and his alliance with Hitler had brought about his downfall as well as causing the miserable plight of his children, the people of Italy.

The New Italian government surrendered to the Allies, even though German troops still occupied Italy's mainland. After this capitulation, the Germans completed their occupation of the country by disbanding and disarming the hapless, leaderless Italian Army.

Immediately the Germans strengthened their hold on the Italian peninsula. Field Marshall Rommel took responsibility for the protection of Northern Italy and moved five infantry and two panzer tank divisions down from Germany.

With the fall of Sicily, Mussolini, and the Italian Army soldiers simply walked away from the war. They traveled along railway lines in their cracked boots and shredded uniforms, many of them scared or wounded, but singing as they headed south. The songs were no longer fascist tunes, but popular old songs that they hoped would help them forget the horrors they'd seen. They joked and laughed, happy to be anywhere but in the hopeless fight.

It looked as though the war might finally be winding down.

Off the coast, I could even see Allied warships in the distance. Clearly they'd be arriving soon—but I was surprised by just how soon. The next day, September 9, 1943, the Allies invaded Italy on the beaches of Salerno, just thirty miles south of Napoli. For the first time since 1940, Allied troops had set foot on European soil, a domain the Nazis had ruled for three years. Germany immediately sent more troops south to repel the combined British/American invasion.

A couple days later, I was at the house, dressed as Russo in the wheelchair. Carlo, Renzo, Antonio, and I had just returned from a dawn meeting with a smuggler. Forenzo came to the house in a frenzy. "I was down there, in Salerno, the day the Allies invaded."

"Good Lord, Forenzo. Why?"

"History, I wanted to witness it. But, oh, my . . . Americans stormed the beach, but the Germans fought back and tried to push 'em right back into the sea. Huge tanks, 'Tigers,' shot day and night at the Americans on the beach. I st . . . st . . . stole binoculars from a drunk German soldier and watched American officers run away and abandon their men. P . . . p . . . panic everywhere in Allied troops. German foot soldiers stormed the beach and the Americans began shooting each other in con . . . con . . . con . . . turmoil."

"Lord, they're going to get pushed right off the beach," Carlo said.

Forenzo continued. "The next night, in the dark, after the fighting cooled down, I went to the beach into the American camp."

"What were you thinking?" I cried. "You could've been killed!"

"I was ca . . . careful. Soldiers ran every which way to get ready for another German attack."

We all shook our heads in amazement at Forenzo's story. "It doesn't sound like the Americans and Brits will survive," Renzo sighed.

"Looks bad," Forenzo agreed. "Lots of German troops setting up position in the h . . . h . . . hills."

Carlo's eyebrows rose. "So you know where they are, and how many?"

"Sure."

· "We should contact the Partisans and give them any German positions," Carlo suggested as he moved toward the door. "Maybe they can do something to help the Allied forces."

We all agreed. Carlo, Antonio, Forenzo, and I went to the Piazza near the University of Napoli. Fast Talk, our Partisan contact, was the clearinghouse of information in Napoli, and he dispersed and collected most of his intelligence reports from the piazza.

People swarmed the area, trying to find out what was happening with the Allied invasion. We found Fast Talk in one of his usual spots, by the fountain in the center of the piazza, smoking a cigarette. We positioned ourselves near him, but we didn't immediately acknowledge him for fear of Nazi spies.

No one was close enough to hear us, so I said, "Nice weather?"

"Yes, it is, but I hear the breeze from the south has slowed," Fast Talk replied at the speed of one of the machine guns we'd sold him.

"That's what I'm hearing, too. We came to give you some information that Forenzo obtained. He was down in Salerno during the invasion. He has knowledge of German positions and strength. And I'm sure our brothel in Salerno will have useful information, too. There are always loose-lipped German officers."

Fast Talk smiled. "We always need good intelligence."

I prompted Forenzo to give him details on German troop positions, strengths, and lines of supply.

Suddenly, several German trucks sped into the piazza and more than a hundred German soldiers piled out, wielding machine guns. As always, my gut reaction was that they were coming after us. I froze as people all over the square screamed and ran in every direction. The soldiers halted anyone attempting to flee. At the sight of this I actually relaxed a bit; clearly, the Germans weren't interested in singling our group out.

More soldiers arrived, herding hundreds and hundreds of additional people into the plaza. We overheard people say that the Germans had rousted them from their homes.

"What are they up to?" Antonio asked.

"We're going to find out soon," Carlo replied.

"*Silenzio! Silenzio!* There will be an announcement shortly," a German voice snapped over a loudspeaker. Major Kappel appeared and dragged a single teenage Italian soldier onto the stage. One of Kappel's assistants carried a small briefcase.

Over the speaker, Kappel ordered, "Citizens of Napoli, kneel down."

We looked at each other, confused. A few people got down on their knees but most continued to talk and mill about.

"What are those crazy Nazis doing?" Carlo asked.

Suddenly, a deafening cannon blast fired. The main structure of the university exploded into flames.

"Kneel!" Kappel ordered again.

People dropped to their knees. I stayed in my wheelchair.

Major Kappel held the young Italian soldier in front of the crowd and shouted, "This hoodlum has thrown bombs at the German soldiers who protect you! His suitcase is full of hand grenades, ready to kill those of us who provide you security!"

Kappel's assistant displayed the suitcase full of ammunition. Kappel gestured to the terrified teenager to enter the flaming doorway of the university. The young boy stood frozen. Kappel repeated the order. As the Italian soldier shuffled toward the door, Kappel's assistant shot him in the back.

Kappel turned back to the piazza and yelled over into the microphone, "Cheer for Hitler and Mussolini, your protectors!" The crowd provided a half-hearted shout. "Cheer for the glory of Italy and Germany! And now, Colonel Scholl, our great commander in charge of Naples, will say a few words."

Colonel Scholl came to the microphone and spoke in Italian. "Germany will continue to protect the citizens of Napoli from Allied attack, but we need your cooperation. All weapons held by citizens must be surrendered for the safety of everyone in the city. We can only continue to protect citizens if they behave in a calm and disciplined manner. There will be no tolerance for those who act against the innocent German officers and soldiers defending you. Each German soldier wounded or killed will be avenged a hundred times. Be calm and reasonable. These orders and the reprisal already taken against this rogue Italian soldier are unfortunate but necessary. Please obey these instructions for your own safety." With that, Colonel Scholl left the microphone.

"All men move to the north side of the piazza," shouted Kappel. "Women, children, elderly and the disabled to the south end." He kept repeating these instructions, punctuating them with gestures. Soldiers strode through the crowd and pushed the men to the north end.

"What do they want?" Antonio wondered.

"I'm afraid we're about to find out," Fast Talk said with a scowl.

The piazza offered no opening into the underground through which to escape. The soldiers provided no place to run.

A soldier motioned with his machine gun in the direction he wanted Antonio, Carlo, and Fast Talk to walk. *"Schnell!"* he ordered. They started to move. Forenzo started to go with them, but the soldier pushed him back. "Too young."

As Russo, I shouted to the soldier and pointed to my wheelchair, "I need them!"

The soldier ignored me and marched them off. "Then take me, too!" I wheeled toward them.

The soldier motioned for me to go back. *"Nein! Nein! Gehen Sie dorthin."*

An officer announced over the microphone for the women, children, and elderly to return to their homes.

The Nazis marched more than five-thousand men out of the piazza and down the street. As I watched them go, the blood drained from my face.

Chapter 42

FIGHTING EVIL

"Should I take you home, Signore Russo?" Forenzo asked as the women and children scattered around the square in a panic.

"No, Forenzo. Mobilize every Scugnizzi you can find. The first two you see, tell them to gather my brothers and Carina's brothers. Have them take the underground to my house. Next, tell the Scugnizzi to follow those damn Nazis and find out what the hell's going on. They need to learn where they're taking Antonio, Carlo and everyone else. Have them report back to me at the house. Tell them they'll be rewarded well for their efforts, as will you. But be careful, Forenzo. If you see a soldier, disappear. Don't take any chances. Did you get all that?"

"I got."

"Now run like a tiger," I said. Forenzo vanished into the crowd.

The remaining German soldiers continued to disperse the few groups of women and children that remained in the square. One instructed me to move along. An older woman pushed my wheelchair out of the piazza. I directed her to leave me by a quiet alley. She seemed puzzled that I wanted to be left in such an odd location. In fact she would not leave me that way, so I finally just jumped out of the chair and ran to a nearby underground entrance, where I ripped off my disguise.

In the safety of the city below the city, I raced home. My brothers Giacomo, Luigi, and Giorgio, along with our guard Mario, were already there. Within a few minutes, Russo's brothers Benito and Alonzo arrived.

Still in a panic, I told them about the Germans taking away Antonio, Carlo, and Fast Talk. We stayed in Russo's office near the entrance to the underground, just in case the Germans showed up. I stationed two Scugnizzi by the front door to alert us if any soldiers approached or if any Scugnizzi came with information.

"What the hell are the Nazis doing?" Benito asked.

"It's not good, whatever it is."

"Let's go after them," Giacomo said angrily.

"No!" I waved my arms emphatically. "There are more than a hundred heavily armed soldiers."

Forenzo arrived, breathless. "I got five Scugnizzi to follow them. They'll report back here."

"Excellent." I realized Forenzo had been with Russo in the piazza and now here I was dressed as myself. "Russo told me how brave you were in the piazza, Forenzo. With my Brother Luigi's help, the Prince has gone to meet with some of the other Partisans."

"I'm glad he's all right."

"Forenzo, I want you to go through the underground and call on Aldo at City Hall. Ask him if he knows anything, or if he can help us in any way."

I opened the entrance to the underworld. Forenzo held up a fist, signifying unity, and then disappeared down the stairs.

I sent another Scugnizzo to contact the Partisan Firecracker to see if he knew anything, or if there was any way we could help if he and his men were plotting an attack against the Germans.

We still hadn't come up with any plan by the time Forenzo returned. "Aldo doesn't know anything, either. Since the Italian surrender to the Allies, the Germans have ju . . . just taken over the city."

"I want to kill every fucking Nazi in sight," Georgio shouted.

A half-hour later, the Scugnizzo returned with news from the Partisan. "Firecracker said they followed them but they couldn't attack. Too many Germans, plus they have an armored vehicle."

We stayed awake trying to formulate a strategy, but nothing seemed viable. Early in the morning one of the Scugnizzi returned to the house with information. "The Nazis led thousands of men out of the city northeast on Arenacci. Along the way, stragglers and those attempting to escape were shot and left along the road."

I gasped. "Dear God!"

"It was midnight before the Nazis let them stop and rest. After a couple hours of sleep on the roadside, they resumed their march. The soldiers don't provide them food or water. Just marching."

"*Bastardos!*" Benito said.

"What about Antonio, Carlo, and Fast Talk?" I asked.

"Don't know. No one could get close enough."

We continued our anxious vigil. Around noon, another Scugnizzo returned. "They continue marching north. Dozens of men collapsed from lack of water. I overheard a soldier say in German, 'I'll be glad to be rid of this Italian scum—bunch of weaklings.'"

"Dear Mother of God, they're going to kill them all!" I moaned.

Mario made several obscene gestures, something I'd never seen him do before. But what else could we do? I opened a bottle of whisky and we drank ourselves into a stupor as we waited to hear the final pronouncement. Before the sun set, another messenger arrived. We all rose to our feet, preparing for the worst.

To our astonishment, Antonio walked through the door, followed by Carlo.

"You're all right! They're all right!" I shouted in disbelief, as I ran and embraced them both with a clamping hug. "Mother Mary," I said, crossing myself.

Everyone rushed to greet them. Antonio's body drooped from the ordeal and even Carlo's usual perfect constitution showed signs of fatigue.

"What happened?" Giacomo asked.

"It's beyond strange," Carlo said. "They marched us for twenty-four hours without water or food. They only allowed us a few winks of sleep."

"My asthma kicked in," interrupted Antonio. "But Carlo helped me. I might not have made it without him."

"Carlo to the rescue again." I patted his wide shoulder.

"Then," Carlo continued, "about noon today, the Germans stopped us. We thought it was all over. But they told us that those with proper identification would be freed. No explanation—nothing. They took our money and valuables, but then they let us go, even those without ID."

"Why?" I asked.

Carlo ran his hands over his weary, unshaven face and added, "I overheard one of the officers say in German that they planned to send us to a German labor camp, but no vehicles could be spared to transport us. A logistical fluke or we'd be knee deep in gunpowder in a munitions plant in Germany now."

"Dear Jesus. It's good to see you both," I said. "We didn't think we'd ever . . . Oh, God, it's good to see you." I embraced them again to make sure I wasn't dreaming.

"Unbelievable!" I shook my head. "How could they let it happen?"

"The headline is, 'Mussolini Liberated by the Nazis.'" Antonio quoted from the newspaper a Partisan had given him. "'After Mussolini's capture, the Italian Military Intelligence (SIM) continually moved him from one holding location to another in an attempt to keep him hidden from the watchful searching eyes of the Germans. For a month, the German Gestapo and the SIM have played a cat-and-mouse game of hide and seek. On September 12, the cat found the mouse. Eight gliders, carrying SS Colonel Otto Skorzeny and his men, landed near the resort of Grand Sasso and captured Mussolini without a single shot fired from his Italian guards.'"

"Incredible! Absolute lunacy," Carlo said in disbelief.

"Yes, it says the Germans caught them by surprise," Antonio said. "'The *Carabinieri* assault guards holding Mussolini refrained from fighting because the Germans had brought a Carabinieri general with them.

"'With their trophy in hand, Skorzeny's commandos still faced the problem of getting Mussolini off the mountaintop. They brought in a tiny Fiesler-Storch plane that they hoped could take off fast enough from the only available airstrip, a short downhill stretch of grass that ended at a precipice.

"'Mussolini, a pilot himself, was leery of the plan, especially when Skorzeny insisted on stuffing his six-foot-seven body into the tiny plane along with the pilot and Il Duce. Overloaded, the plane bounced along the grass, hit a rock, dropped over the precipice, then gained altitude and flew to safety.'"

"The Nazis won't go quietly," Carlo said.

Later that day, with everyone still buzzing about their march from the piazza, an announcement came down from Colonel Scholl, the German commander running Napoli. All males between the ages of eighteen and thirty-three were required to report for mandatory labor in two weeks. Evidently, the Germans had finally found transportation.

In response, the men of Napoli disappeared from the streets altogether and hid in the bowels of the city.

Surprisingly, German soldiers didn't search them out. The Germans faced bigger problems as the Allies continued to push Nazi forces back along the coast. They were now close enough to the city for us to hear artillery fire.

But there was a down side. As the Germans became increasingly preoccupied with the Allied dogs nipping at the heels, the city began disintegrating. Soon it was an unlivable place, with conditions that made the previous three years seem like paradise.

One day the running water, something everyone had taken for granted since the time of the Romans, stopped, which forced people to draw the vital liquid from one of the three fountains around the city that continued to dribble. Electric power and telephones had been out for weeks. Trash multiplied along every street, and the smell of decomposing garbage mixed with the putrid tang of rotting flesh that welled from under the collapsed buildings. The stench saturated one's skin. Flies and mosquitoes delighted in the decay and swarmed in dense clouds, making it difficult to breathe without ingesting their tart bodies.

From my Partisan contacts, I knew that the British Eighth Army and America's Fifth now pounded German positions to force them north, toward Napoli. But no ground was gained easily. The Germans used the rough terrain to make every Allied step one of pain and death. The Nazi defenders destroyed everything that could be used by the Allies as they retreated. On one seventeen-mile stretch of road, the Germans blew up twenty-five major bridges. Just as bad, constant rain and mud made mother nature the Allies' second enemy.

The Nazis prepared Napoli for the Allied arrival. Kesselring ordered his Tenth Army, which held Napoli, to remove all the machinery from the Alfa Romeo plant as well as from all other factories in the city. The Germans demolished every railroad track, train switch, power plant, phone line, sewer, and water main. They confiscated every remaining bus, truck, car, motorcycle, and homemade motorized vehicle in the city.

Day and night, explosions blasted away the face of Napoli. Word spread that the Germans planned, before the Allied arrival, to demolish every building in the city except for museums and churches. Apparently Field Marshall Kesslring specifically wanted to spare the museums, as someone quoted him saying, "I never realized what it was like to wage war in a museum until I came to Italy." But surprisingly, the German army's motor-transport actually contributed valuable gasoline and trucks to the Italian effort to evacuate its masterpieces to safety.

Some sections of the city never saw daylight; they remained shrouded under perpetual clouds of smoke. The Germans clearly planned to leave nothing for the Allies to liberate.

Since the Allied invasion, some Italian troops had changed sides and now fought the Germans. Rumors circulated that the German high command had ordered that no more Italian prisoners be taken alive. On the Greek island of Kefalonia, 5,170 Italian soldiers were gunned down even though they surrendered without resistance. The Italian prisoners already in the Germans' charge were shipped from Greece in overcrowded vessels not properly marked as prisoner-of-war transports. British and American planes sank the ships, and the Germans refused to initiate a rescue. This caused the death of another 13,288 Italians.

Hitler reinstated Mussolini's power, as head of a new Italian fascist government in the North, but this time the once-revered leader received no cheers from his subjects.

On the September 25 deadline, less than a hundred men in Napoli complied with the German order to report for forced labor. That same day, the Nazis mounted a reprisal; they ordered anyone living within three-hundred meters of the harbor or shoreline to move to the inner city by the eight o'clock curfew that night. Tens of thousands took their few belongings with them and left their homes. Some families found refuge with relatives. Others camped in the street or moved to the underground.

All around the city, buildings burned. As I watched from my home on the hill, my eyes shrank from the series of bright flashes at the Hotel Excelsior, near the docks. The shock from the enormous blast hit me and buckled my legs. My ears rang from the explosion as the grand hotel collapsed into itself.

Carlo and Mario ran up to see what had happened.

"For hundreds of years, foreign dignitaries and royalty from around the world have stayed at the Excelsior," Carlo said as a quaver ran through him.

"It only took the Nazis a few seconds to turn it into rubble," I said.

Before the dust settled at the Excelsior, two more explosions erupted along the Via Partenope. The equally famous Vesuvio and Santa Lucia hotels sank to the ground. Smaller charges continued to pop by the docks as the Nazis blew up building after building along the evacuated shoreline.

Forenzo sprinted up the hill. "I know a secret! I know a secret!"

"Tell us."

"The armory . . . the Italian Army armory still holds weapons."

"How do you know?" I asked.

"I snuck in. Look!" Forenzo produced a rifle from under his coat. "There are many weapons and no one is guarding it."

Carlo and I exchanged knowing looks.

"Good boy, Forenzo," I said. "I want you to find one of the Partisans—Firecracker, Count Sureshot, Fast Talk. Tell them to have their men meet us at the armory. Now, go!"

Carlo, Mario, and I headed toward the armory, less than a mile away. I decided not to change into my Russo persona; there was no time.

As we walked down the hill, the chaos in the city became more apparent. A young man raced across the street in front of us; behind him a German soldier rounded the corner, aimed his rifle and fired. The man fell face down in the street, his blood painting the asphalt red. The soldier saw us, directed his weapon toward us, and shouted, *"Halt!"*

The crack of a rifle shot echoed down the street and the soldier toppled over. I looked up to the rooftop and saw a citizen waving to us with his rifle. The three of us returned a thankful gesture as we hurried down the street.

We peered around the corner and saw a group of fifteen Nazi soldiers conducting a house-to-house search. They dragged men from their houses and forced them into transport trucks. One man struggled as soldiers pulled him into the street and searched him. When they found a revolver in his jacket, they shot him in the head.

On the ready, Carlo and Mario held their pistols under their coats.

"This is too dangerous. Let's take the underground," Carlo suggested.

"It's only a few more blocks," I said.

Suddenly, armed only with brooms and sticks, women and old men rushed the German soldiers. Startled by the attack, the Nazis jumped back into their trucks and drove off, leaving behind the able-bodied men they had rounded up.

"No one cares anymore that the Germans carry machine guns and have tanks," Carlo said with pride.

We were nearing the armory when several huge blasts knocked us back against a building. A second later, a row of huge cargo cranes collapsed into the harbor and fresh clouds of smoke drifted high into the sky.

We hurried on and finally reached the armory. Through a gap in the fence, we looked into the courtyard. No sign of anyone. A shiver ran up my back at the suspicious calm. Carlo motioned for Mario to scale the six-foot stone wall. Despite his hefty size, his strength allowed him to easily shimmy over the fence and push open the metal gate. Carefully, we approached the side door of the building. Carlo pressed his ear to the door and listened before pulling on the handle. The door swung open.

Inside, five long rows of neatly stacked racks filled with rifles stood before us, with ammunition piled high along the wall.

"How can this be?" I gasped.

"Maybe the Germans have forgotten an Italian Army ever existed," Carlo suggested.

The sound of footsteps came from outside. Mario and Carlo drew their weapons and we crouched behind the racks. Near the door, several men whispered to each other in Italian.

"It's Forenzo," I said. "Forenzo, in here!"

Forenzo entered with Fast Talk, Count Sureshot, and a dozen more Partisans.

"We just destroyed a German armored car!" Fast Talk babbled. "People are shouting, 'Insurrection!'"

"The battle has begun," said Count Sureshot.

Firecracker gaped at the weapons. "Look at all this!"

"We need to hurry and distribute them around the city if this uprising is to be successful," I told them.

"We've got to stop the Nazis before they destroy any more of the city," Sureshot said.

"Are you Signore Russo's wife?" Fast Talk asked.

"Yes."

"Thanks for sending Forenzo to tell us about the armory," Sureshot said in his dignified tone. "I think this is the firepower we need to drive the Nazis out."

"We'll distribute the weapons around the city," Fast Talk rattled. "We have thousands of loyal Partisans now. We should have a clearing-house for information: German positions, distribution of weapons."

"I can do that from our house on the hill," I said.

"Where's your husband?" Fast Talk asked.

"Out in the streets, doing what he can to stop the Nazis." I turned to my young helper. "Forenzo, get the word out to the Scugnizzi to report to me at the house. I want German troop movements and strength, as well as supply needs for the citizens battling them. I'll also have a great vantage point up on the hill to see what's going on around much of the city."

"Yes, Signora," Forenzo said. "For months, my friends and I have been stealing gasoline from German cars and trucks. We were selling it on the black market; now we'll make it into Molotov cocktails."

"Be careful," Fast Talk cautioned, before turning to his men. "Okay, let's start dispensing these weapons."

Mario and Carlo escorted me back to my house through the underground. Both my brothers and Russo's, along with others from our organization, were there stocking up on weapons.

"Please be careful," I urged Giacomo and Antonio, as I hugged them. They nodded before heading out with Benito and Alonzo. Carlo and Mario watched them take off into the streets.

Carlo turned to me. "Carina, would you be . . ."

"Go ahead, Carlo. Mario, you too. I'll be fine." I hugged my two guardians and they ran off to catch up with the rest of our family. I didn't want them to go, but knew they needed this moment. I prayed to the Virgin Mary. We'd all need her protection to survive the next twenty-four hours.

Chapter 43

FINALLY LOVE, FINALLY CAUGHT

Holding a shotgun, I looked out over Napoli through the dining room window. All around the city, more and more flashes of gunfire showed where citizens had taken up arms against our Nazi occupiers. Scugnizzi came with information and weapons gathered from around the city and left with my reports on German positions and strength to give to the Partisans.

The Germans quickly abandoned their plan to destroy the city block by block as they encountered strong resistance and were forced to constantly defend themselves. When they tried to counterattack, the citizen soldiers disappeared into the mysterious maze of back streets, alleys, and the underworld. If the Nazis retreated in their trucks, they often were stopped by roadblocks of rubble, burning trash, or overturned trolley cars. Live or die, everyone seemed ready to stand up to the Nazis and prevent the leveling of their city. Ten-year-old boys, ex-soldiers from the Italian Army, mothers, and eighty-year-old grandfathers fought side by side.

From my position at the window, I caught a glimpse of someone rushing up to the house. I grabbed my shotgun and peered out. The man wore a dark coat and hat. He pounded on the front door. I cocked the gun.

"It's Domenico, Carina!" He pulled back his hat. I unbolted the door and opened it, and clamped him in a tight embrace.

"I'm leaving for the North," he said.

"Why? We—we're finally ridding ourselves of the Nazis."

"SS troops have been rounding up Jews in Rome, Milan, Florence, and other northern cities and sending them to concentration camps in the north."

"Why must *you* go?"

"The Nazis are abducting Jews in clear sight of the Vatican, Carina, and still the Pope stays neutral. He's convinced that Stalin's godless Communism is a greater evil than Hitler's Fascism. But how can he still have nothing to say? I've got to do what I can to help the Jews."

"Don't leave!" I pleaded.

"Some people within the Church want me dead for speaking out against the Pope. The Nazis may be after me, as well. I must go."

I clutched at him. "Why must you always be the one to help? Stay here."

"People are suffering."

"Where will you go?"

"To Assisi. The padre at the monastery there, at the instruction of his bishop, has found homes and hiding places for hundreds of Jews from Trieste. He hides many of the refugees at the monastery and dresses them as monks and nuns to hide them during Nazi searches. 'Preach the gospel at all times, if necessary use words,' St Francis of Assisi taught us."

I kissed Domenico and ran my fingers through his wavy hair. "Stay," I whispered. "We can find a way to be together now."

"Carina, you'll always be my love, but we've chosen different paths," he said.

"Domenico, you own my heart."

He gazed deep into me. My heart thrilled to see so much love in those eyes. "You're intoxicating," he murmured. He seemed to see the person I was deep within my essence, not the harsh person I had become. With a sweep of his hand, he buried his face in my hair, brushed it over his cheek and breathed deeply into it. A rush of exhilaration filled me as his lips kissed their way down my neck.

"Domenico, so many times thoughts of you have gotten me through the night."

"Every day, no matter how difficult the circumstances, I can always find happiness by thinking of your lovely face. I've never loved another."

"Is it finally our turn to be happy together?"

He smiled sadly as he ran his hand through my hair again. "I wish it were so."

"Let us enjoy happiness for this moment, then. Some memories can be enough to last a lifetime. Can't they?"

He smiled, and I kissed him with all my soul. Years of repressed desire bubbled up within me. Taking his hand, I led him to a nearby servant's bedroom. With the chaos around us, this seemed the wrong time to make love. But for us, no right time would ever come. Soon Domenico would be gone.

Once inside, we fell back against the door and his chest pressed against me. Feeling his weight sent a wave of desire through me. My fingers followed his eyebrows.

"Oh, Domenico."

He kissed my eyes, my cheeks, my shoulder.

I took his hand and placed it on my breast. "Can you feel my heart beating so fast?"

His mouth widened into a smile. Reverently, he undid the buttons on my dress and let the garment fall to the floor. With slow precision, he pulled my slip down until it drifted around my ankles like a silken cloud. He looked at me as if memorizing every part of me. Not even Russo with all of his skills as a lover had ever made me feel this way—so uninhibited, so loved.

He touched my face and whispered into my ear, "Carina, gazing at you makes me believe in the beauty of Heaven."

After taking in a shaky breath, I began to undress him. I hesitated when I reached his frock. "It's all right." He pulled the robe over his head and tossed it aside. "It's only cloth."

The key-of-dreams necklace that I'd given him dangled on his chest. He had nearly worn it smooth from rubbing.

"You see," he said, "your heart is always close to mine."

I smiled, happy to know I'd been so much in his thoughts. I noticed a little scar on his shoulder and traced it with my finger. "From the time you fell out of the tree on the cliff above our beach back home?"

Domenico nodded. "A pleasant reminder of some of the happiest days of my life." He moved to kiss me. His lips pressed against mine and his energy surged into me.

Suddenly, he scooped me up, lifted me into his arms and placed me onto the bed. His kisses were as wild and frantic as my heartbeat.

Ever so softly he ran his hand over my breasts, down my abdomen, and lower still. "Domenico, Domenico," I whispered. Our kisses grew more anxious and intense. I felt as if I were floating above the bed.

Suddenly he was inside of me, where I had always desired him. From deep within me, a moan escaped.

"Carina, you make me burn," he said, his voice husky.

He started moving slowly, like gentle waves brushing over the sand. Pleasure filled me until it seemed as if my body glowed and saturated the room with heat and light. I couldn't maintain myself any longer. "Oh, *dio glorious*," I said as I shuddered and gripped Domenico's shoulders.

"Carina," he cried as he climaxed. "*Dio bello nel cielo!* Beautiful God in the sky." He collapsed on top of me.

I realized he had tears on his cheek.

"Domenico?" I wrapped my arms around him. "What is it?"

Propping his weight on his hands, he said, "I can't believe that I almost missed this incredible gift from God because of the Church. Now I know my decision to leave it is right. God couldn't want us to deny ourselves such a thing." He smiled. "If this is our one moment to cherish, Carina, then remember how beautiful it was, and how very much I love you."

"I could not forget it."

While gazing into each other's eyes, grins formed and we started to laugh. After so many years of dreaming of it, I felt Domenico's heart beating against my body. He wrapped me in his arms and I never wanted him to move.

The echo of wood splintering ripped through the hall. We jumped out of bed. The clap of soldiers' boots thundered across the hardwood floors outside the bedroom. Cracking open the door, I peered out and saw half a dozen Nazi soldiers rushing into the house. "We want them alive!" Major Kappel shouted. The soldiers scattered through the house.

"We've got to get to Russo's study," I whispered. "We can escape to the underground from there." Quickly, we slipped into our clothes.

I peered down the hallway; it was empty. We hurried to Russo's study, where I pulled back the big map on the wall and led Domenico into the stairwell to the underworld. "One second." I rushed to Russo's desk and grabbed my pistol from the drawer.

The door burst open.

"*Halt!*" a soldier ordered, and aimed his rifle at my head. I let go of the gun and raised my arms. "*Sie ist innen hier!* She's in here," he shouted over his shoulder. Domenico stood motionless behind the map hiding the stairwell.

Several more soldiers rushed in, followed by Major Kappel, his forehead bleeding. As I looked at the soldiers, I noticed they were all disheveled—not the usual pristine uniforms we'd come to expect from the Nazis. It made me happy to see that the insurrection in Naples was taking its toll.

"Rough day, Major?" I said.

"Signora Russo, we understand your husband has been busy help-ing Jews take flight."

"You know that's not true. He's not capable of—"

"Evidently, you look remarkably like him in an overcoat and hat."

Chapter 44

LOVE LOST

Major Kappel threw me against the wall and waved his pistol in my face.

"I'll let you judge how serious I am. You and the priest, Domenico, have been busy bees helping Jews flee the country." He jabbed me in the stomach with the barrel of his pistol, and I doubled over. "I don't like being made the fool. Your family isn't as trustworthy as you think. One of them preferred to save his own life more than the lives of Jews. You would've been wise to do the same."

"None of my family would—"

"Oh, but one did. I'll let you puzzle over which one. He needed to bargain for his life when we caught him stealing German supplies earlier today. He directed us to the hiding place of several Jews. From there, we found information that you and Domenico were the ones helping them."

"I don't believe you."

"Oh, we didn't even need to persuade him. He seemed happy to help. I must admit, spending time and resources rounding up Jews seems a terrible waste of energy. What threat are Jews to the New World Order of the Third Reich? Nevertheless, I'm loyal to my country. I have orders to carry out. We all follow such dictates in life in order to keep the world running with precision, don't we?"

"Go ahead and kill me. Get it over with," I said.

"Kill you? You're a wealth of information about how the Jews escape Italy. No, we're taking you with us now that we're relocating to Rome."

"I won't help you!" I shouted.

"Maybe, maybe not. We'll see."

I started to fidget. At first the major didn't notice, so I exaggerated the motion.

"What's wrong with you?"

"I need to go to the bathroom."

He squinted at me, but I continued to squirm.

"Oh, for God's sake!" Major Kappel exclaimed. "Why do women always need to use the toilet at the most inopportune times?"

He and several soldiers followed me to the bathroom. One of the soldiers rummaged through the drawers, under the sink, even inside the toilet bowl, I guess to make sure I didn't have a weapon stored inside.

Finally the major let me go in. I closed the door, and then made a retching sound to cover the noise I made opening the panel in the wall. The bathroom shared a common wall with Russo's study, and I shimmied through the secret opening and I rushed back to the stairwell. Domenico was still waiting there. I grabbed a lantern and we raced together down the stairs into the darkness. From behind came the sounds of soldiers breaking down the bathroom door. *"Gottfluch Schweinhunt!"* Major Kappel roared.

Flashlight beams shot down the stairwell, followed by shouts and thundering footsteps.

"They're not far behind," Domenico said.

"They don't know the underground like I do." My heart pounded wildly, but this time it was for fear of Domenico's safety, not my own. We reached the bottom of the stairs and I led Domenico to the hall on the right.

A hundred paces back, the soldiers' flashlight beams struck along the stone walls. They fired a volley as we ran down the ancient aqueduct. The blasts sparked brightly and lit up the hall. Bullets whizzed past my head. The thunderous discharge reverberated through the caverns.

I turned down a hallway and pulled Domenico into an area that contained adjoining corridors. We crisscrossed through a maze of halls.

"Should we stop and hide?" he asked.

"Too risky." I heard the soldiers, Major Kappel barking orders.

We continued running until we entered the large cavern, where I stopped to catch my breath. I found my gaze drawn to the Roman painting on the wall depicting Caesar defeating the German barbarians "I've got a plan," I said.

"Lead on."

We took a turn and went through several halls ending in high archways before entering the *Cimitero delle Fontanelle,* the underground cemetery. As light from the lantern struck the human skulls tucked into their chambers in the wall, they looked disturbed by our noisy presence. A group of shocked shouts came from behind us as the Germans entered the chamber of the dead.

We entered a passageway that split in two directions. One stone archway read, "Mater Dei Hill—Holy Mary of the Carmelites." This was the exit. The hallway sloped upward toward the surface. After fifty paces it ended at a large door. We pushed it, but it didn't budge. The sound of running soldiers drew closer. A rifle fired at us from down the hall. The soldier yelled out, "*Hierhin gekommen! Comenzi!* This way, come."

With all our strength, Domenico and I propelled ourselves against the door. It creaked open and daylight struck us. We ran into the courtyard of the small church. The sound of gunfire echoed through the courtyard from the top of the wall that surrounded the church and from the street on the other side of it.

Ten Partisans were stationed at the top of walls, as the Scugnizzi had informed me less than an hour before.

"Down here! Down here!" I shouted.

Several familiar faces—Fast Talk, Count Sureshot, Forenzo—peered over the top of the ten-foot wall into the courtyard.

"Look, it's Carina!" shouted Forenzo, his unmistakable thick mop of hair blowing in the wind.

I pointed at the door to the underground. "The Gestapo's right behind us."

The Partisans trained their weapons into the courtyard as Domenico and I ran for cover behind the large statue of the Virgin Mary in the courtyard. A moment later the Nazis pushed open the door and rushed into the courtyard. Half a dozen of them dropped to the ground, wounded or dead, under Partisan fire. Major Kappel ignored the men on the wall and headed straight toward Domenico and me. From the wall Forenzo fired a shot, and the major fell.

The remaining Germans returned fire at the Partisans on top of the wall. I was horrified to see Forenzo slump forward and topple into the courtyard.

"No! No!" I gasped and started toward him, but Domenico held me back.

A second Partisan volley dropped the remaining Nazis, and I rushed to Forenzo. His shirt was soaked with blood and he struggled to speak. I drew him close, and he whispered into my ear. "I never told anyone . . . no one. I knew your secret, Signora Russo. I knew you were the Prince. I knew, but I never told anyone." He looked at me with adoring eyes.

I ran my fingers through his thick hair. "You've always been such a good boy, Forenzo. I feel like you're my own son."

A sputter escaped his lips.

"No Forenzo, no! Don't go!" I felt him take a last breath, and his body sagged in my arms. Once again I cursed God. I scolded him for not sending raining thunderbolts down on the Nazis long ago.

Above all, I felt guilty I hadn't done more to protect this noble, loyal spirit from the harshness of the city. Forenzo deserved a better life than the one he'd lived.

Domenico helped Fast Talk and the Count climb down into the courtyard. He walked over and knelt beside me. "I'm sorry."

"He was such a sweet boy," I said in a cold voice, "good to his core. Such a difficult life. He didn't even know his own birthday, he'd been on the street so long." I needed to cry, but no tears escaped my hardened eyes.

"This war takes many good people," Domenico said. He motioned toward the Partisans, who anxiously waited to continue their mission. "They said they can help get me to the North."

"Must I lose everyone I care about?"

"There's no time; I must go."

"Will I ever see you again?"

Domenico ran his hand along my cheek and smiled. "Some day, Carina, when peace comes."

He leaned over and kissed me. I wanted to hold him and not let him go, but I had to conserve my strength to free him. We exchanged mournful smiles before I watched him disappear into the streets of Napoli with the Partisans. War brings great loss to everyone, but the emptiness it leaves in your soul is unbearable.

After several days of insurrection, the German commanders abandoned their plans to demolish the city. With the Allies advancing ever more strongly up the coast, the once arrogant Nazis retreated—exhausted and humiliated, their spirits broken. I understood the grief that filled their faces, but I blamed them for mine.

From the high window of my house I watched the enemy drive past in vehicles filled beyond capacity with sullen, used-up soldiers. They had commandeered anything with wheels: buses, tractors, horse-drawn carriages, oxcarts.

After the dismal parade of vehicles passed, the dirty-faced and bloodied German soldiers of lesser means—unshaven, in filthy tattered uniforms, even barefoot—walked on foot behind them, quietly dragging themselves along with no hint of formation or military discipline left.

It was an amazing sight. Just a few years before, the Nazis had arrived with a bounce in their goose-step, feeling superior to everyone. Now they retreated with their heads hung low and faces full of fear, saying not a word.

Napoli fell ominously quiet; the German departure had left a void. Hours passed without any movement apart from the plumes of smoke drifting into the sky from all around the city. In its 2500-year history, I couldn't imagine that the city had ever been so still, so quiet, so lifeless.

I sat with my brothers and Russo's family, looking out our dining room window. On a day like today, words seemed meaningless. The whole city sat waiting for its new future to begin. We watched for the arrival of the Allies, but we waited for more than that. Maybe those of us who had survived the cruelty of Nazis, the bombings, the hunger, and the despair were waiting for a rebirth, a resurrection of spirit.

In the quiet atmosphere my mind drifted to what Major Kappel had told me about one of my brothers betraying me. Could it be true, or had Kappel lied to create distrust within my family? If the latter, it was working; his words burdened me with a cloud of uneasiness.

I couldn't help thinking about Sergio. He was my brother, and he had intended to not only betray me, but kill me.

A dog bark broke the silence, and then the expectant hush returned.

Chapter 45

REUNITED WITH TRAGEDY

"There!" shouted Antonio, pointing to the south end of the city. A faint smile crept onto his face. I strained to see, but the smoke from hundreds of burning building carcasses drifted into the sky in dark pillars that obstructed my view. Finally, a slight movement became visible. A convoy of khaki green Allied tanks and trucks was entering the city.

It had taken the Allies three weeks to push the Germans the thirty miles from their invasion point on the beaches of Salerno to our city, a trip of less than an hour by train.

The civilian attitude toward the arrival of the Americans seemed one of stunned indifference. No cheering in the streets, no confetti. Like our group, the rest of the weary citizens of Napoli peered out from behind ragged curtains and blown-out windows.

Debris from demolished buildings blocked most of the city's two hundred narrow streets. From our house on the hill, we watched as American tanks and heavy equipment slowly pushed through one street at a time to reopen the clogged arteries of the city.

A platoon of American soldiers passed by our house. They appeared surprised that no one greeted them in the streets. Both the liberator and the liberated seemed unsure what to expect from one another.

Most of the Allied troops passed right through the city, chasing after the German Army. Three days later, they reached the Volturno River, fifteen miles north of Napoli, where German forces had withdrawn behind the river's natural barrier. Both sides stopped to regroup.

With the city secure, the Americans and British set out to resurrect Napoli. It seemed an impossible task.

Napoli had clearly been a key objective for the Allies because of its strategic harbor, but the retreating Germans had sunk every single ship in the port, adding to those already destroyed by Allied bombings. More than 130 scuttled ships now clogged the port: ocean liners, tankers, destroyers, tugboats, and trawlers. For good measure, the Germans had dumped damaged locomotives and trucks, cranes, ammunition, and mines into the harbor. Along the docks, piles of smoldering coal burned so stubbornly that the American Army Corp of Engineers could find no way to extinguish them. Every pier, wharf, grain elevator, dockside crane, and office building at the water's edge was gone. The once pristine port now resembled a giant layer cake of wreckage frosted with a thick smoldering topping of oil scum.

The Germans had destroyed all transportation in the city, telephone lines, electric power lines, the power plant, the sewers, the water system, and hundreds of buildings. Would Napoli ever return to the modern world, or would it forever remain in a war-imposed Stone Age condition?

Now that the Allies had taken the South from the Germans, it seemed safe to visit my children.

Antonio and I took the organization's only truck that hadn't been destroyed or confiscated by the Germans and headed south. A multitude of checkpoints and patrols inspected the vehicle and our papers along the way, but unlike the Germans, the British and Americans weren't confiscating vehicles.

After several days we made it to Cosenza, where we rented four horses and left the truck as collateral. On this warm September night, we rode with supplies to the remote farmhouse, which seemed oddly quiet as we approached.

"Hello! Mother's here!" I called as Antonio and I dismounted. There was no sign of anyone.

"It's Mommy!" I called again, running into the house. It was empty.

A feeling of dread filled me and then the cabinet by the sink inched open.

"Mommy!" Adriana swung open the door and burst out. Tears dripped down her cheeks. Behind her, my other two little ones emerged from the cabinet.

I squatted and gathered them to me. "I'm so sorry it took so long to come and see you. The war made it impossible. Why were you all inside the cabinet?"

"We were afraid when we saw someone coming toward the cabin," Adriana explained soberly.

"I wasn't afraid," Giorgio said.

"I'm sure you've all been very brave," Antonio assured them.

Lucia still hadn't said anything; she clung to her sister's dress and looked at me with apprehension. I thought back, and couldn't believe it had been more than four months since I'd seen my little *angeli*.

"Where is Auntie Gianina?"

"It was terrible, Mommy," Adriana whispered.

"What? What happened?"

"Auntie Gianina . . ." she began, and then paused, starting to cry. "Months ago, a German soldier came here. He . . . he did terrible things to her, but he didn't see the three of us. We hid in the cabinet."

Giorgio produced sand from his pocket. "We all held on to the magic sand you gave us from the beach. The sand you said would make us invisible."

"And it did," Adriana went on. "The soldier searched the house, but he didn't find us." She took me by the hand and led me outside, with Lucia still clinging to her skirt. Antonio put his arm around Giorgio. "After the soldier left we came out of the cabinet to check on Gianina. She was . . . she was . . . Oh, Mommy!"

Adriana walked out to the porch and pointed to a mound of dirt beside the house, and then buried her face in my bosom. A cross made with two branches stuck out from the top of the grave. The spring grass that covered it had already turned brown from the summer heat.

I went to the spot and knelt down. I pounded the earth. Tears attempted to fill my eyes, but I held them back. With so many people to grieve for, if I allowed myself to cry even once, I'd never stop.

"My dear Gianina," I gasped. "How can this be?" I forced my fingers into the soil, yearning to reach her.

I struggled to my feet and pulled my children into a tight embrace. "Oh, my little *angeli*. What you've been through!"

I had the children mount one of the horses, and we left the sanctuary that had proven to be no safer than the front lines after all. We took nothing but the goat with us—no reminders. By sunset, we had arrived back at the truck and headed back toward Napoli.

"Where's father?" Giorgio asked suddenly.

"Well, he wanted to come, but he . . . he's . . ."

"He's dead," said Adriana coldly. "Isn't he, Mommy? Dead from the war, like Aunt Gianina." The pain in her voice surged into me and seemed to infect my blood. It was a feeling I never wanted to experience again.

But I didn't know what to tell her.

Chapter 46

REBUILDING

Finally I told my little ones that their father was away on business, but he wanted to see them and would return as soon as he could. Of course, by now I knew it was unlikely Russo would ever return. But I wanted to protect our children from the tragedy of their father's condition as long as possible. They had already lived through too much pain.

By the time we reached Napoli, the American Army Corp of Engineers had started to resuscitate the city; the streets had been cleared, the sewers repaired, and the aqueduct was functioning. They had also set up an ingenious makeshift power station using the generators of three captured Italian submarines linked through a trolley station.

The American and British salvage crews had also made miraculous progress in the harbor. Only four days after the Nazis decimated the port, the Americans unloaded their first cargo ship along the repaired docks. Miraculously, within two weeks, the Army engineers made it possible for American supply ships to unload thirty-five hundred tons of cargo a day. By the end of a month that amount doubled, returning the harbor to prewar capacity.

Despite the furious pace of rebuilding, Napoli was still a wasteland. One million Neapolitans depended upon the Allies for food and other basic necessities.

With Naples, as the Americans called it, and the Foggia airfield under their control, the Allied Operation AVALANCHE had come to an end. To achieve this goal the Allies suffered 12,500 casualties—two thousand killed, seven thousand wounded, and thirty-five hundred missing.

With the city secure, the Allies turned their attention north, using Naples as a silo to supply the voracious consumption of the war beast. And I asked myself, *What would Russo do in this situation?*

Through Aldo's influence at city hall I arranged a meeting with an American supply officer, Colonel Berry. Carlo, Antonio, and I headed down to the harbor. On our way, we noticed a large public building with eight American trucks parked in front. Soldiers streamed into the large building. It didn't appear to be any kind of military installation, so we went inside to satisfy our curiosity.

Hundreds of soldiers, each carrying a tin of rations, stood in lines inside the warehouse-sized room. It looked like a rush for tickets at a train station. One GI approached me and offered me his can. "How about it?" he asked. Unclear what he was asking, I shook my head. He moved on.

We walked to the side of the lines to see what everyone was waiting for in front of the room. A long row of women who appeared to be housewives sat arm's length apart. Their dresses were bunched up around their thighs and a pile of ration tins of varying heights rose next to each of them. It became clear what a tin of food bought. These family providers kept absolutely still and said nothing, their faces expressionless—no solicitation, no enticement. Like a token for a rollercoaster, men deposited a tin, enjoyed a minute of violent action, and, without an utterance, slipped away from the amusement ride.

I motioned to leave and we returned to the fresh air outside. It seemed cleansing after the base smell of the makeshift brothel.

We arrived at Major Berry's office. "The Colonel will be with you shortly," said the clerk in the reception room. I understood his words. Carlo spoke English well, and I had learned a little from him.

We took a seat near two Italian Army majors. They were discussing the Allied attack on Italy, and it sounded as though they had been privy to information that was no longer classified. The three major Allied powers had found it difficult to agree on a plan to attack Germany. Churchill urged expansion of Allied operations in the Mediterranean to keep the Germans away from British soil. Roosevelt wanted to undertake a massive buildup of men and equipment for a cross-channel invasion of France. Soviet leader Joseph Stalin, preoccupied with the battle for Stalingrad, demanded an immediate military assault to draw German forces out of Russia.

The Allied leaders had finally agreed to invade Sicily—Operation HUSKY—in order to secure the Mediterranean.

"Major Berry is ready to see you," said the clerk. He escorted us down the hall into an office and then retreated.

Major Berry, a giant of a man with a ruddy complexion and a constant grin on his face, greeted us.

"Sorry to keep ya'll waitin', Mrs. Rusto. I'm Major Berry. How can I help ya?" His accent was so heavy, I wasn't sure he was speaking the same English I had picked up from Carlo. He exchanged a powerful handshake with both of us.

"We're in the trade business," Carlo told him, just as I had asked him to. "If you have any excess supplies you're looking to sell, we'd be most happy to handle the transaction for you."

"Sorry. I just don't have anything for ya." The major rose and showed us out.

"Well," I told Carlo as we stood in the street, "he's not the only supply officer in the U.S. military."

To my surprise, later that day, Russo received a call from Vito Genovese. I answered it in Russo's voice. I knew of Vito's reputation in the Sicilian mafia, although he had grown up in America from the age of fifteen. Suspected of murder in New York, he had fled to Italy in 1937. Our organization had run into his a few times, as his operation included Napoli. His group was very powerful and entirely ruthless.

Genovese requested a meeting with Russo. I saw no choice but to agree. What did a man as powerful as Genovese want with Russo? I felt apprehensive about meeting with him in my disguise . . . but what choice did I have?

What choice did I *ever* have?

Chapter 47

THE NEW MASTERS ARE AS CRAZY AS THE OLD

The next morning, Carlo and I met with Genovese. I was carefully dressed as Russo. This meeting terrified me more than any other had. Vito Genovese was not just some Russo lieutenant who could be dealt with if I made a slip-up.

Genovese walked in alone, with not even a single body guard. He seemed puzzled by the dim lights in the house, but made no comment as he showed me a mimeograph of a letter from one of the American commanding officers. It read:

> The bearer of this introduction, Mr. Vito Genovese, is an American citizen. Mr. Genovese met me and acted as my interpreter for over a month. He accepted no pay; paid his own expenses; worked day and night and rendered most valuable assistance to the Allied Military Government. This statement is freely made in an effort to express my appreciation for the unselfish services of this man.

"I understand you want to move American goods," Genovese told me.

"Yes." I was surprised that he had learned of our visit with the American supply officer.

"I am in control of all such goods, but you have a respected organization and I would be most honored to have you distribute goods to the general population in your territory."

After a little negotiation, we worked out a deal where he would start us with a small supply of food rations. But within two weeks he realized we could handle most any quantity or type of goods, so our truck began pulling up to his distribution center south of the city every single day to pick up cigarettes, food, boots, military clothing, medicine, and other items to feed the black market's ravenous hunger.

Most people had prayed for the Allies to liberate Napoli. Their presence brought a sense of safety to a city filled with fear. The citizens no longer worried about executions in the street and forced labor camps. The Americans treated us more like an ally than an enemy.

Russo's men started to feel safe again, and with American goods to sell on the black market, they were making good money again, too. The problem is, when people aren't fearful, they're much harder to control.

I sensed increasing discontent not only amongst Russo's family, but from some of my own brothers as well. I felt unappreciated, as it had been no small accomplishment for me to get us and our organization safely through the Nazi era of the war. The problem was that these men just couldn't accept having a woman in charge. But I wasn't ready to relinquish power. I enjoyed building a strategy and executing it. I enjoyed being feared, just a little bit. I enjoyed seeing the money flow in. Moreover, I was still the only one cunning enough to run the operation, and I needed to prove that to everyone else.

And the proof would have to go through the Americans. The impoverished conditions experienced by the average Neapolitan hadn't improved much under Allied occupation. Citizens still had no food, no water, no salt, no sugar, no soap, no sewage disposal, no jobs, no money, and no hope.

One thing was available in abundance, though: typhus and smallpox claimed thousands of lives every month in families already overwhelmed by three years of grief and misery.

As if the city's deplorable conditions didn't provide enough to worry about, booby traps set by the retreating Nazis threatened thousands of structures and lives. Delayed-reaction bombs had been bricked into the walls of public buildings, and at least one detonated each day.

About a month after the German retreat, American Army officials received word that thousands of delayed-reaction devices were set to explode at two o'clock. The officers ordered an evacuation of the entire city. All one million residents retreated to the heights of Voermo, Fontanelle, and to the observatory. The city stood still below us for many hours, nothing moving except an occasional flock of birds.

Around four o'clock the order came for everyone to return to their homes; the scare had been just another rumor.

Later I heard that the Germans had left one lone soldier behind during their retreat. His mission was to give false information designed to disrupt the Americans as much as possible. At least one day had been wasted because of him.

Rumors of spies surfaced everywhere, and Allied Army Intelligence followed up on every accusation, even though most proved to be false. A mysterious stranger tinkering with a powerful radio transmitter turned out to be a man trying to tune in the BBC. An investigation of flashing code lights in the night proved to be some poor citizen holding a flashlight on the way to the cesspit in his backyard. Such accusations often stemmed from someone's vendetta against a neighbor.

The American commanders managed to create a few serious blunders of their own as well. Antonio approached one American GI about buying a watch. The soldier handed him a note printed in Italian. The message started out, "I'm not interested in your syphilitic sister." Every soldier had been issued this document by army headquarters; it was to be shown when approached by any Italian they believed was offering the services of a woman. The high command was apparently ignorant of the fact that such taboo remarks to Southern Italians instilled vendettas. Many soldiers who presented this note received a beating or worse.

Another ridiculous plan conceived by the Americans was implemented later that month. A Major Smith approached me through one of our whorehouses and presented me with an interesting example of American logic. Under the control of the Gestapo, our brothels had maintained strict medical supervision to halt the spread of syphilis. But this American officer said, "The operation objective is to locate prostitutes who have syphilis but register no outward signs of the said disease."

"Why would you want prostitutes with syphilis?" I asked.

"The second phase of 'Operation Bed Bug' will be to deploy said infected joy girls throughout Northern Italy to reduce the effectiveness of the German army, one soldier at a time."

I wondered if he'd thought this plan through. It seemed a total waste of time, and the Germans, with their strict inspections, would quickly thwart such an effort. "I'm sorry to disappoint you, but we don't employ diseased prostitutes." Nothing more was ever heard about this plan.

This isn't to say that prostitution didn't continue to run rampant in the city, and certainly some of the women had contracted a disease. Major Berry showed me a report from Army Intelligence that said nine out of ten Neapolitan women had lost their men to battle, prisoner-of-war camps, or to the ranks of the missing. According to the study, out of a nubile female population of 150,000, some 40,000 engaged in prostitution, selling the only thing they still possessed just to buy a meal.

Hunger wasn't the only discomfort experienced by Neapolitans. With the Allies occupying the city, we now suffered frequent bombings by the German Luftwaffe. After one terrible raid, I passed a bombed-out building where a long neat row of dead children had been placed in the street. Someone had rested new dolls in their arms. City workers continued to dig children out of the structure while the tears of professional mourners supplemented the weeping of the grieving families.

A large crowd ran through the streets yelling, "Give us peace! Give us peace!"

This All Souls Day, I had plenty of people to visit. The children and I went to the graves of Bruno and Forenzo, and said a prayer for Gianina and even Sergio. And we prayed for Russo.

"Mama, when is Papa coming home?" Adrianna asked as we left the cemetery.

"I don't know, my love," I said, glancing at Carlo. "Soon, I hope."

As worried as I was about my children's' future, I was also tormented by Domenico's absence from Napoli. Before he left for the North, I had gotten through many a day with the comfort of knowing he was nearby, at the Duomo. Now I worried about the Nazis uncovering his dangerous work in the North. I knew he was still at it because he continued to send Jewish families to me for help. I provided them housing and transportation. At least with the Americans in control, they found safety in the South.

In the North, the war continued its destructive path. Late in December, a Partisan attack dismantled a train carrying ammunition to Monte Cassino, killing five hundred German troops. The assault was just one of more than two thousand Partisan actions reported in 1943.

Under these circumstances, it amazed me that the Allies had the resources to set up the Sub-commission for Monuments, Fine Arts, and Archives. The MFAA briefed bomber crews and infantry commanders on monuments to avoid. The "Venus Fixers," as GIs referred to the MFAA, also helped Italian authorities trace lost or stolen works of art.

On the other side of the scale, the Allies could be horribly unfeeling. Nick, our Scugnizzo, showed up at my kitchen window one day with fresh blood staining much of his shirt.

He opened his left hand, revealing that one of his fingers was missing.

"Oh, Lord, how did this happen?" I wrapped the injury with a dish towel. I pulled the first aid kit out of the drawer and began to clean and bandage the wound.

He winced and bit his lip. "All I did was jump onto a British Army truck." A rash of missing fingers had been plaguing boys ever since the Allies' arrival. Hundreds of orphaned, half-starved boys found that the only way to survive was to jump into the back of Allied army trucks stopped in traffic and grab anything that wasn't clamped down. The Allies had chosen quick work with bayonets as their solution to the problem.

"Oh, dear God." I hugged him. "Why did you do it? You have plenty to eat; we make sure of that."

"I was showing some young homeless boys how to stay alive."

Chapter 48

FORMING THE CARTEL

On March 19, 1944, spring announced itself with the dramatic blossoming of Mount Vesuvius. A great cloud of smoke formed above the mountain and expanded all day long, until it seemed to reach to Heaven. At night you could see the orange glow of lava streams flowing down its side. Periodically, the crater exploded and fiery plumes of smoke burst out of the huge chimney. For days the mountain snowed gray ash onto Napoli.

On the fourth day, the erupting volcano still showed no signs of relenting. In fact, it had increased its violent rage. Lava ten meters deep covered half of the small town of San Sebastiano.

The eruption of Mount Vesuvius damaged the U.S. 340th Bombardment Group more than any previous German air raid. They lost all eighty-eight B-25 bombers in the attack of hot ash.

People worried that the volcano's destructive path would reach the streets of Napoli. But on the fifth day, Vesuvius began to subside. That same day, another kind of eruption hit in Rome; ten Partisans, university students posed as street cleaners, attacked a heavily armed column of SS police with a bomb. The attack left twenty-four dead Nazis in the cobblestone street, then additional Partisans fired on the remaining column of Germans, killing another nine.

The Nazi SS seized 335 men and teenagers. None were connected to the attack in any way, yet they were taken to the caves at Ardea where the SS completed Hitler's standard method of reprisal by executing ten innocent citizens for every German soldier killed. This practice was inspired by the ancient Roman Army's tradition of "decimation," in which a mutiny was punished by dividing the soldiers into groups of ten, each group cast lots, and the soldier on whom the lot fell was executed by his nine comrades.

From that day on, Partisan recruitment grew rapidly. The Germans action had mobilized Roman civilians against them.

A few months later, the strengthened Partisans worked with the Allies to take back Rome. I continued to supply the Partisans in Napoli with weapons and food. I heard from local contacts that Fast Talk, the Count, and Firecracker had also joined the effort to expel the Germans from the Eternal City.

On June 4, the Allies and Partisans liberated Rome—the first Axis capitol to be freed by the Allies.

The next day, the Allies invaded a beach in Normandy with a massive force.

The Germans were on the run.

While our organization generally did well, our success now revolved around the price and quantity of whatever goods American supply officers were willing to pilfer and sell to us. Battles to the north stopped us from smuggling shipments by land, and the American Navy didn't allow any boats in or out of the harbor. They vigorously patrolled the coastline, which cut off our sea operations and made the American military our only source of goods for the black market.

Genovese worked with supply officers to acquire these goods, but American commanders, fed up with losing nearly half of their supplies to pilfering, ordered the losses stopped. These commanders still hadn't figured out that Genovese was behind most of the disappearances. They sent military police out into the streets to enforce this policy. We spent a lot of money on bribes and attorneys to keep our men out of jail.

Restaurants began to reopen, catering mostly to British and American officers. This trend proved good for our business, too, since restaurants needed black-market goods such as wine, meat, and cheese. Bistros extracted outrageous prices, upwards of twenty U.S. dollars—a month's pay for the average Italian—from their new patrons.

Benito, Giacomo, Antonio, and I met at an outdoor café to discuss the difficulties of moving merchandise in the current environment.

"I hear that the top American brass plans to crack down even harder on the black market," Giacomo said.

"It'll never fucking happen," Benito snorted. "They'll round up a few people on the street, but they'll never go after the American supply officers."

I motioned as if I were counting out money. "A few bribes and our guys are back on the street. It's the price of doing business."

"And business is good," Antonio told us, as he filled his briefcase with the food and medicine we'd brought him. "Thanks." He returned to the street and immediately found a prospective couple to approach. We watched him pull them aside, open his case, and reveal the contraband inside. The couple's eyes sparkled as they viewed the fresh salami, a highly prized and rare item in Napoli. The man produced several bills and the exchange was consummated.

"That didn't take long," Benito said with a chuckle.

As soon as the couple went their way, an American in a black coat approached Antonio, opened his coat and revealed the Military Police uniform underneath.

"Oh, merciful God," I said. "No!"

Antonio tried to pay him off but the MP refused the bribe. He marched Antonio away.

Fortunately, we had the means to buy justice.

We called on our barrister, Signore Tintoretto, the finest criminal attorney in Italy. He had never lost a case. With a well-placed bribe, he knew how to end many cases before they went to trial.

But Antonio's case did go to trial. Tintoretto delivered a stirring speech that lasted four hours. Several times it reduced both the judge and jury to tears, leading the justice to call for a recess. At the end of the day it would be an understatement to say the jury found Antonio innocent; the judge even shook my brother's hand, apologized, and hugged him.

Another example of justice that I witnessed occurred while we were loading goods into the truck at the dock. We saw three Italian dockworkers arrested by American MPs, and learned they had been caught grabbing a couple of tins of rations. I read in the paper later that they'd been sentenced to ten years in prison, even though they'd stolen the tins to keep their families from starving.

Another case involved a man falsely arrested for looting his own bombed-out house. He missed his trial date because the prison system couldn't find which facility they'd assigned him to. As a penalty for not appearing at his trial, the judge levied fines and a mandatory three-month prison sentence.

Such inequities became commonplace.

Every type of American military supply showed up on the streets. In spite of this, our profits were dropping. A variety of factors conspired against us. For one, most people couldn't afford black-market prices, which made the enterprise a hotbed for robbery. We even discovered that some of the Pollini brothers' men were stealing from our guys. The continued crackdown by American Military Police cost us court fees, bribes, and the loss of goods. But the final and most crucial factor driving up the cost of business was the bidding wars that broke out for American commodities, as they were the only source of goods.

Rather than continuing to battle our competitors, I—as Russo—organized a meeting with the major players who were buying American supplies from Genovese.

The groups represented were the Pollini brothers, our main competition in the city; Vito Catallino, who ran a very powerful organization built on controlling the smaller towns between Napoli and Rome; Gino Bellini, who controlled northern cities like Pisa and Genoa, which remained under Nazi control; and, of course, ours.

I had never met any of these other leaders. Benito told me Russo had worked with Vito Catallino on a couple of deals many years ago and that Russo had maintained a good relationship with Vito on the telephone. He'd also met the Pollini brothers.

Disguised as Russo, I represented our group as the negotiator and to strategize for the organization. Antonio and Benito Russo joined me. Antonio's insight on the value of goods and their marketability would be helpful. And Benito was the only one who knew all the other families.

Fabroni Pollini wasted no time showing his aggravation at our organization. "We're tired of getting the crumbs left by the Russo organization. We deserve—"

Benito bellowed, "Hey, we're fucking sick of you stealing from our guys on the street—"

"Bastard!" shouted Michel Pollini. "You're accusing us of stealing from your morons?"

"I don't have to accuse you; we know your gutter thugs rob our men." Benito shot to his feet. "Years ago some of your guys even tried to kidnap the Prince's wife, but they paid the price for that!"

I had to control myself to stay in the wheelchair. Why had no one ever told me the Polinis were behind that kidnap attempt? Antonio gave me a subtle look that showed his equal surprise. He pulled Benito back to his chair and calmed him down.

"Gentlemen." Vito Catallino held his hands up in a calming gesture. "Vincenzo went to a lot of trouble to form this summit. Let's leave the back-alley squabbles at the door."

Everyone finally calmed down, and Catallino turned to me. "Vincenzo, first may I say how sorry I am to see how difficult this war has been for you."

"Thank you, Vito," I replied. "Who has not suffered in this war? I'm sure we've all experienced losses of loved ones and valued members of our organizations." Everyone nodded. "And I agree, we need to set aside any disputes we've had in the past."

"Vincenzo," Catallino said, "I'm certain you have some ideas that will help us all prosper. I'd like to hear what you have to say."

"Well, gentlemen," I began, "as you know, we all compete for the same goods that the Americans sell to the black market. Since their arrival, we've all come to rely on these goods for the majority of our incomes."

"Tell us something we don't know," Fabroni Pollini grumbled.

"Exactly," Gino Bellini said. "American goods certainly represent a major income source for our organization, and we all must compete for them with others." He sounded more like a banker—a man with a college education—than a street thug.

"Exactly," I said as I maneuvered the gold coin across the back of my hand, Russo style. "While plentiful, the Americans have only so much merchandise. However, we can all afford to receive fewer goods if—"

"We already get the short end of the stick!" Michel Pollini shouted. "We're not going to take less."

"I'm talking about *all* of us making a great deal more than we're currently earning," I said. "The way it stands now, we're competing against one another, and other smaller groups, for this limited supply of goods. All it's doing is driving up the price we pay to the Americans."

"I think I see where you're going with this," Bellini said thoughtfully.

I acknowledged him with a nod. "I propose we form a cartel. That way we can cut the price we pay for American goods in half, if not more. We'll agree not to bid above a certain price. Of course I'll need to convince Vito Genovese as well."

"Why would Vito accept less for the goods?" Catallino asked.

"Because the American commanders are trying to end the black market; they could put Genovese out of business all together. Many of the small operators are sloppy and noisy about their work; they even sell American soldiers goods still in army containers. I will propose to Genovese that our organizations will keep the black market stealthy and out of sight to the Americans, making it more politically palatable for American brass. That will keep Vito in business."

"I like that," Catallino said. "I like it a lot. No reason to make the Americans wealthy at our expense."

Bellini smiled and nodded.

I went on. "We'll repackage all American goods. Blankets will become Italian made overcoats. GI rations will filter through restaurants and be served with Italian flare."

"Wait, wait," Fabroni Pollini cut in. "Who decides how much each organization gets to buy off Genovese?"

"A fair question," I said. "I have some ideas, but we need to work it all out before we go forward. As an example, if we each receive the same amount of goods we do now, but sell them at double or triple the profit, I don't think any of us would complain much."

Everyone liked this plan; even the Pollini brothers agreed. We quickly hammered out a pricing structure, percentage of goods each organization would receive, how we'd handle questions from the Americans, and penalties for breaking the quotas of our new organization. The Napoli Import Cartel had opened for business.

Only one big question remained unanswered. Would Genovese himself accept a pay cut?

It was an unnerving question to have to ask the most dangerous man in Italy.

Chapter 49

LIFE AFTER THE NAZIS

A year after their liberation from their Nazis and their allies, not to mention the repression of Fascism, the people of Napoli sat wearily in their squalor with polite smiles on their faces. They were hungrier than they had been under German rule and more diseased than during the plagues of the Middle Ages.

With Mussolini and the fascists out of power, political party banners sprouted up faster than weeds in spring. Italians had a host of choices, including the Communists, the Separatists, Italian Socialists, Party of Actions, and a dozen others. But it was the Christian Democrats that quickly emerged as the strongest group. Its power came from the support of large landlords and, more importantly, the Church. Nuns went door to door to explain the sin of voting for any other politicians. They handed out pasta to needy families that pledged their support. An unemployed man stood a greater chance of being hired if he joined the Christian Democrats.

All parties produced mountains of words, but no one seemed to take any action toward rebuilding the country. Politicians, and the people they represented, seemed content to complain and, perhaps, hope that the Americans would fix things.

Everyone looked for miracles of one kind or another, political or religious. For the crowds of believers, every church in Napoli seemed to claim a miracle: a statue that talked, bled, sweated, or healed.

Neapolitans anxiously awaited the next one. I concluded that most people preferred hallucinations to reality.

But no other miracle in Napoli captured the hearts of its citizens more than those provided by the city's patron saint, San Gennaro. Each September, Gennaro's blood predicted the fate of the city for the coming year. The omen relied on whether the fourth-century saint's blood liquefied or stayed congealed, a miracle that baffled even modern science. This year, as always, the streets filled and the shops and cafes emptied as everyone waited for the saint's prediction. Despite discounting such superstition, I couldn't help but anticipate San Gennaro's verdict.

The children, Carlo, and I arrived at the Chapel of San Gennaro, and we inched down the magnificent arched aisle toward the altar where I'd married their father. The Parenti di San Gennaro took their positions in front. The Church claimed that these aged women were the actual descendants of the saint.

The Archbishop lifted the vials of blood high above his head for the anxious crowd to see. Several people shouted, "San Gennaro, do it quickly!" How had Napoli come to depend so on the blood of the 1600-year-old martyr?

During Roman Emperor Diocletian's persecution of Christians, around 300 A.D., Timoteo, the ruler of the Napoli region, imprisoned Gennaro for his Christian beliefs and proceeded to torture him. He hurled Gennaro into a blazing furnace, but Gennaro emerged without injury. Gennaro then survived the torture of the rack unscathed. Timoteo condemned him and his friends to be fed to wild beasts. But instead of tearing Gennaro apart, the animals crouched in submission to him. Timoteo again sentenced him to be executed—and was promptly struck blind. But Gennaro prayed to God to restore Timoteo's vision. Even though this immediately happened, Timoteo ordered Gennaro decapitated.

On September 19, Gennaro met his fate. The saint's nursemaid promptly collected some of his blood.

The weariness from war brought a greater tension and expectation for the saint's verdict. If the blood liquefied, the church would announce the miracle by firing twenty-one cannon shots.

When the cannons fired, Lucia cried at the harsh sound. As for the rest of the crowd, it murmured uneasily.

Word passed back from the front of the assembly suggested that the blood had liquefied in a slow, deliberate manner, which cast doubt on the quality of the coming year. Still, slow liquefaction was better than none at all.

That same day, again made up as Russo, I met with Genovese. The mafia don was well dressed but this couldn't hide the broad, scared face of a thug, albeit a charming one.

"You expect me to take a 40 percent pay cut?"

His tone was biting, but I didn't back down, because I knew that the plan would ultimately serve him well. "Keeping the black market out of sight will only strengthen your ties with the Americans," I said. "The stolen goods are too visible now. The American's are losing face."

He had a sharp mind and knew I was right. So he agreed, on a trial basis, to sell pilfered American supplies only to our cartel.

That summer, Neapolitans discovered new lines of clothing: overcoats made from military blankets, army undergarments, smart new outfits constructed from stolen uniforms dyed and altered into sharp forms, even GI socks and boots re-crafted with Italian style. In Italian restaurants appeared exciting new culinary creations made from everything from boring k-rations to fine caviar, all supplied by the American war machine.

In August, much to my surprise, American MPs arrested Genovese. It seemed one of the MPs had been a New York City cop, recognized Genovese and knew he was wanted for murder in the States.

With Genovese so conveniently removed from the picture, our cartel moved in and made its own deal with the Americans. No longer needing to pay Genovese his share, we saw our profits skyrocket.

Sadly, although our organization saw a strong rise in prosperity, the winter of 1944 provided the bleakest time of the war for most Neapolitans, with so little food and so many hungry. The ranks of the Italian Partisans grew, but so did the number of deaths. Important strikes were made against the Germans, but always at high cost.

The Allies' progress in driving back the Germans remained slow. The Allies invaded Anzio, a beach a hundred miles north of Napoli. On a daily basis we saw the aftermath of the bloody offensive as thousands of wounded arrived in Napoli, along with endless stacks of coffins. Once again we began to worry that the Americans might not win the war.

Refugees from the north continued to migrate south to Napoli, including a Jewish family that came to me for help.

"Did Domenico send you?" I asked.

The bearded man looked at me wearily. "Domenico Saldino was killed by the Nazis in Terni."

The next thing I knew, the man was catching me as I fell.

"I'm sorry," he said as he eased me back onto my chair. "I didn't realize you hadn't heard. Are you all right?"

I nodded, but my wounds were serious; my heart had just shattered. I got to my feet and steadied myself against the doorframe. I stared ahead, but saw nothing except sorrow ahead of me.

Chapter 50

AN UNEXPECTED PROPOSAL

The year 1945 brought even more death and disease to the people of Italy. Many simply gave up and died from despair. If not for my children, I might have done so, too. With the shell of my husband in the basement and the love of my life dead, I found it difficult to see much meaning in life.

Then, on May 2, the Germans finally surrendered. The brief yet intensely destructive Nazi Third Reich—our one-time ally, then despised occupier—evaporated. The Roman Empire had dominated Europe for a thousand years and brought prosperity, education, and safety to the regions it conquered. The Nazis ruled Europe for only a few years, but left every country they touched in poverty and ruin.

I went to church, got on my knees and thanked God for ending this hell.

The dismantling of the German war machine inspired a collective cheer in Napoli, but that shout soon faded into despair. For most, fear over finding their next meal weighed too heavily on them to find much joy even in this.

"Now, with the war ended, will Daddy come home soon?" Adriana asked.

"I don't know, my little *angeli*," I said. "He travels so much. You must be brave and never mention to anyone that you haven't seen your father. It would hurt and anger him if you told anyone he was away."

"Why doesn't he come home?" Giorgio asked.

"So often life doesn't allow you to do what you want. You must be strong and make the best of what comes your way." I was getting tired of lies and deception.

With the war over, the black market thrived like never before. Both supply and demand now favored our organization. Our shipments were no longer seized by the Nazis or the Americans; every port and land route opened up to us again; the constant spying that had threatened to expose us during the war disappeared, although I still felt as if people watched us. We also continued to purchase goods, using cartel pricing, from the American military. I made certain that Russo's organization controlled the docks after the war, since Italy needed to rebuild and the necessary materials would have to flow through Napoli's harbor. Few groups had the money, influence, or resources to acquire large quantities of goods from foreign countries and transport them into Italy. Ours did, and we profited.

Waves of cash flowed in as we imported everything Italians needed or desired: lumber, coffee, tires, auto parts, industrial equipment, building tools and nails, clothing, lipstick, seeds, and wine by the vat-full. But nothing sold like American cigarettes—every Italian had become addicted to Yankee smokes.

While most Neapolitans still struggled to survive, American servicemen partied. And we were very happy to accommodate them. We opened dance halls with gambling and brothels in the back.

In the six months following the end of the war, we made more money than we had during all five years of the war combined. Although politicians spouted that they planned to "get tough" on crime, we saw no change.

All seemed well, but still, a haunting feeling of being watched continued to hang over me. Several times I thought I saw a man following me. Perhaps the war had simply left me with an indelible feeling of paranoia.

Or perhaps the problem was that one business condition did not improve at all: Russo's health. One night I confided to Carlo, "My husband didn't celebrate the end of the war. He doesn't celebrate the growth of his organization. He didn't even celebrate the return of his children two years ago. Except for his body, my husband is dead." I put my hands over my face but didn't cry. I just wanted to hide from the constant reality of Russo's condition.

With the war over, Russo's family, who no longer even spoke of him, started talking about the future. "We appreciate all you've done, Carina," Renzo told me. "But it's getting too dangerous for you to continue impersonating Vincenzo. Someone's bound to discover you, then who knows what could happen?"

Benito added, "A more permanent decision needs to be made about the future of the organization. I'm worried about your safety and that of your children. They, too, would be in danger if you're discovered. Maybe you should return to just running the financial side of things and leave the street decisions to us."

This time I knew they were right. It was time for an eremitical life, an existence away from the world of making judgments over others and determining punishment. It was time to transfer power. But everyone still recognized my leadership position and knew I'd make the final decision about when to leave.

Since the war had ended and the cartel brought peace between rivals, I'd become lax about keeping a bodyguard with me. One morning on my way to the marketplace, my feeling of being watched became reality. A man grabbed me from behind and pushed me into the alley. Before I could see his face or even cry out, he latched handcuffs onto my wrists. "Carina Cunzolo-Russo," he said into my ear, "you're under arrest by Interpol for smuggling, racketeering, and various other crimes."

"What's Interpol?" I demanded, furious at myself. "Are you after ransom, or are you just going to kill me?"

The man reached around from behind me and flashed a badge. It identified him as Giuseppe Dante Lorenzo Vannini of "Interpol." I had never heard of such an agency. The man led me to a car and forced me into the back. He sat in the driver's seat, slammed the door, and drove off.

I peered through the wire mesh that separated the back seat from the front. The man looked familiar, even from behind.

"I know you, don't I?" I demanded.

He didn't respond. I thought of opening the door to jump out, but saw that the interior handles had been removed. "Why are you arresting me?" I asked. But what I was wondering was how this man and this Interpol organization, if it really existed, know that I'd been running Russo's organization in the first place. Had someone betrayed me—again? Perhaps the brother who had informed on me to Major Kappel?

The man still said nothing, but I saw him looking at me in the rearview mirror. I was sure I had seen those eyes before.

I expected him to take me to the police station, but he pulled the car up the driveway of an old, abandoned warehouse in an industrial part of the city. He drove inside the bombed-out building's loading dock. I decided he must work for the Pollini brothers or another competitor of Russo's. Clearly, he planned to kill me.

He opened my door. "Please get out."

"I can pay you a handsome reward for my release," I said, as I exited the car.

"Please walk straight ahead, if you would be so kind." He was a very polite killer. I knew the voice, too, but couldn't place it. We walked until we entered a room with an old desk and several chairs. Debris covered the floor.

"Are you going to rape me?" I asked.

He led me toward the chairs.

"Has someone hired you to kill me?"

No response. He forced me into one of the chairs, and I finally got my first good look at him. His face was familiar, but I still couldn't place him. He took off my handcuffs, and then leaned against the desk and rubbed his chin. That was it—he used to have a beard. When I pictured him with one, I knew immediately who he was. "Count Sureshot!"

He smiled. "Actually, I'm Giuseppe Vannini with Interpol, Europe's new inter-country police agency; but, I'm glad you remember me a little."

"Of course I remember you. But . . . why would the police want me? I'm just a mother and housewife."

"Please, Carina. I know the whole story. I know that your husband, Vincenzo Russo, is in the basement of your house and has been since early in the war. I know you run all of his businesses. I even know about the men you've killed." He placed a pistol on the table. "I know all of your sins, Carina."

I summoned up my most innocent voice. "What are you talking about?" I wondered if I could reach the gun before he snatched it up again. No. What about my trusty stiletto, still hidden in my belt. Again, no. Sureshot—Vannini—was too far away.

"I imagine you're considering how to kill me right now," he said matter-of-factly. "Well, good luck. The Greeks tried, the Croatians tried, the Nazis tried. While I've come to realize how accomplished you are at this task, I hope you'll focus on my proposal for a moment before attempting to take my life."

"Take your life?" I said. "I don't know what you're talking about. I'm a housewife." The truth was, this man frightened me. He knew so much about me, seemed so certain of my thoughts, so certain of the outcome he'd planned—whatever that might be.

"Stop with the innocent act, Carina. As the Partisan who bought guns from you, I checked you out carefully before purchasing those weapons. We needed to be certain we could trust you. I determined back then that you were impersonating your husband. I told no one."

"You're crazy!" I said.

He laughed. "More than likely. Your husband became incoherent after the Allies bombed your house during an air raid. He remains in that condition to this day, locked away in the basement."

"How is it possible you could—"

"Not much gets by me. I followed you before we purchased the guns. You're so beautiful when you're dressed like a woman—not so much when you're wearing Russo's clothes. Portraying your husband all these years . . . you're a gem." He chuckled and shook his head.

"Who told you these ridiculous tales?"

"I'm very good at uncovering the truth. A little perception combined with a bit of deduction." He shrugged. "Interpol recruited me after the war. It had your husband's smuggling organization on its radar. Of course, they didn't know you had taken his place. I asked for the assignment to watch your activities, but in order to protect you, as I knew your secret. Any other agent would have already turned in enough evidence to put you away for a hundred years, and your brothers, too. For months I've watched you and collected the evidence on you . . . but if you handle this the way I hope you will, nothing will ever be seen by the authorities."

"So. Blackmail."

"No, Carina. Our fates will be decided here and now, in this room." He emphasized his point by touching his finger to the gun on the table.

Normally, I was so clear-headed, but this . . . this was insane. Baffling. All through the war, I'd known what needed to be done, what step to take next. Now I had no clue what move to make.

"What do you want from me?" I asked. "Money? A percentage?"

"No. I want to marry you."

"Excuse me? What?"

"I know, it sounds crazy, but somewhere in all of this I realized I love you. I've never wanted an ordinary woman, the kind who's never left the kitchen her entire life. I want a smart woman, strong enough to stand up to me, to challenge me." He smiled. "I want a woman exactly like you. In fact, you're the only woman for me, Carina."

"How . . ." I shook my head. "You're mad."

"Hear me out. You'll find me to be a good match. I'm offering safety to you and your children. I'm offering you a different kind of life before Interpol, the Italian authorities, or one of your competitors catch up with you. I'm offering to make you and your children royalty, as I am indeed a count . . ."

"It's not just a nickname?"

"No. I am Count Giuseppe Dante Lorenzo Vannini of Ponza—a lesser count, but nevertheless of royal blood. I'm not rich, I don't own property, but I do have a modest income. I'm offering you a new life, free of crime, violence, and danger. I only hope you won't get too bored."

"It's so . . . so . . ."

"I know. I'm almost as surprised as you are that I'm asking. But I've given it a lot of thought. I'll leave Interpol and we'll both start a new life, together, wherever you want to go. This is my proposal. The alternative is that neither one of us leaves this room." He stroked the gun again.

"You *are* mad."

He shrugged. "Don't tell me you've never considered taking this way out."

Again, he was right. It was unnerving how sure he was about my thoughts and actions. And how accurate he was.

As for his proposal, or proposition, I found it simultaneously romantic, homicidal and suicidal. Absolute insanity . . . yet also sincere and inexplicably charming.

I looked at him more closely. Guiseppe was a handsome man. He had thick, wavy black hair dashed with streaks of gray, and a stately stance and elegant presence that did in fact give him the look of a royal. Would it be so bad to start a new life?

He said, "I fought as an Italian soldier in Greece. I fought to free Serbs and Gypsies in Croatia. I battled the Nazis for years as a Partisan. Carina, both of us have lived lives of great danger. What other woman could relate to all that I've done in my life? And don't tell me you didn't feel something between us the first time we met, even though you were dressed as a man at the time." He smiled.

This was also true.

I finally relaxed in the chair. Truly relaxed . . . and only then realized how long it had been since I'd enjoyed that sensation. I said, "How would you feel about running a luxury hotel outside of Rome?"

"A hotel?"

"If you're nobility, you've got the connections to bring in the finest guests. I have an eye for decoration and some skill at managing personnel and money."

"Yes, I've noticed." He rubbed his chin with his free hand. "No selling guests' jewelry out the back door?"

"No."

"Would your brothers work as porters or bellmen?"

"That would be up to them." I had to smile at the thought.

"So it's a deal?"

"Yes," I said. "I accept your offer."

"A hotel . . ." He grinned and let go of the gun.

Life is a series of decisions; I was learning to take the best one presented to me.

"You've made the right decision, Carina. You'll see. We'll be very happy. Besides, if you decide you don't like me, you can always kill me in my sleep."

I chuckled. That exact thought had crossed my mind. "There is one small problem," I said.

"What's that?"

"I'm already married."

"Are you?" he said.

Chapter 51

THE END OF THE PRINCE

Marrying Giuseppe would be utterly impetuous, but the moment I said yes to him, I knew it was the right decision. Still, I wondered how many times a woman could fall in love and give away her heart. Maybe this time mine wouldn't be broken. Maybe this time life would be kind.

A few days after Giuseppe made his request, an attorney arrived from Rome. My beloved Uncle Salvatore had died. He'd made me the executrix of his will and bequeathed me the ownership of the Hotel Augustus. I would retain 51 percent of the profits, with the remainder to be equally divided amongst my siblings.

After the attorney left, I sat in silence for a long time. What I felt was shame. How many times had I cursed God for his cruelty? For letting Mama treat me the way she did? For denying me my love for Domenico, not once but over and over again? For permitting me to be married off to a man I did not know or love? For forcing me to kill and kill and kill in order to keep that same man's business functioning . . . ?

But without all those things, all that trauma and difficulty, would I be in the position to own or operate a hotel? No. I would be fit only to cook and clean and order servants about, the way Mama had always wanted.

They say that God works in mysterious ways. Perhaps he has a mysterious sense of humor as well.

I arranged Uncle Salvatore's funeral as he had requested. He was buried in Cosenza, his birthplace, next to his and Papa's parents.

Upon my return to Napoli, Vito Catallino called Russo for a meeting of the Import Cartel.

Carlo drove me to the meeting that evening as fog drifted over the city. The guards for the other members already sat outside as we drove up to the warehouse. Carlo helped me into the wheelchair and pushed me to the door.

I wheeled myself in and was surprised to see everyone already seated around the table.

"I'm not late, am I?" I said in my Russo voice.

Everyone remained silent. I began rolling the gold coin over the back of my hand.

"What's wrong?" I asked.

"I still can't see it," Vito Catallino said to no one in particular.

"What are you talking about?" I said.

"Oh, the hell with this." Fabroni Pollini rose, walked over to me and tore the hat off my head, pulled open my coat and ripped the fake mustache off my lip. I heard the gold coin ping off the floor.

"It's Russo's wife!" Michael Pollini shouted.

"What the fuck?" Bellini said.

Fabroni pulled out his stiletto. "I say we each cut a piece out of her face."

Vito raised a hand. "Wait! First, I want to know what the hell's been going on."

I told them everything. I described Russo's condition and explained how I'd controlled his organization for almost five years.

"You've been running things that long?" Vito said in disbelief.

"Fuck it, let's kill her and be done with it," Fabroni said. "We should take out Russo's entire organization, too."

I sat up straighter. "Listen, I don't even want to be part of the organization anymore. I was trying to work out a way to transition power anyway. Please don't harm anyone because of me. If you need reparations, kill me, but don't let anyone else suffer. We all had to do whatever was needed to survive during the war. Now that the war is over, Vincenzo Russo will never be seen again."

Vito gestured to the four bosses. "Let's make a decision." They huddled while I prepared for the final judgment and once again pondered God's sense of humor. Still, I said a prayer of intercession for all those in Russo's organization.

At last the four leaders got to their feet walked over to me. Each drew his stiletto, and I took a deep breath and shut my eyes. My body felt warm but not with fear. Surprisingly, tranquility enveloped me.

I heard Vito's voice close to my ear. "Never again will you have any involvement in the Camorra. That's our first condition."

I opened my eyes. "Of course."

"If it wasn't for my longtime friendship with your husband, you'd be dead. And, we all have to admit that you've helped us prosper. But now you must leave Napoli and the South altogether."

"It's done. I'll be out within the week."

"Russo is dead, correct?"

"Yes. He's gone."

"We don't want war . . . well, some do." I suspected that "some" meant "almost everyone." I suspected that without Vito's forgiveness of my sins I would already be a pool of blood on the floor. "So avoiding a battle over Russo's territory will require restitution."

I nodded. "Of course."

"You will pay twenty-five percent of Russo's total earnings for the next five years. That's our price to not encroach on his territory or his men."

As had become my habit, I quickly weighed all the parameters of the offer. Vito controlled the most powerful organization among us; the Pollini brothers wouldn't dare go against him. I let out a sigh. My brothers and Russo's family would be safe from danger.

"If any of these rules are broken . . ." he went on, and then paused. "Well, you don't want to see that happen."

"That's true," I said. "I don't."

The following day, holding a carafe of brandy and two crystal goblets, I walked down the cool, dark stairs to the basement. I wore my new red stiletto heels, and each clicking step stung at my heart until I reached the bottom and unlocked the door.

Russo sat motionless on the couch.

I looked at him for a long time. If anyone from the Cartel ever learned that he was still alive, they'd consider the terms of the agreement broken and everyone in Russo's organization would pay dearly. Then there was the matter of my own future, a possible future with Guiseppe. Sharing the hotel outside Rome. My children, my happiness.

The time had come for the past to catch up to the present.

"Brandy?" I offered. I placed the brandy and glasses on the table and poured us each a drink. I looked into Russo's eyes, but no one looked back. Trapped within his secret world, he stared into the distance.

"You're not Vincenzo Russo," I said, reaching to my belt. "The great Prince of Napoli died five years ago. You're his ghost, and it's time to give up your haunt."

I swung my hips to straddle him.

"I'll always protect you, my Prince."

I drew my scarf across his chest and wove the silky material around his arms.

The stiletto did the rest.

Hundreds of people came to the Prince of Napoli's funeral—everyone in his organization, people he had helped over the years, public officials, and all the members of the cartel. People brought so many flowers that I imagined every garden within one hundred miles lay barren.

I made sure that Russo received the best of everything: the finest church, the premier mahogany coffin with brass handles, the most expensive plot, and the finest headstone. He'd always liked the finest of things.

No one questioned the circumstances of Russo's death. Even his brothers seemed relieved at the finality of the situation. I told the children that their father had died in the war but his body had only recently been discovered. They hadn't seen him in so long that the news didn't seem overly devastating to them.

The day after the funeral, I met with Russo's relatives and my brothers at Caruso's Restaurant to inform them that I planned to move to Uncle Salvatore's hotel. I had already warned them that the cartel had uncovered my impersonation of Russo. Under my guidance, they elected to reorganize with each member concentrating on his own area of expertise: Antonio moving merchandise on the street; Giacomo directing smuggling and handling the City Hall connections; Renzo controlling street crime and the Scugnizzi; and Benito overseeing gambling and prostitution.

After the meeting, Carlo rose and said, "Well, it's time for me to move along."

"I'll see you back at the house." I patted him on the shoulder.

"No—I meant that I plan to leave Italy."

"Carlo, you've been my protector for so long. I rely on you in so many ways. I was hoping you would come with me to Rome."

"No, Carina. It's time for me to go. It's time I started seeing some of the world instead of just reading about it. I plan to visit Egypt, Jerusalem, the Amazon, China."

"I don't know what to say. You've been such a wonderful friend."

"You, too, Carina."

"I feel like I'm losing a limb. I wouldn't have survived without you." He had been my protector and mentor twenty-four hours a day for ten years. I would feel naked without him.

Tears attempted to reach my eyes. Out of habit, though, I held them back. "How will I continue without you?"

He kissed my cheek. "You'll do just fine, Don Carina."

A NEW BEGINNING

The time had come for me to leave Napoli. No one wanted me here to remind them that a woman had once run the largest crime organization in the largest city in Southern Italy.

I had told no one, not even Antonio, about Giuseppe. Russo's funeral was still too fresh in people's minds.

It was a pleasant spring day in 1946 when the children and I left Napoli with Giuseppe behind the wheel. Adriana, Giorgio, and Lucia sang songs as we drove; they also seemed eager to leave behind the memories of the South and the war. Except for a few clothes, we took nothing with us; I wanted an entirely new start without reminders of the past.

We arrived at the hotel around dusk. The building was much smaller than the grand memories of a palace I'd nurtured in childhood. In addition, the war hadn't spared Uncle Salvatore's Hotel Augustus. Several burned-out German Army trucks and tanks greeted us as we entered the driveway. Bombs had ripped part of the skin from the façade, and fire had devastated a large section of the structure. I saw the disappointment in the children's eyes, and it hurt me deeply to disappoint them yet again.

"*Bel niente.* Sweet nothing."

Giuseppe parked the car in the back of the hotel. A sign hanging on a roped-off area warned: "Active Minefield."

Bullet holes decorated both the entry doors to the lobby and much of the exterior. With caution, we stepped into the stench of urine and gasoline. The smell permeated every step I took down a blackened, fire ravaged hallway.

I looked inside one of the rooms. Dried blood spotted the once white mattress on the bed, the only piece of furniture remaining in the room. An old, tarnished mirror caught my reflection. My hair stood on end from the drive in the convertible, but Papa's silver comb was still firmly planted in my black mane. Using my fingers I attempted to smooth my hair into place. The effort was futile. For the first time in a long while, I really looked at myself. My face had aged during the last five anxiety-filled years. I'd lost the last glow of youth.

Unsure what I was searching for, I stared deeper into my eyes. I wondered how my children judged me. You so want to be your children's champion. Perhaps my redemption rested with them. Every day of our lives we face so many choices, each with the power to alter our direction, each leading us toward a different possible fate. You wonder if you've taken the right path, what reparations you need to make for all the wrongs you've committed. I had always felt so certain about my decisions, but in that tarnished piece of glass and silver, a haze obscured my resolve.

Who was this in the mirror? In many ways, I still felt like the young girl climbing Spartacus Summit, excited to be setting out on her own course, but I didn't see her in the mirror today. With a slow sweep I brushed my hands over my tired face, hoping to see it more clearly. In the reflection, I watched a tiny tear trickle down my cheek. I let out a nervous chuckle. With all the horror, pain, and suffering I'd endured, this was the first tear I had allowed to escape.

I grabbed the mirror and turned it toward the wall. On a day like today, I didn't want to look at my past.

For the first time in a decade I broke down and sobbed. I cried for Papa, Bruno, Gianina, Forenzo, Sergio, Russo . . . and Domenico. Strong arms embraced me from behind. "Ah, Carina. It's all right. You can cry now. I'll be strong for you," whispered Guiseppe.

I turned and looked up at him. "I've never been allowed to cry."

He took out his handkerchief and dabbed my tears. "Tears can be good. They clear away many things so one can start anew."

More tears came.

"Come, my sweet Don Carina."

We went outside and found the children sitting on the bumper of a burned-out jeep, looking dejected.

"I'm sorry it's not what you hoped to find, Carina," Guiseppe said. He laid his hand across my shoulder.

Looking at the ruin of the building again, I found some inner strength well up within me. "Well, if this isn't the hotel I remember, we'll just make it into the hotel of my dreams."

Guiseppe smiled.

I turned to my children. "My *angeli,* I want you to always remember one thing. In this life, you must do what needs to be done."

The next day we began to rebuild. No, not just rebuild.

We would make everything better than before.

EPILOGUE

Hopefully, the words I have laid down here will help clarify some of the myths that continue to waft through the streets of Napoli.

After leaving the city, I went on to rebuild Hotel Augustus into a top hotel, which opened the door for me to create a chain of luxury hotels throughout Italy. That is not to say my past did not return like an unpleasant aquaintance you hope never to see again. But those trials are beyond the scope of this limited space.

Guiseppe, now my husband, stayed with Interpol for a time, but then quit to help me build up the hotel business. It's curious that both my husbands were royal: one by birth, the other one honorary peer decree based on his street deeds.

As my four children grew, yes, Guiseppe and I added a little one quickly, I found that the scars of the war had left their mark on them. Georgio missed his father even more than the girls and wanted to follow his footsteps into the Russo family business, but more about that another time.

Let me just say that our lives are better now than the war torn years in Napoli. Thank the Father, the Son and the Holy Ghost.

ABOUT THE AUTHOR

Author, artist, composer, restaurateur are just a few of Ronald Russell's titles. A multiple award-winning journalist, Mr. Russell's human interest stories have appeared in publications including the *Los Angeles Times, L.A. Weekly,* and national magazines. His play, *Beethoven: Heaven's Voice,* received critical and audience acclaim. Mr. Russell's restaurant, SunCafe, has won various culinary awards for its unique organic cuisine.

The love of animals has motivated Mr. Russell throughout his life. He works to improve the treatment of both companion and farm animals. He has hosted and organized fundraisers for various animal organizations, as well as provided catering for their events.

Visit www.DonCarina.com to read deleted scenes from *Don Carina,* read the stories of amazing WWII herioines, learn more about Napoli during WWII, or to contact Ron Russell.

Other Books by
Bettie Youngs Book Publishers

The Maybelline Story
And the Spirited Family Dynasty Behind It

Sharrie Williams

A woman's most powerful possession is a man's imagination.
—**Maybelline ad, 1934**

In 1915, when a kitchen-stove fire singed his sister Mabel's lashes and brows, Tom Lyle Williams watched in fascination as she performed what she called "a secret of the harem"—mixing petroleum jelly with coal dust and ash from a burnt cork and applying it to her lashes and brows. Mabel's simple beauty trick ignited Tom Lyle's imagination, and he started what would become a billion-dollar business, one that remains a viable American icon after nearly a century. He named it Maybelline in her honor.

Throughout the twentieth century, the Maybelline company inflated, collapsed, endured, and thrived in tandem with the nation's upheavals. Williams—to avoid unwanted scrutiny of his private life—cloistered himself behind the gates of his Rudolph Valentino Villa and ran his empire from a distance. Now, after nearly a century of silence, this true story celebrates the life of an American entrepreneur, a man whose vision rocketed him to success along with the woman held in his orbit: Evelyn Boecher—who became his lifelong fascination and muse. Captivated by her "roaring charisma," he affectionately called her the "real Miss Maybelline" and based many of his advertising campaigns on the woman she represented: commandingly beautiful, hard-boiled, and daring. Evelyn masterminded a life of vanity, but would fall prey to fortune hunters and a mysterious murder that even today remains unsolved.

A fascinating and inspiring story, a tale both epic and intimate, alive with the clash, the hustle, the music, and dance of American enterprise.

A richly told juicy story of a forty-year, white-hot love triangle that fans the flames of a major worldwide conglomerate.
—**Neil Shulman, associate producer,** *Doc Hollywood*

ISBN: 978-0-9843081-1-8 • $18.95

In bookstores everywhere, online, or from the publisher:
www.BettieYoungsBooks.com

Out of the Transylvania Night

Aura Imbarus

An epic tale of identity, love, and the indomitable human spirit.

Communist dictator Nicolae Ceauşescu had turned Romania into a land of zombies as surely as if Count Dracula had sucked its lifeblood. Yet Aura Imbarus dares to be herself: a rebel among the gray-clad, fearful masses. Christmas shopping in 1989, Aura draws sniper fire as Romania descends into the violence of a revolution that topples one of the most draconian regimes in the Soviet bloc. With a bit of Hungarian mysticism in her blood, astonishingly accurate visions lead Aura into danger—as well as to the love of her life. They marry and flee a homeland still in chaos. With only two pieces of luggage and a powerful dream, they settle in Los Angeles where freedom and sudden wealth challenge their love as powerfully as Communist tyranny.

Aura loses her psychic vision, heirloom jewels are stolen, a fortune is lost, followed by divorce. But their early years as lovers in a war-torn country and their rich family heritage is the glue that reunites them. They pay a high price for their materialistic dreams, but gain insight and a love that is far richer. *Out of the Transylvania Night* is a deftly woven narrative about finding greater meaning and fulfillment in both free and closed societies.

Aura's courage shows the degree to which we are all willing to live lives centered on freedom, hope, and an authentic sense of self. Truly a love story!
—Nadia Comaneci, Olympic gold medalist

If you grew up hearing names like Tito, Mao, and Ceauşescu but really didn't understand their significance, read this book!
—Mark Skidmore, Paramount Pictures

This book is sure to find its place in memorial literature of the world.
—Beatrice Ungar, editor-in-chief, Hermannstädter Zeitung

ISBN: 978-0-9843081-2-5 • $14.95

In bookstores everywhere, online, or from the publisher:
www.BettieYoungsBooks.com

On Toby's Terms

Charmaine Hammond

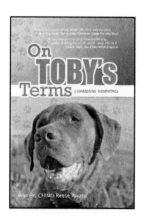

When Charmaine and her husband adopted Toby, a five-year-old Chesapeake Bay retriever, they figured he might need some adjusting time, but they certainly didn't count on what he'd do in the meantime. Soon after he entered their lives and home, Toby proved to be a holy terror who routinely opened and emptied the hall closet, turned on water taps, pulled and ate things from the bookshelves, sat for hours on end in the sink, and spent his days rampaging through the house. Oddest of all was his penchant for locking himself in the bathroom, and then pushing the lid of the toilet off the tank, smashing it to pieces. After a particularly disastrous encounter with the knife-block in the kitchen—and when the couple discovered Toby's bloody paw prints on the phone—they decided Toby needed professional help. Little did they know what they would discover about this dog.

On Toby's Terms is an endearing story of a beguiling creature who teaches his owners that, despite their trying to teach him how to be the dog they want, he is the one to lay out the terms of being the dog he needs to be. This insight would change their lives forever.

Simply a beautiful book about life, love, and purpose.
—**Jack Canfield, Coauthor** *Chicken Soup for the Soul* **series**

In a perfect world, every dog would have a home and every home would have a dog—like Toby!
—**Nina Siemaszko, actress,** *The West Wing*

This is a captivating, heartwarming story and we are very excited about bringing it to film.
—**Steve Hudis, Producer, IMPACT Motion Pictures**

ISBN: 978-0-9843081-4-9 • $14.95

In bookstores everywhere, online, or from the publisher:
www.BettieYoungsBooks.com

Diary of a Beverly Hills Matchmaker

Marla Martenson

The inside scoop from the Cupid of Beverly Hills, who has brought together countless couples who have gone on to live happily ever after. But for every success story there are ridiculously funny dating disasters with high-maintenance, out-of-touch, impossible to please, dim-witted clients!

Marla takes her readers for a hilarious romp through her days as an L.A. matchmaker and her daily struggles to keep her self-esteem from imploding in a town where looks are everything and money talks. From juggling the demands her out-of-touch clients, to trying her best to meet the capricious demands of an insensitive boss, to the ups and downs of her own marriage to a Latin husband who doesn't think that she is "domestic" enough, Marla writes with charm and self-effacement about the universal struggles all women face in their lives.

Readers will laugh, cringe, and cry as they journey with her through outrageous stories about the indignities of dating in Los Angeles, dealing with overblown egos, vicariously hobnobbing with celebrities, and navigating the wannabe-land of Beverly Hills. In a city where perfection is almost a prerequisite, even Marla can't help but run for the BOTOX every once in a while.

Marla's quick wit will have you rolling on the floor.
—**Megan Castran, international YouTube Queen**

Sharper than a Louboutin stiletto, Martenson's book delivers!
—**Nadine Haobsh,** *Beauty Confidential*

Martenson's irresistible wit is not to be missed.
—**Kyra David, author,** *Lust, Loathing, and a Little Lip Gloss*

ISBN: 978-0-9843081-0-1 • $14.95

In bookstores everywhere, online, or from the publisher:
www.BettieYoungsBooks.com

Living with Multiple Personalities

Christine Ducommun

Christine Ducommun eloquently shares her story of her descent into madness, struggling to regain her sanity as four personalities vie for control of her mind and protect her from the demons of her childhood. A story of identity, courage, healing, and hope.

Christine Ducommun was a happily married wife and mother of two, when—after returning to live in the house of her childhood—she began to experience night terrors, a series of bizarre flashbacks, and "noises in her head." Eventually diagnosed with dissociative identity disorder (DID), Christine's story details an extraordinary twelve year ordeal of coming to grips with the reemergence of competing personalities her mind had created to help her cling to life during her early years.

Therapy helps to reveal the personalities, but Christine has much work to do to grasp their individual strengths and weaknesses and understand how each helped her cope and survive her childhood as well as the latent influences they've had in her adult life. Fully reawakened and present, the personalities struggle for control of Christine's mind and her life tailspins into unimaginable chaos, leaving her to believe she may very well be losing the battle for her sanity. Christine's only hope to regain her sanity was to integrate each one's emotional maturity while jettisoning the rest, until at last their chatter in her head could cease.

Anyone who has ever questioned themselves—whether for a day, a week, or longer—will find themselves in this stunning probe into the often secret landscape of the mind.

A powerful and shocking true story. Spellbinding!
—**Josh Miller, Producer**

ISBN: 978-0-9843-0815-6 • $15.95

In bookstores everywhere, online, or from the publisher:
www.BettieYoungsBooks.com

Blackbird Singing in the Dead of Night
What to Do When God Won't Answer

Gregory L. Hunt

"Blackbird singing in the dead of night,
take these broken wings and learn to fly…" —The Beatles

Pastor Greg Hunt had devoted nearly thirty years to congregational ministry, helping people experience God and find their way in life. Then came his own crisis of faith and calling. While turning to God for guidance, he finds nothing. Neither his education—a Ph.D. in theology— nor his religious involvements—senior pastor of a multi-staff congregation, and a civic and denominational leader—could prepare him for the disorienting impact of the experience.

Days turned into months. Months became seasons. Seasons added up to a year, then two. He began to wonder if his faith had been an illusion. Was God even real? In the midst of his struggle, he tries a desperate experiment in devotion: Could he have a personal encounter with God through the red letters of Jesus, as recorded in the Gospel of Matthew?

The result is startling—and changes his life entirely.

Sometimes raw, always honest, and ultimately hopeful, *Blackbird Singing in the Dead of Night* speaks to the spiritual longings of the human heart. **—Julie Pennington-Russell, senior pastor, First Baptist Church, Decatur, GA**

In this most beautiful memoir, Greg Hunt invites us into an unsettling time in his life, exposes the fault lines of his faith, and describes the path he walked into and out of the dark. Thanks to the trail markers he leaves along the way, he makes it easier for us to find our way, too.

—Susan M. Heim, co-author,
Chicken Soup for the Soul, Devotional Stories for Women

ISBN: 978-1-936332-07-6 • $15.95

In bookstores everywhere or from the publisher:
www.BettieYoungsBooks.com

Amazing Adventures of a Nobody

Leon Logothetis

In a time of economic anxiety, global terror and shaken confidence, Englishman Leon Logothetis, star of the hit series *Amazing Adventures of a Nobody* (National Geographic Channels International, Fox Reality), shows us what is good about mankind: the simple calling people have to connect to others.

Tired of his disconnected life and uninspiring job, Leon Logothetis leaves it all behind—job, money, home, even his cell phone—and hits the road with nothing but the clothes on his back and five dollars in his pocket. His journey from Times Square to the Hollywood sign relying on the kindness of strangers and the serendipity of the open road, inspire a dramatic and life-changing transformation.

Along the way, Leon offers up the intriguing and charming tales gathered along his one-of-a-kind journey: riding in trains, buses, big rigs and classic cars; sleeping on streets and couches and firehouses; meeting pimps and preachers, astronauts and single moms, celebrities and homeless families, veterans and communists.

Each day of his journey, we catch sight of the invisible spiritual underpinning of society in these stories of companionship—and sheer adventure—that prove that the kind, good soul of mankind has not been lost.

A gem of a book: endearing, engaging and inspiring!
> —**Catharine Hamm,** *Los Angeles Times,* **travel editor**

Masterful storytelling! Leon begins his journey as a merry prankster and ends a grinning philosopher. Really funny—and insightful, too.
> —**Karen Salmansohn, AOL Career Coach, and Oprah.com Relationship Columnist**

ISBN: 978-0-9843081-3-2 • $14.95

In bookstores everywhere, online, or from the publisher:
www.BettieYoungsBooks.com

It Started with Dracula
The Count, My Mother, and Me

Jane Congdon

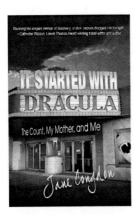

The terrifying legend of Count Dracula, silently skulking through the Transylvania night may have terrified generations of filmgoers, but the tall, elegant vampire captivated and electrified a young Jane Congdon, igniting a dream to one day see his mysterious land of ancient castles and misty hollows.

Four decades later, she finally takes her long-awaited trip—never dreaming that it would unearth decades-buried memories of life with an alcoholic mother. Set in Dracula's backyard, the story unfolds in a mere eighteen days as the author follows the footsteps of Dracula from Bucharest to the Carpathian Mountains and the Black Sea. Dracula's legend becomes the prism through which she revisits her childhood, and lays claim to a happiness she had never known.

A memoir full of surprises, Jane's story is one of hope, love—and second chances.

Unfinished business can surface when we least expect it. *It Started with Dracula* is the inspiring story of two parallel journeys: one a carefully planned vacation and the other an astonishing and unexpected detour in healing a wounded heart.
—**Charles Whitfield, MD, bestselling author of**
Healing the Child Within

An elegant memoir of discovery, of dark secrets dragged into the light.
—**Catherine Watson, Lowell Thomas**
Award-winning travel editor and author

An elegantly written and cleverly told real-life adventure story, proving that the struggle for self-love is universal. An electrifying read.
—**Diane Bruno, CISION Media**

ISBN: 978-1-936332-10-6 • $15.95

In bookstores everywhere, online, or from the publisher:
www.BettieYoungsBooks.com

Bettie Youngs Books

We specialize in MEMOIRS
. . . books that celebrate
fascinating people and
remarkable journeys

VISIT OUR WEBSITE AT
www.BettieYoungsBooks.com

CPSIA information can be obtained at www.ICGtesting.com
Printed in the USA
LVOW061114050312

271323LV00004B/1/P